SILENCE
IN THE
LIBRARY

ALSO BY KATHARINE SCHELLMAN

LILY ADLER MYSTERIES

The Body in the Garden

SILENCE IN THE LIBRARY

A LILY ADLER MYSTERY

Katharine Schellman

CROOKED
LANE

NEW YORK

Copyright © 2021 by Katharine Schellman Paljug

Published in the United States by Crooked Lane Books, an imprint of The Quick Brown Fox & Company LLC.

Crooked Lane Books and its logo are trademarks of The Quick Brown Fox & Company LLC.

Library of Congress Catalog-in-Publication data available upon request.

ISBN (hardcover): 978-1-64385-704-6
ISBN (ebook): 978-1-64385-705-3

Cover design by Nicole Lecht

Printed in the United States.

www.crookedlanebooks.com

Crooked Lane Books
34 West 27th St., 10th Floor
New York, NY 10001

First Edition: July 2021

10 9 8 7 6 5 4 3 2 1

For my parents, Jim and Andrea Schellman,
who turned all of their kids into readers.

And for Brian, the only adult I could handle
living with during a pandemic lockdown.

CHAPTER 1

London, 1815

The sound of angry voices cut through the sleepy morning quiet. There were never raised voices on dignified, out-of-the-way Half Moon Street, and certainly never from Lily Adler's own terrace. Her butler, Carstairs, was conscious of his youth spent as a boxer and prided himself on his decorum. But as she drew closer to her home, she could see him standing on the front steps, facing another man in a dark suit and gesturing broadly, his voice just barely controlled enough not to be a shout. Lily was so surprised that her steps slowed to a halt.

"Is . . . are those fellows carrying luggage into your house?" her companion asked, stopping beside her and frowning in confusion.

"Of course not, Captain, that would be . . ." Lily trailed off, watching as two postboys finished unloading the pile of trunks and cases from a carriage and began hauling them one by one inside her home, pushing past the two arguing men with the dogged determination of those who intended to finish their task, collect their pay, and depart as quickly as possible.

For a moment Lily panicked. The house on Half Moon Street was let to her for the indefinite future, and it had finally begun to feel like home. She had nowhere else to go. If she was forced to leave . . .

Lily squared her shoulders. She would *not* be leaving. Forgetting about the captain and not caring which of her too-curious neighbors might be watching, she stalked toward her house.

The postboys, who hadn't expected a well-dressed lady to elbow past them, fell back. At the top of the steps, Carstairs was nose to nose with a man in the dark suit and painfully starched collar of a valet. Their heated voices tumbled over each other so rapidly that Lily could barely make out what either of them was saying. Mrs. Carstairs, the cook and housekeeper, stood in the doorway just behind her husband, hands on her hips and a duster in one hand as she harangued both men at the top of her lungs. Just as Lily drew in a breath to speak, the strange man turned enough for her to see his profile.

Her resolve crumbled into weary fury, and though she managed to keep her voice from growing too loud, it still cut through the noise. "Branson."

The two servants stopped arguing abruptly and turned toward the foot of the stairs where she stood, one hand gripping the banister so she wouldn't tremble. Carstairs, a vein visibly throbbing in one temple, opened his mouth to speak, but Lily held up a hand to forestall him.

"Branson, where is he?"

"Miss Pierce." Robert Branson winced, then quickly corrected himself. "Beg pardon. Mrs. Adler. He is waiting in the drawing room. Your servants—" He cut a quick, irritated look at Carstairs, who instantly jumped in.

"Mrs. Adler, this man is claiming that—"

"No one told *us* about anything—" Mrs. Carstairs started speaking at the same time.

The small scene began to descend into chaos once more. The postboys took advantage of the confusion to resume their task, and Lily could see the luggage piling up in her front hall. She took a deep breath.

"If you please," Lily said, pitching the words to carry, though she tried to keep any sharpness out of them as she gestured for everyone to move inside, away from any prying eyes.

They obeyed promptly, all three looking embarrassed, and Lily sighed. She resented being caught in the middle of the confusion and uproar, but the three servants weren't to blame for it. The man responsible was, no doubt, currently making himself comfortable in the drawing room and growing irritated that no one had yet brought him any refreshments.

"Carstairs, see these men paid and sent on their way. I assume," Lily said to Branson, fixing him with a narrow-eyed stare before indicating the piled luggage with a sweep of her hand. "I assume that he intends a visit?"

Branson frowned. "I understood you were aware of his plans."

"No doubt he believes everyone is aware of them and prepared to accommodate him at a moment's notice. Which I must endeavor to do, I suppose. Mrs. Carstairs." Lily turned to the motherly woman who kept her home comfortable and her life running in perfect order. "It seems we will have a visitor with us. For some time, judging by the amount of luggage he has brought. Will the two of you see his things installed in the best spare room and accommodations for his valet as well? And Branson?" Lily managed to smile, though the expression felt stiff. It wasn't Branson's fault his employer was so damned difficult. "You might start by introducing yourself to my servants and explaining the situation. I do not want to hear shouting in my house." She gave each of them a pointed look. "From anyone."

"Of course, Mrs. Adler," Carstairs rumbled, looking embarrassed. "May I ask, madam, who our visitor . . ." He trailed off, eyeing her warily.

Lily tried to school her expression back to its normal calm, wondering what she must have looked like to make her stoic butler so uneasy. "Our visitor is Mr. George Pierce," she said. "Branson will explain, I have no doubt. And Mrs. Carstairs, if you could first see tea and some light refreshments brought into the drawing room? No doubt Mr. Pierce is famished after his journey."

As they nodded and began to move about their tasks, Lily became aware of someone standing just behind her. Glancing over her shoulder, she found that her companion had followed her inside and was watching, his arms crossed and his brows raised as he leaned against the doorway.

"Is everything all right?" he asked, the concern in his voice in direct contrast with his casual attitude.

"Yes," Lily said immediately, and a little defensively, before she shook her head. "No. I have a visitor."

"I gathered. Is it really—"

"Yes." Lily's expression grew grim. "You ought to come say hello, Jack."

Taking a deep breath, she gathered her composure, lifted her chin, and walked briskly to the drawing room door. Throwing it open, she met the eyes of the man waiting for her.

He sat in the tall chair across from the door as regally as if it were his own home, two hands resting on top of the walking stick planted between his feet and, oddly, a small pile of books on the floor beside him. His familiar eagle-eyed stare bored into her.

"Hello, Father," Lily said, her voice dripping with false pleasantness that she knew didn't fool him for a moment. "How good to see you. And how unexpected. May I ask what in God's name you are doing in my house?"

CHAPTER 2

"Lily." George Pierce stared at her, brows raised. There were wings of gray in his dark hair, just above his temples, and the effect was quite distinguished. Lily knew others thought her father handsome, but she never could—whenever he looked at her, lines of disapproval appeared between his eyes. They were there now, along with a tightness in his jaw as he eyed her from head to toe. "What a lovely way to greet your father. I had a tolerable journey; thank you for inquiring. May I ask why there was so much noise in the hall just now? Your servants do not seem particularly well trained."

"I could say the same of Branson, Father, as he contributed equally to the noise." Lily took a deep breath and sat across from him, glancing out of the corner of her eye at Jack. He had strolled in with his usual swagger but was hanging back in the doorway, watching the small scene unfold with an unreadable expression on his face. Lily turned back to her father, not yet ready to draw Jack into the line of fire by making an official reintroduction. "The noise was due entirely to your own arrival. So I ask again, what are you doing in my house?"

"Where else am I supposed to stay? Is it truly so much of an imposition to have your own father staying with you while he must be in town? Or is it an issue of household management?" He sighed. "Your dear mother was a perfect manager, you know. She would never have allowed shouting in her home. Or trash like this," he added, gesturing to the small stack of books on the floor by his feet. "I was disappointed to find several novels on your shelves. I will instruct your butler to see them disposed of."

Behind her, Lily heard Jack draw in a breath, and she spoke quickly to prevent him from saying anything. "Is it truly so much of an imposition to send notice before you descend on my home?" she asked, trying to direct the conversation back to her original point and biting the inside of her cheek to stop herself from adding more. Arguing with her father would only draw things out, and she refused to let him see that he was provoking her.

Mr. Pierce sniffed. "I wrote to you of my plans."

Lily knew her father well enough to ask, eyes narrowed, "*When* did you write?"

He waved a hand absently back and forth, as if the question were unimportant. "A day or two ago, I suppose. I don't concern myself with details, as you know. I have more important things to keep track of."

"Your letter has yet to arrive."

"Well, in that case." Mr. Pierce sighed, leaning heavily on his walking stick as he rose slowly to his feet. Lily wondered if it was from fatigue or simply to show that he was disappointed with her. Again. "I suppose my presence here is too much of a burden on you. I shall find accommodation elsewhere."

Lily gritted her teeth. "Father, please sit down," she said quietly. Drawing in a deep breath, she looked toward the ceiling for a brief moment while he obeyed. "I have already instructed my servants to prepare a room for you," she continued, keeping her voice as pleasant as possible. "You are, of course, welcome to stay."

"I suppose that will have to do. Though I hope your beds are more comfortable than your chairs," he said, looking down at his own seat and grimacing. "Wherever did you purchase such monstrosities?"

"The house came furnished," Lily said, her jaw so tight that it was a struggle to get any words out at all.

"A furnished house?" Mr. Pierce sighed. "Well, I suppose if that is the best you can afford." He settled back into his chair—looking quite comfortable, Lily noted, though she managed not to point that out—and glanced toward the doorway, acknowledging Jack's presence at last. "Who are you, and what are you doing in my daughter's home?"

Lily's hands clenched into fists before she carefully relaxed them, one angry finger at a time. "Father, this is Captain Jack Hartley. The captain was Freddy's boyhood friend in Hertfordshire, and he has been most gallant since I returned to London. Captain, you of course remember my father, Mr. Pierce."

Jack's expression was carefully neutral as he bowed. "Indeed, sir, you are not the sort of man one ever forgets."

"The Indian boy," her father said rudely, making a dismissive gesture with one hand. "I know you."

Jack smiled. "My mother will be so pleased to hear that you remember her."

He was, strictly speaking, half Indian, with a British father. That meant different things to different people, especially to those who, like her father, had particular ideas about good breeding. Jack's family was unapologetic about his parents' marriage, though such unions were becoming increasingly uncommon. For the most part, his naval career and his family's comfortable wealth were enough to smooth aside any objections that might otherwise have been voiced publicly.

But Jack seemed unconcerned by Mr. Pierce's comments, giving Lily a quick conspiratorial wink before he took a seat at last. Lily tried not to let her relief show—she had years of experience handling her father and could do so again without support. But it was still comforting to have a friend here.

"What brings you to London, sir?" Jack asked. "I was not aware that Mrs. Adler was expecting the pleasure of your presence."

"Private concerns," Mr. Pierce said. "Where is the damned tea?"

Lily's maid Anna, her timing impeccable, entered only a moment after he spoke. She bobbed a quick curtsy as soon as she had set the tray down. "Mr. Pierce."

"Anna."

He had known her for years; she had been a housemaid in the Pierce home before becoming Lily's personal maid and leaving with her upon her marriage to Freddy Adler. And after Freddy's death, Lily had been grateful to have Anna still by her side, a single familiar thread she could cling to until she found her feet once more. But George Pierce hadn't seen Anna since Freddy's death, and as he looked her over, Lily waited for him to say something critical.

Instead, he pursed his lips. "I see you were not chased away by Miss Lily's odd choice to remove to London. I admire your loyalty."

"It is a pleasure to serve Mrs. Adler, as always," Anna said politely.

But Lily heard the subtle reminder that she was a grown woman in her own home, and she could have hugged Anna with gratitude. Instead, she met the maid's eyes and smiled. "Thank you for the tea. Will you please see that Branson is settled in and has everything he needs to make Mr. Pierce comfortable?"

"Yes, ma'am." Anna curtsied again. "Sir. Captain."

After she left, Lily poured the tea, measuring out a careful teaspoon of milk and adding it in while her father watched with narrowed eyes. Apparently she did that right, at least, because he took the cup and turned to Jack once more.

"And what brings you to London, Hartley? I should have thought you would be in French waters." If it had been a trifle less dignified, the expression on his face might have been a smirk. "Or are you one of those spare captains without your own ship?"

"Only in the strictest sense," Jack said, leaning back in his chair while Lily silently marveled at his easy manner. Nothing ever seemed to fluster him. "My frigate has been undergoing repairs since the spring, so I unfortunately missed the final action in France." Accepting his cup from Lily with murmured thanks, Jack continued. "With Napoleon defeated once more, I may be kept in London or Portsmouth even after repairs have been completed. At least until the Admiralty gets organized and decides where it is best to send me."

"And what brings you to my daughter's home?"

"Father," Lily said, her voice tight with warning. "I'll thank you not to interrogate my guest."

"I've a right to know," Mr. Pierce said, reaching for a slice of cake from the tea tray.

Lily tried not to clench her jaw. "No, you haven't."

"Well." Mr. Pierce shrugged.

Jack laughed, breaking the tension in the room. "Well, there is no need for secrecy. Mrs. Adler had received a letter from our mutual friends, Sir Edward and Lady Carroway, that she was going to share with me. But perhaps I shall return another time for news of Ofelia and her new husband." Rising, he bowed politely. "Mrs. Adler, Mr. Pierce, a pleasure. I am sure we will meet again soon." As he turned, he caught Lily's eye and made an exasperated face—more suited to a boy of ten than to a man of his rank—before smiling encouragingly.

Lily held back an unladylike snort as he took his leave, before a long sigh from her father interrupted her. She turned to him. "Are you well, Father?"

Mr. Pierce sighed again. "Tired from the journey. It is not a comfortable trip."

"You are welcome to go rest," Lily said, trying not to sound too hopeful. Fifteen minutes in her father's company was very nearly too much.

"Already eager to be rid of me?" he asked, poking at his cake without enthusiasm before settling backward with a sigh and closing his eyes.

"What brings you to town, Father?" Lily asked, taking a moment to study him while he couldn't see. There were deep lines around his eyes and jaw that she didn't remember noticing before. Her father had always been a man of robust health and too much vitality. She wondered if this time there was something actually wrong.

"Seeing a doctor," he muttered, his eyes still closed. "I was sick over the winter, you may recall. My lungs are still troubled with wheezing, so the physician in the village suggested I see a colleague here in London. I've no notion of him being able to improve anything, but you know I am not one to argue."

Lily bit her tongue. Her father liked nothing better than to argue, unless it was to argue and be proved right. "Well, I shall be glad to have you," she lied.

He opened one eye. "No, you shan't."

"I shall be as glad to have you as you are to be here," Lily said, her smile fixed firmly in place. She refused to let him rattle her.

"Don't know why you choose to live in London," he muttered, sitting up once more. "I cannot stand it here."

As he spoke, Lily's butler entered, offering Mr. Pierce a folded letter and making a hasty retreat. Lily sipped her own tea, watching her father warily over the cup's edge while he read the note and crumpled it up with a sigh.

"The doctor can see me this afternoon. Which is quite the bother, because I also need to call on Sir Charles Wyatt. You'll remember him, of course? And Frank?"

Lily resisted the urge to roll her eyes. "Of course I remember them."

The Wyatts' property had been less than three miles from her father's, and the two families had spent a great deal of time together when Lily was young. Sir Charles and Mr. Pierce had liked nothing better than to argue over a glass of sherry in the evenings. Sir Charles's son Frank was Mr. Pierce's godson; when Frank was home from school, he had often been included in their evening discussions or taken along when Mr. Pierce went riding or hunting.

Lily, who spent more time with a governess than with her father, was never invited to join.

"Well, he and his new wife have been in town," Mr. Pierce said.

Lily couldn't hide her surprise. "Frank Wyatt has married?"

Her father snorted. "No, Sir Charles has."

That was almost more surprising. Lady Wyatt had died about sixteen years before. Lily vaguely remembered that she had been pregnant not long before her death, but as Frank was Sir Charles's only child, she presumed that the child had died in infancy and that Lady Wyatt had never recovered from the birth. Sir Charles had been as much an established widower as Mr. Pierce.

Lily hadn't thought about the Wyatts since before her marriage, and certainly not in the last few years of her mourning. But if she had, she would have assumed that Sir Charles was as unlikely to marry a second time as her own father.

"They will be leaving London any day now for the country," Mr. Pierce said, shaking his head. "I must pay my respects before they depart. I cannot think why he got married again. But one must be polite to a bride, especially when she is married to an old friend. All this doctor business is damned inconvenient."

Lily knew what he wanted. "I would be happy to call in your place, Father. I am sure Sir Charles will not be offended. And then when your appointment is finished, you will be free to return here and rest with no social obligations."

Mr. Pierce smiled, clearly pleased to get his way. The expression he turned on Lily was very nearly approving. "That is very considerate of you."

Lily smiled back so she wouldn't sigh.

"Poor Frank is none too pleased with Sir Charles's marriage." Mr. Pierce shook his head again, already standing to show himself from the room. "So would any man be if his father took a fancy to some flibbertigibbet. But I've no doubt it will be an enjoyable visit for you. The Wyatts have always been pleasant people."

★   ★   ★

When Lily emerged from the house with Anna accompanying her, she was surprised—and yet not at all surprised—to find Jack lounging against a nearby hitching post, watching the door with a small smile on his face. He tipped his hat. "I thought it might not take you long to flee."

Lily sighed. "He has never been an easy man. Where are you headed, Captain?"

"With you, of course," Jack said, giving a slight bow. "I suspected you might be in need of a confidant after he chased you out."

Lily protested that she could not keep him from his plans for the day, and Jack shrugged his shoulders and insisted he hadn't any other plans. Anna was free to return to the house while they set off toward Wimpole Street, where, Branson had informed Lily after her father neglected to provide any information, the Wyatts lived.

"He did not chase me from my home, I will have you know," Lily said, her pride stinging a little. "He had an appointment he could not miss, and so I offered to pay a visit for him. A friend of his recently wed, and someone from our family must pay our respects to the bride."

Jack snorted. "Your family being you and Mr. Pierce?"

"Well, my father does have a sister, so it is not *only* us," Lily said. "But as she is not in London, yes."

"I see," Jack said dryly as he stepped toward the street to hail a passing hack carriage. When it stopped beside them, he opened the door, then turned to offer Lily his arm. "While your father may think—"

Whatever he might have said was lost as a flurry of bodies pushed past them, four young dandies in striped waistcoats and top boots all laughing and talking at the top of their lungs to be heard over each other. Lily and Jack were jostled out of the way as the young men crowded toward the carriage door Jack had just left open.

"Any string of bad luck has to break—"

"You'll earn it all back at the Leger Stakes—"

"Just don't let the old man know!"

"No fear of that," one replied, as he swung himself into the carriage, waving at his friends to walk on. "Have to go meet my cousin. We will see you at ten o'clock?"

"—at Rogerson's club before that—"

"—learn to judge horseflesh one of these days—"

"Best not mention it to Crawford, but I saw his wife last night—"

The whole exchange happened in a moment, and before Lily and Jack could protest, their carriage had clattered off without them. The remaining young men were about to saunter off when Jack planted himself firmly in their path, his walking stick swinging menacingly.

"Not so fast, whelps," he growled.

The three of them stuttered into silence, staring in confusion at the broad-shouldered figure who was now blocking their way. They did not look like fellows who knew their way around a fight, and they were clearly uneasy when faced with Jack's intimidating stance.

"You nearly pushed the lady into the street just now," Jack said, eyeing each of them in turn. "Not to mention that your friend took the lady's carriage. So what have you to say for yourselves?"

In spite of the fact that they outnumbered him, all three seemed to shrink back, looking at each other to see who would be willing to step forward. It would have made Lily laugh if she hadn't been so irritated.

"Well?" Jack barked. "Speak up."

Part of Lily wanted to see him put the dandies firmly in their place. But the other passersby were beginning to stare at the small altercation, and she didn't want to be involved in a public scene. She stepped forward and laid a hand on Jack's arm.

"While I should dearly love to see you teach them some manners, Captain, this pack of fools is not worth your time," she said. She looked them up and down scornfully, and only one of them was able to meet her eyes, though he flushed a fierce red. The other two looked away, shifting awkwardly from foot to foot. "And we have somewhere to be."

"We can summon another carriage for you," the red-faced one burst out, though he immediately glanced at Jack and fell silent with an audible gulp.

Lily pursed her lips. "That would be acceptable. Quickly, now. I am not in a mood to be kept waiting by ill-mannered boys."

They were all blushing now, and the one who had spoken darted out into the street to flag down another carriage for hire. While he did so, Jack crossed his arms and glowered, and the other two young men cleared their throats uncomfortably and tried to look anywhere but at Lily. When a carriage at last arrived, Jack handed Lily in and narrowed his eyes at each of the boys in turn before climbing in himself.

"So, what did the new Lady Carroway have to say in her letter?" he asked by way of making conversation as the carriage began to move through the snarl of London traffic.

"Ofelia and Sir Edward are both enjoying their wedding trip, though she wishes things in France had stabilized in time for them to see sights on the Continent as well. Though we should not expect them home for some weeks yet . . ."

Lily shared what news she could remember. Jack made interested noises, but his attention was clearly elsewhere; she thought he was still irritated over the loss of their first carriage, until she fell silent at last.

He gave her a look out of the corner of his eye. "He dislikes seeing you in control of your own life," he said. "Your father, I mean."

Lily leaned back against the seat of the carriage as she considered his words, then nodded. "He was happy enough to have me out of his house when I married," she said, shrugging off the familiar tension that tried to worm its way down her spine. Though Jack's concern touched her, she had long ago stopped expecting things to be easy between her and her father. "Had I returned to his home after Freddy's death, he would have thought it an imposition. Yet it offends his sense of propriety to see a woman of my age living on her own. Or having friends, apparently." Lily shook her head. "I am sorry you had to deal with him. Really, he ought to be grateful. I could be a great deal more troublesome and embarrassing if I chose. Encouraging a brawl in the middle of a public street, for example," she added, shaking her head.

"You should point that out to him," Jack suggested, looking entirely unrepentant.

Lily's eyes glinted. "If he makes himself a guest in my house for too long, I very well might."

CHAPTER 3

"Lady Wyatt, I am sorry not to see Sir Charles—it has been several years since I have had the pleasure. My father sends his best wishes for your marriage, and I offer my own as well. You seem to be most happily settled."

Lily kept a bland social smile on her face as she spoke, then hid behind her teacup as quickly as possible, hoping the woman in front of her wasn't astute enough to notice her surprise. Sir Charles was a contemporary of Mr. Pierce's, and Lily had expected to find the sort of wife so many older men seemed to choose when they remarried: old enough for her parents to consent to the union, young enough not to disrupt her husband's comfortable routine. Instead, the woman was nearly a decade older than Lily, confident and self-possessed. And she was shockingly beautiful, in the way that only a woman who had left her girlhood behind could be.

Lily, who normally prided herself on her composure, felt tongue-tied. And Jack wasn't faring much better. He had somehow ended up coming in with her when she gave the Wyatts' butler her card and now was holding a cold cup of tea in one hand, watching Lady Wyatt in rapt silence as they all sat in the Wyatts' cozy drawing room. Wimpole Street wasn't in the most fashionable part of town, but you would never have known it from the inside: the room was elegantly papered in cream and gold, and the large arched windows flooded the space with light. At one side of the room was a writing desk, its cubbies stacked with papers and letters. Just behind the settee Lady Wyatt occupied sat a card table, three unbroken packs of cards waiting on its surface as if a party might begin at any moment.

"I am quite fortunate in my situation," Lady Wyatt agreed as she served them each a slice of cake. "Though I must ask for your thoughts, Captain, as I am in need of a male perspective. My husband gave me free rein to redecorate this spring, but I am worried that I have perhaps created too feminine a retreat. Be honest." She leaned forward, her voice dropping as though she were about to impart a great secret, an engaging smile flirting around her lips. "Are there too many tassels?"

Jack laughed. "I am sure your husband would put up with any number of fripperies to enjoy your presence, ma'am."

"That is a yes, then. I suspected as much." Lady Wyatt sighed, shaking her head dramatically before her smile returned. She turned to Lily, a perfect hostess who didn't let either guest sit unacknowledged for too long.

"I know Sir Charles will be sorry to have missed you, and your father as well, Mrs. Adler. He speaks so highly of Mr. Pierce. What a shame we did not know you were in London sooner." Lady Wyatt's voice was cordial rather than warm, but Lily didn't hold that against her—she had never been considered a particularly warm person herself, at least not on first meeting. "We will be leaving within the week. Perhaps we will have the chance to receive Mr. Pierce before that."

"Perhaps," Lily agreed vaguely, unwilling to make any promises on his behalf. If Mr. Pierce disapproved of his friend's marrying again, there was every chance he would avoid seeing them in the country as well. "Will you be glad to finally see your husband's home in Devonshire?"

Lady Wyatt's grimace was so slight that Lily might have thought she'd imagined it. "I enjoy town life more, I must admit," Lady Wyatt said. "But as the city will be rather deserted during the summer, one cannot really object to departing. And I shall be glad for the chance of a real ride again. I confess I do not much enjoy the timid trotting that one must adhere to in Hyde Park." She took another sip of her tea, then asked politely, "Do you ride, Mrs. Adler?"

"Acceptably, though not skillfully," Lily admitted. "And being in London does not afford me the opportunity to become more skillful."

Before Lady Wyatt could answer, there was a small commotion at the door and two young men, talking animatedly, pushed their way into the room. As soon as they realized it was occupied, they stopped and fell silent.

"Beg pardon," the younger one said, his face and neck flushing red. "We did not realize you had guests, madam."

Lily glanced at Lady Wyatt, catching the woman's small sigh of annoyance before she smiled and stood to make introductions.

"Mrs. Adler, Captain Hartley, may I present Sir Charles's son, Mr. Frank Wyatt, and nephew, Mr. Percy Wyatt."

Frank stepped forward very gallantly to bow over Lily's hand. "Surely you remember that at least one of those introductions is not necessary, Lady Wyatt?" he said. He was the elder of the two, around thirty, handsome and sensible looking, with dark hair and broad shoulders. "Mrs. Adler and I are old friends. How do you do?"

She would never have described them as friends. They had been thrown together often, certainly, even when she hadn't particularly wanted to be. And part of her had always wanted to dislike Frank—so clearly singled out and favored by her father while she was overlooked. But she had never quite managed to do it. He was too friendly, too charming, too at ease with himself and the world. She knew why her father liked him better; he was everything Lily was not. Even now she couldn't help smiling in response to his grin.

But there had been something dismissive in the way he spoke to Lady Wyatt, as though he was laughing at her for having made a polite introduction when she didn't need to. So there was an edge of censure to her voice as she replied, "I am very well, Mr. Wyatt, thank you."

"Oh no, have you found something in me to disapprove of so quickly?" Frank laughed. "Was it because we interrupted your visit?

My sincere apologies for being so boorish. I shall have to be on my guard to gain your approval once more. And Captain Hartley, was it?" He turned to bow to Jack, polite and personable in spite of his awkward arrival. "A military man, then? You must be glad to see the end of our action in France, and it came none too soon. Mrs. Adler, I think you have met my cousin Percy, have you not?"

Percy, in contrast to his cousin's ease and friendliness, was red-faced, the blush clearly visible against his pale skin and light hair. Though taller, he looked younger than his cousin, perhaps only slightly older than Lily's own seven-and-twenty years. Lily had met him only once before at his uncle's house, when they were all still children, though she knew he and Frank were close because they had overlapped at school.

He was, however, very familiar. She wouldn't have recognized him as Sir Charles's nephew without the introduction, but she knew his face well: Percy Wyatt was the young man who had snatched the carriage from her and Jack less than an hour before.

Lily narrowed her eyes, wondering if he would notice and apologize. But he didn't say anything, and she supposed he must have been too preoccupied to spare a glance for the people he had treated so rudely. He bowed to Lily and Jack from the doorway, glancing around the room as though wondering whether he should join them or make his escape.

"Your father had several matters to see to. He left about an hour ago," Lady Wyatt told Frank as she resumed her seat, gesturing for Lily and Jack to do the same.

"I am amazed that he was persuaded to leave your side," Frank said, his words so gallant that they were clearly mocking. Lady Wyatt stiffened as Frank, grinning, reached over his stepmother's shoulder and helped himself to a piece of cake. His smile didn't quite reach his eyes as he added, "You two have been so inseparable, it is quite charming."

"Your father is a most charming man," Lady Wyatt replied, her voice sharp.

Jack glanced at Lily, his brows raised and an uncomfortable smile hovering around the corners of his mouth. Lily gave him a quick warning look, struggling to keep her expression appropriately disinterested and afraid that he would make her laugh.

"Have you any notion of when he will return, ma'am?" Percy asked, finally moving from his position by the door. Ignoring the tension, he crossed to the writing desk at the far side of the room. "Excuse me, Captain Hartley, if you would be so good. I just need to fetch some correspondence from—yes, most obliging, thank you."

"I am afraid not," Lady Wyatt said, responding to Percy's question as he retrieved a leather writing portfolio and paged through it as though looking for something, keeping it angled away from Jack. "Will you two be joining us this evening, or have you plans of your own?"

"Oh, Percy's got some scrape he wants to drag me along for," Frank said carelessly as he finished his slice of cake. "You needn't worry about feeding us; we can always dine at Percy's lodgings."

"Haven't any food there, sad to say," Percy said.

Glancing at Jack, who still stood close by him, he took a small step to the left, a frown creasing his forehead. Not finding what he wanted among his letters, he turned back to the desk to continue his search, though he kept glancing over his shoulder as if checking to see whether anyone was looking at him. Lily watched him curiously out of the corner of her eye, though she kept her face angled toward the rest of the room so he wouldn't notice.

"The club, then," Frank said, still smiling his not-quite-mocking smile at Lady Wyatt. "You see, I am happy to make shift for myself."

"You are always welcome at your father's table, Frank," Lady Wyatt said, sighing.

"But not yours?" he asked, leaning carelessly over the back of the settee so that he could look at Lady Wyatt's face. A faint blush appeared high on her cheeks, though the tight line of her jaw made Lily guess it was from anger rather than embarrassment.

There was an uncomfortable silence in the room as Lady Wyatt very pointedly did not contradict him.

"And how is your father?" Frank asked, straightening as he turned back to Lily, apparently unbothered by his interaction with Lady Wyatt. "I've not had a letter from him since May."

"He is well, and I am sure he will be pleased to hear that you asked after him." Lily silently wondered when she had last had a letter from her father; it had been long enough that she couldn't remember. "As a matter of fact, he arrived in town just this morning."

"And does he stay with you for this visit?" Frank's grin had the look of a naughty schoolboy. "Who will emerge victorious from such an occasion? For I do not doubt it will be quite the battle of wills."

"I say, Frank." Percy looked shocked at such familiar speech, and even Lady Wyatt's eyes grew wide with surprise.

But Jack snorted with laughter from his spot by the window, which made Frank's smile grow even wider. Lily couldn't keep the corners of her mouth from twitching.

"Mr. Wyatt knows us of old, as you see," she said, shaking her head. Jack caught her eye, and her wry expression grew into a real smile. "A battle of wills indeed."

"I shall be sure to pay a call," Frank added. "It has been too long since I have seen him."

"To take my side or his?" Lily quipped.

Frank laughed. "I will stay on neutral ground, as always. But as I can scarcely credit that he has come to London at all, I will have to see him in person to confirm that it is true." As if remembering all of a sudden that there were others in the room, he glanced at Lady Wyatt, his smile once again taking on that mocking edge. "How strange that Mr. Pierce has not called to pay his respects, if indeed he is in town. He and my father have been friends these many years, as you know, ma'am. Since the time of the first Lady Wyatt."

Lily drew in a sharp breath. She was about to take Frank to task, propriety be damned, for such an unkind speech. Her father might be deliberately snubbing the new Lady Wyatt, but there was no need for Frank to point that out so bluntly. But Percy Wyatt spoke first.

"Well, we shall leave you to your visitors," he broke in, gathering up his papers as quickly as possible and hurrying across the room to take Frank's arm. His own blush had returned, and he tugged his cousin toward the door before Frank could say anything else. "Mrs. Adler, Captain Hartley, a pleasure to meet you both."

"A pleasure," Frank Wyatt echoed, laughing as his cousin shooed him from the room.

Lady Wyatt sighed as the door closed behind them. "I apologize for them," she said. "They mean well, but like many young men, their manners are not always what they ought to be." She glanced at Jack. "Begging your pardon, Captain."

"You will find no disagreement from me," Jack said. He had remained standing while the young men were in the room; now he crossed to take a seat near Lady Wyatt, and his teasing expression made her smile. "We are a sorry lot indeed, not fit for company, as my mother and sisters often remind me."

"Fortunately, I think you are no longer classed with the young men," Lily put in, wondering whether he was thinking of Percy's rudeness or Frank's sly remarks.

"You wound me, Mrs. Adler."

"I think, under the circumstances, it was a compliment," Lady Wyatt said, an edge to her voice that tugged at Lily's sympathy. How uncomfortable it would be to marry and find yourself sharing a home with a stepson who made his dislike so plain.

They had almost outstayed the polite length of time for a visit, and she and Jack would need to leave soon. Lily impulsively found herself asking, "Lady Wyatt, if you are not engaged tomorrow morning, perhaps I might call again? There are so few people left in London these days, we who remain must stick together. That is," she added, her wry tone matching Lady Wyatt's own, "if you think you will feel the need for friendly company."

For a moment, Lady Wyatt looked as though she didn't know whether to be embarrassed or grateful. A warmer smile than she had yet offered crept over her features. "Perhaps you would join me for a ride tomorrow morning, Mrs. Adler? And you as well, Captain, of course. Sir Charles keeps a number of horses in town," she added politely, too tactful to ask outright whether either of them had the funds to keep their own stables in town. "But he is too gouty of late to join me. And I dare not ask Frank for his company."

"Oh, if you ride in the mornings," Lily tried to demur. "I've no wish to impose—"

"Nonsense," Lady Wyatt insisted. "My other riding companions have already left London for the summer. And riding alone, or even with a groom for company, is no pleasure at all when one is confined to a walk or trot. Perhaps at ten o'clock—"

She was cut off by the sound of a commotion from farther back in the house. Lady Wyatt started, frowning as she turned toward the door, clearly expecting the disturbance to be quelled as quickly as it had arisen. But the shouting only grew louder, and a moment later a housemaid burst into the room.

"Ellen, what on earth is happening?" Lady Wyatt demanded.

"Oh, ma'am." Ellen wrung her hands, glancing uncomfortably at the visitors but unable to delay her message. "There has been such a to-do, you must come at once, they're saying Thomas *stole*—" She broke off with another panicked look. "You must come, please. Mr. Percy—and Mr. Wyatt—"

Lady Wyatt rose, and Lily was impressed all over again by her composure as she turned to her guests. "If you will excuse me, I am sure I will not be a moment."

Lily and Jack exchanged a glance once they were alone.

"Well," Lily said at last, her gaze still turned toward the noises emanating from outside the room. "She was charming."

"Shame she has to deal with those two, though," Jack said. "Seems rather unpleasant for her." He gave her a considering glance out of the corner of his eye. "Mr. Frank Wyatt seemed very friendly with you, at least."

"But otherwise behaving very badly," Lily said, frowning. "It is not like him. Witty and sly, certainly, but not unfriendly. I would have expected him to go out of his way to make Lady Wyatt like him, even if she had been inclined to dislike him when they first met."

"Maybe he was the one who started off on the wrong foot," Jack pointed out, scooting across the settee to be closer to the remaining cake.

"Mr. Percy Wyatt at least seemed aware of his cousin's bad behavior."

"But not his own," Jack grumbled, cutting himself a large slice. "He was the one who stole our carriage, after all."

Lily couldn't help chuckling. "I wondered if you recognized him too."

Glancing at the door, she went to the writing desk and knelt down. In his haste to remove his cousin from the room, Percy hadn't noticed the piece of paper that had fluttered out of his grasp, but Lily had spotted it immediately.

"Snooping?" Jack asked around a mouthful of cake.

"Always," Lily agreed, unashamed. Percy Wyatt's shifty manner had piqued her curiosity, and his snatching their carriage had left her disinclined to behave politely toward him if she didn't have to. She scanned the paper, unconcerned that he had said it was a private correspondence.

It was, as she had suspected, nothing of the sort. In fact, it didn't seem like much of anything. It contained only two lines, the first reading *King, Dublin's Boy, Wednesday* and the second an address with *Seven Dials* noted in parentheses afterward.

The back of Lily's neck prickled.

"Jack, do you remember the name of the moneylender that Bernard Walter got into such a scrape with in the spring?"

"The whelp who cost Lord Walter five hundred pounds and made you wonder if his lordship had gambled himself into dire straits?"

"That one, yes," Lily said, standing. "Was it a Mr. King?"

"I've not your memory for names and faces, but that sounds right," Jack agreed, standing and crossing the room to peer over her shoulder at the paper. "Why?"

The sound of crying in the hall made Lily pause instead of answering. Letting the paper fall, she went to open the door and found the maid who had rushed in earlier crumpled on the bottom step, her head in her lap and her sobs shaking her whole body.

"What is the matter?"

The girl jumped to her feet, wiping her tearstained face and stumbling a little. "I beg your pardon, ma'am. I didn't mean to disturb—"

"Nonsense, we weren't doing anything that could be disturbed," Lily said, stepping forward. "Are you well? Can we help?"

"No, there's nothing wrong with me," said the maid—Ellen, Lily remembered her name was. But her posture was rigid with distress, and her hands were clenched into fists among the folds of her dark dress.

"Not with you, then, but with someone you care about?" Lily asked gently.

"My brother. They're saying—" Ellen broke off again.

Jack had joined them in the hall, and he was the one who finished her sentence. "They are saying he stole something?"

Ellen's face crumpled once more, and she hiccupped her way through another sob. "They're saying he stole money right out of Sir Charles's study—and someone sent for a constable. Thomas cleans Sir Charles's study is all, and when Mr. Wyatt went in there, he found the drawer unlocked and the money missing—" Ellen gulped, her shoulders hunching miserably as she remembered to whom she was speaking. "I'm sorry, I oughtn't say anything," she said in a small voice. "I'd be dismissed if she heard I was gossiping. Please, can I get you anything? More tea?"

"No, no tea." Lily eyed Ellen's tearstained face unhappily and turned to Jack. When she saw that he was watching her with an expectant look, she shook her head. "Captain, we cannot simply interfere in their family business."

"I know," he sighed. "But I thought you might—"

Whatever else he might have said was cut off by a tremendous crash from upstairs and a loud shriek that sounded like Lady Wyatt's voice. Jack's eyes went wide and his shoulders stiffened in a moment of indecision before he ran toward the sound.

Clearly there was no choice but to follow. Lily jerked her chin at the wide-eyed maid, then hiked up her skirts, her long legs taking the steps two at a time as she ran after Jack.

★　★　★

Servants clustered in the hall, peering into Sir Charles's study, though the household's grim-faced butler was clearly trying to shoo them away. As Lily pushed past, she could see why.

The scene that met them in Sir Charles's study was chaotic. Lady Wyatt lay on the floor next to her husband's desk; it looked as though one of the heavy drawers had come all the way out and knocked her off-balance, landing half on top of her while its contents were strewn across the floor. Frank bent over her, offering his hand. Lady Wyatt, grimacing with discomfort but clearly unwilling to accept his help, ignored him as she tried one-handed to shift the drawer aside so she could stand up.

A few feet away, Thomas, the accused footman, hovered awkwardly half in, half out of his chair, clearly not sure what he should do, while Percy kept a firm hand on the servant's shoulder to keep him in place and endeavored to look stern, though a green tinge of distress had replaced his earlier blush.

As Lily paused behind Jack in the doorway, Frank took Lady Wyatt's arm to pull her to her feet. She gave another cry, this one sounding pained rather than surprised, and yanked her arm away, falling back once more.

"Oh damn, did it hurt your arm?" Frank growled, looking genuinely concerned. "Hold still—"

As he bent down, the footman started forward. "I can help, sir—"

"Thomas, stay where you are," Frank snapped. "Percy, for God's sake, can't you—"

"Allow me," Jack said, stepping forward. Frank cast him a look of gratitude as they bent together to help Lady Wyatt to her feet.

She looked pale and swayed on her feet as they helped her to a chaise longue tucked under one window, and Lily stepped forward. "I've a vinaigrette," she offered, pulling the silver vial of salts from her reticule and kneeling next to the chair. "If you do not object, Lady Wyatt . . ."

"Thank you, Mrs. Adler." Lady Wyatt winced in pain as Jack brought her a pillow and she settled her arm on it. Frank watched from a few steps away, apparently content to leave her care to them. "I thought to prove the drawer would be locked, but it came out so quickly I lost my balance, and I landed so awkwardly . . ."

As Lily and Jack helped to settle their hostess, Lily took the opportunity to glance around. Ellen had somehow made it past the glowering butler and gone to her brother, dropping to her knees beside him and gripping his hand tightly. Frank's face was rigid with displeasure, and his gaze landed with equal frustration on his stepmother and the accused footman before traveling to the disturbed desk.

"Well, as you can see, Lady Wyatt, the drawers were indeed unlocked, and my father's money is gone from its customary place," he said, running a hand through his hair. "And if you had allowed me to deal with the matter, you would not have injured yourself."

"I am mistress of this house, Frank," Lady Wyatt said sharply, sitting up. "As I hope you remember. Whatever has happened, it is mine to deal with until your father returns. How much money was taken?"

Frank hesitated, glancing at the disturbed desk. Lily followed his line of sight; from her position near the floor, it was easy to see that the drawers were undamaged and their locks unscratched, their keys nowhere in sight. She let her gaze wander around the room, pausing when she got to the doorway before she was recalled by Frank's answer.

"I do not know," he said stiffly. "I only know that is where my father keeps his account books and his ready money, and now only the account books remain. Do you know, ma'am?"

Lady Wyatt shrugged, but Lily thought she looked a little irritated, or perhaps even embarrassed, as she said, "You know your father does not care to have me concern myself with his accounts."

"And Thomas." Frank looked unhappy as he turned to his servant. "You were the last one in here before the money went missing. I saw you leaving before I came in myself."

"Maybe it was not what it seemed, coz," Percy put in, his voice cracking a little. He looked deeply uncomfortable in his role as unofficial guard and rested his hand as lightly as possible on Thomas's shoulder. But there was a hopeful edge to his voice as he said, "We cannot say for sure whether there was money in there. Perhaps my uncle took it with him when he went? To pay a tradesman's bill or some such thing?"

Frank considered the suggestion. "Lady Wyatt, do you know what errand Sir Charles left on this morning? Is it possible he took the money to settle his monthly accounts around town?"

"It is possible, but it did not happen."

Everyone jumped, and the servants hastily stood and bowed, even the wretched-looking Thomas. Sir Charles stood in the doorway, arms crossed and a thunderous frown on his face. Though Lily hadn't seen him in years, his lion's mane of white hair and steely eyes were instantly familiar. But there were lines of irritation on his face, and he walked stiffly, as if his knees or feet were in pain. Lily remembered that Lady Wyatt had mentioned her husband suffered from gout.

"Mrs. Adler." He nodded at Lily. "A pleasure, my dear. You are looking very well. And I hear your esteemed father is in town? I shall take him to task later for not calling himself. But first . . ." He turned to Lady Wyatt, looking grave as he approached her. "Are you well, Winnie?"

"Banged my arm a bit," she said, smiling up at him, though she winced a little.

"Frank." Sir Charles glowered at his son. "How could you let your mother end up in harm's way?"

Even from a distance, Lily could see Frank's jaw clench. "Sir, she is *not* my—"

"It wasn't Frank's fault," Lady Wyatt broke in, looking uncomfortable. Frank shot her a look of surprise, apparently unaccustomed to her coming to his defense, but she kept her eyes and her smiles for Sir Charles as she continued. "He tried to stop me, actually. And it is nothing too terrible, I am sure."

"We shall summon a doctor to be certain of that," Sir Charles rumbled, still glowering. "Once we have dealt with this other matter. Now, am I to understand that we have been burgled?"

"Thomas would never—" Ellen burst out, only to be interrupted by her brother.

"For God's sake, Ellen, hold your tongue—"

"Truly, Father, we cannot say for certain what happened—"

"Uncle, do you mind? I think you must not need me here anymore—"

"All of you be quiet and tell me what the devil has happened!"

Lady Wyatt sank back onto her chaise, her eyes closed and a small sigh of frustration escaping her lips. Thomas and Ellen stumbled over each other trying to explain what he had been doing that day and how he could not have been responsible for the theft.

Lily ignored them, crouching down to look at the fallen desk drawer. She barely heard Sir Charles agree that his nephew could leave. While Sir Charles began to question Frank, she beckoned to Jack. Eyebrows raised, he came to her, looking as if he was trying not to grin.

Lily scowled at him. "What on earth is so amusing?"

"Simply thankful I have no household to manage." He shrugged and bent down to her level. "What can I do for you?"

"Do you know anything about the outcome at the Oaks Stakes at Epsom?"

"Horse racing?" Jack looked baffled. "What the devil do you want to know about horses for at a time like this?"

"Answer the question, please. Did anyone lose unexpectedly this week?"

Jack stared at her. "As a matter of fact, one did. Read about it this morning. One of Lord Templeton's racers, name of Irish Boy or something like that. Lot of people lost money on that race when he stumbled on the turn. The Duke of Grafton's three-year-old, Minuet, placed first."

Lily let out a satisfied sigh. "Was the horse named Dublin's Boy, perhaps?"

"That would be the one." Jack looked at her sharply. "How did you know that?"

Her smile grew. "Captain, will you do something for me?"

"Certainly, though you are annoyingly mysterious."

Lily patted his arm sympathetically. "I expect you'll figure it out in a moment. In the meantime, find Mr. Percy Wyatt and do not let him leave the house."

"Find . . ." A grim smile spread across Jack's face. "Aye, aye, ma'am."

He left so quickly that the door banged shut behind him, and the others in the room jumped, suddenly remembering that they were not alone.

Frank turned to Lily. "Is the captain well?" he asked.

"He is." Lily stood, dusting off her dress. "I apologize for interrupting, but I have rather an important question, Sir Charles." He frowned, clearly irritated, but gestured for her to continue. "Do you know of any moneylenders in the neighborhood of the Seven Dials?"

"Do I know of any . . ." Sir Charles's brows snapped together. "Lily—Mrs. Adler—I have no dealings with moneylenders or with that appalling neighborhood. And if I did know any, I would not share that information with a lady such as yourself."

"I am not asking for my own benefit, sir. In fact, though I have never had cause to deal with him personally, I know there is one by the name of Mr. King."

"The fellow who backs the horse races?" Frank asked, frowning. "Mrs. Adler, I really think—"

"That one precisely, and I am glad you are able to confirm his reputation, Mr. Wyatt." Lily nodded in satisfaction. "Sir Charles, Thomas did not steal your money."

They were all staring at her again. Even Lady Wyatt had opened her eyes. "Mrs. Adler?" Frank asked, hesitating, when no one else said anything.

"Your footman is innocent. I am afraid it was your nephew who stole the money."

"Percy?" Sir Charles shook his head. "Surely not. I provide him a generous allowance."

"Which I expect he exceeds greatly, like all young gentlemen." Lily shook her head. "Just one of those waistcoats must have cost at least thirty pounds. And he hasn't even the money on hand to keep food in his lodgings."

"But—"

Sir Charles was interrupted as the door banged open to reveal a grinning Jack hauling Percy in with a hand around the back of the younger man's neck. "Look at who I found trying to hurry out the door," he said, as cheerfully as if he were inviting them to fire-works at Vauxhall Gardens. In his other hand he held Percy's writing portfolio.

"Take your hands off me!" Percy's cheeks and neck were red with embarrassment and anger as he struggled to free himself. "And return my things to me at once—you have no business . . . Those are my personal letters . . ."

Ignoring his continuing protests, Lily took the portfolio that Jack handed her. She admired the workmanship for a moment, then opened the case. A slow smile spread across her face. "Tell me, Sir Charles, how much did you have in that drawer?"

"Seventy-six pounds."

"What a strange coincidence." Lily offered Sir Charles the portfo-lio. "That is exactly the amount Mr. Wyatt has here."

"That isn't—" Percy tried to protest but was cut off when Jack shook him firmly by the scruff of his neck.

The captain was still grinning broadly; even a glare from Lily didn't dim his enjoyment. "He seemed in a dreadful hurry to leave the house," Jack explained. "I asked where he was going, and the chucklehead tried to run for it. Stupid trick to pull. Boys in the navy run as fast as those who work on land, you know." He shook Percy again, looking cheerful. "Figured it out as soon as he tried to run and brought him straight back here." He bowed to Lily.

"But . . . Percy, why the devil . . ." Sir Charles shook his head, at a loss for words.

"He planned to win back his money before anyone knew he was in debt." Lily said. "I imagine you took the money Mr. King lent you—"

"How the devil do you know about King?" Percy demanded.

"Try not to interrupt, Mr. Wyatt." Lily shook her head. "You are in enough trouble already; forgetting your manners will only make it worse." He stared at her, mouth agape. "Now, where was I?"

"Mr. King," Jack said helpfully.

"Thank you. As I was saying, you took the money Mr. King lent you and went to the Oaks with your school chums." She raised an admonishing eyebrow at Percy. "You really ought to be more careful about snatching carriages, Mr. Wyatt. There is always a chance the people you steal them from will remember what you were discussing. I imagine Mr. Wyatt was one of those unfortunates who lost his whole purse when Dublin's Boy stumbled on the turn." Lily tried to sound authoritative, though she knew next to nothing about horse racing. She could feel Jack holding back laughter but refused to meet his eyes. "Of course, that put him in trouble with Mr. King, who was expecting to be paid, and who no doubt would go to you, Sir Charles, if he did not receive his money." She glanced at Sir Charles. "I imagine you would be displeased if you discovered he was in debt?"

"He will be lucky if he gets any allowance at all after this," Sir Charles said coldly. "And if I do not hand him over to the law first."

Percy went from red-faced to pale so quickly it was almost comical. Lily shook her head. She could guess that Sir Charles would never subject his family to such public embarrassment, but Percy was too overcome to realize that.

"But Mrs. Adler," Sir Charles continued, "one question you have not answered. How the devil did he get the money at all? Are you saying my nephew can pick locks?"

"If I thought he could do something half so clever, I would not suspect him of such a clumsy robbery in the first place. No, he simply used the spare key you keep on the lintel above the door, then put it back when he was done. Though it seems he was silly enough to leave a drawer not only unlocked but open." She shook her head. "You really should have a more careful hiding place. Even I noticed it, and I was not planning to rob you."

They all, even Jack, stared at her in astonishment. Lady Wyatt began to laugh.

CHAPTER 4

Given the way she hadn't hesitated to interfere in the Wyatt family's affairs, Lily expected Lady Wyatt to politely rescind her invitation to ride the next morning. But she had insisted, saying her arm was sure to be better by morning. So after breakfast, Lily instructed Anna to lay out her riding habit.

Though she had forgone her usual routine of breakfasting in her own room and instructed Mrs. Carstairs to lay breakfast in the parlor, Lily hadn't seen any sign of her father. She didn't mind. If she couldn't be cozy while she dined, she was at least happy to be alone. And it gave her the opportunity to go over the week's menus with her housekeeper and offer several suggestions for managing her father's requests while he was with them.

"And do you know how long might that be, Mrs. Adler?" Mrs. Carstairs asked carefully. "Mr. Branson was unable to say when I spoke to him last night."

Lily pursed her lips. "For as long as he needs, Mrs. Carstairs. Or as long as I can bear his company. My record on that score is fifteen years, however, so let us hope it will not come to that."

The housekeeper wisely didn't say anything else.

Lily's pleasant solitude lasted until she was making her way back upstairs to change, when she found her path blocked by her father's belligerent frame. Unwell he might be, but George Pierce was still a solid, imposing man, and Lily had to remind herself to square her shoulders and meet his scowl with a smile as he did his best to tower over her from the step above.

"Good morning, Father."

He didn't return the greeting. "I am going to breakfast," he announced, eyebrows raised.

Lily waited for a moment and then, when no more information was forthcoming, nodded. "I hope you enjoy it. Mrs. Carstairs is an excellent cook."

He sniffed. "And I assume your excessively early rising is an attempt to avoid my company?"

"It is past nine o'clock, father," Lily said. "Hardly excessive. And I have an appointment this morning, so if you will excuse me——"

"What is your appointment?"

He couldn't curtail or dictate what she did with her time, Lily reminded herself. Even if having him in her home left her feeling as if her independence were being slowly stripped away once more, in practical terms he had no say in her life anymore. Answering his question was only polite. "An engagement with a friend——"

"That sailor again, I assume?"

Lily took a deep breath. "Captain Hartley was also invited, but no, the engagement is to ride with Lady Wyatt this morning. Which I assume you would approve of?" Seeing that she had momentarily surprised him into silence, she took the opportunity to push past her father. "You would like her, I think. She is charming and elegant."

"And her husband's a fool for marrying again," Mr. Pierce grumbled, but Lily was already heading down the hall and didn't answer.

Jack was coming just before ten to escort her to the Wyatts' house, and Lily was in a hurry to dress and escape her father once again. Her room was empty when she walked in, but Anna had laid out her riding habit on the bed, pressed and ready, its military-style buttons glinting in the morning light amid folds of emerald-green fabric.

Lily stared at it without moving. She had forgotten that her habit wasn't suitable to wear when she was in mourning.

She was still staring when Anna returned, the freshly brushed riding hat in her hands. When she saw Lily's posture, Anna paused.

"You don't have another, I'm afraid," she said gently.

Lily nodded, unable to speak. One hand reached out to brush the heavy fabric of the habit; the other clenched a fold of the gray dress she wore. She had stopped wearing colors even before Freddy died—in those last months of his illness, she had traded all her pretty dresses for drab gowns more suited to nursing an invalid who would never recover. And even after full mourning was complete, she had lingered in the muted shades of half mourning long past when anyone would have required it of her, even Freddy's own family. Laying aside the visual reminders of her grief felt too much like leaving behind her marriage.

But that had meant more than two years of sorrow. And in the last few months, since she had come to London and taken control of her life once more, something had shifted inside her.

"Yes, thank you, Anna," Lily said quietly, her voice catching a little. She cleared her throat and said, more firmly, "I will wear this one."

★   ★   ★

She managed to leave the house without encountering her father again. When Carstairs sent word that Captain Hartley was waiting in the front hall, Lily felt a pang of anxiety. Jack had loved Freddy like a brother. And he had never given any indication that he thought her mourning had gone on long enough.

Jack was in the middle of removing his hat, and his hand stilled at the brim as he caught sight of her. Even Carstairs fell still as they watched her come down the stairs, the heavy folds of her green skirts buttoned up on one side to allow her to walk freely and a single dyed-green feather curling over the brim of her hat and flirting with her brown curls.

Lily felt exposed as she descended the final few steps, though she was bolstered by the approval that softened Carstairs's smile. She had never considered herself a shy person, but she could barely meet Jack's eyes as she crossed the hall to give him her hand.

For a moment neither of them spoke, and when she raised her gaze at last, Lily thought she saw the captain blinking something from the corner of his eye. "That was Freddy's favorite color," he said at last, his voice catching.

Lily nodded. "I know."

Jack's jaw tightened for a moment as he swallowed. But he smiled. "Well done, Lily," he said quietly. "Good for you."

★   ★   ★

There was a lightness between them as they made the quick journey to Wimpole Street. As Jack waved down a hack carriage and handed her in, Lily found herself laughing at all of his quips or droll pieces of gossip, even the ones she normally would have chastised him for repeating. And Jack kept glancing at her out of the corner of his eye.

"Do I look that dreadful?" Lily asked at last as he handed her down from the carriage in front of the Wyatts' home.

"Quite the opposite," he said, rubbing the back of his neck as he released her hand. "Did you know, you are actually quite pretty?"

"You mean you did not find me pretty before?"

"I think I had forgotten to consider it one way or another," Jack admitted, grinning. "What a shame everyone has left London already; you would cause quite a sensation."

Lily shook her head. "I know full well I am not handsome enough for *that*."

"Surprise can cause as much of a sensation as admiration," Jack pointed out.

"Captain!" Lily exclaimed in mock indignation. "You were supposed to argue with me!"

They continued bantering as they mounted the steps to Sir Charles's townhouse, only to fall silent and exchange a puzzled glance as they realized that the door was half-open, the sounds of raised voices echoing from within.

Lily glanced at Jack, an uneasy sensation beginning to curl in the pit of her stomach. "Should we knock?"

He shrugged and did so, rapping firmly on the wood of the door. There was no response, but it swung open a little more. After hesitating a moment, Lily bit her lip and said, "Well, we ought to at least make sure Lady Wyatt knows we've come. If it is no longer convenient to ride, she can certainly tell us to leave."

"And you were already happy to interfere yesterday," Jack pointed out, though she could hear the unease lurking beneath his playful tone. "We might as well do it again."

"Very true." Lily pushed the door the rest of the way open and strode in, Jack following close behind.

The front hall was empty, but they could still hear voices not far away, now low and urgent, and the sound of quiet crying from somewhere just out of sight. The uneasy feeling began to spread through Lily's chest and arms, and she reached out her hand in blind anxiety. She was relieved to feel Jack take it and press it reassuringly into the crook of his arm.

She had just decided that they should leave after all when quick steps echoed down the stairs. A moment later Frank Wyatt came rushing down, checking himself at the bottom as he stared at them in surprise.

His face was pale and his eyes red as he gaped at them, his easy manner vanished. "Lily? And Captain . . . I've quite forgot your name. You must excuse . . . what are you doing here?"

"The door was open, and no one answered our knock," Lily said, feeling a little ashamed of their hastiness in entering. "I apologize, Frank; we did not mean to intrude, but we had an appointment to ride with Lady Wyatt this morning. Is everyone well?"

"Is everyone . . . No. No." Frank gripped the banister with one hand, his knuckles white. "I am afraid that Lady Wyatt will not be able to ride today. My father . . ." He swallowed. "My father has died."

Lily stared at him, unable to make sense of his words. They had seen Sir Charles just the day before. If he had seemed a little older and weaker than she remembered, he had still been utterly vital and alive. "Died? But . . . how?"

"In point of fact," a new voice said quietly from behind them. "It seems Sir Charles Wyatt has been killed."

CHAPTER 5

The man who emerged from the library should have looked out of place in the Wyatts' elegant entrance hall. But he carried himself with confidence, as if he were a frequent visitor in the houses of his superiors—which, Lily knew, was not entirely untrue. His clothing was too professional for a guest but too well made for a servant. His accent was neither cultured nor deferential, his age neither old nor young. His appearance was in almost every way unremarkable—except for his eyes, which took in the shocked tableau with a quick, intelligent gaze.

He was the last person Lily would have expected to see, and she very nearly opened her mouth to say so. But those perceptive eyes caught the motion, and the man gave his head a minute shake.

She saw it, though, and obeyed the unspoken request. If he didn't want Frank Wyatt to know they were acquainted, she wouldn't give it away yet. Jack, she could see from the corner of her eye, had noticed the silent exchange and was holding his tongue as well.

Neither of them had completely hidden their surprise, of course, but that wouldn't matter. A suggestion of murder was reason enough for anyone to look shocked.

"I will thank you not to say such things, especially in mixed company," Frank was saying, oblivious to the undercurrents between his guests. "We have no reason to believe my father suffered from anything but an extremely unfortunate accident. Mrs. Adler, Captain, I

apologize. Mr. Page is here from the Bow Street offices, and his presence is, I assure you, a mere formality."

"As you say, Mr. Wyatt," Simon Page said. It seemed he had
learned something about dealing with the members of London's upper
classes since Lily had first met him. Where he once would have bristled at Frank's presumption, Mr. Page simply nodded and accepted
the correction, though his expression lost none of its shrewdness or
determination. "But I am afraid I cannot allow you to have visitors in
the home until I have made a thorough observation of the premises
and questioned everyone in residence." His eyes glittered a little as he
added, "As a mere formality."

"Of course," Frank said, looking flustered. "I did not—"

"Mr. Wyatt was unaware that we were arriving," Lily put in, feeling
obligated to rescue Frank from Mr. Page's imposing stare. "When we
were here yesterday, Lady Wyatt invited us to go riding, and of course,
with the tragedy of Sir Charles's death, no one remembered to—"

"You were here yesterday?" Mr. Page broke in.

Lily bristled a little at the interruption, but she decided to for-
give him, considering the circumstances, and nodded. "Both Captain
Hartley"—she gestured to Jack—"and I called on Lady Wyatt. I am
Mrs. Adler."

"Mrs. Adler, Captain." Mr. Page bowed, and his gaze fastened
first on Lily, then on Jack as he straightened. "If you will permit a
question: did either of you see Sir Charles during your visit?"

Lily exchanged a glance with Jack. "Yes, we both saw him when
we were here yesterday afternoon. That was when we engaged to ride
with Lady Wyatt this morning." She felt a pang of sympathy as soon
as she said the words and turned to Frank Wyatt. "How is she?"

Frank swallowed visibly. "I am not certain she has overcome the
shock. But she will be devastated." He glanced toward the stairs, his
expression lost. "We all are."

"Regrettably, I do need to speak to Lady Wyatt," the Bow Street
officer said. "But I'll only need a moment of her time. If you'd be so
good as to ask her to see me?"

Frank hesitated. "I am not sure that is . . . wise." He glanced back up the stairs, then shook his head. "She is unlikely to come down, I am afraid. She and my father were very fond of each other, and she . . ." For a moment, an expression like irritation crossed Frank's face, but it was quickly swallowed back into his general distress. "It seems she is not the sort of woman who bears up under difficulty."

A day before, Lily would have been surprised at the statement. Lady Wyatt had seemed exactly like the sort of woman who would handle difficulty with forbearance. But to lose a husband you cared for, and without even the warning an illness could provide . . .

Lily closed her eyes, the reality of Lady Wyatt's loss hitting her like a blow. But a moment later she felt Jack's hand on her elbow, warm and comforting and understanding, and she opened her eyes. She couldn't quite bring herself to smile at him, but he seemed to sense her gratitude, because he gave her arm a slight squeeze before releasing her.

"I need only ask Lady Wyatt a few questions about last night," Mr. Page said. "To have as clear a picture as possible of what happened. And if I do not ask now, I will have to return another day, which may be more difficult for the family."

"Very well," Frank said, his voice as stiff as his posture. The expression he turned on the constable was not quite a glare, but it was certainly a warning. "As long as I have your assurance that you'll make no mention of this preposterous theory that my father was killed deliberately. We are all distressed enough, sir. We don't need any more reasons for grief."

The constable bowed. "I will certainly do everything in my power not to add to her distress."

"Then, of course, we should be leaving," Jack said to Frank. "If there is anything we can do . . ."

"Unfortunately, Captain, I must ask you both to wait a moment as well," Mr. Page said. "As you and Mrs. Adler saw Sir Charles yesterday, it would be most helpful if I could have a moment of your time to hear your impressions of how he appeared. Perhaps you'd be so good as to answer a few questions while Mr. Wyatt fetches his stepmother?"

Frank looked unhappy, but there was little he could do when both his guests readily gave their assent. He nodded, told them he would return as swiftly as possible, and, with a final warning glance toward the constable, hurried upstairs.

As soon as they were alone, Mr. Page crossed his arms and took a deep breath before bringing his stern gaze to rest first on Lily, then Jack. "And how is it," he asked, keeping his voice quiet, "that I find you yet again in such close proximity to a suspicious death?"

"Bad timing," Jack said, shrugging before reaching out a friendly hand. "Good to see you in any case, Page."

There was a glimmer of a smile in Mr. Page's eyes as he shook the offered hand, and Lily couldn't help but marvel at the friendliness of the gesture. When they had first met, neither Jack nor Mr. Page had been willing to see anything of value in the other, each of them caught up in a tangle of resentment and misunderstanding arising from the gulf between their different positions in the world. And Mr. Page's opinion of Lily herself had been as far from flattering as could be. Only gradually had they come to feel anything like respect for each other. When the Harper affair had finally resolved with the murderer of three men arrested, Mr. Page had been willing to admit that both Lily and Jack—and Ofelia, Lady Carroway, whose practical mind Lily suddenly found herself missing immensely—had been vital to uncovering the truth.

"And you, Hartley." Mr. Page turned to Lily. "Mrs. Adler."

"Sir. Mr. Wyatt does not seem to think there is anything to be suspicious of," Lily replied, keeping her voice low to match his. "Why did you not want him to know we are acquainted? I have known the Wyatts for years, and Frank trusts me. He might be more cooperative if we tell him you are known to us."

Mr. Page eyed them without answering for a moment, then, seeming to make up his mind, reached for the door behind him. "Come into the library."

Lily hesitated. "Is that where . . . ?"

"Yes." The constable raised his brows. "Never say you're becoming squeamish now, ma'am."

"Here, now," Jack said, though there was little heat to his objection.

But Lily had already lifted her chin and, meeting Mr. Page's challenging gaze with her own defiant one, stepped through the door he was holding open.

"What do you want us to see?" she asked, once all three of them were inside with the door closed behind them.

"Mr. Wyatt may not think there's anything suspicious, but I hope you'll allow me to know more than he does," Mr. Page said in clipped, professional tones, walking toward the windows. "Or at least, to have more reason to be suspicious than he has."

There was a heavy desk near one wall of windows. Mr. Page stopped next to it and gestured toward a spot Lily would rather have avoided looking at. One jutting corner was smeared with red-brown stains, which had dripped down the wooden leg beneath it. Below, a darker puddle had soaked into the expensive carpet. It was a jarring sight, especially with no other signs of struggle or disorder in the room. Lily swallowed.

"The family would assume that he tripped, correct? And hit his head?" Jack asked.

Mr. Page nodded. "He was found dead on the floor this morning. Wound to the head. This was what did it." He gestured toward the bloody desk. "At least, that's what seems obvious."

"But you doubt it?" Jack asked, squatting down to gaze at the unfortunate scene before them. Though he moved without hesitation, Lily was gratified to see that his expression was nowhere near calm; seeing death in the middle of a war was a far cry from being confronted with a puddle of blood in someone's library, and Jack clearly thought so too.

Mr. Page nodded. "I think it's too tidy. My instincts say there is more under the surface here. But I've no way to prove anything, especially if these Wyatts keep me out of their life the way most of your class does." His hands clenched into fists as he spoke, a rare moment of emotion for the stoic constable.

Lily exchanged a quick look with Jack. He raised his shoulders in a quick shrug, then nodded. She nodded back. "What do you need from us, Mr. Page?"

He couldn't hide his surprise at the quick agreement. "Just like that? You'll believe me and offer to help, with no more proof than my instincts?"

"I am familiar with not being believed about something important, sir," Lily said, and though her tone was mild, she couldn't keep the pointed expression from her face. Mr. Page, who had been dismissive of her insight more than once when they first met, flushed as she continued. "You know your business, and you have proved more than once that your instincts do not lead you astray." She pursed her lips, then added, "Though they do sometimes bias you against widows of a certain class."

Jack let out a short bark of laughter, which he quickly smothered. "Beg pardon," he said. "Not the time for humor, I know."

Mr. Page was smiling too, though the expression was more self-deprecating. "As you say, Mrs. Adler. I'll be certain to hear Lady Wyatt out, you may be sure. But it's not just instinct that makes me suspicious."

"What, then?" Jack asked, standing.

Mr. Page hesitated, then gestured toward the fireplace. "One of the irons is missing."

Lily followed the motion of his hand, frowning. The stand of implements on the hearth was indeed missing a poker. The absence would never have struck her as odd—but as soon as Mr. Page pointed it out, it did. Everything about the room was tidy and organized, each book and knickknack in its place. For something to be missing was incongruous. And an implement like a poker wasn't something that was inclined to break easily.

"You think it was used for nefarious purposes?" Lily asked quietly.

"It's a possibility," Mr. Page agreed quietly. "Though a difficult one to prove. But it's enough to make me curious." He cleared his throat, then pulled a small memorandum book from his pocket, flipping through a few pages. "Mr. Wyatt is fetching his stepmother at the moment. Perhaps you'd be willing to stay while I speak with her, Mrs. Adler? I imagine she'll feel more comfortable with you than with me."

"Of course," Lily said, surprised at the request. As grateful as Mr. Page had been for her help in the past, it had taken more than a little effort to convince him to accept it. For him to now seek out her assistance, and Jack's, must mean he was convinced indeed that his instincts were correct—and convinced that the members of the Wyatt family would do their best to hide the truth from him.

Her suspicions were confirmed as Mr. Page glanced at the door, then lowered his voice even further. "For now, what can you tell me of the Wyatt family?"

He was looking to both of them, and Jack shrugged. "Just met them for the first time yesterday when I accompanied Mrs. Adler on her visit."

"I have known them for years, except for Lady Wyatt. Mr. Frank Wyatt is my father's godson, and they are quite close," Lily said, moving slowly around the room as she spoke, her gaze traveling over every object there without settling in any one spot. "Sir Charles and my father have long been acquainted, but before yesterday, I had not seen any of the family in years." She swallowed, suddenly feeling a surge of emotion, and grasped the edge of the mantelpiece to steady herself. "I can hardly believe he is truly gone."

"And you called yesterday because . . . ?"

Lily grimaced. "Because my father didn't want to. Sir Charles and Lady Wyatt married recently, and I was calling to pay my family's respects, offer our best wishes, that sort of thing." She glanced up, shaking her head. "My father does not approve of second marriages, so I was dispatched in his place."

"And then you met Lady Wyatt?" Mr. Page asked, his fingers steepled together as he tapped them thoughtfully against his lips. "What did you think of her? And of the young Mr. Wyatt?"

"I know Frank from childhood, though he was several years my senior and away at school a great deal of the time." Lily shook her head. "He was always the sort who aspired to being a popular man about town, and it seems he has achieved that goal. Lady Wyatt was charming and, from what I could see, devoted to her husband."

"Which did not seem to endear her to her husband's son," Jack put in. He shook his head, grimacing. "They were quite the pair."

"Sniping at each other," Lily explained, seeing the question in Mr. Page's expression. "It surprised me in Frank. But there didn't seem any real harm in it. I think there is very little difference in their ages, which could account for it. She was injured yesterday, not badly I think, and while Mr. Wyatt seemed annoyed, he was also perfectly helpful."

"And did you see Sir Charles?"

"Briefly," Lily said, hesitating, her gaze darting back toward the blood at the other end of the room. She shivered, tucking her gloved hands around her elbows for comfort before glancing at Jack.

"He seemed well enough," Jack said slowly. "In full command of himself and his household, except for his nephew."

"And except for his gout," Lily added.

"A nephew?" Mr. Page's brows rose. "I hadn't heard that there was a nephew as well."

"Mr. Percy Wyatt. I had met him only once before yesterday, when we were still children, and know him not at all. Except that now I know he steals carriages from other pedestrians," Lily said, though there was no heat in it. With a man dead, Percy Wyatt snatching their carriage was hardly of consequence. She glanced around the room again, this time looking anywhere but at the blood by the desk. She was going to have to tell her father that his friend was dead.

"He gambles," Jack added. "And he is a very poor thief. At least when Mrs. Adler is around to catch him. And he doesn't live here, though he and Mr. Frank Wyatt seem to be friends."

Lily listened with only half an ear. How was she going to break the news to her father when she could barely believe it herself?

There was so little about the library that was remarkable. Comfortable chairs before the fireplace, two walls of books. A wheeled chair sat in one corner; Lily eyed it, puzzled, before she recalled Sir Charles's gout. Such an affliction often caused swelling in the knees and feet, and a wheeled chair would likely prove a comfort on days when the sensation was particularly painful.

The desk . . . She shuddered and looked away again, her eyes going to the windows beyond it. The curtains were only partly open, which made sense. If a maid had started to air out and clean the room, she would have gone to the curtains first, then been interrupted as soon as she caught sight of Sir Charles's body on the floor.

"Theft? I'm going to need you to elaborate on . . . Mrs. Adler, what are you doing?"

Lily was walking slowly over to the windows. Something had just struck her as odd—but what was it? She looked round once more, hoping something would jog the thought loose, and her eyes fell on the hearth where she had just been standing.

"Mrs. Adler?"

That was it. There was a streak across the hearth, as though someone had begun wiping the ash and soot away before abandoning the task.

"Look," Lily said quietly, pointing. Both men came to where she was standing, frowning at the hearth.

"Someone did a poor job of cleaning," Jack said, then broke off. "No, that makes no sense. If a maid had been cleaning the fireplace yesterday, she would have finished the task."

"And the one this morning didn't even finish opening the curtains before discovering Sir Charles," Mr. Page said, turning to look back at the half-covered windows.

"She certainly would not have begun cleaning the hearth." Lily stepped closer. "Was something dragged across it?"

"Sir Charles cannot have done it, after he collapsed," Jack said. "And look at this." He reached out as though to touch something on the carpet, then drew his hand back, looking uneasy. "Unless I mistake my guess, those are spots of—"

"Blood." Lily crouched down to look at them as well, swallowing back a wave of nausea.

"And yet Sir Charles supposedly collapsed near the desk," Mr. Page said, his voice rising slightly with excitement as he strode briskly toward them. "Which was how he hit his head. So why was someone by the . . . Mrs. Adler, what are you doing?"

Lily was twisting her neck to look in the fireplace, and as she did, something white behind the lintel caught her eye. She reached in, grabbing a corner of it, and tugged. "There is something stuck in here, some kind of fabric." She tugged again, then let out a startled yelp as whatever it was came free and tumbled into the fireplace with the clanging sound of metal and a shower of soot.

Jack grabbed Lily's arm and hauled her to her feet while Mr. Page stepped quickly back. All three of them were coughing as the door to the library flew open.

"What the devil?" Frank Wyatt demanded, staring at them from the doorway. Behind him stood Percy Wyatt—newly arrived, judging by the hat and gloves clutched in his hands. Lily, her arm still clasped by Jack while dust and soot swirled around them, tried to think of some explanation. "Mrs. Adler, what are you . . . And Mr. Page, what is the meaning of . . ."

He trailed off, staring toward something at their feet with confusion that was slowly growing into horror. Lily followed the line of his gaze.

At her feet lay a pile of toweling that had clearly once been white. Now, though, it was stained and discolored—not just with soot from being stuffed in the chimney, but with the reddish brown of blood that had not yet had time to dry. And sticking out of the bundle was the missing iron poker.

CHAPTER 6

For long moments there was deep silence in the room, broken only by the swish and trickle of soot that still fell from the chimney. Lily was suddenly grateful for Jack's steadying hand at her elbow. Gathering her composure, she met the two pairs of eyes staring at her from the doorway.

"I am terribly sorry, Mr. Wyatt," she said, amazed by the steadiness of her own voice. "But I am afraid someone stuck that up your chimney."

Frank and Percy both gaped at her. "But what—" Percy began.

"Step back please, madam, sir." Mr. Page stepped forward, herding Lily and Jack out of the way. His voice was that of an officer of the law once more, serious and impersonal.

He crouched down in front of the hearth, peering into the chimney, then turning to examine the bloody pile of cloth in front of him. Lily stepped back, drawing Jack with her and trying to discreetly brush the soot from her clothing.

Mr. Page rose at last. "How often are your fireplaces cleaned?"

"The fireplaces?" Frank asked, sounding dazed. "The maids sweep them out daily, of course. I suppose the chimneys are swept once a season? I really could not say; you would do better to ask the housekeeper."

Mr. Page eyed him coldly, then turned back to the hearth. "It was bunched up tightly, it seems. The blood has not quite dried."

He glanced up at his audience. "This has certainly not been up there more than a day. Which means this is likely your father's blood, Mr. Wyatt. And someone tried to clean up and hide the mess of murdering him."

"That is . . . it could not . . . preposterous," Percy stammered from the doorway.

"Have you another explanation?" the Bow Street constable demanded. The younger man went very red, then very pale, and did not answer. Mr. Page turned back to Frank. "I think we may now safely conclude that your father's death was *not* natural. Which means that I'll need to speak to all the servants as well. Are there any other members of the family, in town or otherwise?"

"An uncle of my mother lives in Lincolnshire, and my father has a second cousin—I think he and his family reside in Oxford?" Frank looked ill as he stared at the hearth. "But other than that, no. It was just us." Suddenly scowling, he rounded on Lily and Jack once more. "What the devil were you doing in here?" he demanded.

"Mrs. Adler was feeling unwell and needed a moment to collect herself," Jack said quickly, lying with a perfectly straight face.

"And I thought I heard an animal in the chimney."

"She was afraid it was a bat."

"I cannot abide bats," Lily agreed, resisting the urge to kick Jack in the shin for such a ridiculous explanation. Instead, she pressed a hand to her heart in a picture of feminine distress. Men, in her experience, rarely questioned a visibly upset lady too closely. She clutched Jack's arm more tightly, wondering if she should fan herself for good measure. But that might be pushing it too far; she didn't want Frank to remember that she wasn't the sort of woman to grow squeamish around small animals.

She was saved further scrutiny by Mr. Page, who stepped forward. "Gentlemen, Mrs. Adler, as this room is now definitively the scene of a murder, I must ask that we leave it immediately. Mr. Wyatt, we'll use the parlor that you and I spoke in before." He raised his eyebrows when none of them moved quickly enough to suit him. "Now, if you please."

"Certainly," Jack said, steering Lily toward the door. Percy and Frank, who were still blocking the way, had no choice but to step out into the hall.

Mr. Page followed swiftly and pulled the door shut behind him. "Mr. Wyatt," he said, fixing Percy with a stern gaze. "I'll need you to fetch the housekeeper. This door must be locked and stay that way until I give leave otherwise."

"I say—" Percy began indignantly, only to be cut off by his cousin.

"Do it, Perce." Frank sounded weary beyond belief; his expression was dazed, as if he still couldn't quite believe what he had just seen. "Please."

When Percy, with a belligerent look, had trotted off into the depths of the house, Mr. Page turned to Jack. "Captain, as an officer of the navy, I trust I may rely on you? No one is to go into or out of that room until the housekeeper arrives to lock it. And then the key must go to no one but myself."

"Certainly." Jack looked far more serious than usual as he let Lily's arm fall and took up a post by the door. But Lily caught the quick glance he gave her out of the corner of his eye. "I trust Mrs. Adler will not object to delaying our departure while I do my duty."

The pretense was for Percy and Frank's benefit, of course, since Mr. Page had specifically requested their assistance. And Frank, still looking dazed, nodded. "Of . . . of course. Lily . . . Mrs. Adler, would you care to come into the drawing room to sit down?" He ran a hand through his hair as he opened the door across the hall and bowed her in. "I know it is highly irregular . . ."

"I will await the captain, certainly," Lily said, her voice as serious as her expression. "I am so, so dreadfully sorry, Frank. Will you sit down? You do not look well."

"I do not feel well," he said, shaking his head. "In fact, I think I don't feel much of anything." But he sank into a chair as she urged, then glanced up at Mr. Page, who had followed them in and shut the door. "What happens now?"

Mr. Page regarded him without speaking for a moment, his expression unreadable. Lily took a seat of her own, watching the interplay between the two men. "Now I must speak to Lady Wyatt. And your cousin, and the servants who were in the house last night."

Frank grimaced. "Unfortunately, Lady Wyatt has informed me that she is not well enough to come down." There was an edge of frustration in Frank's voice, and the fingers of one hand drummed against his thigh in a sharp, agitated beat.

Mr. Page nodded, looking more sympathetic than Lily had yet seen. "Of course, it's very understandable that she'd resent my presence at such a time. Perhaps if someone she knew, who could sympathize with her position, could speak with her . . ."

He glanced around the room, his eyes landing on Lily as if he had only just remembered her presence. Lily kept her own expression impassive, though it took effort. She turned to Frank.

"Perhaps I might go to Lady Wyatt?" she offered gently, seizing on the opportunity to follow Mr. Page's request without arousing too much suspicion. "I could help her prepare herself, perhaps sit with her during the interview." She didn't have to contrive the sympathy in her voice as she added, "I lost my own husband far too early, and I can well imagine the pain and confusion she must be feeling."

"That is very good of you," Frank said, swallowing roughly. "But she said . . . she said she is not yet ready to pick over her husband's corpse. And that was before we knew he was . . ." He broke off, looking suddenly horrified. "Good God, do I have to be the one to tell her?"

"Frank," Lily said gently. "I can tell her, if you wish. It might be easier to hear from a family friend than from . . ." She hesitated.

"From someone she does not like? At all?" Frank shook his head. "No doubt she would, but I cannot ask you to . . . such circumstances . . ." He trailed off. It was the first time she could ever recall seeing him at a loss for words.

"The circumstances are very unusual, and very grim. But also not so unfamiliar to me. Were you aware of the unfortunate incident at the home of Lord and Lady Walter this April?"

Frank looked uneasy. "You mean the . . ." He hesitated, still clearly unable to say *murder*.

"Lady Walter is a dear friend, and I was with her during much of that incident. This"—Lily cast a sideways look at Mr. Page—"this is not my first experience with Bow Street, I'm afraid. I think I may well be able to be of assistance to Lady Wyatt."

Frank puffed out his cheeks, hesitating, and it took all Lily's will-power not to glance at Mr. Page. He had wanted her to speak to Lady Wyatt. What would he do if Frank turned down her offer?

But at last Frank nodded. "Very well. If anyone can be of assistance to her . . ." He shrugged again. "I confess I haven't the faintest notion of what to say."

Lily stood decisively. "If you will be so good as to show me to her," she said.

As Frank held the door open and followed her into the hall, Mr. Page called, "If you would return as swiftly as possible, Mr. Wyatt, I've a few questions to ask you. And your cousin as well."

Frank nodded curtly, not bothering to glance back as he allowed the door to swing closed behind him.

Lily cast a glance at the parlor, then leaned conspiratorially toward Frank, speaking in an undertone as they began to climb the stairs. "Such an intrusion on what ought to be a private family matter. One cannot bring these things to a close too quickly."

At that, Frank nodded firmly. "Indeed, it is most unfortunate. And to suggest that it might have been one of the servants . . . It does not bear thinking of." He sighed and raised his voice. "Ellen?"

A moment later, the young maid Lily had met the day before appeared at the top of the stairs. "Yes, sir?"

"Show Mrs. Adler to Lady Wyatt's chambers," Frank said. "I am afraid I must . . ." He gestured toward the parlor and sighed.

"He does not seem the type to browbeat you," Lily said, pausing with him at the top of the staircase.

"We shall see. Thank you for offering your assistance to Lady Wyatt." For a moment, Frank gazed at nothing; then, meeting Lily's eyes, he scowled. "I am glad she will have someone else's backbone to borrow, since apparently she has none of her own."

Lily bit back a sharp retort at the unkind words. Frank's father had just died, she reminded herself. He could be forgiven for whatever petulance or unhappiness he might currently feel. And better he said it to her than to his father's widow. "I will see what I can do for Lady Wyatt."

He nodded. "Thank you, Lily." Shaking his head, he muttered, "God knows how we are going to get through this."

Lily watched him leave. Mr. Page had not, in fact, suggested that it had been one of the servants. He had merely said he wished to speak to them.

He had also said he wanted to speak to the members of the family. Which meant . . . Lily held back a shiver. She had known the Wyatts for as long as she could remember. It was almost impossible to believe that Sir Charles was dead.

It was even more impossible to think that someone in the house had likely killed him.

Lily watched the parlor door swing closed behind Frank, then turned to the young maid. "Lead on, Ellen." She squared her shoulders. "Let us see how I might be of service."

★ ★ ★

"There must be some mistake."

The utter certainty in Lady Wyatt's voice was heartbreaking. She looked as if she had made it halfway through her preparations for the day before her husband's death was discovered. She had dressed, and someone had begun fixing her hair, but enough curls were still loose to create a wild halo around her head. Her face was pale and splotchy, and her eyes were red. And though her denial was firm, there was an undercurrent of desperation, almost panic in her expression. She shook her head, her fingers worrying at a handkerchief over and over until Lily wondered if there would be anything left of it but threads before the day was done.

"I am afraid I saw it with my own eyes, Lady Wyatt," she said, as gently as possible. "And the gentleman from Bow Street will now need to speak with you."

Lady Wyatt shook her head, her expression suddenly furious. "My husband has *died*, Mrs. Adler, and that man down there wishes—" She broke off, her entire body suddenly wilting, the energy and fury gone. "Does he think I did it, then? Is that why—" She raised her handkerchief to her mouth, unable to cover the sob that escaped.

"I am sure it is nothing of the sort," Lily said quickly, taking Lady Wyatt's hands in her own, wanting to offer some kind of comfort. The rich green fabric of her riding habit suddenly seemed inappropriate, and for a moment Lily wished she were still wearing her mourning colors. "He needs to speak to everyone, not only you. And Frank—"

"Wants nothing to do with me, I am sure," Lady Wyatt snapped, pulling away suddenly and rising. She paced around the room, her hands fluttering at her sides, clenching and unclenching as if she had no idea what to do with them. "You needn't try to pretend that it occurred to him to offer me any comfort or assistance."

Lily, thinking of Frank's unkind remarks, couldn't argue. Unkind and untrue, it seemed. Watching Lady Wyatt visibly pull herself together, Lily reflected that the woman had plenty of backbone.

"I am grateful for your kindness, Mrs. Adler, but I will not speak to the man from Bow Street." Lady Wyatt finally drew to a halt in the middle of the room and lifted her chin. But she wrapped her arms around herself, as if she were trying to hold herself together through sheer force of will. Her fingers dug in so sharply that they dimpled the skin, and Lily feared they would leave bruises. "You will, I hope, be so good as to tell him."

"Then he will return," Lily said gently. "Please, allow me to help you prepare yourself. If you speak with him today, that can be the end of it."

"I cannot." Lady Wyatt turned away quickly, but not before Lily saw tears breaking through her composure. Lady Wyatt sank onto the settee at the foot of her bed. Holding back a sob, she gasped, "I wouldn't even know what to say. Please." For a moment she sounded very young. The tears were visible on her cheeks now. "I don't know what to do."

Lily hesitated for only a moment. She barely knew Lady Wyatt. But she remembered what it felt like to be that lost, that overwhelmed. She crossed the room and took a seat as well.

"Start by letting yourself cry," she said, taking the other woman's hands in her own once more. "Hold yourself together in public, if you must. But first, give yourself a moment to grieve."

Lady Wyatt dropped her head onto Lily's shoulder, and her sobs shook both of them for several minutes. Lily didn't move, not even to brush away her own tears, until Lady Wyatt lifted her head at last.

"Thank you, Mrs. Adler." She took a deep, shaking breath, wiping away the tears that lingered on her cheeks. "And I am sorry. God knows what you must think of me."

"You needn't apologize," Lily said past the lump in her own throat as she stood. On the dressing table on the other side of the room, she found a bottle of lavender water and a handkerchief. Upending the bottle onto the soft cotton, she handed it to Lady Wyatt so the woman could bathe her face. The light floral scent made Lily feel calmer as well, and she took a deep breath of her own.

Lady Wyatt nodded. "And yet you still advise me to speak to the man from Bow Street?"

"I do," Lily said gently.

Lady Wyatt nodded again. For a moment she stared ahead, unseeing, her fingers again twisting the handkerchief in her lap. Then she stood, gathering her composure around her like a cloak. Lifting her chin, she moved to sit at the dressing table, meeting Lily's eyes in the mirror. "You said when you came in that you have had cause to deal with Bow Street before?"

"I have. It was not . . . It is not something any lady would choose," Lily said carefully. She had great respect for Mr. Page, but having to deal with the new police force would make anyone uneasy. "But I can say with confidence that Mr. Page is a respectful and respectable man."

Lady Wyatt opened a box of pins, her movements deliberate and careful though her hands were still shaking. "What do you think he will want to know?"

Lily watched in the mirror as Lady Wyatt began to fix her hair. "I imagine he will wish to know where you were last night."

"Here, of course." Lady Wyatt frowned. "Where else would I be? Nothing is happening in town this time of year."

"Will you be able to tell him what time you retired for the night?"

Lady Wyatt's hands fluttered helplessly for a moment. "Early, I suppose. Does anyone ever know what time they retire for the night?"

It was a fair point, Lily had to acknowledge. "Likely not. And . . ." She hesitated, unsure how blunt to be. But Mr. Page had asked her to find out what she could. And Lady Wyatt would be less guarded with a woman of her own class than with her unwanted inquisitor downstairs. "He will wish to know whether you were concerned when your husband never came to bed."

Lady Wyatt turned to stare at her, aghast. "Surely he would not expect me to . . . Not something so private!"

Lily grimaced, deeply uncomfortable. "I am afraid he will. If it is anything like the . . ." She hesitated, knowing how odd it would seem if she appeared overly familiar with either the new police force or the investigation of murder. "If it is anything like the last time I had to deal with one of the Bow Street gentlemen, he will need to account for the whereabouts of everyone in the family and house at the time of Sir Charles's death. Merely as a formality, I am sure," she added quickly. "I am sure he does not believe you will tell him anything untoward."

Lady Wyatt's cheeks were bright with fury. "If he is a gentleman as you say, he would not ask such questions," she bit off, stabbing pins into her chignon.

"I do not think he has a choice in the matter," Lily said, momentarily wishing Mr. Page were there so she could let him know exactly what she thought of his putting her in such an uncomfortable position.

But Lady Wyatt's anger—an easier emotion to express than grief, no doubt—made her realize he had been right to ask. Better for Lady Wyatt to hear such questions from her first, with the chance to bring her emotions under control and prepare herself, than from Mr. Page, likely with her stepson's eyes on her at the same time.

Lady Wyatt's laugh was mostly a sob, and she dropped her head into her hands, pins scattering on the dressing table in front of her. "We keep separate rooms," she said, her voice muffled by her palms. She was very still for a moment. Then she lifted her head once more, her expression grim as she continued to apply herself to her hair. "Surely this Mr. Page will find nothing surprising in *that*."

He likely would not. It was common among the upper classes for a husband and wife to maintain separate bedrooms—sometimes entirely separate wings of the house, depending on the resources of the family and the size of their home. Mr. Page would have been among them enough to know that.

"I am sure that is all he will need to ask you, ma'am." Lily swallowed, remembering how lost she had felt after her own husband's death. And what Lady Wyatt would now suffer was a thousand times worse—not only was her husband dead, but someone had taken his life deliberately. And, whether she realized it or not, unless the murder could be accounted for, suspicion about his death would always hover at the edges of her life.

Lily glanced at the mirror, taking in the hard line of Lady Wyatt's mouth, the carefully controlled panic that edged her movements. She understood. Perhaps better than anyone else in the house, she realized where suspicions would fall.

"And then the matter will be done," Lily said quietly, knowing it wasn't true.

"Done," Lady Wyatt repeated. For a moment, her eyes closed, as if she were in pain. Then she stood, her jaw firm and her shoulders back. "Then I shall prepare myself to confront him."

★ ★ ★

Simon Page could already feel a headache growing between his eyes.

Usually he enjoyed this part of his work. Not the death of a stranger, but the chance to observe, to begin putting the pieces together that would help him understand how and why something had happened. Often the answers were unremarkable: a petty theft, a misunderstanding, an accident, an illness. An ordinary death that perhaps could have been avoided but wasn't the product of any criminal activity.

But then there were the times when something was off, someone was suspicious, a piece of a story didn't add up. Making the connections between those inconsistencies depended entirely on the nimbleness of the mind considering them, and Simon had discovered early in his education that he had a unique facility for doing just that. And then there were new advances being made, sometimes every month, it seemed—such as the tests being created by doctors in Spain to actually detect poisonous substances in a slain corpse. It felt like his work was changing and growing daily, and Simon wanted to be part of that.

He also knew that being part of it meant the men in front of him—and those like them—would always look down on him. Normally, he didn't let that bother him. He knew the value of what he did.

Today, though, that sense of disdain was grating on him more than usual. Mr. Frank Wyatt he could have borne; it would have been easy to forgive the man his condescending manners so soon after his father's death. But Mr. Percy Wyatt took snobbery to new heights.

"I object strongly to such questions," Percy was saying, his pale brows drawn down into a scowl. He had been complaining since the moment he came into the room. A footman had been sent to summon him the moment Sir Charles's death had been discovered that morning. Simon had arrived after the footman departed, which meant Percy had been completely taken aback when he arrived and realized he would have to answer the Bow Street officer's questions. "I don't see why you need to know anything about my evening."

Simon wanted to fold himself into one of the very comfortable-looking chairs that dotted the parlor and rub his temples with both hands. But he remained standing, his hands clasped behind him and a neutral expression on his face. "I need to know so that I can determine where you were when Sir Charles Wyatt died last night."

"I must have misunderstood, sir," Percy said, his voice icy. "Surely you do not mean to imply that someone in our family may have had something to do with my uncle's death."

"That is precisely what he is implying, Percy," Frank said in a weary voice. "Please answer his questions so we can be done with this."

He sounded as if he wanted to rub his own temples. Instead, he sat with his head tipped back against his chair and his eyes closed. He would have looked absurdly relaxed were it not for the tight lines around his clenched jaw and eyes. Frank Wyatt, Simon could say with certainty, was not taking his father's death lightly—though, of course, that could mean any number of things.

"This is beyond belief," Percy said, jumping to his feet. "Am I to be faced with accusations yet again? It was not enough, yesterday, that I was accused of theft—"

"You were guilty of theft, as I recall, Mr. Wyatt," Captain Hartley said amiably as he entered the room. He nodded to Simon, polite and deferential. "My apologies, Mr. Page, for interrupting. The housekeeper has locked the door to the library. And as requested, I have come to hand the key to you personally." He did so with a polite bow, a small flourish of respect that Simon suspected was purely for the benefit of the other two men in the room. Then he installed himself by the windows, lounging at his apparent ease.

"You!" Percy turned on the navy captain, his face splotchy with rage at the reminder of his actions the day before. "Should you not depart now that you have accomplished your task?"

"Oh no, sir, I must await Mrs. Adler, who is upstairs assisting your aunt," Captain Hartley said, holding his hands palm out in front of him in a disarming gesture that would have been mocking if his expression hadn't been so carefully polite. "And I imagine Mr. Page would prefer that I remain in this room while I wait. Is that not so, sir?"

"It wouldn't do to have him wait somewhere where the servants might speak to him, or he to them, before I have a chance to question them myself," Simon said, scrupulously polite himself. In reality, he wanted the captain to remain in the room and observe the two Mr. Wyatts so he could have the impressions of a man of their own class in addition to his own. "I am sure the captain will give his word not to repeat anything said in this room."

"Do you really have to question the servants too?" Frank asked, opening his eyes and sitting forward. The tense lines around his face had deepened. "Really, I cannot see any reason that would be necessary."

"I'm afraid I will have to speak to everyone in the house," Simon said gravely.

"Everyone." Percy glanced at his cousin as he spoke, the expression clearly pointed, though Simon didn't have any idea—yet—what it was intended to convey.

Clearly Frank did, though. He scowled at his cousin, then blew out a long breath and nodded. "Then I shall say again, Percy, please answer his questions so we might be done with this as soon as possible." He swallowed, his voice catching a little as he added, "I have a parent to bury, after all."

"I shall be quick, Mr. Wyatt," Simon said. He turned to Percy, who had taken his seat once more, scowling ferociously and looking queasy with nerves. "I have had your cousin's account of his activities last night, but I'd appreciate hearing your own recollections on the matter. Particularly after you parted ways for the evening." He smiled. "And rest assured, I will be confirming whatever you have to tell me."

Percy looked as if he wanted to protest once more, but evidently he realized it would get him nowhere. He let out a long-suffering sigh. "Well, as it seems you have heard—" He scowled in Hartley's direction once more, but Simon didn't turn to see how the captain reacted this time. "Yesterday was a rather disheartening day for me. But my uncle called me back around seven o'clock, and we had a cozy chat over drinks in his library." Percy swallowed, looking suddenly ill as he realized he had just named the room where his uncle had died. "We made things up, and he was quite kind and encouraging. I left feeling much better."

"And when was that?"

"Perhaps eight? Frank was already out, but we had made plans to dine at the club, so I went straight there to meet him. We ate, had a game or two of billiards with some friends. Frank suggested we go out. There's not much to do in town this time of year, but we ended up at a gaming hell with some of the fellows from the club. I left early. Midnight or so. I went home."

Simon nodded. So far, the two men's stories matched up well enough. They had given slightly different times, but that made them more trustworthy in Simon's eyes, not less. If they had given all the same details, he would have wondered if they had planned their stories out. He glanced at Frank. "And you, as you said, stayed to play cards until quite late?"

"I had a streak of good luck at the faro table," Frank said quietly. "I can't imagine I made it home before three in the morning, though that is mostly a guess. I doubt I could have seen straight enough to read a clock by that point."

"You always play better when you're foxed," Percy said, shaking his head. Simon couldn't tell whether Percy was impressed or jealous. "No inhibitions."

Frank grinned at his cousin, and for a moment they looked like nothing more than a pair of mischievous boys. Then they both seemed to remember where they were and why. Their expressions grew grim once more, and they looked away from each other. Frank stared at his hands, clenched in his lap. Percy glared at Simon.

"Is that all you wish to know?" he asked, an edge of angry sarcasm to his voice.

"Not quite," Simon said, his own voice growing sharp. He regretted it as soon as Percy's eyes narrowed—it would have been better to remain impassive and civil, but sometimes that was impossible for him. "Where did you go after you left at midnight?"

"Home."

Simon waited a moment, his brows rising when no other information was offered. It was the shortest sentence Percy Wyatt had spoken since he arrived. "And what did you do there?"

Percy glanced toward the ceiling, sighing. "Sleep."

Simon's brows climbed even higher, and he resisted the urge to glance at Captain Hartley, not wanting to remind either of the young Wyatt men that the captain was watching them. "Was that all?"

"That is generally what one does during the night," Percy snapped, still not fully meeting the Bow Street constable's eyes.

"And was there anyone at your home who can attest to that?" Simon asked. "A servant, perhaps?"

"One of the maids at my lodging house comes to make coffee and clean in the morning," Percy said, his voice tight. "That is all."

Simon was surprised that the young man didn't have a valet or other servant waiting up for him—Frank had mentioned his own valet when he recounted his comings and goings the night before. But looking at Percy's disgruntled expression, Simon decided not to press the matter—though he would check with the captain later to find out whether the younger Mr. Wyatt's claim that he lacked domestic help was surprising for a man in his position.

Instead, Simon changed tactics. "You mentioned that you were feeling disheartened after the events of the day," he said, noting the way Frank's eyes suddenly snapped open, the flush that crept up Percy's neck and ears.

"No doubt you have already been informed," Percy said, glancing once more toward where Captain Hartley lounged against the window. "I've no wish to speak about it."

"Perhaps not, but I wish to hear about it," Simon said, his voice steely.

It was a tone he had learned directly from his father, a school-teacher responsible for keeping a dozen rowdy village boys in line each year. He had discovered, after joining the Bow Street force, that it was particularly effective with a certain kind of young man. Percy Wyatt was, as he expected, one of those. His flush spread, and he shifted a little in his seat.

When he finally met Simon's eyes, the Bow Street officer softened his tone slightly. "Mr. Frank Wyatt has shared the details of what happened yesterday afternoon," he said. When Percy turned to glare at his cousin, Frank shrugged, looking apologetic. "But I'd appreciate knowing what happened later that evening, Mr. Wyatt, when you spoke with your uncle. You said that he requested you call again?"

He kept his eyes on Percy, but he noticed that Frank sat up at that, his eyes locked on his cousin with surprising intensity. Percy, who was turned away from Frank, didn't notice. Instead, he frowned to himself.

"Well, you know, it was surprising. Uncle had been furious that afternoon, practically threatening to cut me off—really, it was a huge fuss, and the interference did not help." He took a moment to glare in Hartley's direction before shrugging. "When I came back, I thought for certain that it would be more of the same, but in fact, he wanted to mend things between us."

"Really?" Frank interrupted. "Did he tell you what changed his mind? He was still furious when I left for the evening."

"He didn't say. Something was on his mind, certainly. But he said he wanted it put behind him." Percy's expression was growing almost buoyant. "He said that he had overreacted, when really a boy in debt for some horse racing was really nothing when one thought about the sort of things people *can* get up to. And in fact, he was going to—"

Percy broke off suddenly, looking uncomfortable.

"He was going to what?" Simon asked. His tone was mild, but the way his eyes fixed on Percy was anything but.

"Ah. Hmm." Percy's face grew red again. "Well, he was in a pensive mood, you know. Thinking things out loud. But he said that he had been wrong when he talked of cutting me off earlier. He wanted to, ah, assure me that I would continue to receive my allowance." He offered Simon a weak smile. "I was glad to patch things up with him. I should never have forgiven myself if he had died while we were still quarreling."

"Your uncle forgave you for your theft?" Simon asked, his brows rising. It was hard for him to imagine that Sir Charles had been so understanding, let alone forgiven his nephew so quickly. And he had the distinct impression that Percy had been about to say something quite different before he cut himself off.

"Completely." Percy didn't meet Simon's eyes as he spoke. In fact, he glanced briefly at his cousin, a look so quick Simon almost missed it, before returning his gaze to a spot just to the left of Simon's ear. "He said he would pay my debts, so long as I gave up my private lodgings and removed with him when he left town. He wanted me away my friends from the club, I suppose." Percy shrugged. "I did not much care for the idea, but the temporary trial of leaving town would have been worth reconciling with the old fellow."

"And how do you think your uncle would have felt about you going out to a gaming hell mere hours after attempting to rob him because you had no money left to pay your debts?" Simon asked, unable to keep the dry disapproval from his voice.

He had expected Percy to bristle; instead, the young man shrugged again, looking surprised by the question. "What else is a fellow supposed to do at this time of year?" he asked. "Surely even a man like you knows that nothing happens in town during the summer." He glanced at Captain Hartley, for the first time without malice. "Tell him, Hartley. I am certain a man of your position understands."

"Mr. Wyatt is certainly not the only gentleman in town who gambles with nothing but his vowels to offer," said Captain Hartley dryly.

"There, you see?" said Percy, clearly not having paid enough attention to catch the captain's obvious disapproval. "There really is nothing else to entertain one at the moment."

"And yet you did not want to leave town," Simon pointed out. "Even though, as you say, nothing is happening. Why is that?"

Percy hesitated, his eyes darting to his cousin before snapping back to the Bow Street constable. "A fellow likes his independence," he said at last. "I had not intended—"

He was interrupted as the door to the parlor swung open, and Simon did not miss the look of relief on the young man's face. Percy Wyatt, he was sure, had a specific reason to want to stay in London— and he clearly did not wish to discuss it. Whether his cousin knew about it, Simon couldn't be sure. That last look might have been a plea for Frank to come to his rescue or a moment of panic brought on by the threat of discovery.

But Percy Wyatt had already been caught in the act of stealing from his own relatives. What else could he be trying to hide?

Simon had to push the thoughts away. Percy and Frank had both bounded to their feet, Percy looking distressed and Frank's face impassive as they regarded the woman entering the room. By the expensive look of the black gown she wore and the redness of her eyes, he could guess instantly who she was. But he still waited politely for Mrs. Adler, who followed the woman into the room, to close the door and make the introduction.

"Lady Wyatt, you will remember Captain Hartley." Mrs. Adler nodded at the captain, who had come forward to bow over Lady Wyatt's hand.

"My deepest sympathies, madam," Hartley said, his usual playfulness replaced by a serious expression. Simon abruptly remembered that the captain had been boyhood friends with the late Mr. Adler. The navy man, like Mrs. Adler, would no doubt be predisposed to sympathize with the new, young widow.

"Thank you, sir," Lady Wyatt murmured.

Percy stepped forward and took her hand. "Aunt, I am so . . ." He shook his head, looking as though he were at a loss for words. "So very, very sorry. It is a loss to us all. But I cannot imagine how it must feel to you."

Lady Wyatt's mouth trembled a little before she schooled her expression back into steadiness. "Thank you, Percy. It is a comfort to be surrounded by those who cared for him as I did." She glanced over at her stepson. "Frank."

"Lady Wyatt." He took the hand she held out to him and bowed over it, though the gesture was a little stiff. Simon watched them closely. "Are you certain you are well enough for this?"

"It seems I have little choice in the matter," Lady Wyatt said, stepping back from him and taking a seat. She looked expectantly toward Simon, though there was little other emotion to be read in her expression.

Mrs. Adler took the hint. "Lady Wyatt, may I present Mr. Simon Page, of the Bow Street force," she said. Percy politely retreated to another chair so she could take the spot on the settee next to Lady Wyatt. Captain Hartley moved to take up a position just behind Mrs. Adler, not far from where Frank was standing.

Simon looked them all over as he gave a brief bow in response to the introduction. "Lady Wyatt." He usually didn't like to extend too much social courtesy when he was in someone's home in a professional capacity, but the woman's husband had just died, after all. "My own deep condolences. I'll try not to take up too much of your time."

"Mrs. Adler has been good enough to give me some sense of what you will wish to know," Lady Wyatt said, her head high and her voice steady, though Simon noticed her hands twisting together in her lap before she clasped them into stillness. "I would ask, though, that we speak more privately." She glanced toward Percy and Frank, and her voice trembled a little as she added, "You will understand my disinclination for an audience."

"I do not like to leave you at such a moment, Aunt," said Percy, looking doubtful.

Lady Wyatt's expression softened. "You are very good. But perhaps you could go upstairs and check on Ellen?"

"Ah yes, of course." Percy stood abruptly. "If you will excuse me."

Simon frowned, racking his brain for a clue as to who Ellen was. The name obviously had some meaning to the three Wyatts, but he couldn't place it. "Who is Ellen?"

There was a moment of stiff silence, all three Wyatts looking surprised that he had asked. "One of our maids," Frank said at last.

It was an answer that told him nothing at all. "And why must Mr. Percy Wyatt check on her?"

"Merely to offer her some comfort and assistance at the moment," Lady Wyatt said. It was hard to tell from her tone whether she was bored or irritated by his inquiry into her household affairs. "Ellen has been most upset by my husband's death—so many of these girls in service are quite young and emotional. Percy always has a way of speaking to them that helps them calm down and go on with their work."

A flicker of movement caught Simon's eye; Mrs. Adler had leaned ever so slightly forward in her chair. When she saw him looking at her, she gave her head the barest shake, narrowing her eyes as they glanced between Lady Wyatt and the two young men. Clearly, something about Lady Wyatt's explanation didn't sit right with her. He'd have to find out why.

But he could also tell by the expressions of the three suspects before him—for that was what they were, even if they didn't yet realize it—that now was not the time to press for more. Simon wanted to sigh.

"Very well. Mr. Percy Wyatt, thank you for your time and patience. Mr. Frank Wyatt, if you would stay a moment longer, though. We're not quite done."

Frank's eyes darted toward his stepmother, and he didn't hide his look of irritation quickly enough. She looked equally unhappy, though she kept her gaze turned resolutely away from him. That was the exact reason Simon wanted to keep them in the room together for as long as he could. He wanted to observe the undercurrents of animosity between them—though in truth they were so obvious that they weren't really under the surface at all.

"Mr. Wyatt mentioned that he went out for the evening. What time was that, Lady Wyatt?"

"He left sometime after half seven, I believe, since that was when Sir Charles and I—" Her voice wavered for a moment. "We dined together. Then we sat together in the library for a while, as we often did when we had no company."

"And Mr. Wyatt, do you usually dine at home?"

"From time to time. I am more likely, though, to dine at the club or with friends." Frank stood rigidly upright, meeting Simon's eyes as he spoke. Though his voice was steady, his knuckles were white where they gripped the back of the chair in front of him.

Simon considered Frank, his own hands clasped behind his back. "I would have expected that a young man such as yourself would keep your own lodgings, the way your cousin does."

"I have often wished to," Frank said, shooting a quick, narrow-eyed glance at his stepmother. "But my father preferred to have me here. It had been just us until *very* recently." A note of sarcasm entered his voice as he spoke, and Simon didn't miss the way Lady Wyatt's posture stiffened. But the sarcasm faded, and Frank's shoulders slumped. His voice was quieter when he spoke again. "Father and I enjoy . . . enjoyed each other's company."

"And now?" Simon asked, looking between Frank and Lady Wyatt.

They both stared at him blankly. "Now?" Frank asked.

"Which of you will inherit the property, now that Sir Charles is gone?"

"Oh." Lady Wyatt raised a hand to her mouth, her eyes wide. "I do not . . . That is, I had not even considered the question."

"We will have to consult with Hammond," Frank said impatiently. "At one time, of course, all my father's property was left to me. I cannot say what the arrangement is now. The Devonshire property is certainly still mine—it is entailed in the male line."

"You've no idea, Lady Wyatt, how your husband left his estate settled?" Simon asked, raising his brows.

"It never occurred to me to ask," Lady Wyatt said faintly. "His health was so vigorous, I never would have dreamed . . ." She broke off. "Please, I cannot bear this talk of money so soon after . . . I cannot." She raised her handkerchief to her mouth, catching a sob.

Frank made a sudden movement with his hands, as though he wanted to reach for his stepmother or shake her. But he jerked them back just as quickly, a flurry of emotions chasing over his features before he schooled them back into proper English calm. "Do try to have a little composure, Winnie," he said. "The fellow is only trying to do his job."

The stare that Lady Wyatt turned on her stepson was blistering; if looks could kill, the Wyatt family might have lost another member right then. "Mr. Wyatt," she said, enunciating each word so sharply that Simon nearly winced. "I will thank you not to speak down to me."

Frank flushed. "I only meant that I would like this whole monstrous business to be concluded as swiftly as possible," he said, his voice catching. "I find myself ill suited to answering questions or engaging with company at the moment."

"You are entitled to grieve for your father," Lady Wyatt said, turning her head away and taking a deep breath. "But you are not entitled to tell me how I should grieve for my husband."

There was a long pause, then Frank nodded. "My apologies. Do you wish me to leave?"

Another long pause. "I would prefer it, yes."

Frank stood, bowing to his stepmother and to Mrs. Adler before turning toward the door. Simon's jaw clenched; clearly, it hadn't even occurred to Frank Wyatt that he ought to check with the constable in the room before excusing himself. But Simon knew he wouldn't get much further with his questions if he upset the lady of the house too much. And he could always come back to Mr. Wyatt. Still . . .

He could see some of the tension fading from Frank's shoulders as he crossed the room, clearly glad to be done with facing questions.

So he waited until Frank's hand was on the doorknob, inches from freedom, before he spoke again.

"A moment, Mr. Wyatt," Simon said. Frank paused, glancing back over his shoulder, suddenly tense once more. "Did your cousin give you any indication last night that he and your father had reconciled?"

"He told me when we met at the club that they had left things on good terms, though he did not say much else. Seemed a little shifty about the whole business, but I was glad to hear it."

"And are you equally ready to forgive your cousin?"

"To forgive him?" Frank looked surprised, then frowned in consideration, staring at his hand on the doorknob. "I suppose I already have. I was upset at the time, certainly. Percy might not always display the best judgment, but I shouldn't have expected him to do something so underhanded. But now . . ." Frank looked up again. "Under the circumstances, it seems rather trivial, does it not? My father clearly did not wish to hold a grudge over the matter. I've every intention of following his example. Boys make mistakes, after all."

Simon held back a retort. Percy Wyatt was hardly a boy, and his "mistake" had nearly cost a man his livelihood—and possibly his life, if the Wyatts had decided to bring charges against the footman for such a significant theft. But his job wasn't to correct the people he was interviewing. It was to find out what they were thinking and, more specifically, what they had done. He kept his hands firmly behind his back so no one else in the room could see that they had clenched into angry fists. "Thank you, Mr. Wyatt. My sympathies, once more."

As soon as Frank was gone and the door closed behind him, Simon turned to Lady Wyatt. "Now, ma'am, I'm afraid I must ask you a few questions as well."

Lady Wyatt lifted her face toward him. Her hands still twisted the handkerchief in her lap, but her gaze, as she met his, was steely.

"Do your worst, sir," she said softly. "Nothing you can say will hurt me more than what has already happened today."

Simon met her eyes, his expression equally steady. "I hope that is the case, Lady Wyatt. But we shall see."

CHAPTER 7

Lily expected Mr. Page to begin his questions right away. Instead, he regarded Lady Wyatt for several long, assessing moments. She met his eyes steadily, but her own were brimming with tears, and she continued to twist the handkerchief in her lap so tightly that the fragile fabric looked as though it might rip. Lily glanced briefly at Jack, and he met her eyes with a frown, his own flickering toward Mr. Page in an obvious question. Lily gave the barest shrug of her shoulders. She didn't know what the constable was waiting for either.

Just when the silence had grown painful, Mr. Page spoke.

"Lady Wyatt, who do you know who might have wished your husband harm?"

Lily caught her breath at the bluntness of the question. Out of the corner of her eye, she saw Jack start forward before Mr. Page gestured him back sharply. He never took his eyes off Lady Wyatt.

She had stood abruptly as he spoke, so abruptly that her feet knocked against a tufted footstool and sent it tumbling. She didn't seem to notice; instead, she regarded Mr. Page with an expression that was somewhere between fury and horror. "*No one.* This all must be a mistake, mustn't it? An accident, a terrible joke . . . surely no one could . . ." She met his eyes. "But I see you are not the sort of man who even has a sense of humor, are you?"

"Not much of one, no," said Mr. Page mildly, seeming unperturbed by the woman's outburst.

Lady Wyatt took a deep breath, gathering her calm once more as she sat. "Had Mrs. Adler not told me what was discovered in the library, I would never have believed it possible that Charles could have been . . . There is no one who could have wanted to harm him. *No one.*"

"No one?"

Lady Wyatt looked around the room, an appeal in her eyes. "Mrs. Adler, Captain Hartley, you saw our family just yesterday. Did it seem to you that any of us harbored any ill will toward my husband? Did you detect any secret vendettas?" Lily and Jack glanced at each other uncomfortably. "Well?" Lady Wyatt demanded, clearly unsatisfied with their silence. Her breathing was deep and erratic with emotion, and Lily hoped the woman wasn't going to work herself into a faint.

"I did not," Jack said at last.

"And Mrs. Adler, your family knows ours no little amount. Surely you cannot think of anyone who wished Sir Charles harm?"

"No," Lily agreed, though she hesitated a little. "There was the issue of the theft, of course, but even Mr. Percy Wyatt seemed to treat Sir Charles with great respect. And according to him, your husband was almost unaccountably forgiving."

"There, you see?" Lady Wyatt said, rounding on Mr. Page once more. "There is absolutely no reason for anyone in our family to wish him harm."

"Your family aren't the only ones to consider, Lady Wyatt. There are other people living in this house."

Her lips parted as she stared at him, stunned. "You mean the servants?"

"It is a possibility."

"But . . ." She shook her head, her brows knitting together in thought as she sank back onto the settee. She shook her head firmly. "It is impossible. My husband was a strict man, certainly, who expected a great deal of those in his employ. But he was always fair."

"What would have happened to your footman yesterday if Mr. Percy's theft had not been discovered?" Mr. Page asked pointedly.

But Lady Wyatt only sighed, leaning back against the settee and briefly covering her eyes with one hand. Her voice, when she spoke again, was weary. "He would have been let go without a character. Which even you must admit would be far preferable for him when compared to charges for theft." She opened her eyes to glare at the constable. "And, since you seem to know all our business, you also know that Percy's theft *was* discovered, thanks to Mrs. Adler." Lady Wyatt took a moment to nod in Lily's direction before turning back to Mr. Page. "Our servants have no cause for complaint against us." She closed her eyes again and added, her voice growing smaller, "So ask your questions and be done."

Lily's heart twisted in her chest, and she had to take her own deep breath against the renewed memory of grief. She felt a gentle hand settle on her shoulder and turned to smile at Jack. She pressed her hand briefly against his before sitting forward, her gaze fixed on Lady Wyatt once more.

Mr. Page seemed to relent, and he asked his remaining questions in a gentler voice. Lady Wyatt was pale but resolute as she answered, telling him much the same information she had offered Lily.

No, Frank had not joined them for dinner. She and Sir Charles had dined early together, as they had no evening plans. Yes, she had been sitting with her husband in the library that evening, as they often did. No, there was nothing odd in them having retired at different times. Sir Charles liked to stay up late and spend time by himself. He had been without a wife for many years after the death of Frank's mother; she had not expected him to change his ways so soon—one hand pressed against her mouth, she closed her eyes as if to hold back more tears—so soon into a new marriage. No, they did not share a bedroom; she would have had no way of knowing whether he ever retired. No, she had not heard anything odd after withdrawing to her room for the night. She had gone to bed early after her maid helped her change.

Through it all, Lady Wyatt's voice grew smaller, and one hand pressed her temple briefly as if warding off a headache. At one point, she reached out blindly for support, and when Lily took her hand, she discovered that it was trembling.

Mr. Page's sharp eyes caught the gesture, and he hesitated. "Lady Wyatt, are you well?"

"A trifle . . ." She briefly closed her eyes once more, before shaking her head and attempting to square her shoulders. "Continue, if you please. I would rather this be over and done."

"Very well." Mr. Page had not moved throughout his questions, his hands still clasped behind his back and his face impassive. "You said you were sitting with your husband in the library before you retired for the night."

Lady Wyatt frowned. "We often do after dinner."

"And yesterday evening was one of those times."

"I believe so." There was an edge of faintness to the woman's voice, and she swayed in her seat as she spoke.

Lily, casting a distressed look at Mr. Page, pulled a vinaigrette out of her reticule and held it out. At Lady Wyatt's brief nod, Lily held it before the other woman's face, and the sharp smell of the salts made her catch her breath and sit up straighter. But she was still pale.

Mr. Page was eyeing Lady Wyatt, his mouth twisted in a way that Lily could not interpret. It might have been sympathy; Lily remembered too well his opinions about the sensitivity and weakness of women of the upper class. Or it might have been frustration that he was clearly not going to be able to ask any more questions at the moment.

"We're done for now, ma'am," he said at last. "I thank you for your time. Perhaps we can call your son and nephew to help you back to your room?"

"No, not them." Lady Wyatt stood. But she still swayed a little, and Jack quickly held out his arm over the back of the settee. She steadied herself with it, giving him a small, grateful smile. "If Mrs. Adler will lend me her assistance just once more, I believe I need to retire."

"Of course," Lily said quickly, slipping her smelling salts away and standing. "Captain, if you will wait, I shall return immediately."

She took Lady Wyatt's arm, helping the other woman from the room. Just before they left, she glanced over her shoulder. Mr. Page was watching them go, his forehead creased in thought.

★ ★ ★

Lady Wyatt did not speak as they made their way upstairs once more, and Lily, knowing the twisting emotions grief could cause, did not press her. After helping Lady Wyatt to her bed, Lily murmured her condolences once more, preparing to depart.

But when she would have turned away, Lady Wyatt caught her arm. "Mrs. Adler, I know you'd not seen my husband in many years. But you and your father know him, know his character." Lady Wyatt's grip on her arm was surprisingly tight. "You must tell that man that no one had any reason to harm him, that—" She broke off, dropping Lily's arm abruptly and turning her head away. "I cannot bear to go down and speak to him again. But please, you know our family. You must tell him . . ."

"I cannot imagine my words would have any influence," Lily said, hesitating. Mr. Page had grown to respect her, certainly. But she doubted he would leave off his inquiries simply because she'd told him Sir Charles had been a man of character and that Frank cared for his father.

"But surely—"

She was interrupted by the door swinging open.

"Lady Wyatt?" A woman in a dark-blue dress and white apron stood in the doorway, her uniform just different enough from those of the other maids of the household to tell Lily that this must be Lady Wyatt's personal maid or dresser. She held a dark bottle and an empty glass in her hands. "I've brought some of Mr. Frank's laudanum."

Lady Wyatt hesitated, shooting a sideways glance at Lily. "Why did you do that, Wilkes?" she asked. Lily was surprised by how cross she sounded.

The maid Wilkes clearly was too. "The doctor who came this morning, Lady Wyatt, to look at . . ." She hesitated. "You'll remember, he suggested you take some to help you rest after the man from Bow Street was finished."

Lady Wyatt hesitated again. Lily, wondering if she was worried about being seen as one of those unfortunate people who depended on the laudanum bottle to get through the day, spoke up. "If the doctor recommended it, there can be no harm. And surely you need your rest after such a morning."

Lady Wyatt gave a sigh and nodded. "Very well, Wilkes. You may pour a small dose." Turning, she clasped Lily's hand. "I thank you for coming to help, Mrs. Adler. It truly was a kindness."

"I could not have done otherwise," Lily said quietly. "My heart goes out to you for such a horrible loss, truly."

Lady Wyatt nodded, her mouth trembling as she closed her eyes and lay back upon the bed. Lily suddenly felt that she could bear to stay no longer. Murmuring condolences once more, she slipped out of the room.

Lily closed the door softly behind her, her body feeling suddenly heavy and exhausted. There were little gilded chairs tucked in alcoves along the hallway, and Lily sank into one of them with a sigh. Witnessing Lady Wyatt's grief had brought back too many memories, and she wanted nothing more than to retreat to her own comfortable home on Half Moon Street and be alone with her thoughts.

Then she remembered that she wouldn't be alone—not with her father there. For a moment, she wanted to scream with frustration. She whimpered slightly, dropping her head into her hands.

"Are you well, ma'am?"

Lily started to her feet to find that Wilkes, the lady's maid, had emerged soundlessly from Lady Wyatt's chamber and was watching her with concern.

"Perfectly well, thank you," Lily said, standing hastily and shaking out her shoulders. The assertion came out just a bit too loud, and she cleared her throat, trying to bring her wayward emotions back under control. "Lady Wyatt will be able to rest, I hope?"

The maid's face softened with sympathy. "Aye, she's lying down now. Poor dear," she said, her warm voice surprisingly deep for such a small frame. "And her so newly a bride too." Lily nodded, unable to speak past the lump in her throat. "I hope it don't weigh on her too much, that they didn't have a chance to make up their quarrel," Wilkes continued, shaking her head sadly. "Sir Charles was married before; he knew those little spats never lasted. But her never being married before, she already took it so seriously."

Lady Wyatt hadn't mentioned a quarrel when Mr. Page was questioning her. Lily hesitated, not sure how to find out more without seeming like a gossip. "I think it must weigh on her," she said at last, watching the lady's maid closely out of the corner of her eye. "She wouldn't even say what it was about."

"No, no more would she say last night." Wilkes sighed. "First her not wanting to go on his walk with him, then her shutting herself in her room like that, refusing to sit with him as she usually did of an evening after he was shouting about leaving London. Poor dear." She sighed, then curtsied. "Begging your pardon, ma'am. I don't mean to keep you. You're sure you're well?"

"Of course." Lily stood, her mind reeling. Why had Lady Wyatt lied about being with Sir Charles last night? "Thank you for your concern."

★ ★ ★

When Lily finally made her way downstairs, her feelings back under control and her face serene once more, she found a strange tableau in the front hall. Jack stood at the foot of the stairs, trying to look as though he were concerned only with waiting for her. Mr. Page was talking to the butler, watched over from no very great distance by both Frank and Percy Wyatt. Percy's arms were crossed belligerently, while Frank had his hands in his pockets, and they had identical scowls of disapproval on their faces.

Lily paused before she reached the bottom of the stairs, the better to watch everyone below her. Jack laid one hand over hers where it rested on the banister before cutting his eyes back toward the polite interrogation happening in the hall. They stood quietly facing each other, both of them watching the others out of the corner of their eye and listening to every word.

"And you didn't wake Sir Charles when you found him sleeping in the library?" Mr. Page asked, pointedly not looking at either of the Wyatt men, who were watching him.

The butler couldn't stay quite so impassive; he glanced uncomfortably at them before he spoke. Lily saw Frank gesture impatiently, while Percy's scowl deepened.

"No, sir," the servant said at last. "He often sat in the library in his chair after dinner. If he fell asleep there, we all had specific instructions not to wake him."

"And why was that?" Mr. Page asked.

"Because—" Frank began, but he fell into a scowling silence when Mr. Page held up a hand.

"I should like to hear it from Mr. Clewes, if you please," he said pleasantly, only glancing at Percy and Frank before returning his attention to the butler. "Mr. Clewes?"

Clewes cleared his throat. "On account of his gout, sir. He often slept poorly when it was paining him, so if we found him asleep in such a position—it happened from time to time—we were to let him sleep."

"And all the staff knew this?"

"Yes, sir."

"And his gout was paining him yesterday?"

"Yes, sir."

"And you're sure that he was asleep when you saw him? He was well and uninjured at that time?"

"Oh yes indeed," Clewes said, sounding shocked. "I had to approach him to be certain he was actually asleep, you see. And . . ." The butler cleared his throat again, then lowered his voice, as if afraid of giving offense. "I'm afraid Sir Charles snored quite loudly at times. There was no mistaking it."

"Was he still in the library when you retired for the night?"

The butler hesitated. "Yes and no," he said at last. "He was there when I first retired—snoring loudly, as I said. But Mr. Wyatt had lost his key, so I had to come let him in when he arrived home—"

"And what time was that?" Mr. Page interrupted.

"Around half three in the morning, I should think," Clewes said. "I didn't look too closely at the clock, so it might have been a bit earlier or a bit later. I am . . ." He glanced at Frank and cleared his throat. "I'm not used to arising at that hour, I'm afraid. I wasn't at my most alert."

"By that, do you mean it was uncommon for Mr. Frank Wyatt to return home in such a state during the small hours of the morning?" Mr. Page asked, glancing at the young man in question. Lily saw Frank grimace a little and shrug.

"Yes, sir," Clewes said, looking uncomfortable at having to discuss his employer's drinking and gaming habits right in front of him. "But at that time I did glance into the library on my way to the front door to see if Sir Charles was still there. I didn't see him, so I assumed he had gone on to bed. I helped Mr. Wyatt upstairs, and Mr. Randall and I—Mr. Randall is valet to Mr. Wyatt and Sir Charles both— helped him undress and put him to bed. Then Mr. Randall and I both returned to our own rooms."

Lily raised a hand to her mouth, feeling cold. If Clewes hadn't seen Sir Charles sitting before the fire, that meant the man was likely already lying on the floor, slowly bleeding to death. And no one had known. She glanced at Jack, whose face was equally grim, then at the others. Percy looked ill, while Frank's face was stony with repressed emotion. Clearly, both of them understood the implications of the butler's words as well.

Mr. Page was the only one who looked unbothered by the news. He nodded slowly, his expression thoughtful. "Thank you, Mr. Clewes." The Bow Street constable glanced at the grim-faced Wyatt men briefly, an ironic smile on his face as they both scowled back at him. "I am grateful for your time this morning."

"That will be all, Clewes," Frank said, his tone final. Only as the butler was bowing to leave did Frank notice that Lily had come down; she thought he jumped a little in surprise. "Actually, Clewes, a moment. Mrs. Adler, how is my mother?"

"Lady Wyatt is resting," Lily said, coming fully down the stairs with Jack at her side. "She is as well as can be, I think, under the circumstances." Struck by a moment of daring, she added, hoping to find out something about Lady Wyatt's quarrel with Sir Charles, "She wished to know if you will leave London as planned or if you will be staying now."

"When were you planning to leave town?" Mr. Page asked, his tone mild even as his brows drew together.

Frank's sigh was audible throughout the hall. "I was not. My father wanted me to stay in town and handle some of his business affairs. But he decided last night after dinner that he and Lady Wyatt would be leaving for his property in Devonshire today. Mrs. Adler, as you came expecting to ride, I hope I may offer you our carriage to convey you home?"

Lily thought he might be reaching his limit at last and nodded quickly. "Certainly, it is kind of you to think of it," she said, glancing at Jack. The navy captain raised his eyebrows. His expression was relaxed enough, but she could feel the tension in him where her hand rested on his arm.

Frank nodded. "Clewes, see to it, please."

"Yes, sir," the butler said, bowing and looking relieved to have a reason to be gone from the hall.

"For how long?" Mr. Page asked.

Frank frowned. "How long what?"

"For how long was your father planning to remove to Devonshire?"

"I do not know when he planned to return," Frank bit off, visibly bristling at the question. "Or when he was going to want me to join them again."

"And do you know why?"

"He does not usually stay in town in the summer."

"But why the decision to depart so suddenly? Did he give an explanation?"

Frank hesitated, his gaze darting to Percy. "He did not say, but I, ah . . ." He cleared his throat. "I had the impression that yesterday's events . . ."

"You mean, he wanted to get me away from town." Percy scowled, then sighed.

"Devonshire is rather far away," said Mr. Page, his expression giving no hint of his thoughts.

"Yes, it is," Frank said sharply, seeming to lose his patience all of a sudden. "And I should like to convey my poor father's body there for burial as quickly as possible. Have I your permission to do so, Mr. Page? Are we done with this nonsense?" His voice was trembling as he finished speaking, and his hands were clenched into fists.

"Mr. Wyatt," Lily said quietly. "Frank." When he turned to look at her, she shook her head. "He must do his work."

"His work should end at our front door," Percy snapped. His voice rose as he stepped belligerently forward. "And my cousin wants him on the other side of it immediately."

"Unfortunately, Sir Charles was murdered on this side of that door." Mr. Page's voice cracked like a whip on the word *murdered*, and every movement in the hall ceased at the reminder that this was no simple death they were faced with. "So here I must come."

Lily shivered. Before her return to London, when the worst thing she had seen was her own husband's final illness and too-early death, she would have had a hard time believing a killer could lurk in such beautiful surroundings. She would have believed that well-brought-up people did not do such things.

But the Harper murders had taught her a brutal lesson. It didn't take a monster to kill, just someone who was so convinced of their own rightness and righteousness that they ceased to think of the living obstacles in their path as people at all.

Such people could lurk in a beautiful drawing room as easily as in a London slum—or in a beautiful library.

The silence was broken by the return of the butler, Clewes. He glanced at Frank Wyatt, then at the police constable, before clearing his throat. "The carriage is waiting outside whenever Mrs. Adler is ready to depart," he said, as polite as if nothing were out of the ordinary at all.

"Yes, thank you," said Frank quickly. "Mrs. Adler, Captain Hartley." His chin lifted. "Mr. Page. I think we now wish to be left alone. As a family."

For a long moment, Mr. Page said nothing, merely regarding the younger man with a steady, unreadable gaze.

"The coroner's inquest will be held tomorrow morning," Mr. Page said at last. "He will judge whether you may be permitted to remove your father's body for burial. I need not trouble you or Lady Wyatt any further for the moment, but I will need to speak to your staff after I see Mrs. Adler and the captain to their carriage."

Lily held her breath, wondering whether Frank would actually take the step of having the Bow Street officer thrown out and what would happen if he did.

"Certainly, Mr. Page," Frank said at last. "Clewes, please have them assemble in the servants' hall."

"And we shan't trouble you any further," Jack said, already heading toward the door. Lily, who still held his arm, had no choice but to follow unless she wanted to create a scene by trying to stay put. "Our sympathies, once more, Mr. Wyatt, Mr. Wyatt."

Lily murmured something polite as well, but there wasn't time for extended pleasantries. Jack, clearly uneasy, managed to get them out the door with record speed. Mr. Page stalked after them.

As the front door closed behind them, Jack cleared his throat. "Well, that was a horrible discovery you made," he said quietly. Then, glancing at the groom waiting by the carriage, he added in a slightly louder voice, "Such a tragedy for the family. Was there anything else you needed to ask us, Mr. Page, or are we at liberty to depart?"

"Nothing else at present, I thank you for your patience," Mr. Page replied, bowing politely and distantly. "Mrs. Adler, may I assist you into the carriage?"

Lily dropped her voice as they made their way down the terrace steps. "Lady Wyatt lied."

Both Jack and Mr. Page faltered in their steps a moment, but they recovered quickly. Mr. Page turned his head away from the groom.

"I cannot stay out here and speak with you long," he murmured. "So I'll request that both of you record your impressions while they're fresh in your minds. Send them to me at the Bow Street offices."

"Certainly," Lily said quietly. Jack nodded his agreement.

"And then it will be safest if you stay as far away from this business as possible." Mr. Page waved the groom back to his perch in the driver's seat, then opened the carriage door and held out his hand to help her in. He stepped back so that the captain could climb in as well. "Good day, Mrs. Adler. Captain Hartley."

"Good day, Mr. Page." Jack swung the door closed and tapped the ceiling of the carriage with his walking stick as he settled onto the seat across from Lily. Leaning toward the window, she caught a last glimpse of Mr. Page touching the brim of his hat to them, his eyes narrowed in thought, before they rolled away.

It was two miles back to Half Moon Street, and for a long while they were both silent as the carriage made its way slowly through the crowded London streets. Finally, when there was enough clamor outside that Lily judged the driver would have no chance of hearing them, she asked in a low voice, "What did you make of that?"

He snorted. "That there was a great deal no one in that family wanted to say." He was silent a moment more. "Do you think one of them did it?"

Lily thought of Frank, willful and sunny and obsessed with attention, displaced in his father's affection by a new marriage. Of Percy's claims to have reconciled with his uncle in private, though he couldn't prove where he had been for half the night. Of Lady Wyatt's cool composure, reduced to faintness in the face of Mr. Page's inquiry as she quietly lied about her quarrel with her husband. She thought of Sir Charles, the impression he always gave of a studious, friendly lion, arguing cheerfully with her father over the glass of port he always liked in the evening. She shivered. "Someone did."

"And likely someone in the house," Jack said grimly. "I checked the door and windows of the library; there was no sign of a break-in at all. And the clock on the desk was plated in gold. Any proper burglar would have stolen that." He leaned forward, elbows resting on his knees as the carriage jostled over a series of uncomfortable bumps. "You aren't planning to leave it alone, are you?"

"I grew up with them," Lily said quietly, staring at her hands.

Out of the corner of her eye, she saw Jack start to rise, then sink back down. She wondered if he had been about to come sit next to her, to offer a shoulder to lean on. For a moment she felt forlorn, alone on her seat, and wished he had. She understood why he had stopped: the gesture would have felt shockingly intimate while they were in a closed carriage together. But she would have been grateful for the comfort, though she would never bring herself to say so out loud.

"And Mr. Page asked for our insight," Lily pointed out, lifting her chin and trying to inject some confidence into her voice. "Which does not stop with a single observation of the family. Well-respected country knight murdered in his own home? You know as well as I that the gossip will be everywhere by tomorrow. And we can learn a great deal from what is and is not said in response."

Jack raised a brow. "Every lady needs a hobby?"

"And you were the one who suggested I make poking my nose into things mine."

"I believe the phrase I used was *discreet inquiries*," Jack said.

"And *confidential investigations*," Lily pointed out.

"And I meant it as a way to use that clever brain of yours from time to time. I did not think you would get involved with another murder."

"And yet a murder it seems to be." Lily smiled at him, though the expression took some effort. "Do not fret, Captain. I have every intention of being both discreet and confidential, as you suggested."

"God help us," he muttered, rolling his eyes heavenward as the carriage came to a halt.

CHAPTER 8

After Jack left her at the door, departing with a bow to return to his lodgings and record his own observations for Mr. Page, Lily had two unpleasant tasks in front of her. She had to seek out her father, whom she would rather have avoided altogether. And she had to tell him of his friend's death.

She found him in her book-room, the cozy space at the back of the house to which she often retreated herself. Yet today looking around the room made her shiver. It was too much like the Wyatts' library. She couldn't even glance at the carpet on her own floor, remembering too clearly the stains of Sir Charles's blood. She was happy to let her father claim the space for the time being.

Her father cleared his throat impatiently, recalling her to the present moment. "What is it? You oughtn't to daydream like that; it makes you look unfortunately vacant."

Lily bit down a sharp reply. "I have some news, Father. And it is . . . It is not good."

He raised his brows at her, one finger marking his place in his book as he let the pages fall closed. "From your morning ride? How peculiar."

"We did not end up riding." Taking a seat in the chair opposite his, Lily told him as gently as she could of Sir Charles's death.

Mr. Pierce's face remained impassive until she got to Bow Street's involvement and the investigation of the murder. His eyes grew wide, then narrowed, and his hands tightened on the carved arms of his chair.

"Nonsense," he said sharply, glowering at her. "Nonsense. Well-bred people simply do not do that sort of thing. I hope you'll not repeat such slanders to anyone else."

"Father, I was there. I saw—"

"The Bow Street riffraff is always trying to puff itself up with importance, making trouble for their betters. You should know not to give them any credence."

Lily shook her head. "Sir, the evidence was . . ." She shivered, remembered the pile of bloody linens. "It was damning. Someone killed your friend."

Mr. Pierce looked away from her, his chin lifted and his expression unreadable. "Well, I am sorry for them, having to deal with such unpleasantness," he said, taking up his book once more. "I shall pay a condolence call, of course, and offer my services as I might."

Lily stared at him. "Is that all you have to say?"

"What do you want from me, Lily?" he replied, looking up from his reading. For a moment she thought there might be the glimmer of a tear in his eye, but he blinked and scowled and it disappeared before she could be sure it wasn't a trick of the light. "It is a terrible accident, to be sure, but I am not going to cry over it. When you get to be my age, you begin to expect that your fellows will soon pass from this earth."

"You are barely past fifty, Father," Lily pointed out. "And even so, one would think that the murder of a friend deserves more than a cold acknowledgment."

"I will thank you not to discuss my age," he snapped, and Lily nearly threw up her hands in defeat. "And Sir Charles was older than I am. He was a friend, true, but my going to pieces over his death does no one any good." He looked back down at his book.

This time Lily caught the slight tremor of his shoulders as he took a deep breath. He was upset, perhaps even devastated, and pretending as hard as he could not to be.

He was a man who could and did feel deeply, as evidenced by the mourning he still wore for her mother more than twenty-five years later. But he would have died himself before he let those feelings be shown in his manner or his words. It made her want to seize the book he was reading and throw it at his head. It made her want to cry for him. And for herself. "You can have feelings, you know, Father. The world will not stop turning."

He didn't look up. "Yesterday's mutton was too tough. Tell your cook to prepare tonight's dinner more carefully. I am already concerned about my health, as I hope you recall. Surely you do not wish me to suffer from indigestion as well."

Lily opened her mouth to reply, then shut it sharply, her hands clenched around the arms of her chair.

Her father glanced up. "Well, go on. And you really ought to avoid making faces like that, unless you want to give yourself wrinkles ahead of your time. Your dear mother had the most beautiful complexion," he added, his voice dropping to a murmur.

There was no point in arguing or even answering. She stood and made to leave the room.

"*What* are you wearing?"

Lily's hands clenched in the folds of her skirts, and she didn't turn to face him. She knew exactly what he meant and what he would think of it. But she wouldn't give him the satisfaction of a discussion. "A riding habit, Father. They are customary, you know, when a lady intends horseback riding."

"But it is *green*." He pronounced the word with shock bordering on outrage.

"Yes, it is," she said. Without waiting for his reply, Lily stalked out of the room, unable to resist slamming the door behind her. Ignoring her father's instruction to speak to Mrs. Carstairs—the mutton had *not* been tough—she didn't stop moving until she was in her own room.

Lily leaned back against the door as soon as it was closed, her fingers pressed to her temples. Was this going to be her life now—dodging her father's demands and suffering through his moods until he finally had enough and left?

Straightening, Lily shook her head, though there was no one else there to see the gesture. However he might choose to act, she was mistress of her own home. Her life no longer revolved around his whims.

Whether or not he wanted to admit it, he was as upset by his friend's death as she was—and no doubt even more concerned for Frank's well-being. And she had made a promise to Mr. Page to write while the morning was still fresh in her mind. So that was what she would do.

Pulling out a fresh sheet of paper, Lily settled at her writing desk, dipped her pen with a quick, decisive stroke, and began to write.

Chapter 9

"And apparently we must find a new governess before the end of the month, and how we shall do that I've no idea; it took us the better part of six months to find this one—Lily? Lily, are you paying attention?"

Lily jumped, suddenly realizing she had been staring at the same shelf of books for over a minute without seeing it. "I apologize, Margaret, my mind was elsewhere. You were saying?"

Lily had hoped to hear from Mr. Page the next day, at least a note if he didn't have time to call. But the pressing desire to avoid her father had driven Lily from the house before the day's first post arrived.

Margaret Harlowe had called that morning. After exclaiming in delight to find Lily dressed in colors once more, Margaret had asked for her company on a shopping expedition.

Lily had just sat through an entire breakfast of her father's criticism of her breakfast room, thinly veiled as a litany of the merits of the breakfast room in his own home. She'd jumped on the invitation, then suggested they turn their steps toward the shops on Oxford Street. The closer they stayed to Wimpole Street, she reasoned, the more likely she would be to overhear any gossip about Sir Charles. She had followed Margaret from the stationer's to the lending library, keeping up with the conversation without really paying attention. Now she looked up to find her friend frowning at her.

"Is it your father?" Margaret asked, grimacing in sympathy. "I cannot believe he has simply *installed* himself in your home. The nerve." She shook her head. "And how revolting that he'll not even say how long he intends to stay. We're to visit Mr. Harlowe's parents near Clapham soon. You are welcome to come with us if you need to escape him."

"I may take you up on that offer," Lily said, feeling grim. "I've no wish to be chased from my own home, but if it is a choice between standing on principle and seeing him every day . . . But it isn't only him."

Margaret gave her a sideways glance as she carried her books toward the desk. "You're thinking of Sir Charles?" she asked. The notice of his death had appeared in the paper that morning, with plenty of hints in the gossip columns about the suspicious circumstances. Lily had, after only a little hesitation, told her friend what had really happened.

Lily nodded.

Margaret looked thoughtful while the titles of her books were entered in the ledger and the librarian took them away to make a parcel for delivery to her home. "I've not heard any particular gossip about it, but I shall keep my ears open. It seems this is becoming a habit for you, Lily," she added as they made their way out of the library. "If twice makes a habit. It seems so odd to think about. A murder on Wimpole Street!"

"No odder there than in the middle of Mayfair," Lily pointed out.

"Well, I do not know about that," Margaret said thoughtfully as they linked arms to stroll down the street. "If one goes by the reports in the paper, murder so often has to do with money, and there is plenty of that in Mayfair. Which was the trouble for the Harpers—or the lack of money, as I recall. Do you think this Sir Charles was killed for his fortune?"

"If he had one," Lily said. "I haven't any idea if he did. He has property, certainly, but that does not always come with money."

"You could ask your father," Margaret pointed out. "It seems like the sort of thing he would keep track of—"

"Would you mind if we stop for a bite?" Lily asked suddenly as they passed a confectioner's shop. She wasn't particularly hungry, but a glance through the windows had shown her that the shop was an almost exclusively feminine retreat, suitable for ladies who would otherwise have been looked at askance for dining in public. It was exactly the sort of place where the sort of woman she wanted to find might pass an hour or two.

As soon as they entered, Lily laid a hand on Margaret's arm, keeping them both by the doorway for a moment while she evaluated the room. In one corner, a young lady read a letter while a woman who looked like her governess enjoyed a decadent pastry. Close to the door, two young matrons shared their opinions on the recent theatre season at Drury Lane. And by the windows, two older women, one in a resplendent turban, were talking in loud whispers about two of their neighbors, living in adjacent houses on Cavendish Square, whom they suspected of having an affair.

Lily hid a satisfied smile and, beckoning to Margaret, chose a table by the window as well. While an aproned waiter took their order, eventually returning with a pot of tea and several small confections, Lily returned to what Margaret had been saying about her struggles to find a suitable governess for her two daughters, whether they would need to learn Italian rather than French, and the likelihood of finding someone who could prepare girls with sufficient knowledge to be successful political wives.

After the tea arrived, however, Lily leaned forward, beckoning her friend to do the same. "I need to be indiscreet for a moment," she whispered. "And I need your assistance. Do you think you can gossip loudly enough to be overheard by those two women?"

"Gossip about what?" Margaret whispered back.

"About how you found out Sir Charles Wyatt has been murdered." Lily smiled briefly before assuming a shocked expression, raising her voice just enough to carry to the next table. "Surely not! The notice in the paper this morning gave no such details of his death. How can you be sure?"

Margaret looked panicked for a moment before an encouraging nod from Lily made her clear her throat and speak in a loud whisper. She stumbled a little over her words but performed her part creditably. "The . . . the butcher boy. Who delivered our meat this morning? He also delivers to their house, and . . . and the cook told my dresser. Who told me."

"But—murdered in his own library! And not five blocks from where we sit at this moment. I cannot believe it to be true. Sir Charles was always such a gentleman—"

"Excuse me, dear ladies." The woman in the splendid turban cleared her throat, leaning closer to Lily and Margaret's table. "I don't mean to intrude, but I could not help overhearing. Were you by chance speaking of that tragic incident on Wimpole Street and the death of Sir Charles Wyatt?"

"Good heavens, yes," Lily said, while Margaret receded gratefully into her chair. "I read about it only this morning, which was a great shock, as he had been a close acquaintance of my father for years. And yet my dear friend here"—a nod to Margaret, who jumped a little at being included once more—"tells me there is a rumor afoot that he was in fact murdered. I can scarcely credit it!"

"Oh, my dear." The second woman shook her head, though there was an edge of delight to her expression as she leaned forward. "Your friend is tragically correct. We know everything that passes in this neighborhood, and we have it on good authority that Sir Charles's death was certainly not a natural one."

"Indeed," agreed the one in the elaborate turban. "We of course heard of it mere hours after that Bow Street fellow found evidence of"—her voice dropped—"*murder*. And when I was at Fowler's not one hour ago to purchase new draperies for the back parlor—with the most delightful rose pattern—I ran into Mrs. Hammond, who told me that *she* had it directly from her husband. His brother is Mr. George Hammond, you see, who is one of the family's solicitors. He had to attend them last evening to discuss the provisions of the will.

And they had to explain the whole matter to him. So you may be sure it is a reliable report and not simply some rumor."

"How horrid!" Lily said, gazing at them with rapt—and encouraging—attention. "But a gentleman like Sir Charles! So respected, so upstanding. Who could have any reason to do such a thing?"

The woman in the turban lowered her voice. "My understanding of such things is that they are nearly always to do with money. And from his style of living, I imagine Sir Charles had plenty of that."

"But he had only a son and a nephew to inherit from him," the second lady pointed out. "And judging by *their* style of living, he was already more than generous. No, there are always two possibilities, not one: love or money. Perhaps Sir Charles was having an illicit affair—"

"Surely not at his age," Margaret interrupted, shocked into speaking up.

The two women exchanged a look, then chuckled. "Oh, my dear," the one in the turban said, still laughing. "Such appetites do not wither with age. And they certainly did not for Charles Wyatt, who . . . well, one does not like to speak ill of the dead, but before his first marriage—and before the second one as well—he apparently was quite the skirt chaser." She dropped her voice nearly to a whisper. "I have even heard rumors that he has a natural child tucked away in the country somewhere."

"Some men are insatiable," the second woman said darkly, punctuating her pronouncement with a glower over the rim of her teacup.

"That was when he was unmarried, as you said," Lily said. She knew plenty of rumors about Frank's own amorous tendencies—starting with stories of him kissing various village girls behind more than one stable when they were young and only growing when he was old enough to become a man about town. But Sir Charles had been a man her own father's age. If there had been rumors about his affairs, they had never been repeated where a young girl might hear them. "I thought he and the new Lady Wyatt were quite attached. Could he truly have betrayed her?"

"Well, he was certainly fond of her or he'd not have married again. But whether she was strongly attached, I could not say," the first woman said, a thoughtful frown drawing down her brows. She absently poured herself a second cup of tea, considering the question. "I had the pleasure of meeting the new Lady Wyatt several times during the spring season. As you say, she is both charming and beautiful—"

"But her family was quite penniless before her marriage, which accounts for her staying single so long, you know," the second woman put in. "Young men must worry about such things as an income; it puts us ladies at quite a disadvantage. A man in Sir Charles's time of life, and with his wealth, can ignore such concerns and marry only to please himself."

"And he certainly was pleased," the first woman agreed. "But I could never tell whether there was any true affection on *her* part."

"She seemed fond of him when I saw them together," Lily said slowly, remembering the friendly rapport she had witnessed after Lady Wyatt was injured.

"Oh, she was always every inch the doting wife in public," the turbaned lady agreed. She leaned forward, her eyes glittering. "But who knows what her private feelings were? With him so much older and her family so poor, one can only assume a mercenary motive for the union. If she were only passingly attached, and if it became apparent after the wedding . . . well, he may not have considered it a betrayal."

"But who then would have"—Lily leaned forward again, dropping her voice further—"done it?"

"Lady Wyatt or the other woman," said the second woman, still looking grim. "Or the other woman's husband."

"Gracious, Angelica!" the woman in the turban exclaimed. "What a morbid turn of mind you have. Depend upon it, my dear, there is a much simpler explanation. Mrs. Hammond told me the family believes it was a burglar."

The second woman tittered, looking embarrassed. "Oh, certainly, that is the most likely answer. Or one of the servants."

"I am afraid we must be going," Lily said, standing abruptly. Margaret, a confused moment later, followed suit. "Thank you for your assurances. Doubtless, as you say, it was a burglar."

"You are most welcome, dear ma'am . . . I did not catch your name?" the woman in the turban hinted, her eyes alight at the prospect of more gossip.

Lily pretended not to hear, occupying herself with gathering her things, saying polite farewells, and herding Margaret toward the door. Behind her, she heard the ladies resuming their tête-à-tête, still eagerly speculating about their neighbors:

"Poor Lady Wyatt. First the shock of losing her husband, then to discover that he was actually murdered . . . Did you hear the news about Lydia Sanderson? She claimed they were going to Bath for her husband's health, but it turns out they had been forced to let their property to satisfy his creditors . . ."

Margaret waited until they had gained the park at Cavendish Square before collapsing dramatically to a bench, fanning herself. "Gracious, Lily, how do you do it? With such wide eyes and innocent looks? I could barely keep my countenance or think of anything to say when you needed me to."

"You did marvelously, and I am so grateful for your help," Lily said, as warmly as she could while her mind was still occupied with thoughts of the Wyatt family. "I'll not ask it of you again, I promise."

"Yes, I should prefer to stay as far away from murder as possible," Margaret agreed, shuddering. "Now, I believe we left my carriage back on Oxford Street? After a performance like that, I am dearly in need of a rest."

★ ★ ★

When Lily entered the drawing room of her own home, she was torn between wishing she had stayed away and guilt that she hadn't returned sooner. Jack sat there, clearly waiting for her. And with him, glowering from the chair he had claimed as his own, was her father, cane planted between his feet and his hands clasped around the top as he fixed Jack with a narrow-eyed stare.

"And you sympathize with these radicals, these agents of destruction?" George Pierce's voice was high with outrage. "You, a man charged with upholding the will of King and country?"

"I merely said, sir, that it must be hard on a man to have the skills he has labored his whole life to acquire suddenly valued at naught, and himself replaced by a machine," Jack replied mildly. "The question of destruction and rioting is a separate one."

"They certainly *cannot* be treated separately—"

"Dear me, are you talking politics in my drawing room?" Lily asked, pasting a smile on her face. The last thing she wanted was to get drawn into such a conversation with her father. "It is too beautiful a day for that. Captain Hartley, I hope you've not been waiting long for my return."

"Not more than twenty minutes, I am sure," Jack said, rising to offer her a gallant bow. He kept a remarkably straight face as he added, "And your father has been kindly entertaining me in your absence."

Mr. Pierce snorted loudly, thumping his cane against the floor. "I begin to fear you have introduced unsuitable opinions—or perhaps unsuitable people—into your life. It is unseemly." He gave Jack a withering glance before fixing his eye once more on his daughter. "I strongly advise you to reconsider allowing them in your home."

"The opinions or the people?" Jack inquired politely. If Lily had been closer, she would have kicked him.

Mr. Pierce looked outraged. "Both, perhaps."

"I could never bear to turn away someone who was so important in the life of my dear Freddy," Lily said coldly. "Or who has been such a kind friend to me. Have you offered the captain any refreshment, Father?" she added, taking her seat.

Mr. Pierce snorted again, leaning heavily on his cane as he climbed to his feet. "I'll not play at hostess for you, Lily. I leave you to such entertainments as you can find in your conscience to enjoy." Shaking his head in disappointment, he thumped from the room.

"I wonder what *entertainments* he suspects we shall get up to," Jack said, brows raised. "Do you think he means discussing politics? Or does he believe I intend something more dastardly?"

"Must you be so vulgar?" she demanded. Jack looked at her in surprise—normally Lily would have laughed at such a quip. This time she rolled her eyes toward the door. "He might be listening, and I am the one who has to suffer through his company at dinner tonight."

Jack laughed. "My apologies. I shall do my best to maintain my company manners." Growing more somber, he leaned forward. "I came to inquire whether you had heard anything from Mr. Page today."

"No, nothing." Lily frowned. "I had hoped to. But I did have a most interesting conversation in a tea shop when I was—"

At that moment, they were interrupted by Anna, Lily's maid, who bobbed a curtsy from the doorway. At Lily's nod, she stepped forward. "Begging your pardon, Mrs. Adler, but there is someone here wishful of speaking with you."

Lily frowned. "Well, for heaven's sake, Anna, show whoever it is in. You know I am at home to visitors this morning."

Anna hesitated. "It's not properly a visitor, ma'am. Not as could come in the front door. There's a girl in the kitchen who asked to speak with you. She said she's a maid at the home of Sir Charles and Lady Wyatt. Her name is Ellen."

Lily exchanged a startled look with Jack before standing quickly. "Did she say what she wants? Or who sent her?"

"No, ma'am, but I don't have the sense that anyone sent her. She begged to speak with you. And she's all aflutter. Keeps tripping over her words. I think she's terribly upset about something."

Lily frowned. Lady Wyatt had mentioned the other day, when she sent Percy away, that Ellen was distressed. But the girl she had met had not seemed the fluttery type; in fact, she had been ready to leap forward and take her brother's part with Sir Charles when Thomas had been accused of theft. Lily was about to order Anna to bring the girl to her instantly, but she paused, reconsidering.

If Ellen's visit didn't come at the prompting of her employer, she might have something valuable to share about the circumstances of Sir Charles's death. And while Lily would have been happy to interview the girl in the drawing room, there was every chance her father might overhear if they remained upstairs. That would never do.

She glanced at Jack. "Come downstairs with me, Captain. I expect that whatever the girl has to say, you ought to hear it as well."

★ ★ ★

Ellen jumped to her feet as soon as they entered the kitchen, prompting a startled exclamation from Mrs. Carstairs, who had been presiding over the day's baking. Both women curtsied, though Mrs. Carstairs returned quickly to her task, while Ellen looked down, then up, then down again, her hands clasped nervously in front of her.

"Ellen," Lily said briskly. "I recall you from the Wyatts' home. I hope you and your brother are both well?"

"Very well, ma'am, I thank you for asking," Ellen said, her hands twisting together. "But it isn't me or Thomas I wanted to talk to you about."

"She wants to talk about the murder," said the eager, gangly boy who had been sitting next to her, springing to his feet. Jack had taken the boy into his service after the latter's employer, the shipping agent Hyrum Lacey, had died in the spring. The boy still gave the impression of being an utter ragamuffin, even though he was attired as a respectable servant. His curly dark hair needed to be clipped, and Lily could see that his pants were already too short for him. But he gave a smart bow, standing briskly at attention as he straightened. It seemed the captain had been working on manners with his young charge along with instruction in his other duties.

"Jem." Lily greeted him warmly. "How good to see you again."

Both Jack and Lily felt responsible for the boy. He didn't know that even though his salary came from Jack, the money that covered the clothes he was constantly outgrowing came from Lily's accounts, or that between them they had ensured that his sickly mother would never be responsible for any of her doctor's bills.

Jem ducked his head, embarrassed. "Mrs. Adler, ma'am."

"Still serving the captain well, I hope?" she asked.

"Indeed he is," Jack said, winking at Jem. "Whenever I get my next set of orders, Jem is to come to sea with me to be my body man. I need someone I can trust aboard ship."

Lily's smile grew at the eager look on the boy's face and his obvious pride at being called a man, even if the word was simply a description of a servant's role. "I imagine you will like that, Jem?" she asked kindly.

"Oh, yes, ma'am!" He beamed. "Almost like being a lascar, like m'father. Mam'll be so proud."

The words tugged at Lily's heart. From what Jem had let fall about his family, his mother was only barely sure of his father's identity. She had once said he might have been one of the Indian sailors in His Majesty's navy, and the boy had latched on to that idea with eager hero worship. It was partly why he was so thrilled to be in Jack's service, and why the devil-may-care captain had such a soft spot for the clever little urchin he had taken under his wing.

But he was still a child, and Lily had no intention of pulling him into the questions surrounding yet another unnatural death. "If there is another murder, Jem," she said sternly. "It may be none of my affair, and it is certainly nothing to do with you."

"Oh, but Ellen's already told me all about it," he said eagerly.

Ellen cleared her throat at that, glancing over her shoulder at Mrs. Carstairs, then turned back to Lily, a pleading look on her face.

Lily understood. "Mrs. Carstairs, I wonder if you might give us a moment to talk in private?"

The cook-housekeeper, who had just wrapped her apron around her hands to pull a loaf of bread from the oven, looked up in surprise. "Of course, Mrs. Adler," she said, her curiosity written all over her face, though she was too good at her job to ask any questions. "If you'll give me a moment to . . ." Juggling the hot pan, she slid the loaf onto the wooden kitchen table next to a plate piled high with fresh scones. "There, that's done. Will you be needing anything else?"

"No, thank you."

Mrs. Carstairs curtsied. "I'll continue with the baking whenever you are done, ma'am." She gave Ellen a quick, skeptical look before leaving.

Ellen watched her go, eyes wide, then glanced sidelong at Jem.

Lily caught the look. "Go with her, Jem. Ellen needs to speak with us alone."

"But . . ." The boy looked pleadingly at Jack.

Who shook his head. "Out you go," he said firmly.

"But what if you need my help?" Jem asked.

"Then we will ask for it," Lily said. "Take a scone and make yourself scarce."

Jem's shoulders slumped, his face a picture of betrayal. But he still reached out and snagged two scones from the plate, letting out a squeak of surprise when he discovered they were still hot. Casting one more morose look at them, he trailed out the door.

Lily watched him go, then turned back in time to see Ellen eyeing the captain uneasily. "Do you have any objection to the captain staying while you share your information?"

Ellen hesitated, then shook her head. "No, Mrs. Adler. I recall he . . . you both helped my brother. I couldn't go to them Bow Street officers, ma'am, not on my life. If the family found out I went there, I'd be sacked for certain. But I could pay a visit to another house. So here I am. You listened before when I said Thomas didn't do anything. I'm hoping you'll listen now."

"I will," Lily said, taking a seat at the table and gesturing for both Jack and Ellen to do the same. Selecting a scone from the plate, she pulled it apart, wincing at the hot steam, and gestured toward Ellen. "Would you like one?"

"No, ma'am," Ellen said stiffly. She looked uncomfortable being there and didn't take a seat even when Lily again motioned for her to do so.

"I would," Jack said. He too had remained standing, leaning against the doorway. "Toss one over?"

Lily narrowed her eyes at him in an effort to persuade him to be serious—a useless attempt. He merely raised his eyebrows as if daring her. So she sighed and did as he asked. Jack caught the scone easily, and Lily turned back just in time to catch the surprised look on Ellen's face.

"My apologies," she said. "He is incorrigible, but I have a feeling this is not the moment for levity. You came to tell us something concerning Sir Charles's death, did you not?"

Ellen shook her head, then just as quickly nodded, looking torn. "It may be. I couldn't say for sure, ma'am. That is, I don't think it has anything to do with his death, but I'm worried someone will make out that it does."

"Start at the beginning," Jack said gently, his playfulness gone. "We promise to listen."

Ellen nodded again but hesitated, her hands twisting the folds of her dress. "Sir Charles has another son, and his name is Arthur," she said at last, her words coming out in a rush. "He's but sixteen and lives at home too. All the servants look after him somewhat, but he's in my particular charge. I help him every day, and he's the sweetest boy you can imagine, though not what you'd call friendly, not with strangers or those as discomfort him. But I've never known any harm in him, and I've been with him for years."

Lily's hands, at first busy with the scone, had gradually fallen still as she listened to Ellen. As the maid finished speaking, she demanded, "Why did no one say anything of this to Mr. Page?"

"He asked about other family members," Jack added, looking baffled. "Why the secrecy?"

Ellen hesitated again, and Lily was surprised to see tears fill her eyes. "He's not like other boys," the maid said at last. "He never has been. The family says he's feebleminded, but I don't think that's the case. He just doesn't think quite the way the rest of us do. He doesn't say much, he likes things just so, and he gets upset being around too many people. He's well looked after, but outside the house, it's like he doesn't exist. The family doesn't talk about him to strangers."

"Not even when one of them has been murdered?" Jack asked angrily.

That made Ellen's head snap up. "He had *nothing* to do with that. I told you, he's the sweetest boy, and so bright, though of course his brother could never be brought to see that. Mr. Frank doesn't much like being around Arthur."

Lily held up a hand to silence them both. "If you are not here to say you think he was involved, then why are you here?"

Ellen swallowed nervously. "He's acting . . . odd. Not like he usually does, I mean. He's always a little odd. He seems nervous and upset. And Mr. Frank . . . he never comes to see his brother. But all yesterday he kept stopping by to see him, just to look at him for a bit without saying anything at all, then went away. It's odd. It makes me jumpy."

"Perhaps Mr. Wyatt is concerned about how his brother will handle the loss of their father," Lily suggested. "The death of a parent might well prompt a change in familial feeling."

Ellen nodded. "It might. But I've been in that house years. And it doesn't feel right to me. I'm worried . . ."

They waited, but it seemed Ellen couldn't bring herself to say it. Lily exchanged a puzzled look with Jack, who looked as serious as he ever did, then leaned forward. "Ellen, I promised I would listen. What are you worried about?"

"I'm worried that, whatever happened, someone will blame Arthur for it," Ellen whispered. "Because he's not like them. And if that happens, I don't know what might happen to him. Please, ma'am. Please, Captain." She raised her eyes to them, full of tears once more. "There's something strange going on in that family. If someone does try to blame Arthur, I'm begging you, please, make sure them Bow Street police know he had nothing to do with it at all."

The girl was trembling by the time she finished speaking, tears spilling over her lashes. Lily exchanged an anxious look with Jack, at a loss for how to comfort her. Trying to bridge the class divide between them could only make things more awkward. But she could offer her reassurance.

"We shall have to tell Mr. Page," she said gently. "But—" She held up a hand to forestall Ellen, who clearly was about to burst out in more speech. "We will tell him exactly what you have related to us here. And Mr. Page is a fair man. As you are the person who spends the most time caring for young Arthur, I am sure he will trust your word."

"What will he do with him?" Ellen asked, sniffing.

"Likely he will want to speak to the boy," Jack said, holding out a handkerchief to her. After staring at him in wide-eyed astonishment, Ellen took it gratefully and wiped her eyes and nose. "But we will insist that he be gentle in his questions and defer to you for how to behave. And you'll have time to prepare your charge for the interview."

"He may not want to speak," Ellen whispered. "He doesn't, much."

"We will tell Mr. Page that as well," Lily said.

Ellen still looked nervous and unsettled, but she nodded. "Thank you, Mrs. Adler." She sighed, looking down at her hands. "I thought it best to tell someone rather than risk him being discovered, as if he was being hidden away because he's guilty."

"You did right," Lily said briskly, standing. "And we will do all in our power to ensure that no harm or unmerited blame comes to him. But you," she added, looking the girl over, "are too distressed to depart. Shall I call my housekeeper to come sit with you while you recover yourself?"

Ellen shook her head. "Thank you, ma'am, but no. I ought to get back—Arthur's not used to my being gone so long." She glanced down at the handkerchief in her hands, then back at Jack, her eyes wide. "I'll see this laundered and returned to you, sir."

"No need to trouble yourself," he said, shrugging. "I've plenty more where that came from. And if things on Wimpole Street are in as distressed a state as you describe, you may have need of it again in the next few days."

Ellen let out an expressive sigh. "I don't know what to make of them all, sir, truly I don't."

"Is there aught you can tell us about the family?" Lily asked, curious.

Ellen hesitated, and Lily instantly regretted asking. Ellen's first loyalty was to her employers. She had confided in them to protect her charge, but asking her to reveal the family's innermost secrets and tensions was a very different thing.

"Never mind," Lily said, before the girl figured out how to answer. "You have told us plenty of use already. Thank you for doing so. And if you think of anything else we ought to know, you may write me here. I'd not want you to risk your position by coming again."

"Yes, ma'am, thank you." Ellen looked grateful as she curtsied. "There is one thing I can tell you—that new Lady Wyatt baffled me, she did. She and Sir Charles were thick as thieves when he was courting her, and they always seemed terrible fond of each other, spent hours and hours together. But . . ." Ellen lowered her voice. "Wilkes, Lady Wyatt's maid, says that not a month after they married, Lady Wyatt began to refuse him her bed. And that she never let him return." Ellen blushed. "I oughtn't to have said that."

"You never know," Jack said, glancing at Lily, his look speculative. "We will take whatever information we can just now. You never know what might be helpful."

CHAPTER 10

They made it out of the house without running into her father. Though on principle, Lily detested feeling as though she had to sneak around her own home, she had no desire for Mr. Pierce to discover where they were heading.

Their destination was Bow Street, where Mr. Page was currently attached as an officer of the Runners. Mr. Pierce would have disapproved mightily—and so, Lily knew, would nearly everyone of her acquaintance. Unlike the magistrate's office at Great Marlborough Street, where she had visited before, Bow Street was located at the edge of Covent Garden, perilously close to the squalid neighborhoods of St. Giles and the Seven Dials. Though Covent Garden itself was an area of business during the day and entertainment at night, it was not a place a woman of Lily's class was expected to venture. The Bow Street offices were even less so.

That didn't make her hesitate in her task. But it did make her don a hat with a veil before she and Jack made their way to Piccadilly to find a hack chaise at liberty to take a fare. And she let Jack be the one to speak to the driver as she climbed into the carriage without assistance.

As soon as they were on their way, Jack propped his elbows on his knees, resting his chin in his hands and swaying as easily with the motion of the carriage as if he were back on his ship. "So our plan of attack is to lead with the presence of the hidden younger Wyatt brother?"

"What do you mean, lead with?" Lily asked, folding her veil back over her hat so she could see him more clearly in the carriage's dim interior. "Is there other information you have to convey to him?"

"You expect me to believe we're only intending to share our news and then be gone?" Jack snorted. "I made sure you would use this as an opening to involve yourself further in the matter. But if you are willing to let him dismiss you so easily . . ."

"I never let anyone dismiss me easily," Lily said, putting her nose in the air before giving Jack a sideways look. "As for the rest, we shall see how the conversation goes. But Mr. Page is an intelligent man. I doubt he will need much convincing to realize that his first motive in requesting our help has not really changed. The Wyatts still live in a world to which he has very little access, but where we may come and go as we please."

"And you think that will be enough for him?" Jack raised a brow.

Lily shrugged. "He wants to catch the murderer. I have a feeling he is the sort of practical man who will use any tool at his disposal."

⋆   ⋆   ⋆

"No, absolutely not, *no*," Mr. Page snapped, scowling at Lily and Jack as they sat across the desk from him.

Lily scowled back. It wasn't the reception she had been anticipating.

They had been shown in with relative anonymity, Lily with her veil drawn once more over her face. Mr. Page had been shocked to see them, even more shocked when Lily explained that they had important information about the Wyatts to share.

"Do you not at least want to know what it is?" she demanded.

"I want to know that you will refrain from involving yourself in this matter any further," he said, casting his eyes heavenward as if seeking divine assistance. "Mrs. Adler, I appreciate your enthusiasm. And I don't deny that you—both of you," he added, bowing his head toward Jack, "have been most helpful. But the rest of the matter is my business."

"But I know the family," Lily pointed out. "And you asked for our assistance."

"She has a point," Jack said, crossing his ankles as he leaned back in his chair.

"For one day. Less than one day," Mr. Page said, rubbing his temples wearily. "I asked you to listen to what the Wyatts said and let me know if any of it seemed odd to you, given what you know of them. Which you conveyed adequately in the notes you sent last night."

"We did more than that," Lily argued. "Or have you forgotten how you obtained your proof that the play at hand was, indeed, foul?"

"And making that discovery so publicly may well have put the Wyatts on their guard against me. They already saw my presence as an intrusion. Now they'll see it as an attack and will refuse to deal with me honestly."

"Page," Jack said, leaning forward and looking more serious. "They were already refusing to deal with you honestly. You need to know what we can tell you."

"I already have the observations you wrote down for me—"

Lily interrupted. "Sir Charles has another son."

Mr. Page stared at her blankly. "What?"

Jack and Lily exchanged a glance. Jack cleared his throat. "You asked Mr. Frank Wyatt if he had any other relatives, and he gave you that very small list of distant relations. He was lying."

"He has a younger brother," Lily said. "Living in that very house."

Mr. Page stared at her. "How is it you forgot to mention this?"

"I did not know until today."

"And yet you claim familiarity with the family?"

"I grew up not far from Sir Charles's property, and he and my father were close. Frank and my father were close." Lily swallowed, feeling angry heat rise to her cheeks. "I am sure you can understand that, as a female younger than any of the men concerned, I was not brought into any confidences. What they hid from the rest of the world, it seems, they also hid from me."

Mr. Page's voice, when he finally spoke, was cold and quiet. "And did they conceal this from me because the boy did it?"

Lily winced. "I beg you'll not leap to that conclusion, sir." Quietly, helped by Jack when she forgot to include some detail or other, she related their unexpected conversation with Ellen.

Mr. Page listened in silence, though Lily could follow the emotions that chased their way across his features. His initial anger was quickly replaced by surprise, which gradually gave way to thoughtfulness. By the time she fell quiet, his face had become unreadable.

"And you believed her, when she said he had nothing to do with it, even though you've never met him and his own family wanted to hide him from me?"

"They certainly aren't the only family to hide the existence of an . . . unusual member," Jack said. "It does not necessarily imply that they believed he was guilty, merely that they did not want *anyone* to know of his existence."

"And your suspicion is exactly what the maid was afraid of," Lily said. "That was why she wanted you to know of him now."

"Then why go to you, instead of coming here?" Mr. Page asked, his face still impassive.

"She would have been dismissed if they discovered she told you anything," Lily said. "Coming to a private home—of someone she had met and knew to be fair-minded—" Jack snorted, and Lily glared at him. "Well, I am. And she had reason to know it. She took what seemed the safest course of action for both her and her charge. Rather noble, really, when you think of it."

"That remains to be seen."

Mr. Page looked thoughtful once again as he sifted through the papers scattered over his desk. To one side sat a small stack of pasteboard calling cards; Percy Wyatt's was on top, and below it, Lily supposed, would be one for each member of the family. The other papers were full sheets, each covered in lines of neat handwriting, Lily saw as he shifted them into a tidier pile. It was hard to read upside down, but she could make out the names of various members of the Wyatt family, with careful notes underneath each name. Mr. Page, unsurprisingly, was meticulous in his work.

He was also still speaking.

"I'll have to talk to him myself, however, before I can take her word for his innocence."

"Are you glad you listened to us now?" Lily asked, perversely pleased by the scowl she received in response. "Would you rather *not* know they were lying to you?"

"It is a murder, Mrs. Adler," he said quietly. "I assume that every one of them is lying to me until I know otherwise."

Lily winced. "And what else have you learned?"

"Mrs. Adler," he said, clearly exasperated. "I told you—" He broke off, shaking his head, and sighed. "Well, have it your way. You told me something I didn't know. So fair's fair, I suppose. Let's have an exchange and see what you can tease out of this mess."

"Splendid!" Lily said, sitting forward eagerly. Then she grimaced. "Well, not splendid."

"Terrible, actually," Jack agreed, though he looked equally eager. "But let us see what we can do."

Mr. Page gave them a skeptical look as he rose and began pacing around the room, his hands clasped behind his back. "Sir Charles was killed by a heavy blow to the head. We were clearly meant to think he struck his head on the corner of his desk and bled to death on the floor of the library." He paused and glanced at Lily, one brow raised sardonically. "Shall I go on?"

Lily swallowed but nodded. It was no worse than what she had already seen. "Continue."

"Why go to the trouble of moving him?" Jack asked. "There were plenty of carvings on the mantelpiece. Why not make it appear that he struck his head there?"

"Presumably to confuse the matter and make it seem more accidental. And to draw attention away from the missing poker and what was hidden in the chimney. The coroner confirmed that the poker we found could have been used to strike the blow that killed him. Which, by the way, would have needed to be heavy and strong. Sir Charles was a large man and would have been well able to fight back against an attacker. Our murderer is more likely to be a man, though a determined woman could have done it as well."

"Moving him would have also required a great deal of strength," Lily pointed out.

"Indeed." Mr. Page glanced back at Lily and Jack. "The family wants to say it was a burglar, of course, but there aren't any signs of that. And a burglar wouldn't have moved him."

"What about the servants?" Jack asked, sitting forward.

Mr. Page nodded, pausing in his circuit of the room as he considered the question. "I am inclined against that hypothesis. A servant would likely have had better ways to hide or dispose of the incriminating objects."

Lily nodded, impressed. She hadn't thought of it from that perspective.

"From speaking to the servants yesterday and examining Sir Charles's account books, it seems they were all pleased with their positions, considered him a good master, and were well compensated for their work. And as none of them have private rooms, unless one of them is covering for another, by all indications each was where they were supposed to be." Mr. Page paused, staring at the papers on his desk. "It could have been a servant, of course. Or an outsider, whether a burglar or not. I'll have to examine both possibilities. But these sorts of things are usually in the family, and that is where my suspicion lies."

Lily frowned. "Lady Wyatt's maid mentioned a quarrel between Sir Charles and his wife. Did you ask any of the servants about it?"

"I've not been back there since receiving your note," Mr. Page said, clasping his hands behind his back and resuming his pacing. "But the housekeeper, Mrs. Harris, mentioned something that I consider likely to be the same matter." He paused, his expression growing even more serious. "She overheard Sir Charles shouting at one point in the evening."

"He was not often one to raise his voice," Lily said, surprised.

Mr. Page nodded. "That was what she said as well, which is why she took note of it. He was upstairs and she was down, so she couldn't hear exactly what he said. But she did hear a few choice words."

Lily and Jack exchanged an eager look. "And what were they?" he asked.

"That he was disgusted with someone," Mr. Page said, regarding them grimly. "Or something, perhaps. Something unnatural. She thinks he might have even said that something was an abomination. I wonder if that might have been the quarrel Wilkes was referring to."

"Could he have been talking about Percy's theft?" Lily asked. "He was, by all accounts, furious."

"And yet he forgave his nephew not many hours later," Jack pointed out.

"So Percy says," Lily put in, watching Mr. Page closely as he spoke. "There is no one else who can confirm that, can they?"

"No, no one else," he agreed. "And Mr. Percy Wyatt himself told me something else odd, when I took him aside once more. He had clearly been holding something back in front of his cousin, and I insisted on knowing what it was."

"And?" Lily leaned forward once more; beside her, she felt Jack do the same.

"He said he couldn't be sure, but he almost thought his uncle was saying he wanted to make Percy his heir in Frank's place. Mr. Wyatt says he didn't quite believe that was true but assumed his uncle was speaking extravagantly to let him know all was forgiven."

Jack looked thoughtful. "If Sir Charles was going to disinherit his son, that would be quite a motive for murder."

"But we don't know that Sir Charles intended that at all," Lily pointed out, cold all over at the thought of Frank—sunny, self-absorbed Frank—being accused of murder. "We've only Percy's word for it. Which, as we know from his attempted theft, is not exactly trustworthy."

"And Frank?" Mr. Page asked, fixing her with a stern look. "Is he trustworthy?"

Lily hesitated. "I do not know him well as an adult," she said slowly. "As a child, he certainly would not hesitate to lie if it preserved someone's good opinion of him. But I cannot see him being able to kill his father in cold blood. He has been Sir Charles's closest confidant for half his life. He loved his father. He loved being the most important person in his father's life."

"But was he anymore?" Jack mused. "His father had recently married. And Frank, as we have seen, was not pleased with that marriage. Perhaps his love toward his father soured when Lady Wyatt entered the picture."

Lily made a face. "That is rather melodramatic, Captain."

"So is being disinherited, but I've seen that as a motive for murder before," Mr. Page said ruthlessly.

"But how would he have known?" Lily pointed out. "He was already out for the evening. And even if Percy said something to his cousin, Frank did not return home until around three o'clock in the morning, according to the butler."

"Unless that was the second time he came home," Jack said darkly.

"Which we must confirm, along with Mr. Percy Wyatt's movements," Mr. Page said briskly. "Captain, I hate to admit it, but you're better positioned than me to do so."

Jack leaned back in his chair, looking curious as he clasped his hands under his chin. "How do you mean?"

"I imagine you know—or can discover—the sort of gaming hells that young men like Percy and Frank Wyatt frequent. And you're far more likely to be welcome in them than a man like me. Do you think you could find out where they went that night? We—" He broke off, clearing his throat and scowling. "*I* need to know whether Frank was there as long as he claimed."

Jack's eyes were alight at the prospect of such a chase. Lily wasn't surprised—she knew he felt restless being stuck on land with nothing to occupy his time. "Indeed, I will see what I can uncover."

"Try not to lose too much money in the process," Lily said dryly.

Jack shrugged. "All for a good cause."

"I think you will find that he was out as he said," Lily said staunchly. "And that means that when he did return, according to the butler, Sir Charles was likely already . . ." She swallowed, not wanting to say it, but pressed firmly on. "Likely already dead. So that leaves Percy Wyatt."

"Who, according to his own report . . ." Jack leaned forward and plucked the top sheet off Mr. Page's desk. The constable started to protest, then sighed, shaking his head as he resumed his pacing. Jack grinned and read from the sheet. "Went home around midnight to his lodging on Harley Street—alone—and went to sleep. So that makes him the most likely culprit, does it not?"

"Harley Street is not far from Sir Charles's house," Lily said. "It would have been a simple matter for him to return on foot."

Mr. Page raised his eyebrows at them. "Both of you assume Lady Wyatt couldn't have done it?"

"You said it was more likely a man," Jack pointed out.

"But a determined woman could have done it," Lily remembered. "Lady Wyatt would certainly strike one as determined. And she did lie."

Mr. Page studied her. "How did she seem to you, the first day that you met her?" he asked, turning his head to include Jack in the question.

"She had a pleasant and cordial manner, though I should not have called her exactly friendly," Jack said. "I would say she seemed content, as one would expect in a new bride."

"She seemed devoted to her husband, and he appeared quite fond of her," Lily said honestly. Remembering Frank Wyatt's comments, she added, "Even his son remarked how charming it was that they were always together, though I am sure he did not mean it as a compliment."

"That part does interest me," Mr. Page said, hands clasped behind his back as he stared at the papers on his desk, though without seeming to really see them. "The animosity between them."

"Hardly surprising, in a second marriage," Jack pointed out. "Especially when the child of the first marriage is a man grown and the second wife only a few years older than he."

"Better than a second marriage where she is a decade his junior," Lily pointed out tartly. "And there are a great many of those that happen among the men considered Sir Charles's peers."

"And did the other, did Mr. Percy Wyatt, seem to have the same resentment toward her?" Mr. Page asked. "He treated her with a great deal of solicitude yesterday, but what about before?"

"He seemed a disagreeable, weak-willed sort of boy, with nothing of his cousin's ease or pleasantness," Jack said, tossing the paper back on the desk and scowling as he leaned back in his chair. "The sort to take what he wants, even if it wasn't his in the first place."

"Are you referring to his uncle's money or our carriage?" Lily asked, a little dryly, earning a grumpy stare from Jack. She shrugged. "Both prove your point, I suppose, but I think one is far more worth holding against him than the other."

"He was a weaselly little fellow, either way."

"But when it came to Lady Wyatt, he seemed almost ashamed of Mr. Frank Wyatt's behavior," Lily pointed out, leaning forward enough that she could rest her elbows on the edge of Mr. Page's desk, her chin hovering over her steepled fingers as she frowned in thought. "He was far more polite to her than his cousin was."

Mr. Page had returned to his desk, and he braced his hands on it as he regarded them. "Why didn't you believe Lady Wyatt when she sent him to comfort the maid? A personable young man could talk sense into an impressionable girl."

Lily raised her own brows in response. "Because, not only is Mr. Percy Wyatt *not* a personable young man, it was Ellen's brother who very nearly took the blame for his theft." She frowned, a thought clicking into place. "It must have been the younger brother, Arthur. Ellen said that he was principally in her charge."

Jack's feet thumped on the floor as he sat up. "Asking Percy to go see Ellen must have been Lady Wyatt's way of telling him to see to Arthur. They were all quite active participants in deceiving you on that point, Page."

"Speaking of Lady Wyatt once more"—Mr. Page studied Lily— "did her grief seem truthful to you? At times it seemed overwrought to me. And there were several moments where it seemed she forgot to be grieving and was angry or defensive instead . . ."

"Well, grief is an unpredictable thing," Lily pointed out slowly, considering her words as she spoke. "For her to experience so much grief and shock together, so quickly, and then to be confronted with strangers in her home . . . it would not be unnatural to be over-wrought. But"—she held up her hand when both Jack and Mr. Page tried to speak—"there were times when her grief seemed almost like a performance. When she seemed an entirely different woman from the one we met the day before. But if it was indeed a performance, it may have been intended to hide a different kind of guilt."

Mr. Page frowned. "Explain."

Lily told them of her conversation with the gossiping ladies in the confectioner's shop. "If she was indeed a woman who had married for comfort and not love, who went out of her way to appear affectionate to her husband in public but couldn't bring herself to share his bed, would that not lead to a deep sort of guilt? That she had not loved him better when he was alive, that she could not grieve him as well as she knew she should once he was gone?"

"It could," Mr. Page agreed slowly, looking thoughtful. "Though it doesn't account for her lying."

"Do people never lie to you out of fear—not that they will be exposed as criminals, but that they will be accused wrongly because of a horrible coincidence?"

He raised his brows. "You sound as though you want to persuade me of her innocence, Mrs. Adler."

"I am merely pointing out the possibilities," she said. "I feel for her. It is a terrible thing to lose a husband. And for her, the circum-stances were far more shocking than anything I had to deal with."

"That is true. But, Mrs. Adler . . ." The Bow Street constable hes-itated, then said gently, "I hope you'll excuse me, ma'am, but there's every chance your own sympathy may cloud your perception." His voice became firmer. "Lady Wyatt will have to answer for her con-duct herself, and I'll judge her explanation then."

Lily's hands clenched at her sides as he spoke, and her eyes grew wide with outrage at his presumption.

But he was right. Taking a deep breath, she nodded. "Of course, Mr. Page," she said. "Lady Wyatt alone can and should explain her conduct."

His look of surprise nearly made her throw up her hands in exasperation. "I was expecting more argument than that," he admitted.

"Would you prefer it?" she snapped, annoyed when he chuckled.

"No, thank you, ma'am. I can see well enough that you're furious with me for saying it, so I appreciate your restraint."

"There is something you have not yet considered, though," Lily pointed out archly, refusing to get caught in a debate with him over how she was feeling. "Lady Wyatt injured her arm during the afternoon that Captain Hartley and I were there."

"That's a fair point, Page," Jack put in. "She seemed quite laid up with it. At one point, Mr. Frank Wyatt tried to take her arm to help her stand, and it seemed to cause her a great deal of pain. Even had she been able to bash a man's head in—"

"Captain," Mr. Page barked, glancing at Lily.

She shrugged. The description made her feel ill, but she would never have admitted it to either man. "The captain's point stands. She might well have been able to swing a poker, but I don't see how she could have dragged a man across half the room. Especially not without leaving blood everywhere."

Mr. Page sighed. "So Lady Wyatt was physically unable, Frank Wyatt was physically absent, and Percy Wyatt is unaccounted for. As is the younger brother." He eyed them both, looking almost grumpy. "And that is all I can share with you. Do you have anything else you wished to tell me?"

"I can see if my father knows anything else. They were friends." Lily scowled and muttered, "Or as close as my father comes to having friends."

For a moment, Mr. Page looked curious, but the expression was quickly hidden behind a no-nonsense scowl. He nodded. "If he can shed any light on Sir Charles's life these last few years, it might help me discover what reason someone might have for murdering him.

Here." Pulling a scrap of paper from his desk, he wrote something on it quickly before holding it out to Lily. "My home address. So you may reach me quickly with what you learn and not be tempted to more than merely asking questions." Crossing to the door, he gave them a self-mocking smile as he opened it for them. "So much for my intention of keeping you out of it. I'm still not sure I like it."

"A wise man uses the tools at his disposal," Lily murmured, tucking the paper in her reticule as she nudged Jack to his feet. As they pushed back their chairs, her sleeve caught the small stack of papers on the desk, dislodging several and sending them sliding to the floor. "Oh, I beg your pardon, sir," she said, bending down to gather them up.

"And she would just poke around behind your back if you did not give her a task," Jack said cheerfully, earning him a glare from Lily. He shrugged in response, unbothered, and she snorted as she turned her back on the men by the door to replace the papers and cards on the desk.

When she turned back a moment later, Mr. Page was shaking his head. "But you are to limit yourself to inquiries only. No returning to the Wyatt home for more searching under the family's noses; do I make myself clear?"

"Of course, sir," Lily said as he held the door open for them. "I shall stay away from Wimpole Street." At his frankly skeptical look, she smiled. "I'd not dream of putting myself in danger. Or in your way."

CHAPTER 11

Lily eyed the building in front of her warily and took a deep breath. She had never attempted to practice this sort of deception before, but there was a first time for everything.

"Are you sure it's a good idea, Mrs. Adler?" Anna whispered from her spot behind Lily's shoulder, where she was hovering anxiously.

The answer was no, but Lily had no intention of saying that out loud. "It will be perfectly all right," she said instead, smoothing down the folds of her black gown just to have something to do with her shaking hands. It was strange to be dressed for full mourning again, but at least she still had plenty of clothing to choose from.

Jem, Jack's young servant, had come with them to Bow Street, and it was he who had waited outside, holding the leads of the horses hitched to their hired carriage and crooning to them softly while the driver took a nap on the seat. When they finally emerged, Lily asked Jack if she could borrow the boy's services for a few errands, and neither the captain nor Jem made any objection.

She almost changed her mind before they made it to Half Moon Street, her conscience pricking at her not to involve Jem. But she wasn't going to ask him to do anything particularly dangerous, she reasoned with herself, wondering briefly if this was how Mr. Page felt every time she insisted on involving herself where he didn't want her.

It had been a simple matter to take note of Percy Wyatt's address when she righted the papers on Mr. Page's desk. Lily had bought a pair of men's mourning gloves on Bond Street, then had the parcel wrapped and sent Jem to deliver it to Mr. Percy Wyatt on Harley Street.

From what she knew of young men in London, it was unlikely that he would be spending his afternoon at home. Whether he would be assisting his family at the house on Wimpole Street or loitering at his club, Lily didn't know young Mr. Wyatt well enough to say. But she had no intention of barging in without knowing for certain that he was gone, so she and Anna waited in Cavendish Square Gardens while Jem played the role of delivery boy.

Instead of telling him who it was for, she had folded the paper with Percy Wyatt's name on it and slid it under the string that wrapped the parcel. Jem fortunately hadn't asked any questions and had gone whistling off with the parcel under his arm, returning not more than ten minutes later to say he had left the package with the housekeeper, who'd told him that the gentleman it was for was not at home and not expected back for the rest of the afternoon.

When Lily thanked the boy and handed him a small tip, he pocketed it quickly but gave her a concerned look. "Am I telling the captain about this, ma'am?"

Lily hoped she wasn't blushing. "I've nothing to hide, Jem. Tell him what you wish."

"He mayn't like knowing that you're sending parcels to strange gentlemen," Jem said, looking severe, though he had to look up to do it, as he was still quite a bit shorter than she was.

"I assure you, it will not concern him in the slightest," Lily said. It would have been less risky to hire a delivery boy from the shop than to ask Jem for his help, but then she wouldn't have been able to get a report on the recipient's whereabouts. The best she could do was to convince Jem that he didn't need to tell Jack anything before she had a chance to tell him herself. "Thank you for your help, Jem. Off you go."

He had given her another concerned look but obeyed. Which left Lily and Anna, not five minutes later, standing before the Harley

Street lodging house—*Rooms for Gentlemen, Mrs. Davies, Proprietress* proclaimed the discreet sign on the wrought-iron fence—where Percy Wyatt lived.

"Remember, not a word to the contrary, no matter what you hear me claim," Lily warned her maid in an undertone as they climbed the steps. "I need you to help me look respectable."

"Probably shouldn't be going into a men's lodging house, then," Anna muttered.

Lily deliberately ignored the comment as she rapped on the door. Disapproving mutters were an unavoidable consequence of having a maid who had known her since she was a schoolgirl. But she knew Anna would do as she asked all the same.

The housemaid who answered the door was very young, probably not more than fourteen, and she looked shocked to find two women, one of them elegantly dressed in mourning clothes, waiting on the stoop. "Can I help you?" she asked uncertainly.

Lily held out the card she had taken from Mr. Page's desk, which had Lady Wyatt's name elegantly printed across it. "I am Mr. Percy Wyatt's aunt," she said gravely. "I believe he lodges here, does he not?"

"Oh, yes, ma'am, Lady Wyatt," the housemaid said, curtsying quickly. "But I'm afraid he isn't here at the moment."

"Oh yes, of course, I know. He is attending to some family affairs. As you see, we have suffered a loss," Lily said gravely, making a slight gesture toward her gown.

"Oh! Of course, you have my sympathies, ma'am," the housemaid said quickly. "But—"

"My nephew had a parcel misdelivered, and I am here to retrieve it for him," Lily said quickly, trying to sound the right degree of superior. Just enough and she could elegantly bully her way inside; too much and she would put the maid's back up and be sent away. "If you would show me to his rooms, I can do so quickly."

The housemaid still hesitated. While Lily was trying to decide whether grief or displeasure would be more persuasive, Anna jumped

122 ⌒   Katharine Schellman

in. "Lady Wyatt is not accustomed to being kept waiting at the door,"
she said in an undertone.

The housemaid blushed and scurried backward, holding the door
open wide. "Of course, Lady Wyatt. I beg your pardon, truly. Come
in, please, I'll show you right up. I'm sure Mrs. Davies won't mind."

Lily inclined her head regally as the girl stood aside for them.
When the housemaid's back was turned to close the door again, Lily
gave Anna a quick, grateful smile, receiving a stern look in response
that was almost ruined by the smile her maid was trying to hide.
Together they followed the young housemaid up the stairs.

The inside of the lodging house was well kept, elegant enough to
appeal to the sons of gentlemen without being ostentatious. The bottom floor, Lily guessed, would be the rooms of the proprietress, with
the men living in the upper rooms.

And indeed, as the housemaid led them down the hall, Lily
glimpsed small plaques on the doors, each bearing the name of the
gentleman living within. They stopped toward the far end, in front of
the door labeled *Mr. Wyatt.*

The housemaid knocked. "Mr. Wyatt? Begging your pardon, sir,
are you at home?" When there was no answer, she turned an earnest
smile toward Lily. "We always have to check, you see. Just to be sure.
No gentleman likes to have the maids barging in on him."

"Of course, my dear," Lily said warmly, happy to reassure the girl
that she had done the right thing in letting them in. "My nephew
always says this is such a well-run establishment. You must be proud
to work in such a place."

"Mrs. Davies is most particular," the girl agreed as she unlocked
the door. "She takes real good care of her gentlemen, she does. I'm
lucky she took me on." As she swung the door open, she stood back
and looked at them expectantly.

Lily strode across the threshold of the room as confidently as possible, though inside she was scrambling a little. She had hoped the girl
would unlock the door and then leave them for a few moments, giving her a chance to look through Percy Wyatt's things. But it seemed

the maid was too well trained for that; she might be convinced to let a lady in, but she knew better than to let strangers go through one of the gentlemen's rooms without supervision.

A quick glance around was enough to take in the room; it was arranged as a sitting room, with a comfortable set of chairs by the window, a small shelf of books, and a sideboard. The room had been freshly cleaned and smelled of lemons and beeswax polish. There was no smell of smoke, and no decanters of liquor that she could see, though there was a place for them on the sideboard. Either Mr. Wyatt limited his vices to gambling or he couldn't afford to keep those vices stocked in his home.

Lily could see the parcel Jem had delivered sitting on the sideboard as well, but she made a small *hmm* noise and stepped briskly into the adjoining room, muttering, "Where could he have put it?" just loudly enough for the maid to hear.

The next room was a bedroom, of course, with a tidily made bed against one wall and a tall chest of drawers opposite. A desk sat under the windows; Lily glanced over her shoulder to make sure no one in the other room could see her, then stepped over to examine it. It held very little except a blotter, pen, and inkwell; no papers were scattered over the top, no diary had been left out. Even the open cubbies along the back were empty of papers or cards. Lily scowled. Percy Wyatt was too tidy for her taste. She slid open one of the narrow drawers next to the cubbies as carefully as possible, wincing as it squeaked slightly.

That was more profitable. Lily smiled in triumph as she found a stack of letters, addressed on the outside to Mr. Percy Wyatt in a beautiful feminine hand. There was no direction written on them, which would mean they had been delivered by hand—by someone in London, if they were recent? She reached for one, intending to check the signature and date.

"Did you find it, Lady Wyatt?"

Lily just barely managed not to jump at the sound of the young maid's voice. She slid the drawer closed as quickly as possible before turning back to look at the girl. "I'm afraid not," she said. "But I am so very impressed with the order of this room. Do you have the cleaning of it?"

The girl beamed. "Me'n Sarah, the other housemaid," she said, her bright blush clashing adorably with her red hair. "You're kind to approve, Lady Wyatt."

Compliments were never a bad idea when fishing for information, Lily decided. She gave the girl as warm a smile as she felt she could get away with while supposedly being in mourning. "Well, if you ever tire of your position here, I should be happy to offer you one myself."

The girl swelled with pleasure at the praise as they returned to the front room, and Lily, struck by sudden inspiration, added as carelessly as possible, "That is, of course, if my nephew's sleeplessness hasn't been too much trouble for you. I know he can come and go at odd hours. He mentioned that it had been particularly bad this week."

She had no idea if Percy Wyatt did suffer from trouble sleeping, of course. But she wanted to know if the staff had noticed him coming and going the night of Sir Charles's murder.

The girl giggled. "Oh, is that what it is? I know gentlemen keep odd hours, of course, but he takes the cake, if you'll excuse me saying so, ma'am. There's seven gentlemen live here, and he's nearly always the last one home for the night. And when I say night, I mean mornings. Why, only yesterday morning, I seen him coming in the front door when I had just got up to lay the fires!" The girl laughed and then, spotting the package on the sideboard, asked, "Oh, is that your parcel, ma'am? Let me fetch it for you."

Lily accepted it without really knowing what she was doing. Her heart felt like it stopped for a moment. Percy Wyatt had claimed he had returned home at midnight and gone immediately to bed the night his uncle died. But if the maid was to be believed, he had been out until nearly five o'clock in the morning.

She wanted to press the girl for more information, but a quick glance at Anna, hovering anxiously by the door to the hall, made her change her mind. They didn't know when Percy would be coming back, and Lily didn't want to press her luck. Instead she smiled and nodded her thanks. "Yes, I believe that is the one. If you would—"

"What is the meaning of this?"

The thunderous voice cut through the room, and Lily thought her heart was going to stop before she realized it was the voice of a woman, not Percy Wyatt returned early. Anna shrank back from the door, stiff with terror, her eyes fixed on the woman who filled it. Gray haired and clad in a simple but well-made gown, she would have been a comforting, motherly sort of figure if she hadn't been looking at them with wide-eyed fury. "No women are allowed in this establishment! Edna, what is the meaning of this?"

The girl cringed. "I found them here, Mrs. Davies," she said quickly. "They must've let themselves in the front door. I was just about to call for you."

Lily would have been appalled at the unblushing speed with which the girl lied if she hadn't been so impressed.

"Return belowstairs, Edna," Mrs. Davies snapped. "I will deal with this."

Lily almost wanted to set the record straight on principle. But she had no desire to get the girl sacked, especially when she was the one who had bullied Edna into breaking the rules. So she kept her chin high as the maid scampered off and Mrs. Davies rounded on her.

The landlady looked her up and down, taking in her mourning clothes and the make of her hat. From the way her eyes narrowed, she was the sort of woman who could assess another person's financial means directly from their clothes. Her eyes darted to Anna, who was hovering nearby silently, and her expression said instantly that she didn't like the puzzle of what she saw. Lily was clearly a lady of quality. But ladies of quality did not traipse around men's lodging houses.

When she finally spoke, Mrs. Davies's voice was cold and sharp. "Who are you, and how did you get in here?"

The maid Edna had said she'd found them in the room, and Lily had already decided not to get the girl in further trouble by revealing her lie. So she sighed, trying to sound weary but not too offended. "Of course, I understand that you must ask," she said. She produced the card that she had shown to Edna, holding it out between her fingers with a bored expression. "I am Mr. Wyatt's aunt. It was he who gave me a key." She smiled at the stunned expression on Mrs. Davies's face. "I must say, I am reassured to see how respectable an establishment you run—"

"Balderdash." Mrs. Davies's face was growing almost purple with outrage. "I have seen Lady Wyatt, and however respectable you may try to look, young woman, you are not she."

Lily tried to think of a good reply, but her mind came up blank. It was all she could do to continue meeting the landlady's eyes without trembling. She didn't dare glance at Anna, but she could feel her maid's panic even without looking.

Mrs. Davies wasn't done. "I've held my tongue as Mr. Wyatt comes and goes at all hours of the night. I've forborne to comment on the reek of feminine company that clings to him when he returns. Gentlemen are a law unto themselves, and one does not run a lodging house for fifteen years without accepting that every man will have his foibles and pleasures. But I will not—I will *not*—have such business conducted in my establishment. I don't care what arrangement you and Mr. Wyatt have; you will remove yourself from these premises or I shall summon a constable. And you may tell Mr. Wyatt that if you ever appear here again, he can find himself a new place to live. Do I make myself clear?"

Lily was still trying to come up with a reply when strong hands grabbed her arm and pushed her toward the door. "Yes, Mrs. Davies," Anna said quickly. When Lily tried to hang back, Anna hissed, "Don't *argue*," and continued to drag her down the steps and out the front door, hurrying them down the street until they were finally out of sight of the lodging house.

"Why did you do that?" Lily demanded. Her hands were shaking, she realized, along with the rest of her. What if Percy Wyatt had come back? What if Mrs. Davies had summoned a constable? "I could have—"

"Got us both arrested?" Anna demanded as they finally slowed to a more sedate pace. Cavendish Square Gardens was before them again, the circle of green lawn filled with children and their governesses, with men sitting on the benches talking and women strolling arm in arm. Anna dropped her grip on Lily's arm, falling back a proper step, though her eyes were still wide and panicked. "Heavens, Mrs. Adler, what were you thinking?"

"Well, what was the likelihood of that woman actually having seen Lady Wyatt before?" Lily asked, though she had no idea why she was arguing. Anna was entirely right, but Lily was so shaken that she couldn't seem to keep her mouth shut. "The maid certainly believed me."

Anna gave her employer a narrow-eyed look, clearly seeing straight through Lily's bravado. She shook her head. "Did you at least find what you wanted?" she asked.

Lily sank onto a nearby bench, staring at nothing as she thought through what she had seen and heard. "I found out *something*," she said slowly. "But I'm not yet sure what it means."

Percy Wyatt had lied about where he was the night of his uncle's death. But as Mrs. Davies had revealed, he could just as easily have been in the company of a woman as enacting murder. But those letters . . .

Lily turned the thought over in her head as Anna sank onto the bench beside her, too used to her employer's moods and bouts of thoughtfulness to interrupt and clearly glad for the chance to sit and recover from their ordeal.

One thing was certain: Percy Wyatt was not quite what he seemed to be.

CHAPTER 12

Simon had expected to meet resistance when he asked to be readmitted to the Wyatts' home. To his relief, the butler apparently had orders to let him in. But he was left cooling his heels in what was, judging by the outdated and slightly shabby decor, the lesser of the family's two downstairs parlors. When nearly ten minutes had gone by without a member of the family showing their face, he was nearly ready to growl with frustration. But he was used to these petty games and demonstrations of power. The upper classes played them with each other as well. And he had no intention of being ignored into leaving.

Instead, he did a slow circuit of the room, examining the books on the shelf, the newspapers on the table, looking for any more insights into what sort of people the Wyatts might be and what else they might be concealing. He saw nothing out of the ordinary. And when he went to examine the writing desk tucked under the window, carefully sliding open the drawers, he found that it had been emptied of anything personal. Only unused writing implements remained.

Frowning, Simon stared absently out the window, his mind working. The room was a public place. It made sense that no one would keep private papers there. But for there to be no personal effects at all . . .

Simon's train of thought was interrupted as he realized what he was looking at. A door from the basement of the house opened into the space below the window—likely from the kitchens, which were belowstairs. And Frank Wyatt, who should have been on his way to the parlor, was standing there, talking to a man who was clearly neither a servant nor a neighbor. Simon hesitated, then took a quick step to the side so that he was partly obscured by the curtains.

The sandy-haired man below was dressed tidily but not well, in clothes that had been carefully pressed and mended but whose wear and age were visible even from where Simon stood. He had the broad shoulders of a man who worked with his hands for a living, and he held a squashed hat of an indeterminate brown that might once have been another color entirely. The gesture was respectful, but there was a tension to his posture, and his chin jutted forward belligerently as Frank Wyatt spoke.

Simon could just make out the line of a scar tracing its way down the man's cheek. Combined with his uncommon bulk, it gave his face a sinister appearance.

The window was closed, so Simon couldn't hear what the two men were saying, and opening the window even a crack might draw their attention. But he could see Frank gesturing firmly, then offering the man an envelope.

The man took the envelope, then glanced inside. When he did, his head snapped up, and there was visible shock on his face. Simon had only a moment to wonder whether the shock was of the good or bad variety when the expression folded into a thunderous frown and the man began speaking rapidly, shaking the envelope.

Frank shrugged, said something short, and held out his hand, as if asking for it back. The man hesitated, then shook his head, tucking the envelope into his jacket. But the look he gave Frank was pure venom.

Frank seemed unconcerned, crossing his arms and making a brief, dismissive gesture with the fingers of one hand. The man hesitated, then jammed his cap back on his head and turned away, his steps quick and heavy with anger.

Frank watched him go, holding his dismissive posture until the other man was out of sight. Then he slumped against the door frame, looking shaken and unhappy, his eyes closed for a moment as he took several deep breaths. At last he straightened, shook out his shoulders, and stepped briskly back inside.

Simon stepped away from the window, frowning in thought.

★　★　★

After another fifteen minutes of waiting, Simon was finally rewarded with Frank Wyatt's appearance.

"Mr. Page." The young man's somber expression did not quite disguise his irritation. "I hope you've not been waiting long."

"I don't believe so," Simon answered, setting aside the book he had picked up and standing. He refused to show any sign that he was irritated. "I hope Lady Wyatt is well today."

"As well as can be expected," Frank said, his mouth tightening into a brief grimace. "Was there something you needed to ask her? You may have to return another day; she's not left her rooms since yesterday."

"No, we needn't disturb her at the moment," Simon said, clasping his hands behind his back as he met Frank's eyes. "I've actually come to speak with your brother."

Frank went utterly still, his face going first blank, then pale, then slightly green so rapidly that Simon was worried he was going to be sick.

Only a moment later, though, he gave a bemused smile. "I beg your pardon?"

Simon didn't move. "I said I've come to speak with your brother."

"I expect you mean my cousin, yes? Percy?"

"No, I mean your brother, Arthur. The one your family prefers not to talk of."

Frank's expression slid from polite to outraged. "How dare you."

"Have I been misinformed?" Simon asked mildly. "You do like to talk of him, then?"

"How *dare* you engage in gossip about my family—"

"I dare because it's my job, Mr. Wyatt." Simon drew himself to his full height, which wasn't particularly tall for a man but enough that he could meet Frank's eyes. "Or have you forgotten that your father was murdered? Is there some reason you don't wish us to discover who's responsible? Because that is the only explanation I can think of for your behavior."

Frank visibly deflated in front of him. "Of course I want you to . . . But you must understand, we have worked so hard to protect our family from gossip. To protect Arthur from a world he cannot possibly understand."

"I merely wish to speak with the boy, Mr. Wyatt, and see if he can shed any light on what happened the night of your father's death. I've no intention of repeating anything he says or does as gossip."

"But my brother would have had nothing to do with it, and I don't wish to upset him. He doesn't understand what's going on," Frank protested. "And in any case, he doesn't exactly speak. He barely says a word to me."

Simon was not dissuaded. "Then the interview won't take long." He gestured toward the door. "Lead on, Mr. Wyatt."

Frank looked like he wanted to argue more, but a glance at Simon's face must have told him it would be useless. Sighing, he shook his head. "Come along, then. But don't expect too much."

"Excellent." Simon gestured for Frank to lead the way. "And as we walk, you can tell me about the blond giant who was so unhappy with you just now."

Frank's foot caught on the edge of the rug, and he stumbled. "I beg your pardon?"

"Common-looking man, scar on his face, looked like he wanted to break your arms a moment ago," Simon said pleasantly, crossing in front of Frank to hold the door open, then turning back to meet the younger man's eyes. "Who was he?"

Frank shrugged, pushing roughly past Simon into the hallway. "He was no one."

"If he was no one, why were you paying him?" Simon said, making a shrewd guess about what had been in the envelope.

"My father . . ." Frank paused, then said very deliberately, "The man is a common laborer, and my father apparently hired him to do some work. I very generously gave him a token payment and told him he was no longer needed. He seemed to take it amiss."

Simon paused at the foot of the stairs, refusing to move until Frank turned back and met his eyes. "That was all?"

"That was all," Frank agreed, turning quickly away. "Do you still wish to see my brother, or would you rather discuss our household repairs further? Perhaps you would like to inspect the drains and the roofs?"

"In due time, Mr. Wyatt," Simon said quietly, and there was enough warning in his voice that he could see Frank's back stiffen ahead of him. "In the meantime, please do lead the way."

★　★　★

Arthur's rooms were on the third floor of the house, in what Simon assumed would have been the space for very young children with their nanny or a schoolroom run by a governess.

One of the maids Simon had spoken to during his first visit was up there, reading a book, while nearby a boy hunched over one of the school tables. He was dressed well enough, and though his clothes leaned more toward comfort than fashion, they were clearly well made. He seemed on the small side for a boy of sixteen, as Mrs. Adler had said he was, but it was hard to tell for sure, given his slumped posture. He didn't look up as they entered, but the maid leapt to her feet, casting worried glances between Frank and Simon.

"Ellen, you remember Mr. Page from Bow Street," Frank said, his voice clipped and his expression uncomfortable as he glanced toward his brother. Even the sound of his voice didn't make the boy look up. "He has some questions for Arthur."

Ellen nodded and swallowed, her eyes wide. "Yes, sir," she whispered, glancing once more at Simon.

He resisted the urge to tap his foot. He could understand why the girl looked so timid and upset by his presence, even though, according to Mrs. Adler, she was the one who had come forward about her charge's existence. And he knew impatience wasn't the answer at the moment. "Will he speak to me?"

Frank snorted. "Doubtful. You're wasting your time, I tell you."

Simon ignored him, keeping his attention on the maid.

Ellen met his eyes, and he thought she looked grateful that he hadn't simply accepted Frank's dismissal. "It's hard to say, sir," she replied, still speaking in a soft voice. "He may not speak, but he'll listen."

Frank snorted again. "Forgive me if I do not stay to watch such a useless exercise. I cannot bear to see it. Ellen, take the Runner back downstairs when he has finished."

They waited in silence until they heard his footsteps going down the stairs. Then, to Simon's surprise, Ellen was the one to break the silence. "He has very mixed feelings about his brother, sir, and unfortunately, I think none of them are good."

"Mixed?"

Ellen nodded. "I think he's torn. On the one hand, he thinks having such a brother reflects poorly on the family and resents him. He especially resents how fond Sir Charles was of Arthur. On the other hand, he's offended that he's not one of the people Arthur will speak to." She scowled briefly before she remembered to return her face to the emotionless mask that servants so carefully cultivated. "He wants it both ways, and that never works, does it?"

"Generally not," Simon said dryly. "Why did you tell Mrs. Adler about your charge?"

Ellen bit her lip, glancing nervously toward the door, though her employer had already left. "I hoped it was the right way to keep him safe," she said quietly. "I hoped you'd come see him, sir, and see that he'd never hurt anyone."

"Are you sure about that?" Simon asked, glancing toward the boy, who still had not acknowledged that there was anyone else in the room. Simon kept his voice carefully neutral, giving away none of his feelings, as he added, "People like him can be unpredictable."

"How do you know what people like him are like?" Ellen demanded, growing agitated. "You haven't even spoken to him. Sir," she added, belatedly respectful.

Simon nodded, encouraged by both her outspokenness and her conviction. A parent could have a hazy-eyed view of a child, but servants generally cultivated honest opinions about their employers. It was a necessary survival skill in a world where they were so dependent on the goodwill of people with far more power than they had. If Ellen believed Arthur was unlikely to hurt someone, Simon would believe so too unless shown otherwise. But he still needed to speak with the boy. "Then let's do so. You lead the way, young woman."

Ellen looked panicked for a moment, but then she nodded firmly and turned into the room. "Please move quietly, sir," she said, her voice gentle but not a whisper. "He doesn't like to be startled or interrupted." There was an empty seat next to her charge. She took it and, in the same gentle voice, said, "Arthur? The man I told you about wants to speak to you."

Simon cleared his throat. "I'm hoping—"

He broke off as Ellen shook her head firmly, giving him a quick look over her shoulder that told him plainly to wait. She put one hand palm down on the table and stayed silent.

Arthur continued his work; he was drawing, Simon was able to see now that he was standing closer. The boy had a variety of wax crayons lined up on the table in front of him in a perfectly straight line, with a single empty space between two of them. As Simon watched, Arthur slid the crayon he was using into the empty space, then pulled another one out and began using it without disturbing the alignment of the others.

Frowning, Simon glanced around the school room, noticing for the first time that everything was arranged in the same sort of precise lines. Books of the same color were grouped together on the shelves, even if they weren't from the same set. On another table, wooden alphabet letters were lined up in rigid order. A series of handsome drawings marched around the room in a perfectly even, perfectly spaced line, each one the same size.

Simon peered over Ellen's shoulder, trying to get a glimpse of the boy's drawing. He half expected it to be the rough, ugly work of a child. Instead, he was surprised to find Arthur drawing a landscape, as pretty as anything a girl just emerged from her finishing school might make to hang in her parents' drawing room. Simon glanced back at the line of drawings. They had clearly all been done by the hand of the boy in front of him.

He glanced back down in time to see Arthur slide his crayon back into its place. He didn't take out another one. Instead, he reached out and laid his palm over Ellen's hand.

She glanced up at Simon, looking relieved. "You may ask your questions now, sir. Would you like to sit down?"

Simon felt a little awkward as he took the chair across the table from where Arthur and Ellen sat. The boy had turned in his direction but looked past him, as if uninterested in meeting his eyes. With Ellen's encouraging nod, Simon cleared his throat. "Arthur, do you know what has happened to your father?"

The boy frowned, still looking past him. "My father," he repeated, sounding very young. "My father. My father is gone and not coming back. He's not coming back, like Jolly." There was a distant quality to the words, as if he were repeating a lesson.

Simon gave Ellen an inquiring look. "Jolly was his favorite dog," she explained, still in that same gentle voice. "She died last year. It was the best I could think to explain what happened."

Simon nodded. "Like Jolly," he agreed, trying to keep the gruffness out of his voice. The boy was still looking past him, but it clearly wasn't a sign of disrespect or dismissal. "Did you see your father before he died?"

One of Arthur's hands, the one that didn't rest on Ellen's, was tapping restlessly against the surface of the table. It took Simon a moment to notice that Arthur's fingers were tapping out a careful pattern—seven, pause, four, pause, seven, pause, four, pause—over and over.

"I won't see my father anymore," Arthur said at last. "My father is gone. Like Jolly. He will not come read to me anymore." The tapping began to speed up, and abruptly Arthur moved his hand away from

Ellen's and pulled a crayon back out of his precise line. Not looking at either of them, he bent his head over his drawing once again.

Ellen stood. "Thank you, Arthur. It was good of you to speak with Mr. Page."

Simon cleared his throat again. "Yes, thank you, Arthur," he said gently, standing as well. "Your drawings are very beautiful."

As he turned away, he heard Arthur say, quietly but distinctly, without looking up, "Father said my drawings are very beautiful. Father said always keep drawing."

Ellen swallowed, and Simon caught a glimpse of a tear on her cheek before she brushed it away. Simon pretended not to see, motioning her to lead the way downstairs. "Why did Mr. Wyatt say he wouldn't speak to me?"

"Arthur speaks in his own time, as you saw," she said. "Mr. Frank hasn't the patience to wait for him. And sometimes Arthur just decides not to. He hadn't spoken for a year before I figured out the signal with the hands."

"Are you teaching him to read?" Simon asked, remembering the military-like march of those alphabets across the table.

"No one ever bothered before," Ellen said, sounding defensive. "I'm trying to. He knows most of the letters now."

"You deal well with him."

Ellen nodded. "I knew a similar sort of child," she said quietly. "Me and my brother Thomas, we both did. That's why Sir Charles was happy to take us on, five years ago. He liked having people in the house who could deal well with Arthur."

Her expression was sad as she spoke, and Simon didn't press to find out more. Instead he asked, "There is quite a difference in the ages of Arthur and his brother. Did they have the same mother?"

"Yes, sir. From what I understand, there were two children born between, but neither of them lived long." She sighed. "Mayhap that's another reason Mr. Frank dislikes him so. He was all settled into being the only son, and the apple of his father's eye, before Arthur came along. And then his mother died so soon after Arthur's birth . . ."

She shook her head. "Begging your pardon, sir. It's not my place to speculate."

"Your speculations are useful, Ellen," Simon said with a small smile. "I appreciate them." His expression grew serious once more as they continued down the stairs. "What will happen to him?"

Ellen raised her brows. "If he's lucky? The family will continue to pretend he doesn't exist, and I'll continue to care for him. Otherwise . . ." She shivered, looking bleak. "Children like him can be sent to all kinds of horrible places if their families don't want to care for them anymore. Or if they're suspected of being dangerous." She stopped on the stairs, her eyes pleading as she turned to Simon. "Do you believe me, Mr. Page? That he couldn't have had anything to do with his father's death?"

Simon could feel a lump of uncomfortable emotion in his chest. *He will not come read to me anymore.* Arthur might not quite understand what had happened, but he clearly felt it keenly. And Simon knew enough about how the loss of a parent could affect a child to have a great deal of sympathy for the boy, especially one as gentle and careful as Arthur seemed to be. "Yes, Ellen, I do."

CHAPTER 13

Lily eyed her father warily across the dinner table. The room was not large, but they were seated at opposite ends, and the distance between them felt like a yawning chasm. She would have been happy to let that chasm remain unbridged, but she wanted to find out what her father could tell her of Sir Charles and the rest of the Wyatt family in recent years. She cast about in her mind for some way to bring up the topic without arousing his suspicions.

To her surprise and relief, she didn't have to. Her father did it himself.

Setting down his fork and knife with a sigh, Mr. Pierce gestured for Carstairs to pour him another glass of wine. "Well, I escaped the bride visit, but I suppose I must pay a condolence call on Lady Wyatt nonetheless."

"A condolence call?" Lily asked, her eyebrows raised. "You do remember, Father, that Sir Charles was murdered? And that the Bow Street officer investigating the matter currently suspects someone from the family?"

"One still must be polite," Mr. Pierce said, scowling at his daughter.

"And what will you say?" she asked, unable to resist needling him. " 'My deepest sympathies for your loss, which was likely caused by one of you'?"

"You needn't be vulgar."

"He was your friend, Father. How can you go sit calmly with his family and express your polite sympathies when one of them might have been responsible for his death?"

"Because that means some of them were not," he pointed out. "And whoever was not deserves my sympathies. And no doubt Frank will want my advice."

"On what?"

"On dealing with his brother." He took a sip of his wine and grimaced, gesturing at the butler. "This is an underwhelming vintage indeed, Lily. I thought you had better taste than that."

Lily stared at her father, stunned into silence. She barely registered the complaint. "You know about Arthur?" she asked at last.

"Of course." Mr. Pierce poked fastidiously at his dinner, apparently as underwhelmed with that as he had been with the wine. "Sir Charles was, as you continue to point out, an old friend. He often sought my council on how to best provide and care for the boy. Without being unfair to Frank, of course. Or that other one, what's his name, Percy."

"And what did you advise him?" Lily asked, eyes narrowing. She could just imagine what sort of callousness her father would have displayed. "To have the boy locked up? Sent away?"

Mr. Pierce raised his brows. "Really, my dear, have those dreadful novels gone to your head? Must you always be so dramatic? Do you also think the late Lady Wyatt is locked up in an attic in Devonshire somewhere?" He laughed at his own joke. "Of course not. Sir Charles would never have stood for it, anyway. He always wanted the boy cared for at home." He smirked a little, clearly pleased with himself. "I sent the girl who cares for Arthur now to them, you know—she was the niece of my last housekeeper. Apparently the girl had a brother who was a similar sort of child. Died young, as they often do when there's no one to keep an eye on them. But I guessed she would know how to get along with Arthur."

Lily couldn't stop herself from staring. "Sir Charles cared for Arthur a great deal, then?"

Mr. Pierce scowled at the question. "Of course he did. Sir Charles took family very seriously, especially his responsibilities as a father. And a father does not take the well-being of his children lightly."

Lily would have argued the point, but she knew from bitter experience that she and her father had very different views of what constituted a child's well-being.

"Though I also advised him that if he was going to insist on marrying again—which he seemed determined to do—he ought to wed quickly, rather than giving his intended the chance to find out he had an odd son first," Mr. Pierce added. "She might have been put off, knowing there was such a child in the family. It was a shame that it also meant she could not meet Frank before the marriage, but that sort of thing doesn't matter so much. He is a man grown, after all. It isn't as though she had to agree to raise him."

"Well, your advice on that point may have been well meaning, Father, but I don't know that it was conducive to family harmony," Lily pointed out. "Had you been the one to pay the visit, you would have seen that Frank and the new Lady Wyatt quite despise one another."

Mr. Pierce sighed, sitting back in his chair. He eyed his wineglass a little warily, then seemed to decide that the vintage wasn't objectionable enough to keep him from drinking more. He took a long gulp. "That has proved unfortunate," he admitted. "Sir Charles wrote that he and Frank had been thoroughly at odds since his second marriage. Which I suppose I can understand." He shook his head. "I imagine Frank could not forgive him for moving on after his mother's death."

Up until that moment, Lily had been feeling almost charitable toward her father, and certainly grateful for his insight. But as he followed his last comment with a pointed, narrow-eyed stare, she realized he was talking about her as well.

"Oh?" she said, feeling her skin prickle with hot irritation.

Mr. Pierce took a final, slow sip of wine, his gaze traveling over her. "How many years has it been since Mr. Adler's death?"

Lily gripped the edge of the table so hard that she wondered if there would be bruises on her palms. "Over two years."

"And yet there you sit, wearing *pink*." He spat the word out as though it were a vulgarity, then gestured to his own somber mourning. "It makes me ashamed of you, Lily. God knows what Sir John and your mother-in-law would say." He shook his head. "Anyone who truly loved their spouse would never stop mourning them."

"I beg to differ, Father," Lily said quietly. It would have been so easy to accept the guilt he wanted to heap on her, to agree with his judgment when she herself was so uncertain about her choice. But he had erred in mentioning the Adlers. She knew that, whatever else they might feel, they would also feel joy that she had been able to take such a step forward in her life. And she was determined to feel at least some of that joy herself. "Grief may last, but mourning should not. And anyone who truly loved their spouse would not wish to see them mired in the past forever."

They stared at each other across the table silently, the chasm yawning between them once more. Mr. Pierce's cheeks were red with emotion, and Lily met his furious gaze with one of calm defiance. She would not be cowed in her own home.

At last her father looked away, a sneer lifting the corners of his lips. "Well, I cannot say I am surprised. Given your taste for men."

Lily might have been less stunned at his angle of attack if she'd had any idea what he was talking about. "I beg your pardon?" she demanded. Some people loved to gossip about widows; had anyone been saying such things about her? But if they had, how would it have reached her father? "My taste for men?"

Mr. Pierce glared at her. "How many times has that navy man come by since I have been here? Twice? Yes, Lily, your taste for *men*. It is disgraceful, the way you carry on."

Lily couldn't help it. She laughed. Even when she saw that her reaction had only enraged her father more, she couldn't make herself stop. "Captain Hartley?" she demanded. "Good God, of all the things you could have . . . It is too . . . He grew up with Freddy!" She shook her head. "Really, Father, if you can see impropriety in a simple friendship, then you must be desperate to find cause for complaint.

Was insulting my cook no longer sufficient? Did you run out of novels to steal from my shelves?" She laughed again, wiping her eyes with her napkin. Across the table, Mr. Pierce was almost purple with rage. Lily smiled as if indulging an imaginative child. "If you will excuse me, I have an evening engagement to prepare for. But thank you, truly, for the entertainment."

She managed to make her exit, still smiling and shaking her head, before her father could think of anything to say in response.

It felt like a victory, and she savored it.

★　★　★

Her father made it clear that he was avoiding her the next morning. When they emerged from their bedrooms at the same time, he took one look at her, sniffed in disdain, and retreated back into his room, shutting the door so firmly behind him that it was nearly a slam. Lily, after taking several deep breaths, decided to be amused rather than irritated that he was behaving as though he were the one who had been insulted and injured by the previous night's exchange.

And it wasn't as though she *wanted* to breakfast with him, in any case.

So she enjoyed the peace of a morning to herself. Two letters had arrived for her: one from her aunt, which she was able to read without also having to listen to her father criticize his sister, and another from her old friend Serena, Lady Walter, who was currently at her husband's country house awaiting the arrival of her third child. Lily lingered over sausage and potatoes and a second cup of tea, enjoying the distraction of catching up on her friends' news, before summoning Anna to accompany her for some exercise in Green Park.

The pasture-like space was smaller and less central than Hyde Park, and more likely to be quiet in the morning. This suited Lily perfectly, as she wanted to think without too many interruptions.

The day was hot and muggy already, without even overcast skies to promise the relief from dust and heat that rain would provide. Summers in London were rarely comfortable, which was why so many who could afford it would decamp to their country properties to wait out the season. In the fall there would be hunting parties, but in summer the entertainment was rounds of house parties and travel to the most picturesque parts of the country.

Lily didn't have the money for travel, a fact that she was unashamed to admit to herself, and she didn't own any property. But she was looking forward to closing her London residence while she visited her aunt and a few other friends.

Those visits would not begin for several weeks, however. And when she could leave London now depended on her father's plans, which were still irritatingly vague. He would be outraged if she left before he did, so she was stuck in town for the present.

In the meantime, she was grateful for the reduced population of London's western neighborhoods. Places like Green Park were emptier than they had been in the spring, which gave her more time for uninterrupted reflection. With Anna a few sedate paces behind her, Lily meandered slowly though the park, thinking over what she had seen and heard the day before.

Mr. Page had already suspected that Percy Wyatt was hiding something. Judging by the letters she had found in his room and the reaction of his landlady, there was a lady involved.

The letters in his desk had no direction written on them, which meant there had been a certain amount of discretion involved in their delivery. Could the sender have been an unmarried lady who didn't want their correspondence discovered? If Sir Charles had opposed a marriage that his nephew wanted, would that have been enough to drive the young man to murder?

Or perhaps Percy Wyatt had a mistress. Someone expensive, perhaps. It could explain why his finances were so precarious that he had resorted to theft. If he had debts beyond what he had admitted, could that have turned him against the uncle he was so professedly fond of?

Love or money, Lily thought grimly as she stared at the beautiful park before her. Just as the two gossipy women in the tea shop had said. But which had it been this time?

In either case, Mr. Page certainly needed to know what she had learned. But how to tell him? He would be furious if he discovered she had sneaked into Percy's lodgings.

Sharing her father's information would be easier, since the Bow Street Runner had specifically asked her to find out what she could from Mr. Pierce. But how much would it influence his conclusions to know that Sir Charles had loved the son he kept hidden and wanted to provide for the boy?

Lily paused in her stroll, staring unseeing into the distance. *Had* he provided for the boy? Had he provided for his widow or his sons or his nephew? There had been no mention of how his estate was to be divided, aside from the property that was entailed on Frank.

If Mr. Page hadn't already seen Sir Charles's will, that was the thing that needed to happen next. But though the Bow Street force could ask questions, the family was under no obligation to show them the document. And the family solicitor—what was his name? The two gossipy ladies had mentioned a Mrs. Ha—something . . .

"Mrs. Adler!"

The friendly call jolted Lily out of her reverie, and she looked up to find two gentlemen strolling toward her. One of them she recognized instantly: slightly short, slightly round, and always cheerful, Mr. Andrew Harlowe was her friend Margaret's husband. He stopped before her and bowed, beaming with pleasure.

Lily bowed in return, smiling back. It was impossible not to. Andrew Harlowe was a dear man, and she couldn't begrudge him the interruption. Her mind needed a break anyway. "Mr. Harlowe. A pleasure to see you."

"And you, ma'am. Beautiful morning for a stroll, is it not? I know we shall see you tonight, so I apologize for interrupting your solitary reflection, but of course I could not see you and fail to make my greetings." He gestured to the man beside him. "May I make known to you Mr. Matthew Spencer? Mr. Spencer, this is Mrs. Adler, who has been my wife's friend for years."

Mr. Spencer bowed, and Lily tried not to stare as she returned the courtesy. He was one of the handsomest men she had ever seen, with lightly tanned skin, curly dark hair, and eyes of such a deep blue-black that they looked as if they could have been painted. It was only as he straightened that she took her eyes from his face long enough to realize that he was also missing a limb; his left arm ended just above where his elbow would have been, and his shirt and coat sleeves were folded and neatly pinned.

"Mrs. Adler." Mr. Spencer's very blue eyes met hers, and she had the feeling that he took in every inch of her, from the newness of her gown to the damp grass stuck to her walking boots. The smile he gave her would have been disconcerting on such an absurdly attractive face if it had not been so warm and friendly. "A pleasure to make your acquaintance."

"Yours as well, sir. And how are you and Mr. Harlowe acquainted?"

"I have, on occasion, contributed some work to the efforts of our Parliament."

"*Some work.*" Mr. Harlowe, who currently worked as the parliamentary secretary of a peer and expected one day to hold a seat in Commons himself, laughed. "How modest of you. Spencer here has had many occasions to butt heads with Lord Walter, whom you know so well," he added, glancing between them with poorly disguised pleasure. "I'm surprised the two of you did not cross paths before this. Though of course, Mrs. Adler, your black gloves meant you were not venturing out in company so much at one time."

Though he phrased it politely, Mr. Harlowe's meaning was plain, and she saw him glance at Mr. Spencer out of the corner of his eye as if to see how he would take the news that Lily was recently out of mourning. Lily was starting to guess Andrew Harlowe's intent in introducing them and wondered if his wife had dropped a hint. But she hid her discomfort as she always did: behind a facade of cool intellectualism. "Were you one of those working with Lord Walter on the recent passage of the Corn Law, sir?"

Mr. Spencer looked taken aback by the question. "I am afraid I am more Whiggish in my tendencies. Lord Walter was still kind enough to tolerate my presence from time to time."

Andrew Harlowe laughed. "Be honest, Spencer, you are almost too much a reformer for the Whigs." He beamed at Lily. "Not unlike you."

Mr. Spencer suddenly looked far more intrigued. "Is Mr. Adler in politics? I am afraid I do not recognize the name."

"My late husband had intended to stand for a seat," she said, trying to ignore the tightness in her throat. Even though she knew her father's cruel words from the night before weren't justified, they had stuck with her, making Freddy's absence feel sharper than it had in months. "And you are a member, I assume?"

The look Mr. Spencer gave her made Lily suspect that she had not sounded quite as serene as she'd wanted to. But he responded to what she had said rather than how she had sounded, for which she was grateful. "Not a member. But I have the privilege of making my voice heard to many of them." With a sideways glance at Mr. Harlowe, he added, "Whether they wish to hear it or not."

Lily would have pressed further, curious to find out exactly what he had meant, but she saw him glance surreptitiously at his pocket watch. "That is an intriguing statement, Mr. Spencer, but I suspect I shall have to wait for its conclusion. Please do not let me detain you."

"Not at all, ma'am," he said, looking a little embarrassed at being caught. "I believe we were the ones detaining you." But then a smile tugged at his mouth, and he admitted, "I am afraid I have an appointment soon, and I must abandon both the pleasure of your company, Mrs. Adler, and my conversation with you, Harlowe."

"More like a browbeating than a conversation," Andrew Harlowe said, laughing. "We shan't detain you any longer, then. But of course we will see you tonight at dinner, will we not?" As soon as Mr. Spencer nodded his assent, Mr. Harlowe clapped his hands together, beaming once more. "Splendid! The two of you will have the chance to continue your conversation there."

Lily couldn't protest without seeming rude, but she was thoroughly embarrassed until Mr. Spencer caught her eye. His wry smile said he saw through their mutual friend's machinations as easily as she did, and his obvious good humor about the situation set her at ease.

"Then I shall look forward to making your better acquaintance, Mrs. Adler. Good day, Harlowe."

Lily watched him leave. "What a kind man."

"One of the best," Andrew Harlowe agreed, giving her a pleased look. "I know no one more pleasant or more idealistic, for all that he has reason to be jaded. He lost his arm in Italy and his wife to rheumatic fever, all within a year. Dreadful. But that was some time ago."

Lily tried not to wince at the obvious direction of his thoughts. Andrew Harlowe meant well—and if he was making assumptions, there was a good chance it was Margaret's fault. Lily held back a sigh. She would have to speak to her friend at dinner and make it clear that she was no more interested in finding a new husband now than she had been in April.

Mr. Harlowe beamed once more, oblivious to what she was thinking, and offered her his arm. "May I escort you home, ma'am? Or wherever you might need to go."

Lily yanked her thoughts away from her friends' unwanted attempts at matchmaking. There were more pressing matters to worry over. Taking his arm, she gestured to Anna to follow them. "Home, if you would be so good, Mr. Harlowe. I have some correspondence to catch up on."

Whether he approved or not, Mr. Page needed to know what she had learned. And she, in turn, wanted to know what he could discover about Sir Charles Wyatt's will.

CHAPTER 14

Lily paused at the top of the stairs. Surely she had misheard—but no, there it was again. The murmur of masculine voices was coming from the drawing room. She frowned to herself. If someone had called for her, surely Carstairs would have notified her. But who would her father, curmudgeon that he was, be willing to receive?

A sudden suspicion arose in her mind; there was one man her father would never turn away. Her steps were more forceful as she stalked down the staircase and showed herself into the drawing room.

Her father and Frank Wyatt glanced up from their card game, then both stood politely as she entered.

"Lily," Mr. Pierce said, raising his eyebrows at her gown, a floaty confection of gold-and-bronze silk.

The dress had been a gift from her mother-in-law, Lady Adler, in the hope of encouraging Lily to leave her mourning behind when she returned to London. "So that you have something beautiful to wear when you are ready for colors again, my dear," she had said, wiping her eyes.

Mr. Pierce regarded it with clear disapproval. "I thought you were going out," he said, his mouth drawing into a tight line.

"Captain Hartley will be calling for me at eight," she said. "Good evening, Frank."

"Lily." He bowed. "I understood from your father that you were not at home, or I should have paid my respects more speedily."

"My door is open to you, of course," Lily said quietly, taking a seat on the settee near them. "What brings you to call on us this evening?"

Frank scrubbed a hand through his hair. He wasn't dressed for a formal evening call, she realized; he still wore his daytime clothes and looked slightly disheveled. "Mr. Pierce was named one of the trustees of my father's will, as our solicitor informed us this afternoon. And I needed his advice."

"Come deal for us, Lily," Mr. Pierce said abruptly, tossing down his cards. "I should prefer vingt-et-un, and that's no good with just two people."

Lily's heart sped up. Normally she would have resented her father's imperious tone, especially after he had gone to such lengths to ignore her during the rest of the day. And especially when he was in Frank's company, which he always made clear was preferable to her own. But they had mentioned Sir Charles's will.

She rose without complaint and took her seat opposite them at the card table. "Are we playing for stakes?"

Frank shook his head. "I already told your father I'll not take his money, and I'll not take yours either."

"Then I shall deal only, if you do not mind." She accepted the newly shuffled deck of cards from her father and laid two before each of them. There was a pause while they both considered their cards.

"*Carte*," Mr. Pierce said tersely, and Lily dealt him a third card. He considered it, frowning, then nodded. "*Je m'y tiens.*"

"I shall venture a guess, Frank," Lily said as she turned to him, her voice gentle. "I think my father had an easy time convincing you to stay with us this evening."

His smile was sad as he shrugged. "Home doesn't have much appeal right now," he admitted. "Sitting there in the evening is . . . There are too many memories. And there is no one there I wish to share them with." He peeked at his cards again. "*Carte.*"

Lily dealt him a third. "By that do you mean Lady Wyatt or your brother?"

Frank gave her a look of surprise. "So you know about Arthur, then?" He shook his head. "*Carte.*"

Lily raised her eyebrows. "Really?"

Frank nodded.

Lily dealt him a fourth. "The real question is, why did I not know about him before?"

"No one did. Except your father." Frank bowed in Mr. Pierce's direction, an impressive feat while they were seated. "Which is why he was named one of the trustees. He and I are jointly to oversee Arthur's portion of the inheritance to ensure that he is cared for." He looked at the card and made a face. "Ah, bust." He tossed his hand over. A ten, a two, a three, and a nine.

Mr. Pierce chuckled. "Always so bold, my boy. That is not a bad thing. Nothing ventured, nothing gained." He turned his own cards over, revealing a pair of fours and an eight.

"Though caution sometimes serves us well too," Lily said dryly, collecting the cards and shuffling them. "Or at least logic. *Encore?*"

"*Encore,*" her father agreed.

"I was going to lose either way," Frank pointed out, a little petulantly.

Lily dealt two cards to each of them. "I will guess that it is Lady Wyatt you wish to avoid."

Frank made a frustrated noise in the back of his throat. "She is . . . difficult to spend time with. She didn't even approve of my coming over tonight. But I wanted to speak to you, sir. *Je m'y tiens.*"

Lily turned to her father, who was frowning in thought at his cards. "*Carte,*" he said at last. Examining the one she dealt, he nodded. "*Je m'y tiens.*"

They turned their cards over to discover that Mr. Pierce had won again, eighteen points to Frank's sixteen.

"Where's my bold young friend?" Mr. Pierce asked, giving Frank an encouraging smile. "Come, my boy, this will never do. *Encore.*"

"Your friend is having trouble concentrating tonight, I am sad to say," Frank said. "I also wanted to ask your advice, Lily, on handling the fellow from Bow Street. You said you had dealings with them before?"

"What is this?" Mr. Pierce frowned, ignoring the cards as Lily dealt once more. "What does that mean, you had dealings with Bow Street?"

Lily sighed. "Lord and Lady Walter had some trouble this spring," she said, trying to skirt around the issue. "I was there at the time."

"What made them leave your friends alone?" Frank asked, leaning forward. "All the poking about, all the questions—I cannot abide it."

"Nor should you," Mr. Pierce grumbled. "They should be out finding the burglar who did it, not pestering a gentleman's family. Can you not pay them to go away?"

"You're one of the trustees, Father," Lily said lightly. "How stands Sir Charles's property? Can Frank afford to pay them that much?"

Mr. Pierce scowled. "I've not seen the will yet, Miss Impertinence. But it should not matter. They ought to leave our boy here alone."

Lily bit her cheek, holding back the impulse to protest that Frank was *not* her father's boy. "Does this mean you are both satisfied with your cards?"

They fell silent for the third round. Mr. Pierce excused himself after that, presumably to visit the water closet, saying that he would return in a moment. Lily and Frank were left alone.

Lily was busy shuffling the cards when she noticed Frank watching her intently. "What is it?"

"I am still waiting for an answer," he said, his eyes heavy lidded. "How did the Walters manage it?"

Lily debated what she should say in response. In reality, Lord Walter had very nearly made the whole matter go away by paying an enormous bribe to a magistrate. It was only because of Lily's own interference that the investigation hadn't been abandoned completely. But she didn't want Frank knowing that she had been so intimately involved. It would make it much harder to continue snooping around if he and his family were on their guard against her.

"They found the person responsible," she said at last.

Frank still didn't take his eyes away from her, and the directness of his gaze was becoming unnerving. A prickling feeling began to creep up her spine. "What is it?" she asked.

Frank's voice was soft as he leaned forward over the card table. "Why did you really look in the chimney?"

Lily's stomach dropped, as if she'd tried to climb a staircase in the dark and suddenly found that the step wasn't where she'd expected it to be. "Captain Hartley told you already. I thought there was a bat."

Frank shook his head slowly. "Liar."

Lily felt heat rising in her cheeks and hoped the blush looked like anger instead of embarrassment. "Believe what you like."

"I'll play you for the truth."

Lily lifted her chin. "And if I win instead?"

He considered this. "Then I will answer a question for you." He grinned suddenly, the first expression of genuine enjoyment she had seen on his face since she'd come into the drawing room. "Or I could kiss you. I've been suggesting it for years, as you may remember."

"You suggested it years *ago*," Lily said dryly. "And you weren't any more serious when we were children than you are now."

"Does that mean you won't play?"

"I'll play for a question. Put the cards in a stack."

The stack went on the table between them.

"You may draw first," Frank said, his eyes still fixed on her.

Lily did, and they alternated until each had two cards. Lily took only a single look at hers before laying them back down on the table. "*Carte*," she said quietly, drawing another from the pile. She took a swift look at it before laying it on the table. "*Je m'y tiens.*"

Frank played more slowly, giving the appearance of more caution as he studied her face, then looked at his cards for a second and third time. "*Carte*," he said at last, then examined his new hand. "*Carte.*" Lily held her breath. Frank grinned at her. "Shall I be bold? *Carte.*"

His grin faded as he glanced at the fifth. For a moment he looked genuinely angry, and Lily drew back. She had seen him sour when he didn't get his way, but she had never seen him truly angry before. The ugly twist to his mouth was almost shocking. Then the expression faded as he laughed ruefully, petulant and nothing more. "Bust." He turned the cards over. A five, a two, a two, a three, and a queen.

"So close," Lily said, her smile a little taunting, though she still felt shaken. "*Vingt-deux*, as it were."

Frank shrugged, still looking put out. "What did you have?"

Instead of showing her cards, Lily slid them back into the pile. "I win either way, do I not? Since you overshot."

He sighed. "What is your question, then?"

She tilted her head to the side as she gathered the cards and shuffled them once more. "I believe I shall save it. By the way, you should be kinder to Lady Wyatt."

"She should be more considerate of our Frank," Mr. Pierce said, his cane thumping as he strode back into the room.

"You needn't encourage his rudeness, Father," Lily said, exasperated as she dealt again.

His shoulders stiffened. "I am sure Frank displays no such quality."

"No." Frank sighed, all signs of petulance gone as soon as Mr. Pierce rejoined them. "I am afraid she is quite right. Lady Wyatt and I do not . . . Well, we seem to have gotten off to a bad start and never recovered. I cannot feel easy around her."

"And why should you?" Mr. Pierce insisted. "Your father had no need to go marrying again. It is unaccountable. After all, it is not as if you needed a mother."

"No, she is *not* my mother," Frank said, with surprising force. He immediately looked embarrassed, clearing his throat loudly and fixing his attention on his cards.

But Mr. Pierce, instead of looking disapproving at the burst of emotion, just shook his head sympathetically. "Unaccountable," he repeated.

"Perhaps he married to please himself and not his son?" Lily said dryly. "Some people do enjoy the companionship of others."

"Well, he certainly did not marry to please his sons," Frank said, laughing ruefully. He slid his cards in absent circles on the table, not really paying attention. "The sad part is, I think Winnie and I might have got along well under other circumstances. But suddenly discovering that my father had married—so quickly—and then meeting her like that—" He broke off suddenly, glancing up. "I beg your pardon; I am sure you've no wish to listen to my woolgathering."

"Frank, I need you to be honest with me," Mr. Pierce said, his gaze sharpening under his bushy eyebrows. "These Bow Street fellows, for all I dislike them, seem convinced that your father's death was no accident."

Frank looked ill. "Sir—"

"No, I must say my piece." Mr. Pierce looked uncomfortable but determined. "Do you think there is any chance that this new Lady Wyatt could have been the one to do him harm?"

Frank's eyes grew wide, then narrowed, his brows drawing down into a frown. "A little thing like her?" he said, shaking his head. "I don't see how she could have managed it. And . . ." He shrugged. "She certainly doesn't gain from his death. Once you see the will, sir, you will understand."

"What does the will say?" Lily asked, trying not to sound too eager.

But her father still glanced at her dismissively. "That is hardly your concern, Lily. In fact"—he glanced at the clock—"should you not be leaving for your entertainment?"

Lily would have protested being shooed out of her own home, but her outrage was spoiled by Carstairs entering to announce Jack, who was calling to escort her to the Harlowes' dinner. The captain entered the drawing room with his normal ease, then stopped in the doorway. Lily wondered whether he was more surprised by her father's presence or Frank's.

"Good evening," he said politely. "I hope I am not interrupting."

"Lily was just preparing to leave," Mr. Pierce said, giving her an arch look. "Were you not?"

Lily sighed, rising. "I was."

★   ★   ★

Jack didn't speak again until they were in the hired carriage he had brought to call for her. "What was he doing there?"

Lily didn't have to ask who he meant. "I told you. He and my father are close."

Jack snorted, arms crossed as he glowered from a corner of the carriage seat. "Strange time to be paying social calls, after his father is murdered."

"It was not precisely a social call. My father was named a trustee in Sir Charles's will to share responsibility for looking after Arthur's interests. Frank informed him of it tonight, then stayed for a game of cards."

Jack sat up. "Your father has seen Sir Charles's will?"

"Not yet."

"But when he does—what are the chances you could ask him about it?"

Lily sighed. The thought had occurred to her too. But . . . "He would be unlikely to oblige me. And even if he said yes, it would be a risk. He would want to know why I was asking, and then he might tell Frank."

"And you don't want him to know you are helping the Runners, even though you insist he is not guilty." It wasn't a question but a flat statement, accusatory and suggestive.

Lily stared at him, surprised. "You do not believe me?"

"I prefer proof."

"Which Mr. Page has sent you to find. Have you had any luck?"

There was a clamor out in the street, and Jack glanced out the window briefly before turning back, shaking his head. "Not yet. And until I do, you should not be casually playing cards with a man who might have killed his father." He sat forward, his expression fiercely protective. "Even you must see what a risk that is."

Lily was about to protest, but she remembered the strange intensity in Frank's eyes, the twist of anger to his mouth, and shivered. "I can understand his not wanting to remain at home right now, though. Can you imagine walking past the room where your father was murdered? And then having to do it again, half a dozen times a day?"

Jack fell silent for a moment, and Lily thought it was in sympathy until he spoke again. "Just promise me you will be careful."

"I always am." She smiled at him. "And this time, I promise to tell you before I do something reckless and dangerous."

"I would rather you not do it at all," Jack said, glowering in his corner once more.

Lily reached over to pat his arm. "Yes, but we both know that is unlikely."

★   ★   ★

The gathering that night was small by London standards. Only fourteen people sat down to dinner, including the hostess and her husband. Though Lily knew few of the other guests and only one or two beyond nodding, it was still a cheerful, entertaining meal. The group was lively and friendly, made up of society friends, neighbors from the country who found themselves in town, and acquaintances of Mr. Harlowe's from Parliament. The talk ranged from politics and the many troops being recalled from France to the newest craze among the dandy set for waistcoats striped in five different colors.

Earlier in the year, when Lily had first returned to London society, she had appreciated small gatherings because they gave her a chance to find her feet again without feeling overwhelmed. Now she was glad the small numbers prevented her from getting lost in her own thoughts.

She also did not fail to notice that the party included several single gentlemen, nor the eager introductions from Mr. and Mrs. Harlowe that accompanied them. When the ladies withdrew after dinner, Lily cornered her friend at the tea cart.

"You know you are not at all subtle," she pointed out, holding out her cup. "You seated me between two of the four unwed gentlemen here. And one of the others is Captain Hartley."

Margaret Harlowe only laughed as she poured. "Subtlety is over-rated. I prefer to be successful at my endeavors."

"And if I have no interest in providing that success for you?" Lily asked, trying not to sound too irritated. Or too interesting—the last thing she wanted was for the other women in the room to add their opinions to the discussion.

Margaret shrugged, looking unconcerned. "Then you needn't marry any of them. Or you may marry one in a decade when you change your mind. But I like introducing interesting people to each other." She smiled pointedly. "And you looked as though you enjoyed your conversation with Mr. Spencer and Mr. Clay."

Lily shook her head as Margaret turned to another lady to continue pouring. There was no use arguing over it. Margaret was enjoying playing at matchmaker too much to accept the hint easily, and as long as she wasn't too overbearing, there was no real harm in it. Especially as she was right—it *had* been an entertaining dinner.

"I suppose you are planning to inveigle Major Hastings into sitting by me when the gentlemen come through?" Lily said once they were alone again. "Perhaps to partner me at cards?"

"I had planned to put you on the same side for charades." Mrs. Harlowe was unabashed at having her plan guessed. The crowd around the tea cart had dispersed, the ladies settling themselves throughout the room to gossip and laugh. Margaret looped her arm through Lily's as they strolled toward the windows. "You always carry the day at charades, Lily, and I do love showing off how clever my friends are."

"Assuming Major Hastings is interested in a clever wife," Lily countered. "Or any wife."

"Of course he wants a wife. Soldiers make terrible bachelors. Mr. Clay's conversation is delightful, and Mr. Spencer is the most beautiful man I have ever laid eyes on—he is so handsome that one barely notices he lost half an arm to Napoleon's armies! So what is the harm in spending a few hours enjoying some attention?" She dropped her voice. "You cannot fill all your time with thoughts of murder, you know."

Lily turned just in time to catch the look of real concern in Margaret's eyes before it was replaced by a teasing smile once more. "And what about raising their expectations? I should hate if your machinations gave them the wrong impression. And it *is* the wrong impression."

Margaret shrugged. "Well, I shall still place you on the same team for charades. The poor man needs all the help he can get."

Lily shook her head. "And that just shows how lacking in serious matchmaking intent you are, Margaret. I have met the major at your gatherings before, you know. I doubt he will enjoy the company of a woman who outdoes him at a game of wits."

"No, but Matthew Spencer will be impressed, and I like him the best of the lot," Mrs. Harlowe said, clearly pleased with herself.

"And what is the appeal of Mr. Spencer beyond his excess of good looks?"

"I might truthfully say an excess of good humor, but I am far more mercenary than that. His family property in Hampshire is supposed to be very beautiful, and he breeds marvelous horses. I should love an excuse to visit."

Lily couldn't help laughing aloud at her friend. Margaret smiled cheerfully, unashamed of the admission.

"A lady of seven-and-twenty may still discover that she wishes to find a husband one day, and what are old school friends for if not to help when it is needed?"

"Well, this lady is uninterested in matrimony," Lily said. "But I am quite a wit at charades, and I look forward to dismaying any number of your gentlemen guests."

"Oh, you are no fun." Margaret threw up her hands in mock despair. "Go be practical at someone else."

Rolling her eyes, Lily obeyed.

The ladies had just begun comparing preferences for different seaside resorts when the gentlemen came through and the tenor of the gathering changed. Margaret went to pour once more as the men dispersed themselves throughout the room, the gossip and banter taking on a rather more daring, and occasionally flirtatious, tone. Lily was slightly flustered to discover that the Harlowes had managed to maneuver Matthew Spencer into her group near the windows. She hoped she wasn't blushing as he gave her a friendly smile, but before he could say anything, another woman who clearly knew him well began quizzing him on the subject of his daughter's education.

"And when will you bring Miss Spencer to London?" the older woman demanded, once she was satisfied on points of music, languages, and history.

"Not for some years yet, Mrs. Dawson," Mr. Spencer said. Lily was impressed by how unbothered he seemed to be by the interrogation; if anything, he looked pleased to have the chance to discuss his daughter. "My Eloisa is still some time away from making her social bows, and she prefers the country to town. Her aunt and her governess take good care of her when I must be absent."

"And it's a good thing this year, eh, Spencer?" Andrew Harlowe chuckled. "Or you'd be very crowded at the moment."

"And why is that?" Mrs. Dawson demanded.

"Oh, my second, secret family is living with me in town this season," Mr. Spencer said with a careless shrug.

Mrs. Dawson's silence was stunned. But Lily had caught the mischievous smile pulling at the corner of Mr. Spencer's mouth, and she began laughing at the same time as Andrew Harlowe.

Matthew Spencer's smile grew as he shook his head. "Really, Mrs. Dawson, and here I thought nothing could ever shock you."

"Wretch," she said, swatting him on the arm and blushing, but she laughed as she said it. Lily didn't blame her. Mr. Spencer's smile was like a force of nature. "What is the real reason, then?"

"You have family living with you, do you not, Mr. Spencer?" one of the other ladies said.

He bowed his head in assent. "My second cousin, Mr. Hammond. I was the relative with the most room to spare while his family settled into town."

Lily's mind had begun wandering a little, but her attention snapped back at that. Something about Mr. Spencer's cousin rang a bell in the back of her mind, though she wasn't sure what. She cleared her throat. "And what brought your cousin to London this summer?" she asked.

He shook his head. "My cousin *and* his wife *and* their three children *and* the nanny," he said, though with such obvious good humor that it took any sting out of his words. "The whole brood has taken over the house, and unlike me, my cousin has an excuse to depart each day. He is a solicitor and recently began an excellent position with a firm here in town."

Lily's heart rate sped up. She had a feeling she knew exactly why the name Hammond was familiar to her. Now she just had to figure out how—

Just then, Margaret stood and clapped her hands, calling for charades. Lily cursed silently at the lost chance as Mr. Spencer was shuffled away from her in the excitement.

With a broad smile, Margaret divided everyone into two teams, declaring that she and Mr. Harlowe would act as judges and fetch any props anyone might need. Mr. Harlowe, blue eyes twinkling in his round, red face, decided that Lily's team would guess first. They settled in while the others engaged in a furious bout of whispering. Mr. Spencer was on the other side, so she couldn't even use the opportunity to devise a polite way to interrogate him.

Jack slid into a seat next to her as a curtain was strung across one end of the drawing room and a bustle of preparation went on behind it. "What was that look for?" he murmured.

Lily glanced at him out of the corner of her eye. "What look?"

"You had your *I've just solved something* look when you were talking to Mr. Spencer there," he said, gesturing to where the other man was briefly visible behind the curtain. "What did you realize?"

Lily dropped her voice even lower. "You recall what I said about those two gossiping ladies that Margaret and I spoke with? Well, one of them mentioned a Mrs. Hammond, whose husband's brother was one of the solicitors responsible for managing Sir Charles's will. And Mr. Spencer's cousin, Mr. Hammond, is a solicitor."

Even without looking at him directly, she could see Jack's eyebrows shoot up. "And you think he's the same fellow?"

"I want to find out if he is. Mr. Page needs to see that will."

Before Jack could reply, Andrew Harlowe was calling for attention as the curtain was drawn back.

The other team had staged an elaborate scene. Two tall chairs were draped with fabric and set in the center of the tableau. In them sat Mrs. Dawson and her husband, each with something resembling a crown on their heads, Mr. Dawson with one hand upraised. The other held a silver pomander that looked as if it were meant to represent a monarch's orb. Both of them were draped with lavender curtains that trailed off their shoulders in the manner of imperial robes. Around them, their teammates were frozen in bows and curtsies.

"King!" someone guessed.

"Queen," suggested another.

"King George!" was followed immediately by "Prince of Wales!" and "Debtor!" which earned a laugh from the entire room, including those who were supposed to be frozen. A few more guesses were offered, and then the curtains dropped and the next tableau was hastily assembled.

This time one lady stood at the head of a line of chairs, facing sideways, her arms outstretched. Arrayed behind the line of chairs were the men; one held a rolled newspaper up to his eye and looked out over the lady's head.

When the curtain dropped once more, the group came out and bowed to their rivals' polite applause, and then the guessing began in earnest.

"Well, it is something scandalous, with that many gentlemen and only one lady," one man said at last, and the whole company laughed.

"It was a boat," Jack said with lazy confidence. "Or a ship."

"King boat?" That dry guess was from Major Hastings, whom Lily had managed not to end up seated near; everyone laughed again. "Or kingship!"

But the other players denied it. Several members of Lily's team declared themselves baffled, and Mr. Harlowe asked if they gave up.

"I must say, I am ready to!" Major Hastings said.

Those who had set the puzzle began to congratulate themselves. Lily pursed her lips, unsure whether or not to speak up. She loved being right but didn't much care about winning the game. And she didn't care to push herself forward among a crowd of people she didn't know well.

The decision was made for her; Margaret had seen her indecision and raised her voice. "I believe Mrs. Adler has the answer."

Heads swiveled toward her. "Well?" several voices demanded.

"Well?" Jack repeated next to her, grinning.

Lily tried to give him a stern glance, but she couldn't help the smile that twitched at the corners of her mouth. "Courtship."

"Correct!" Mr. Spencer called out, while the others exclaimed loudly—in admiration or annoyance, depending on their team. Lily glanced out of the corner of her eye at Major Hastings, who looked sour, then at Margaret, who was pressing her fan against her lips to keep from laughing.

The game continued, the teams taking turns, most of the puzzles solved but some not, until Lily's team was giving their final clues.

The players began in combative poses, gathered around Mr. Clay, who stood on his knees so that he was shorter than anyone else, one hand tucked inside the front of his jacket and the other holding a poker aloft like a sword. Everyone had their mouths open, as if they were speaking. Dozens of martial words had been suggested, and Napoleon's name had been thrown about with grim humor, before the curtain fell and the players rearranged themselves.

In the final pose, Major Hastings was at the center of the group, lying on a fainting couch with his hands crossed over his chest, draped in the black cover from the top of the pianoforte. The other players arranged themselves around him in tragic poses while Lily stood behind, one hand on her heart, the other lifted up, her eyes turned heavenward and her mouth open.

"Death," Mr. Dawson called. "No, that is too obvious."

"Funeral," another player suggested.

"How ghastly," someone exclaimed as the curtain fell. They continued speculating and suggesting words as Lily's team emerged into the drawing room, pleased smiles on their faces. The guesses flew across the room, some provoking horror and others laughter.

They were just about to declare defeat when Mary Forsythe, a young matron who had been at school with Lily and Margaret some years before, suddenly asked, "Do you think Mrs. Adler was supposed to be singing at the end?"

"Oh, good thought, Mrs. Forsythe," said Mr. Dawson. "Dirge, perhaps? Or hymn?"

A new set of suggestions emerged, *war dirge* and *battle hymn* included. Lily's team was chuckling, and Mr. Clay leaned close to Lily to whisper, "We have them stumped!" when she suddenly caught sight of Mr. Spencer's face.

She recognized that slow, pleased smile—she had worn it often enough herself.

"Mr. Spencer," she called. "I believe you have found us out. Will you share your guess?"

He looked startled, and then the full force of his handsome smile was turned on her. "I will if you answer my questions first. Was the charade your doing?"

Lily smiled pertly. "It was."

"And another word for a dirge is *lament*, is it not?"

Lily felt her smile growing. "It is."

"Then I am either about to be very clever indeed or about to make a great fool of myself in front of a number of beautiful ladies," Mr. Spencer said, shaking his head, while the rest of his team leaned forward. "But I see there is no escaping now."

"*Pfft*, you will still be pretty even if you are wrong, which is more than some of us can say," Mr. Dawson shouted, prompting peals of laughter. "Spit it out, my boy."

Lily thought she could see the edge of a blush around Mr. Spencer's collar. But he smiled gamely. "Very well, then. In the first tableau, we all recognized Napoleon, may he remain on his island prison forever. But we did not pay enough attention to what he and his fellows were doing. They were all talking, of course. And when the French talk, they *parle*. Thus, my guess is that hallowed and infuriating institution where no few of us here spend our days. Your charade is *Parliament*, Mrs. Adler."

"He got it!" Major Hastings groaned, as the room filled with cheers and exclamations.

"Well done!" Andrew Harlowe laughed.

As the groups mingled together once more, Margaret herded everyone back into the dining room for a small, late supper. This was a lighter, less formal repast than the dinner had been, set out on the sideboard. The men and women laughed and teased each other as they loaded their plates with a variety of jellies, cold ham and peas, candied nuts, white and yellow cheese, pears, melons, and fat slices of spiced cake. As they resumed their seats around the table, the servants refilled the wine.

The fun of the charades and the late hour of the supper had combined to set them all at ease, and the guests were happy to talk across the table rather than confining their discussions to the partners on either side of them. Lily found herself next to Matthew Spencer once more and, recalling the conversation that had been interrupted by the start of the game, took a deep breath. She needed to find just the right way to turn the talk back to his cousin if she wanted to find out whether her suspicions were correct.

He beat her to the opening. "I hope, Mrs. Adler, that you won't hold my guessing your puzzle against me. I'd not have managed if Mrs. Forsythe hadn't made her very well-timed observation." He raised his glass to that lady in a salute.

Lily joined in. "I had rather hoped to carry the day, but I think I can manage to forgive you," she said, prompting chuckles around the table.

Jack caught her eye from across the table, making a small gesture at himself. When she dipped her chin in a discreet nod, he raised his voice. "Seems like quick minds must run in your family, Spencer. Did you not say your cousin is a prestigious solicitor?" Catching Lily's eye once more, Jack dropped one eyelid in the barest wink.

Mr. Spencer laughed. "Well, time will tell how prestigious he becomes. He certainly hopes to be. But right now he is the very distracted father of the very loud brood of children who have taken over my home."

Lily narrowed her eyes playfully. His words were completely undercut by the smile that softened his features as he spoke of his cousin's children. "I have a suspicion you secretly love that they have taken over."

"Guilty as charged," he admitted, shaking his head. "They are at the age of being charming little monsters. My cousin would spoil them if he were at home more, but his wife knows better than that. So I am free to be the bad influence in their lives with candy in my pockets and games in the parlor. I highly recommend the role of favorite relation to anyone who has no taste for parenthood itself."

Margaret caught Lily's eye then, and the very pointed look she gave almost made Lily blush. The Harlowes, clearly, had not given up their matchmaking ideas. But while Lily was thoroughly charmed by Matthew Spencer, it wasn't his fondness for children that she wanted to hear more about. She needed to somehow turn the conversation back to his cousin.

She was saved by one of the other guests, who leaned forward from her spot across the table, a mischievous smile on her face and her eyes alight with the prospect of gossip. "I suspect Mr. Hammond may well be in the way of notoriety, if not prestige, given his current work. I do hope you are going to enlighten us, Mr. Spencer? Summer is so deadly dull in town; we could use the gossip."

Mr. Spencer's good humor transformed almost instantly to unease, though he tried to laugh it off. "I am sure I do not know—"

"Oh, come, sir." The lady's smile was full of expectation. "I live on Wimpole Street, you know. The whole neighborhood is abuzz with the death of Sir Charles, whose legal affairs, as I have heard, Mr.

Hammond is responsible for managing. Surely your cousin has let fall some interesting tidbit that you can share?" She lowered her voice, glancing around to make sure all eyes were on her. "I say death, but of course that death was most *unnaturally* assisted."

"Good gracious!" Mrs. Dawson exclaimed with grisly excitement as a shocked murmur went around the table among the guests who hadn't yet heard that particular piece of gossip. "Mr. Spencer, now we are all curious. Do enlighten us."

Lily glanced at Margaret, wondering if their hostess planned to put a stop to such a discussion. But Margaret was watching her, eyebrows raised as if asking a question. Her lips moved silently. *No?* she mouthed. *Or more?*

Margaret had been there when Lily was seeking out gossip. And now she wanted to know if she should facilitate more of it. Lily hesitated, then nodded. She wanted to know what the conversation might reveal.

"I am afraid I can have very little to add to the story," Mr. Spencer said, the lightness of his tone sounding forced. "My cousin is merely a junior solicitor at the firm that kept Sir Charles Wyatt's will. He does not discuss his confidential business with me."

"Well, the will's damned important in such a business," Mr. Dawson suggested, his words slurring a little as he leaned forward, his face red with wine. "Poor fellow was probably done in because someone wanted his money."

The comments flew fast and thick after that, some eager, as if the discussion were merely an amusing game, others fluttering and distressed. Lily listened silently, frustrated that nothing new was being said.

"Surely it was a servant?"

"How do they know it was even an unnatural death at all?"

"Who is this fellow? I never heard his name before."

"I know Mr. Frank Wyatt, and a more pleasing young man I could not imagine."

"I heard the family thinks it was a burglar—"

"*That* rumor is because they do not wish their little secret to come out." It was the first lady again, the one who had asked Mr. Spencer for gossip. All eyes turned back to her, and she looked pleased to be the center of attention once more. Even Lily couldn't help leaning forward, wondering if this time she would learn anything useful. "Apparently Sir Charles had not one, but two sons. And they never talk about the younger because he is . . ."

The lady paused, either for dramatic emphasis or out of some delicacy. A cold knot settled in the pit of Lily's stomach.

"Not quite . . . right," the lady said at last, lowering her voice. "There is some suspicion that he may have become violent and . . ."

There were gasps and murmurs around the table.

"Suspicion from who?" Lily demanded, the words coming out more heated than she intended. But the cold feeling in her stomach was spreading through the rest of her body. Across the table, she could see one of Jack's hands clenched around his wineglass, though he was endeavoring to keep his surprise from his face.

The lady looked a little affronted at being questioned, but she smiled smugly. "From one of my dear friends, Mrs. Martin Ashwood. Mr. Ashwood has more than ten thousand a year—you know, quite an old family—and Mrs. Ashwood knows Lady Wyatt well." The lady took in her rapt audience once more. "Though even Mrs. Ashwood had never heard of this younger brother before Sir Charles's death. But the cat is out of the proverbial bag, it seems."

"I believe we have all had enough of such grim talk," Margaret broke in.

Lily didn't look at her friend, hoping her distress didn't show on her face, but she was grateful for the sudden change of topic. How had rumors about Arthur begun to spread so quickly?

Margaret rose, leading the group from the room. "Shall we set out the card tables to finish out the night? And Major Hastings, do I remember that you were planning to visit Brighton this summer? I hope you will bring back an account of how the Regent's pleasure palace is progressing. I have heard so many ridiculous things about its construction . . ."

Lily followed slowly, letting the current of conversation flow around her once more. The cold feeling in her body had turned hot and anxious, and she didn't try to keep up with what was being said. If the Wyatts were spreading rumors about Arthur, then Ellen's fears, it seemed, had been well founded. She needed to speak with Mr. Page . . .

"Mrs. Adler, are you well?"

The gentle inquiry broke into her reverie. Lily glanced over to find that Mr. Spencer had taken a place next to her as they walked and was watching her with polite concern. He lowered his voice, keeping his question between the two of them while the other guests chatted and laughed about the extravagance of the Prince Regent.

Lily gave the room a quick glance as she chose a seat. The group had divided itself into parties for cards at two different tables. One lady had been persuaded to take a turn at the pianoforte; after a polite protest, she settled herself and began to play a very pretty, very gentle air that provided a counterpoint to the hum of conversation and eager bets of the card players. Lily and Mr. Spencer were both among those who had abstained from cards, as did Margaret, once she had her guests settled.

Turning back to her companion, Lily managed a smile. "Perfectly well, I thank you. I was only a little surprised by the last turn of the conversation."

"Mrs. Steele does enjoy shocking others," he replied, glancing over to where the lady in question was preening over her hand of cards.

The words were stern but his tone was light, and Lily had the impression that he was trying not to seem too upset. But a moment later he changed the subject, turning back to her and smiling warmly. "I think I remember Mr. Harlowe saying you had not been to London in some time before this spring. How are you enjoying town?"

Having the full attention of such a handsome man was enough to make Lily feel almost flustered, now that they were speaking alone and not as part of the larger group. She guessed him to be around forty, with hair that had the slightest hint of gray around the temples, though he had the fit build of a sportsman. And he smiled as if he really meant it.

"Very much, sir. Though I fear I have still not fully adjusted to town hours." She lowered her voice conspiratorially. "I think I am the only one here who would prefer to be abed at this hour."

That made him chuckle, the corners of his eyes crinkling up into cheerful-looking laugh lines. "Not the only one, I'm afraid. At the risk of sounding dull, I confess I prefer country life—and country hours—myself."

For a moment Lily felt a pang of guilt; there was every chance she was going to use this nice man for access to his cousin and his cousin's information. But that laugh made her wish her only motive was a pleasant conversation.

Her guilty thoughts were interrupted as Margaret joined them, her arm through Jack's. They had caught the last part of Mr. Spencer's comment, and Margaret was shaking her head, her look teasing. "Prefer it! Really, Mr. Spencer, how could you admit such a thing? I ought to be deeply offended."

"Ah, Mrs. Harlowe, your entertainments are all a man might wish for. But there is unfortunately no competing with the pleasantness of being with one's family, or enjoying the beauty of Hampshire. Have you ever been there, Mrs. Adler?"

"My aunt resides in Hampshire, and I always enjoy visiting her. It is indeed a lovely part of the country." Remembering what Margaret had told her of the Spencer family's horse-breeding, she added, "How being stuck in town makes one long for a gallop!" She didn't look at her friends as she spoke, but she could feel their sudden suspicion, even without making eye contact.

"Dreadfully so." His agreement was instant. "There is nowhere in town for galloping, of course, but one can still go riding."

"Alas, I do not keep a mount for riding," Lily replied. "My brother, Sir John Adler, assures me that he will help me purchase one when next he is in town, but he is much occupied in Hertfordshire."

"Then, Mrs. Adler, you must join me for a ride. I keep a number of horses in town, and I believe I have just the mare for you. Perhaps tomorrow?"

He looked so pleased with the idea that Lily felt guilty once more. But then she remembered the last time she had been invited to go riding and the dreadful scene that had awaited her when she and Jack went to join Lady Wyatt that day. Sir Charles had been murdered, and now someone wanted to pin the blame on the son he had loved. That was reason enough for a little deceit. With a smile and a bow, she agreed to the scheme.

After a few more minutes of talk, Mr. Spencer excused himself politely, saying he did not wish to monopolize their hostess as he bowed and moved to join the group around one of the card tables.

Margaret restrained herself for nearly a full minute until Mr. Spencer was out of earshot and she could say in a low voice, "I'm sure you are a decent horsewoman, Lily, but you are no more likely to long for a gallop than I am to sing a solo at Drury Lane. What was that about?"

"Really, Margaret, it is a trot in the park. I do not see anything so surprising in that."

"And yet you will not look at me as you say so."

Lily felt herself blushing. "I have my reasons," she said, tamping down another surge of guilt.

Margaret didn't press any further. Whatever suspicions she might harbor, she was too circumspect to pursue them in the middle of her own gathering.

As Margaret stepped away to see to other guests, Lily was left alone with Jack, who was regarding her with his arms crossed.

"I don't think I have ever seen you flirt to get your way," he said, his arms crossed.

He spoke quietly enough that Lily couldn't tell whether he was disapproving or not. But she felt defensive anyway. "If my accepting his offer of a ride was flirting, what were you doing when you accepted Lady Wyatt's invitation?"

"That was a completely different circumstance." Jack shook his head. "I hope you know what you are about, Mrs. Adler."

"It is worth it," she said quietly.

The Wyatts were hiding something. Knowing what had been bequeathed and withheld in Sir Charles's will might be the first step to learning what that was.

CHAPTER 15

As she dressed the next morning to go riding with Matthew Spencer, Lily wasn't sure what she even planned to do—she had simply seized the chance to find out more about Mr. Spencer's cousin so as to pursue the Wyatts' secrets from another angle. But she had no idea what she thought might happen, or whether she would have the courage to take advantage of such an opportunity if it presented itself.

She even thought, for a brief moment, of sending a note with her regrets. But her resolve held; she was going to be of some help to Mr. Page, even if he didn't know he still needed her assistance. And that meant pursuing every connection and possibility she could.

Her conversation with Jack did give her pause, and she stared at her reflection in the middle of settling her riding cap to perch at a jaunty angle over her dark curls. But her mind was too focused to spend any length of time wandering into such sentimental territory. If Mr. Spencer potentially had amorous inclinations, so much the better. There could be nothing serious in his designs yet, and he might be more likely to let something slip in conversation with just her than he had been last night in company.

And if she came away having learned nothing, all she would have lost was a few hours in the company of a handsome man. There were worse ways to spend a morning.

She was careful not to keep him waiting. She had no desire for him to come face-to-face with her father or to deal with any more of her father's insinuations about men. When she came down the stairs, she was unsurprised to see that Matthew Spencer made a dashing figure in his riding clothes. His hat held carefully under his maimed arm, he took her offered hand in his and bowed over it.

"Mrs. Adler. How lovely you look today."

"You are very kind, sir. Though I must warn you," she added briskly, smiling to take some of the sting out of her words, "I've very little patience for flattery."

"And what of your patience for genuine compliments from a friend?" he asked, not seeming put off by her bluntness.

"We will have to see if we are friends first, will we not?" Lily asked. "After all, I've not yet known you for even a full day."

"So I am to conclude, then, that you are merely using me for my horses?" He looked amused rather than offended.

"Something of that nature. Though I promise to be entertaining enough to make it worth your while." Lily flicked her cap's feather back from where it had fallen over her eye and added, "If you wish, you may compliment me again when we return. We can see how I feel about it then."

He laughed. "I was warned that you are a singular woman, Mrs. Adler. I am glad to find it is so." Placing his hat on his head once more, he offered her his good arm. "Shall we?"

"I should be offended that someone felt the need to warn you about me," she said as she collected her gloves and riding crop from Carstairs, who then held the door open for them to depart. "Sadly, it is not the first time that has happened. Lead on, Mr. Spencer." She laid her hand over his arm and allowed him to escort her from the house.

In front of the house, Mr. Spencer's groom waited with three horses. Even with her limited equestrian knowledge, Lily could tell they were beautiful creatures, including the older one that was clearly meant for the servant.

The groom led forward an elegant chestnut mare with a white blaze on her nose. "I think you and Lady shall get along admirably,

Mrs. Adler," Mr. Spencer said. Correctly interpreting her expression, he smiled sheepishly and added, "It is a terrible, typical name, is it not? But I promised my daughter she could choose any name she wanted, and so Lady it is."

"It suits her, at least," Lily allowed, stroking the horse's nose. "She is a lovely girl."

"I regret that I am unable to assist you to mount," Mr. Spencer said as he gestured with his injured arm. His look was self-deprecating but not embarrassed. "But my man will be happy to provide his services."

Once the groom had helped her into the saddle, Lily settled the folds of her riding skirts, unable to keep from watching her companion from the corner of her eye. The groom held the horse's head steady, and that seemed to be all the assistance Mr. Spencer required. In spite of his missing arm, he mounted quite easily, settling into the saddle and taking the reins from the pommel with great physical confidence.

Lily busied herself with her own reins as Mr. Spencer turned to her, hoping he hadn't noticed her scrutiny. "Where shall we go, sir?" she asked, turning her mare toward the street, surprised to find that she did not feel as awkward in the saddle as she had expected in spite of how much time had passed since she had last ridden. Behind her, the groom mounted up to follow them.

"Sadly, there are not many places to ride in London. But if we make our way to the Row, we can at least have a little bit of a trot."

"That sounds lovely."

In spite of her airy promise to be entertaining, Lily hadn't needed to charm a man in years, and she had wondered what she would manage to talk about. To her surprise, it took very little effort to fall into conversation with Matthew Spencer. He talked easily and pleasantly, asking about her former home in Hertfordshire and telling her about his own property in Hampshire. The ride to Hyde Park passed more quickly than she had expected it to.

The busy hours in Hyde Park wouldn't come until later in the afternoon. As it was just half past eleven when they arrived, the paths of the park weren't too crowded. They were able to trot cheerfully up

Rotten Row—once the Route du Roi, or King's Road, now merely a promenade through London's little remaining wilderness. Past the Row, the crowds thinned out further still, and even Lily found herself tempted by the stretch of open land before her.

Mr. Spencer laughed as Lady shifted restlessly under her rider. "I think our pretty girl wants that gallop as much as you do, Mrs. Adler. But perhaps"—he smiled conspiratorially—"we could satisfy ourselves with a bit of a canter?"

"You are a bad influence, sir," Lily remarked, but the corners of her eyes crinkled up with unvoiced laughter. She was finding Mr. Spencer a more than pleasant companion.

"So I was often told by my dear Harriet," he said, and though his smile was bittersweet, his voice was easy as he mentioned his wife, dead now for many years.

Lily envied him that ease and, to her own surprise, found herself saying, "You speak of her very fondly still."

He cast her a sideways glance. "You are not offended, I hope?"

"Why should I be?" Lily thought of the bitter conversation with her father and shook her head. There was a difference between loving someone and becoming stuck in your own life without them. She wished her father had been able to see that—for her sake and his own. "I think it a mark of high character, both hers and yours, that you still feel so deeply for her."

Mr. Spencer smiled gratefully. "That is a kind thing to say, Mrs. Adler. Harriet and I were . . ." He hesitated. "We cared for each other very much."

"A nice sort of marriage, then," Lily said, and he nodded his agreement. Unable to help her curiosity, she asked, "You said you had a daughter?"

He nodded. "And a son. Eloisa is twelve, Matthew ten. They live in Hampshire, of course. After their mother died, her sister raised them more than I did, since I was away in the Peninsula."

"It must have been hard to have duty take you away from them after their mother died."

"Yes." The single word had so much feeling behind it that Lily had to swallow away the prick of tears. "Almost as hard as her death."

Lily nodded. If she had thought more closely about it, she would have been surprised that they were having such a frank, personal discussion. But somehow it seemed perfectly natural.

He looked pensive, though, so she gave him a sideways smile to lighten the mood. "Your Harriet may have said you were a bad influence, but Mr. Adler always accused me of being a secret harridan. Though of course I am too well bred to show such a flaw in public."

"Ah, but if that is true, you will not be able to resist that canter. Particularly if . . ." Accepting her desire to change the subject, Mr. Spencer smiled. "I should dare you to it."

Lily gave him an assessing look. Then, smiling to hide her nervousness, she kicked her horse forward.

Lady needed no encouragement, and she set out at a brisk pace over the open expanse of parkland. Behind her, Lily heard Mr. Spencer laugh, and then he was thundering past her, much closer to a gallop than anyone should have attempted in the middle of Hyde Park. After that, it was all Lily could do to hold on as Lady took off after her stablemate.

He was still laughing when she caught up to him. "Secret harridan indeed!"

Lily, who couldn't decide whether she was thrilled at the brief exercise or still terrified of falling off, said, a little short of breath, "You are a marvelous rider, Mr. Spencer."

To her surprise, his neck and ears flushed red at the praise. "It took some doing to get my seat back," he said with quiet pride, gesturing with the stump of his arm. "You wouldn't think it would make such a difference, but it did."

Feeling a little awkward, Lily merely nodded. He noticed her discomfort immediately and laughed. "No good pretending it's not there. Or rather, pretending it *is* there, not to put too fine a point on the matter. I learned early on to mention it myself. Otherwise, everyone stumbles all over themselves trying to ignore the fact that I only have one and a half arms, which is far more uncomfortable for everyone. Including me." He smiled.

"To be honest, sir, I had almost forgotten until you mentioned it. Not to diminish your accomplishment," she said quickly. "I can only imagine what coming home must have been like and how your life must have changed." Remembering she had promised to be entertaining, she added, "You will be glad to know, I am sure, that it did not diminish the appreciation any of the ladies last night had for your handsome face and figure."

"Why, Mrs. Adler, that is twice in five minutes now that you have made me blush. But indeed, I was—I am—one of the lucky ones." His smile grew a little sad. "I was a major when I was discharged for my injury. But I no longer find anything glamorous in our military endeavors on the Continent." He shook his head, glancing down at the stump of his arm. "What a horrible, senseless waste war is."

Lily found herself thinking over that moment for the rest of the ride back to her house, though she hid her preoccupation behind pleasant chatter. He had spoken with such disgust and resignation. Hearing someone express that depth of feeling out loud was rare, even more so when they had met as new acquaintances during what was left of London's social season.

"I hope, Mrs. Adler," he said, smiling as they turned onto Half Moon Street, "that you will not hold my bad behavior against me and will grant me the pleasure of your company in the future?"

"I should like that, Mr. Spencer. I might even consider accepting a compliment the next time we meet, in spite of your horses' questionable names."

"Would you truly fault me for being a doting father?" he asked.

Lily merely smiled, still trying to decide whether she was brave enough to ask what she wanted.

"I would take that as a favorable response, Mrs. Adler," he said with good humor. "But you seem a bit distracted. Is something the matter?"

The question made Lily start, and the sudden pull on the reins made Lady prance a little beneath her. "I beg your pardon?" Lily asked, blushing as she settled her mount. It was as embarrassing to be caught in her woolgathering as it was to ride so poorly in front of him.

"You seemed distracted. I hope I did not upset you before, with my talk of the war." He hesitated, falling silent as they steered their mounts around a cart that was waiting in the road, then added, "I meant no disparagement of Captain Hartley, of course. I know you and he are old friends."

"No, it was not that." Lily hesitated, wondering how honest she could risk being with him. On the one hand, he talked like a man of principle, and he was a father himself. On the other, what she wanted to ask him to do would sound unbelievable to his ears. And if he should mention it to anyone else . . .

Lily straightened her spine. He had shown last night that he wasn't a gossip. And perhaps he would be shocked, but if there was even the slightest chance of success, it would be worth it. At worst, he would never ask her to go riding again, and as much as she had enjoyed the outing, that wasn't enough of a risk to deter her.

"It did not upset me," she said quietly, drawing her horse as close to his as she could while they were still moving. She glanced briefly over her shoulder, but the groom was far enough back that he wouldn't be able to hear her. "But it did show me that you are a man of honor and sense."

"You flatter me," he said politely, but his expression was puzzled.

"I hope I do not, or I may soon regret what I am about to ask you." Lily kept her face straight ahead, but she could see her companion's eyebrows shoot up. "You will recall Mrs. Steele's talk about the Wyatt family last night? I was impressed that you would not be moved to gossip, even though you must know something of the matter from your cousin."

"I do," he said, shaking his head and looking a little wary. "But such speculation is not something I enjoy."

"Which is to your credit. And I am not going to ask you to indulge in it now. But I am going to ask you to consider something else." Lily took a deep breath and met his eyes. She wanted to speak quickly, to get it over with, but she forced herself to be slow and deliberate, to sound as credible and reasonable as she could. "When Mrs. Steele said the Wyatts had another son and that the family had kept him from society, she was telling the truth. But I fear that the rumors about his involvement in his father's death are intended to steer suspicion away from the rest of the family. They do not wish that cloud hanging over any of them, and so they would rather let him take the blame than cooperate with the Bow Street investigators."

"Mrs. Adler . . ." He trailed off, clearly at a loss for words.

Lily pressed on. "As a father yourself, you must see how abhorrent such a thing is. The real culprit must be caught. And to do so, the Bow Street Runner in charge of the matter needs to see Sir Charles's will. Which his older son and widow, I believe, are unlikely to share."

"Forgive me, Mrs. Adler, but what can you know of such matters?"

They had arrived in front of her door, and Lily pulled her horse to a gentle halt. Her entire body was prickling with nerves as she removed one riding glove and pulled out the card she had stashed there, just in case she had need of it. "I have been asked to assist the Bow Street gentleman in this matter." She handed the card to Mr. Spencer, who looped his reins around the pommel so that he could reach out to take it. Lily pulled the glove back on, pleased with how steady her hands were. Her eyes never left his face.

His widened as he read. Lily didn't need to glance down; she had the words memorized.

A Lady of Quality
Enquire by Letter
General Post Office, Old Cavendish-street, London
Discreet Inquiries, Confidential Investigations & Mysteries Solved

Mr. Spencer stared at it for several long minutes while Lily held her breath, wondering what he was thinking and if she had made a horrible mistake.

"Are you quite serious?" he asked at last.

Lily swallowed, trying to look as though she knew what she was doing. "The life, or at least the well-being, of an innocent boy may be at stake, sir. I am indeed serious. And I hope I have not misplaced my trust by telling you so."

"And what do you expect me to do with this information?" His tone was mild, but she could sense a sharpness beneath the words—though whether that was directed at her or not, she could not be sure. "Because I can assure you, I will never betray my cousin's trust or illicitly obtain anything for these new constables."

"And I would not ask you to," Lily said. "All I ask is that you present what I have told you to your cousin and ask that he share the will with Mr. Simon Page, a principal officer of Bow Street and the man investigating Sir Charles's death."

"And this request, I gather, is the reason you sought my company today?"

Lily hesitated. But there was no use trying to lie, as the answer was already obvious to them both. "As much as I enjoyed our time together, enjoyment was not my principle motivation."

He stared at her silently, his expression unreadable, then glanced once more at the card in his hand. Lily held her breath until he finally spoke.

"I will consider it."

CHAPTER 16

Lily still had not had any response from Mr. Page by that afternoon, and she had just settled down at her desk to write once more when a gentle tap on the door interrupted her.

"Begging your pardon, but you've visitors downstairs," Anna said, poking her head around the door.

Lily sighed and laid down her pen, rubbing her temples. "Depending on who it is, I might not be at home today."

"It's Lady Carroway and Captain Hartley."

"Oh!" Lily hurried to set her things aside. "In that case, I am most certainly home. Will you have Carstairs show them into the drawing room?"

"Yes, ma'am."

It took Lily several moments to make herself presentable for guests; she had kicked off her shoes and sequestered herself in her room immediately after her ride, wanting to think over her talk with Matthew Spencer and avoid her father as much as possible. After repinning her hair and finally locating one of her shoes under the bed, she hurried downstairs.

She was stopped at the bottom of the stairs by the sound of a deep laugh from the drawing room.

Lily frowned at Carstairs, who was waiting for her in the hall. "Did someone else arrive?"

"Lady Carroway has returned from her wedding trip, madam, and is waiting for you." The butler's normally somber face broke into a genuine smile as he spoke; the new, young Lady Carroway was his favorite of Lily's friends, though he would never have presumed to say so out loud. "Captain Hartley is with her as well. I've taken the liberty of requesting refreshments from Mrs. Carstairs, which should arrive soon. And there is this." He bowed, holding out an envelope. "I discovered this in the hall. I believe it arrived with yesterday's post but was mislaid."

"Thank you, Carstairs." The envelope was rough, not the pristine, smooth paper that usually arrived with Lily's correspondence, the direction on it written neatly in pencil. Lily gave it a puzzled look before tucking it into her palm and turning once more toward the door. "But . . . who is with them?"

"Mr. Pierce was sitting in the drawing room when they were shown in."

Lily stared at him. "And that was *him* laughing?"

"It appears so."

Lily eyed the drawing room door, suddenly feeling unsure. Ofelia, Lady Carroway, not yet twenty years old, was known for being charming, pretty, and popular, especially since her marriage to a wealthy young baronet earlier that summer. But she was also the child of a union between an Englishman and a West Indian woman. As her father's only child, her entrance into London society had been guaranteed by his large fortune and impressive family connections. But there were still rumors about her parentage and unkind remarks whispered behind her back. Lily couldn't imagine that her father would be willing to sit and laugh with her friend, no matter how pleasant and polished she might be.

"Even she could not win my father over." Lily looked back at her butler. "Could she?"

If Carstairs had been anyone else, he might have shrugged. "There seems to be only one way to find out, madam."

He was right. And she *did* want to see her friend. Straightening her shoulders, Lily flung open the door to the drawing room.

There was a pause in the conversation as three heads turned her way.

"Mrs. Adler!" Ofelia sprang up and across the room, her hands outstretched and a wide smile lighting her face. Behind her, the two men rose politely from their seats. "Gracious, it has been an age! You look lovely, as always. And what do you think? Do I look *married*?"

Lily dropped the envelope she was holding on a table by the door, holding out her hands as well. But she didn't get a chance to speak; Ofelia, laughing and giddy, was too excited to let her get a word in edgewise.

"That was the first thing my aunt said when she saw me yesterday, the old dragon. I still cannot decide whether it was a compliment or not."

Lily smiled, forgetting about her father for the moment. "It must be," she said, letting Ofelia tow her to the settee and taking a seat beside her. "Because you look radiant. Either travel or marriage must agree with you."

"Both," said Ofelia, laughing again. "And now I have the added pleasure of seeing my friends once more. We had not expected to be in London quite so soon, but Neddy's sister has a young beau, apparently, that his mother does not quite approve of. She insisted we return as quickly as we could, before they had the chance to rush into anything, and now poor Neddy must decide whether he is going to be a dutiful brother or dutiful son."

"I do not envy him that choice," Lily said, taking the opportunity to lift her head and look around the room at last. "Captain Hartley. Was it a coincidence that brought you here together, or did you have advance warning of our friends' return to London?"

"Neither," he said, leaning back and crossing his legs, looking more relaxed than she had yet seen him in her father's presence. "Lady Carroway sent her card and insisted I join her here to surprise you. She is a devious thing, as always."

"Do not listen to a word the captain says, Mr. Pierce," Ofelia said, turning to bring Lily's father into the conversation. "I haven't a devious bone in my body."

The fact that she was able to say so with a completely straight face made Lily shake her head. The girl had caused no small amount of confusion and suspicion by concealing her engagement to Sir Edward Carroway when she and Jack were helping Lily to solve the Harper murders. And Lily knew, though Jack did not, that this was not the only secret Ofelia had been keeping that spring.

But Mr. Pierce, apparently, was happy to believe the girl. He even smiled indulgently at her while Lily stared in amazement.

"I do not doubt it, my dear," he said, chuckling as he rose, leaning less heavily on his cane than he had the past few days. She wondered if he was genuinely feeling better or if he was simply in a better mood than usual. "I am afraid I must leave you to your friend, but I thank you for entertaining me so charmingly. And when you have the chance, I hope you will remember what I said and do your best to persuade your husband to take you to Italy."

"I shall certainly take your advice, sir."

"You see, Lily?" Mr. Pierce said, giving his daughter a sardonic glance. "There are those who find my advice worthwhile. And speaking of which, I need a moment of your time, if your friends can spare you."

Lily gritted her teeth. She wanted to say no, but it was probably best to get whatever he wanted to say over with. And this way she could use her guests as an excuse if she needed to cut the conversation short. "Of course, sir. If you will both excuse me?"

"Captain Hartley." Mr. Pierce and Jack nodded to each other in cool farewell, and Lily followed her father out into the hall, which was now empty except for the two of them.

"Walk with me upstairs, Lily." It was an order, not a request.

"I have guests."

"And they will, I am sure, grant a moment of your time to your father. Do not make me wait."

Lily sighed but didn't argue again. But she couldn't bring herself to remain silent.

"What is it, then, Father?" she asked as they made their way up the stairs. "I assume you wish to make disparaging remarks about my friends?"

He raised his eyebrows. "Meaning Lady Carroway, I assume?"

"Yes," Lily bit off, before taking a deep breath. "I'll not be snubbing her, no matter what your feelings are on the matter, so you can save yourself the effort of ordering me to."

Mr. Pierce frowned, his mouth pursed as if he had tasted something sour. "I am offended that you would think me so foolish and shortsighted. I have always been glad that you cultivated such a close friendship with Lady Walter, and Lady Carroway is undoubtedly as beneficial an acquaintance. The Carroways are a particularly respectable family, with ties to the Earl of Portland, as I hope you know. And her father is, of course, a Devonshire Oswald, a family with its own impressive set of connections in our county and beyond. No, whatever else may be said of you—and there is plenty I could say—"

"I do not doubt it," Lily muttered.

"—you choose your friendships well." Mr. Pierce turned down the hall and continued toward his room, gesturing impatiently for Lily to follow.

She gritted her teeth and did. "So your opinion is entirely based on their families, not on the women themselves?"

He surprised her by smiling. "I might not have approved of Lady Carroway had she *not* been Lady Carroway. Only a fool says wealth and connections do not matter. But even I cannot deny the girl is charming. She reminds me of your mother, you know. Quite vivacious."

Lily stared at him, trying to ignore the hot surge of jealousy in her chest. Her father had never once said *she* reminded him of her mother. She was always too cold, too introspective, too everything he disapproved of. She knew there was more to Ofelia than her pleasant social mask, but for a moment she bitterly resented the younger woman's ease and prettiness.

"But that is not why I wished to speak with you." Mr. Pierce stopped in front of the door to his room, his voice growing sharp as he pulled something out of his pocket and held it where she could see. "I want an explanation for this."

It was one of her cards. And not one of her everyday calling cards, but the same as the one she had shown Matthew Spencer that morning.

"What were you doing snooping through my things?" she said.

"I found it in the hall this morning. I expect you dropped it."

There was no way of knowing whether he was telling the truth, and Lily chose not to argue the point. She reached out to take the card from him, but he moved it out of her reach. Lily dropped her hand, seething inwardly but refusing to let him see that she was discomposed at all. She would not allow herself to appear any more childish than he had already made her feel by trying to snatch it from him again.

Instead, she lifted her chin. "I really do not see how it is any of your business."

"You are my daughter."

"I am a woman grown."

"If you are involved in anything ridiculous, it reflects on me. I've a right to know."

Lily laughed abruptly, though there was no humor in the sound. "Only you, Father, would call a daughter who unmasks a murderer ridiculous."

He narrowed his eyes. "What on earth do you mean?"

"Oh, come now, Father. I know how you like to keep up with gossip and keep track of my affairs. Surely you heard whispers about me this spring."

"Those were rumors," he snapped. "You would never be so foolish—" He broke off, waving the card around. "And this! What in God's name could you mean by . . ." He trailed off, apparently unable to find words sufficient to describe his outrage. His face was mottled red.

Lily sighed. "I was in a position to assist Bow Street and protect Lady Walter—whose friendship you so recently praised me for cultivating, if you will recall—from a potential scandal. Captain Hartley had those cards printed for me as a kind of encouragement."

"Encouragement?" Mr. Pierce's eyes were so wide they looked as though they might pop out of his head. "To do what? Are you advertising? Are you *working*? Are you associating with those . . . those . . . constables?"

Stung, still battered by his criticism and her jealousy, Lily didn't care if she was being unwise. "I would have thought you had more respect for those who are investigating Sir Charles's death. Or do you not wish to know who was responsible for your friend's murder?"

"Frank says it was a burglar."

"And you believe *him* instantly, of course."

"Why should I *not*?" Mr. Pierce's face was flushed with rage, and his hands trembled around his walking stick. "When has he ever disappointed me?"

"Never, of course. Unlike your daughter, the constant disappointment."

"I am disappointed indeed that a child of mine would fraternize with such a low order of people, and not even with the intent of helping our friends."

"I *am* helping Arthur. Unless you want to see him blamed for his father's murder?"

"I cannot talk to you when you spout such nonsense," Mr. Pierce said, throwing up his hands.

"Then do not talk to me," Lily snapped. "In fact, you may kindly remove your nose from my affairs—"

"Mrs. Adler?"

They both turned to find Carstairs standing a few steps down the hall, looking uncomfortable and apologetic. Lily wondered how much of their conversation—which had been conducted in heated whispers—he had heard.

She turned her back on her father. "Yes, what is it?"

"Mr. Page of Bow Street has arrived and asked to speak with you."

The timing could not have been worse. Lily could feel her father's glare, but she refused to look at him. Keeping her expression as calm as possible, she nodded at her butler, though she could feel her face heating. "Please show him to the drawing room. I am sure he will be happy to see the captain and Lady Carroway again. And invite the gentlemen to pour themselves a drink while they wait for me."

"Gentlemen," Mr. Pierce snorted. "That is questionable."

"I will return in a moment, Carstairs." Lily waited for him to leave before turning to her father. "Was there anything else you needed from me?"

Mr. Pierce opened and closed his mouth several times without saying anything; he didn't look as though he was at a loss for words but rather as if there were so many things he wanted to say that he couldn't figure out where to begin.

"Then I will see you at dinner," Lily said, making her escape as quickly as possible.

"Lily!"

The outraged hiss chased her down the hall, but she did not turn around.

★ ★ ★

"Mrs. Adler, what is this I hear? You have become involved with yet *another* dead body?"

Ofelia's playful demand met Lily as soon as she closed the door to the drawing room. The three of them had clearly made themselves comfortable waiting for her: Ofelia had poured tea and was nibbling at a slice of plum cake, while Jack had poured a glass of sherry each for himself and Mr. Page. The captain was lounging comfortably in the most overstuffed chair in the room, sipping from his glass, but the constable held his as he paced around the room, looking impatient.

Lily raised her eyebrows, trying to put the conversation with her father behind her. "I see the men have gotten right to gossiping. Was it Mr. Page or the captain who started it?"

"Me," Jack said, raising his glass in a toast. "And Page is none too pleased about it."

"I dislike having my work treated so cavalierly," the constable said, looking a little embarrassed. Glancing down at the glass in his hand as if he had just remembered it was there, he took a deep swallow and grimaced.

"We are none of us cavalier about the matter," Ofelia protested. "Not after what happened in April. And why are you here if not to seek assistance?"

"Why?" Mr. Page fixed his eyes on Lily. His color was high, and he was clearly displeased. Lily met his eyes as she took her seat, refusing to be cowed. "Mrs. Adler knows why."

Jack eyed them both over the edge of his glass while Ofelia sat forward in her chair, her eyes darting between Lily and Mr. Page with eager curiosity.

Lily nodded as calmly as she could manage. "I assume you received my letter?"

"Your . . ." Mr. Page stared at her, then laughed shortly. "My God, I'd almost forgotten how angry I was over that. We'll get to that in a moment, madam. First, I want to discuss the man who walked into my office today. I am sure you know who I mean."

Lily blinked at him. "I haven't the faintest idea."

"Really?" Mr. Page snorted, draining his glass in a single gulp and setting it down with a *thunk*. He crossed his arms, eyes fixed on her. It was the most worked up she had ever seen him. "You have no idea that Mr. Hammond, a junior solicitor at his firm, walked into my office not one hour ago to present me with the will of Sir Charles Wyatt, saying that he had been persuaded by a lady of quality that it was his duty to assist my investigation?"

"Well done, Mrs. Adler!" Ofelia exclaimed. "She really can persuade anyone of anything."

Lily could hardly believe her ears. "He made up his mind that quickly?"

"So you did talk to the solicitor!" Mr. Page said triumphantly.

"No." Jack looked oddly relieved as he leaned back in his chair once more. "She talked to his cousin. So that was the result of your ride this morning?"

Lily frowned at him. "What did you think I was doing, husband hunting?"

"And please, as you suggested, let us return to that letter," Mr. Page continued, ignoring their comments. "The letter which confessed that you *stole Mr. Percy Wyatt's address* from my office, impersonated Lady Wyatt, and gained access to his chambers."

"You did what?" Jack demanded, starting to his feet so sharply that he nearly spilled his glass. "Lily, what were you thinking?"

In the silence that echoed through the room while she was trying to formulate her reply, Lily heard Ofelia repeat, in quiet surprise, "Lily?"

Jack's neck and ears flushed a dull, dark red. "How could you take such a foolish risk?"

"I am sure Mrs. Adler had a plan," Ofelia said loyally. "And even if she did not, she is sitting here, well and unharmed, and you, Mr. Page"—her voice grew sharp—"now have a piece of evidence that, unless I am very much mistaken, you had great need of and no way to obtain. So perhaps you could both settle your impugned honor, or whatever has you so out of sorts, and take a seat long enough to talk rationally? And perhaps say thank you?"

Her voice had risen at the end, and she glared at the two belligerent male faces currently looming over them. Lily felt a surge of warmth and gratitude. Once, she had been the one defending Ofelia. Now, even before her friend knew the full circumstances, she was returning the favor without hesitation.

Ofelia's admonishment had an instant effect. Jack looked even more embarrassed, and he turned away quickly to walk to the window while he regained his composure. Mr. Page cleared his throat and took a seat.

He glanced at Ofelia, raising a sardonic brow. "Marriage does, indeed, seem to have agreed with you, Lady Carroway."

"A good puzzle will agree with me as well," she said pertly. "Will you share what was in the will with us?"

"With us?" His brows rose even higher. "I'm already uneasy enough about Mrs. Adler and Captain Hartley's involvement. And I suspect your husband wouldn't wish you to become embroiled in another murder."

"Fortunately, we are still in that delightful beginning of a marriage where Neddy finds it impossible to disapprove of *anything* I do," Ofelia said, pouring a cup of tea and handing it to Lily. "So I might as well assist Mrs. Adler with her murder."

Mr. Page scowled. "I remind you, Lady Carroway, that it's Bow Street's murder."

"Of course, sir, that is exactly what I meant. But you cannot deny that a fresh perspective is often a great deal of help. You might as well include me too. Especially since I do not plan to leave anytime soon, and I have the feeling you wish to continue chiding Mrs. Adler too much to outlast me."

Lily couldn't help laughing at that, and she was relieved to hear Jack chuckle from his place by the window. Even Mr. Page couldn't help smiling. "You are incorrigible, Lady Carroway." Then he sighed. "I'll return to berating Mrs. Adler soon, but first, the will." He fixed Lily with a stern expression. "How'd you manage that?"

"I can be very persuasive, sir," Lily said modestly.

He gave her a sour look. "I'm familiar with that talent of yours."

"I will admit, though, in this case I did not expect it to bear fruit quite so quickly." Lily leaned forward, her tea forgotten. "Will you tell me what it says?"

Mr. Page sighed, clasping his hands behind his back as he paced toward the fireplace and back. "My superiors did not have high hopes for my success in this case," he admitted. "With the lack of cooperation from the Wyatt family and their willingness to cast blame on one of their own, it seemed as though the entire matter would be too easily swept aside." He paused, absently picking up and then setting aside several books that were resting on the mantelpiece without really seeing them. "I assume you have heard the rumors regarding the younger son of Sir Charles."

"Yes," said Lily, sighing.

"Seems after taking so much care to keep the boy and his condition hushed up, they were suddenly all too ready to publicize his existence and let him shoulder the blame," Jack said, his tone bitter. "Did you see the boy, Page? What did you think of him?"

"I agreed with his maid," Mr. Page said quietly. "Arthur Wyatt didn't seem at all likely to have harmed his father. My money would be on anyone else in the household before him."

"Which is how I persuaded Mr. Hammond's cousin to say something," Lily confessed. "I did not expect him to act so quickly, though I am glad he did."

"As am I." The admission made Mr. Page sigh as he turned back to his small audience. "Before Mr. Hammond came into my office today, I fully expected to be told that I was done with the matter by the end of the day. Many of my colleagues . . ." He paused, looking grim as he sorted through his words. When he finally spoke again, there was an undercurrent of deep anger, though it was nearly hidden. Lily wondered if the others in the room heard it. "Many of my colleagues find the family's insinuation that their odd youngest member was responsible to be reasonable. It's the fate of many such children to bear the scorn and blame of those who should be caring for them. So I thank you, Mrs. Adler."

"Even if you are still unhappy with me?"

"I am *very* unhappy with you," he asserted, shaking his head. "But I don't expect that to make much difference to you." He cleared his throat, removing a folded paper from the inside pocket of his coat. "And since I'm alone among the Bow Street officers in my assessment of the matter, I'll accept the offer of help you have made." He glanced at Ofelia. "And the fresh perspective."

She raised her teacup to him in a salute.

"So." Mr. Page cleared his throat. There was silence in the room as he scanned the paper in his hands. "Mr. Hammond was understandably reluctant to leave a copy of the will with me. But he did allow me to read it and take notes. It appears that after Sir Charles's death, Frank inherits half of his wealth and property. Most of the other half is set aside for Arthur's care, to go to Frank after his death if he should outlive his brother."

"Most of the other half," Lily repeated. She steepled her fingers together, pressing them against her lips as she regarded Mr. Page through narrowed, thoughtful eyes. "What about Lady Wyatt?"

"As they had no children together, Lady Wyatt receives little of her husband's estate," Mr. Page said, his voice even. Lily's eyebrows shot up in shock, and she could feel Ofelia and Jack shifting with surprise. "She's entitled to a widow's jointure until she remarries, amounting to about one hundred pounds per annum." He raised his head, taking in their stunned expressions, and scowled. "It's a far greater sum than many in this city have to support entire families."

"But far less than she has grown accustomed to living on," Jack pointed out. "I think that makes Lady Wyatt an unlikely murderer, even if we ignore the physical difficulties."

"She mightn't have known before she killed him," Ofelia said.

"She would have to be a very stupid murderer not to find out that information before she did the deed," Jack said, shaking his head. "And she did not strike me as stupid."

"If money was the motive," Lily said quietly, still watching Mr. Page. Since he had pointed out her blind spot, she had been determined to regard Lady Wyatt with the same skepticism as anyone else in the family, even if her impulse was to sympathize with the woman.

Mr. Page nodded. "The same could be said for Mr. Percy Wyatt. He also receives one hundred pounds per annum, though he also has his own income left to him by his parents."

"Money would be a likely motive for him," Jack said. "We know he has debts and that he is very stupid about managing them."

"And there is the matter of his sneaking out at night," Lily said. "I discovered when I visited his home that he was not telling the truth about his actions the night of Sir Charles's death."

"Visited." Mr. Page snorted. "What a charming word for breaking in, ma'am."

"The servant let me in," Lily said, shrugging. "I did not have to break anything."

Ofelia laughed, but Mr. Page shook his head. "We'll have words about your methods later, Mrs. Adler. But what you learned was helpful. He certainly had the opportunity to kill his uncle. If there's a woman in the case—whether his mistress or one he wants to marry—it could go a long way towards explaining why he chose now to act. Because I doubt his debts are new."

"Unless his uncle *was* going to increase his inheritance," Lily pointed out. "That would give him plenty of motive *not* to kill him before the will could be changed."

"*If* he was telling the truth," Jack said. "Which seems unlikely to me. What man would make the nephew who tried to steal from him his heir? He would be more likely to disinherit him."

"Which would give Percy Wyatt reason to act quickly and secure what he could," Mr. Page agreed.

"But an extra hundred pounds a year?" Ofelia made a face. "That would not do much."

"Plenty of people have killed for less," Mr. Page said, sounding exasperated. "The three of you have very little idea of how much money that actually is."

"But to a gentleman with significant debts, one prone to gambling and horse racing, it is *not* very much," Lily pointed out. "We may have our blind spots, Mr. Page, but you have them as well. Which is why you originally asked us to assist you, if you recall."

He scowled again, then sighed and returned to his notes. "A few small bequests to other relatives and old servants. And then a bequest I can't account for, producing an income of about twenty pounds a year, to someone in Kent. Mr. Hammond could not explain it either. The other bequests make note of the family relationships, the servants' long years of service, Sir Charles's affection or gratitude, et cetera. But this one simply states who receives it." He eyed his audience. "Anyone care to venture a guess?"

The other three shook their heads; Mr. Page nodded, unsurprised, and folded the piece of paper, returning it to his pocket.

"There was one other odd thing," he continued. "The last time I was at Wimpole Street, I observed something peculiar. Mr. Frank Wyatt was making what seemed to be a clandestine payment out the kitchen door to an imposing, rough-looking man. According to Mr. Wyatt, the fellow was a laborer whose services were no longer needed—something about repairs not being necessary since Sir Charles's death. But Mr. Wyatt would have no need to be afraid of a laborer, nor to lie to me about him. And I would swear that both those things are true."

Lily frowned. "Who do you think he really is?"

"I don't know." Mr. Page clasped his hands behind his back. "But it's something odd, as I said. And in a case like this, anything odd might be important."

Before any of them could answer, there was a timid tap on the door of the drawing room. Anna poked her head around the door, her eyes wide and fixed on Jack. "Begging your pardon for interrupting," she murmured as she came in, her voice hoarse with anxiety. "But young Jem just came rushing into the kitchen with a message. He says it's urgent that he speak to you right away, sir."

Lily exchanged a swift look with Jack. Jem had been continuing to spend his time in and around Wimpole Street. If he was rushing to them with a message, there was little chance it was a good thing.

"Do you want to go down to the kitchens to speak with him, or should I bring him up?"

Jack hesitated. "Bring him up, if you please. If he is rushing over here with news, it is either very good or very bad. And either way, Mr. Page should hear it as well."

"Where has he been?" Mr. Page asked, the question so deliberately calm that it made Lily wince. She had forgotten until now that he didn't know what task she and Jack had given Jem.

"I asked him to keep an eye on Wimpole Street, make himself known belowstairs if he could," Jack said, meeting the Bow Street constable's eyes as if daring him to object. "He's an engaging little fellow. And servants are good for news."

Mr. Page looked like he wanted to protest. Then he let out a deep sigh, the fight going out of him, and shook his head. "So it seems. I suppose I thank you."

"You sound as if it gives you a toothache to say so," Ofelia said.

Mr. Page smiled grimly. "It does."

Jem's eyes were wide as Anna shooed him into the room, taking in every inch of the comfortable, luxurious house. He had been in Lily's kitchen before but never upstairs, and he craned his neck to look around before Anna gave him a gentle tap on the back of the head.

"Mind your manners. What did you need to tell the captain?"

The gangly boy planted his feet firmly apart, hands clasped behind his back and chin raised as if he were making a report. But he hesitated, glancing around the room at his larger-than-expected audience. His eyes lingered warily on Mr. Page; and he looked away quickly, shifting his weight with embarrassment, when he realized Ofelia was in the room. Lily would have smiled if she hadn't been so anxious about the message.

Jem gave the room a stiff little bow. "Sir," he said, looking at Jack, but still he hesitated.

"Spit it out, Jem. I can tell by your face you have no good news for us. And that gentleman"—Jack nodded in Mr. Page's direction—"is an officer of Bow Street, so the matter concerns him as well."

Jem's eyes had grown even wider, and he gulped audibly before nodding. "It's no good news, Captain, as you say. There's been . . ." Still he hesitated, glancing at Ofelia again, as if unhappy to say what he must in her presence. He lowered his voice. "There's been another death at Wimpole Street. She felt ill this morning and went to lie down, then started having horrible pains in her belly. By the afternoon she was dead in her bed. The doctor is saying that she was sick.

But Mrs. Harris, the housekeeper, is sure it was not natural. And she remembered Mrs. Adler from her helping Thomas and sent me with the message."

Lily's hand tightened on the arm of the settee; beside her, she heard the rattling of china as Ofelia set down her teacup with a clatter. Jack drew in a sharp breath. Mr. Page showed almost as little reaction as Lily herself, only a sudden tension in his jaw and the muscles around his mouth betraying his unhappiness.

"Who has died?" Jack asked gently.

Jem gulped again. "That girl as came here before, sir. The maid, Ellen."

CHAPTER 17

Simon didn't stay long at the cozy house on Half Moon Street after that. The Wyatts were likely hoping to keep the death of their maid quiet, but thanks to the Captain's servant boy, he had the jump on them. He intended to pursue it when they were least expecting his interference.

Mrs. Adler followed him out to the hall when he took his leave, frowning in worry. It was an expression she would never have let him see once upon a time; Mrs. Adler showed her emotions only to those she trusted.

At the moment, though, he would have been glad to be spared that trust, because it came with an interrogation.

"Why were you angry?" she asked as she handed him his hat.

Simon scowled, then quickly resumed his own cool expression. She wasn't the only one skilled at keeping her feelings hidden. "It's a murder, Mrs. Adler, and a particularly frustrating one at that, when the family is doing their best to keep me at arm's length."

"But that was not it." She studied his face. "You are calm and collected when you discuss your investigation. You are even"—a slight smile—"calm and collected when you discuss your annoyance with me. But you were angry when you were discussing your colleagues at Bow Street."

"They think the matter has been adequately explained away," he pointed out. "And I do not."

Mrs. Adler was silent a long moment. "And that was all?"

It took some effort to meet her eyes impassively. He had surprised himself by how much of his professional work he was willing to share with this unusual woman. But she wasn't entitled to his personal life.

"That was all. Now, I want to get a jump on the Wyatts, but before I go, was there anything else you could tell me about the maid? Anything she said to you that you haven't mentioned yet?"

Mrs. Adler frowned, shaking her head. "There was nothing. I've not even heard from her since . . ." She trailed off, her eyes growing suddenly wide. "Oh no."

Before Simon could ask what was wrong, Mrs. Adler had spun around and dashed back into the drawing room; she reappeared a moment later with a letter in her hand, already ripping open the seal even as she moved toward him. As she read it, her face grew pale. And when she lifted her eyes toward him, they were wide with horror.

"I told her to write me if there was anything else," Mrs. Adler whispered, holding the paper out to him. Simon took it slowly. "But her letter was mislaid yesterday. I did not . . ." She swallowed, blinking rapidly as she turned her head aside.

He looked down at the penciled lines of neat capital letters, feeling a vise clench around his chest.

DEAR MRS. ADLER,

I LEARNED SOMETHING THAT HAPPENED THE NIGHT SIR CHARLES DIED, AND YOU MUST KNOW IT RIGHT AWAY, BUT I CANNOT LEAVE THE HOUSE AS I HAVE BEEN SUDDENLY SICK, AND I AM SCARED TO WRITE IT DOWN IN CASE SOMEONE FINDS THIS BEFORE THOMAS CAN POST IT. I AM SORRY TO ASK YOU TO COME TO ME, BUT PLEASE, MRS. ADLER. IT IS VERY IMPORTANT.

RESPECTFULLY YOURS,

ELLEN COOK

"She knew something," Mrs. Adler whispered.

It took Simon a long moment to look up from the paper. "Yes," he agreed quietly.

"And she . . ." Mrs. Adler looked away, and he could see her swallow rapidly, as if she were about to be ill. "Do you think someone killed her for it?"

"Perhaps." Simon jammed his hat on his head, a sudden wave of anger washing through him. "Whatever happened, I shall find out." Mrs. Adler flinched at the fury in his voice, but he barely noticed. "If you will excuse me."

He was nearly at the door when she spoke, her voice smaller and more pained than he had ever heard it before. "Would she still be alive, do you think, if I had read her letter sooner?"

Simon turned back slowly. Mrs. Adler stood in the middle of the hallway, her hands clenched into fists by her sides, chin up and cheeks pale as she regarded him steadily.

"There's no way of knowing," he said, surprising himself with how gentle his voice sounded. "But I do know one thing, madam— whatever happened, you aren't the one responsible. And I intend to find whoever is."

Mrs. Adler nodded, her mouth trembling. "That is two things," she pointed out softly, attempting a smile, though the effort failed. Simon snorted. "Will you tell me what you discover?"

Another day he might have hesitated to agree. But he could still see her hands trembling, see the brittle stiffness of her shoulders and the guilt that filled her eyes.

Simon nodded. "I will. We'll find who is responsible for this. I promise."

★ ★ ★

"I do not know how you came to be here or to hear of our private affairs, but your presence is most unwelcome."

Simon raised his brows. "Mr. Wyatt, your father has been murdered. And now there has been a second death in your home not even a week later. These are no longer your private affairs. I would like to see the body and the room where she was found."

"The girl became ill and died, sir. It is a tragedy, but not out of the ordinary for the lower classes. They often suffer from poor health."

"Nevertheless."

Frank glanced at the clock, then shook his head. "I am afraid I have other matters to attend to at the moment." He ran an agitated hand through his hair. Then, changing tactics, he offered Simon a wan smile, as if hoping for sympathy. "My father's affairs require a great deal of attention. It isn't as if he had time to put them in order."

"Of course, Mr. Wyatt. I'm happy to show myself down to the servants' hall and ask questions without you accompanying me."

"No, that . . . No." Frank Wyatt's mouth drew into a thin line of irritation. The skin under his eyes was dark with fatigue, and his movements seemed jittery, as though he didn't quite know what to do with his hands and feet. "Wait here," he sighed. "I will see what can be arranged."

"Certainly," Simon said, forcing himself to be polite even in the face of the young man's hostility.

Frank Wyatt returned sooner than Simon had expected, accompanied by a somberly dressed man carrying a large black bag and holding his hat in his hand. His white hair was thinning on top, and his face was creased with a web of cheerful lines. He stood deferentially behind Mr. Wyatt as he entered before stepping forward to shake Simon's hand.

"Mr. Page of Bow Street? How do you do? I'm Dr. Shaw. I understand from Mr. Wyatt that you have some concerns regarding the young girl's death?"

"Indeed." Simon planted his feet wide, his expression stern. He had a great deal of respect for professional men, but Dr. Shaw's posture was too subservient for his taste. It put him on edge. "Given that one murder took place in this house so recently"—out of the corner of his eye, Simon saw Frank Wyatt flinch—"I'm sure you can understand why I'm suspicious of any death occurring so soon afterwards."

"Certainly, certainly." Dr. Shaw nodded, glancing a moment at Frank before continuing. "However, it seems that this particular death is little more than a random act of God. The girl, according to the housekeeper, suffered from some distress of the stomach yesterday and again this morning. Nothing too severe, but enough pain that after the morning's work, she was very fatigued. Mrs. Harris—a very competent woman," he added, beaming. "A most excellent house-keeper, I am sure—Mrs. Harris sent her to bed. An hour later, the girl suffered from intense pain in the stomach and chest, along with a gasping shortness of breath. She died shortly afterwards."

"Poor girl," said Frank, covering his eyes as he turned away. He went to the window and stared out, one hand on the wall, as if his mind were a million miles away. But Simon had the impression he was still listening closely to what was being said.

Simon kept his eyes on the doctor and his thoughts off his face. "And what was your diagnosis, doctor?"

Dr. Shaw sighed. "In a case like this, one usually thinks of a prob-lem with the food. But Mrs. Harris tells me the girl had not yet had her half day this week, nor been out of the house for errands. Every-thing she ate would have also been eaten by the rest of the staff, and no one else showed any signs of distress or illness. One often sees these symptoms—the pain, the illness in the stomach, the difficulty breathing—when there is trouble with the heart."

Simon didn't bother trying to hide his surprise. "I spoke to this girl, Ellen, just the other day. She couldn't have been older than twenty."

"Twenty-two," Frank Wyatt put in, still looking out the window. "Still."

"It is rare but not unheard of, even in a person so young. And Mr. Wyatt tells me that this girl—Ellie, you said her name was?"

Simon could barely keep the anger from his face. For the doctor to not even remember the name of the person he had examined was infuriating. But Shaw continued, apparently unaware or unashamed of his own lack of concern.

"Mr. Wyatt informs me that she was often sickly." Dr. Shaw shook his head. "Medicine has made incredible advances, Constable, but so much of the human body remains a mystery to us."

Mr. Wyatt had said Ellen was sickly. But Simon wondered what the other servants might have to say about it. "Thank you, Doctor. Mr. Wyatt, I would like to speak to the other servants, particularly Ellen's brother. I believe his name was Thomas?"

Mr. Wyatt turned from the window at last. "I am afraid you will have to return tomorrow, Mr. Page. Thomas has been given leave to accompany his sister's body. He left with the undertaker and curate."

Simon hissed in a surprised breath, stunned by their audacity in having removed the body before a policeman even arrived. "When was this?"

"They kindly waited until I had finished my examination," Dr. Shaw said, smiling gently. "As I concluded there was no need for an inquest, there was likewise no need to delay."

Simon hoped the grinding of his teeth wasn't audible. "Very well, Doctor, thank you." He waited to speak again until the kindly, unhelpful old man gave his sympathies to the master of the house once more and departed. "Mr. Wyatt, you have said you were home all day, is that correct?"

"It is. I have spent my time going through my father's papers."

"And have you been down to the kitchens or the servants' quarters at all?"

"Of course not. I can only imagine how in the way I would be down there."

"Can anyone confirm that?"

Frank raised his brows, surprised. "Any number of servants. I never go belowstairs, so my presence down there would certainly be marked. You may ask them, if you like."

Simon regarded him silently for a long moment, his own expression giving nothing away. Captain Hartley still had not discovered, one way or another, whether Frank was telling the truth about his movements the night his father died. But now, as then, he met Simon's eyes with perfect ease. He was either a superb liar or he was telling the truth. And Simon was determined to find out which it was.

"Has your cousin been by at all today?"

"Percy?" Frank looked surprised, then frowned in thought. "He was here this morning, if I recall. It is a little hard to keep track of the days at the moment. Everything feels so strange. But I think it was this morning that he wanted to see my brother." He lowered his voice. "We are all doing our best to keep an eye on him these days. Just in case, of course."

The back of Simon's neck prickled. "Just in case?"

Frank looked uncomfortable. "Of course, none of us believe these rumors that Arthur was responsible for my father's death. People will say anything. But . . . it is hard to shake the thought once it has been put in one's head, wouldn't you say?"

Simon wondered whether Frank had brought up the rumors so that he might tell the constable not to believe them or to make sure that the constable had heard them and was taking them into account. But he let none of his thoughts show on his face as Mr. Wyatt continued.

"And now with Ellen gone, we shall need to decide how to look after Arthur properly. It is a tricky business. And distressing, on top of everything else that has happened."

"How would you describe your relationship with your brother, Mr. Wyatt?"

Frank hesitated, then sighed. "To be quite honest, sir, it would be a stretch to say we have one. Arthur, as far as I can tell, lives in his own world. And it is not one into which I am invited. I will do my duty by him, of course, for my father's sake, but it is rather hard to love someone who doesn't even seem to know you are there."

"If there are rumors that Arthur might have been responsible for your father's death, do you think he might be responsible for Ellen's death as well?" Simon didn't for a moment think there was a chance of that, but he wanted to see how Frank would react.

The younger man stilled, looking suddenly nervous. "If he hurt one person . . . No." He shook his head firmly. "There was no sign that anyone was responsible for Ellen's death. She became unwell, and she died. It was a deep tragedy, but there it is."

"And what does Lady Wyatt think of the matter?"

"I believe she is yet unaware of Ellen's death. She has been staying with her family in Hans Town for the past two nights." Frank grimaced. "I imagine she will soon be moving back there permanently."

"Since she received so little from your father's will?"

"What do you know of my father's will?" When Simon said nothing but merely raised an eyebrow, Frank sighed. "Well, in any case, yes. They had no children, so my father wasn't obligated to provide for her beyond a small maintenance. It is plenty for a widow to live on, I am sure. And I cannot imagine it will matter for long." He shrugged. "A woman like Lady Wyatt can find any number of suitors."

"And what did Mr. Percy Wyatt think of your father's will?"

"You would have to ask Percy that," Frank said, his voice suddenly stiff. "He has not shared his feelings with me. Was that all? I have a busy day ahead of me yet."

★ ★ ★

"Lily, we have a call to pay."

Lily glanced up from her book, shocked to find her father waiting in the doorway of the book-room, dressed for visiting in his ever-present black and gray, his hat in hand. He cast a critical glance over her own clothes, a pretty afternoon gown of pale blue.

"That will do, I suppose. If you have a black spencer or shawl, though, that would be far more polite for a condolence call."

"A what?"

He scowled. "I need to pay a call on Frank to discuss several matters concerning Sir Charles's will. And as you are now acquainted with Lady Wyatt, it would be deeply insulting if you failed to accompany me."

Lily, still distracted by her distress over Ellen's death, struggled to keep her irritation in check. "Did it occur to you that I might have plans for the afternoon?"

"Do you?"

Jack had left with Jem shortly after Mr. Page departed, wanting to see if he and the boy could learn anything else at the Wyatts' house. Lily and Ofelia had waited as long as they could for the Bow Street Runner to return, but eventually Ofelia had felt she must depart. And Lily had been left pacing on her own, wondering what the others were discovering without her.

"No," she was forced to admit.

"Well, then. I will wait in the front hall for you. You shouldn't need more than five minutes to ready yourself."

He left the room before she could protest further. And, other than on principle against her father's high-handedness, she didn't really want to.

If Mr. Pierce was paying a condolence call, that gave Lily an opportunity she had no intention of passing up.

★   ★   ★

"The inquest into my father's death has returned its expected verdict, of course." Frank sighed, settling back into a chair. "It seems we must be resigned to this Mr. Page doing his poking and prying."

"Ruffians and upstarts." Mr. Pierce sniffed. "I cannot understand how it has become so commonplace for them to meddle in the business of their betters."

Lily, perched on the edge of her chair, clenched her jaw to stop herself from uttering anything unwise. She kept her gaze fixed on Frank Wyatt, not wanting to imagine what her expression would look like if she turned it on her father.

Frank's own expression as he leaned forward was as serious as she had ever seen it. "They have at least given us permission to proceed with my father's burial, so we will be leaving as soon as we can for Devon. I wanted to speak to you before we go. As one of the trustees responsible for overseeing my brother's welfare, sir, I need your advice. There have been some . . . troubling rumors."

"Yes, of course. I am happy to give whatever advice I might be able to offer," Mr. Pierce said, his expression grim. "Though perhaps . . ." He gave Lily a sideways glance.

"Ah, indeed." Frank looked a little flustered. "Another time, if you think—"

Lily was about to protest—she wanted to hear what Frank might say about his brother—when Mr. Pierce continued. "Perhaps Lily might seek out Lady Wyatt while we have a more private discussion? Since her presence was of so much comfort before."

"I should not like to be the reason you delay seeking my father's advice," Lily said quickly, trying to sound sympathetic rather than eager. As much as she wanted to stay, an excuse to leave the room and see if she could find the housekeeper was even better. "I am happy to see if I may be of assistance to Lady Wyatt once more."

Frank hesitated again, then nodded. "Indeed, perhaps you may. Lady Wyatt just returned from her mother's house, and she is . . ." His mouth twisted into a grimace. "Well, however she is feeling, she has not cared to inform me." He sighed. "She was not satisfied with the way my father left his estate. I know she and my father were fond of each other, but I cannot help but be pained by how very mercenary she appeared when the will was read."

"I am sure, Frank, that no matter how much you loved your father, you would be distressed had he not provided for you after his death," Lily pointed out. Her voice came out a little sharper than she'd meant it to.

"Now, Lily, you've no idea how Sir Charles settled things, and it is not your business to know," Mr. Pierce said, giving her a pointed look as he claimed the most comfortable chair in the room. "Frank, pour us a drink, lad. I shall be happy to help how I can." He waved a dismissive hand. "Lily, you run along and take care of all that feminine nonsense."

It took all Lily's willpower to maintain her bland, polite mask, though it was of some comfort that Frank looked embarrassed on her behalf. "If you will give me a moment, Lily, I will be happy to summon a maid to escort you to her."

"No need." Lily rose. "I remember the way to Lady Wyatt's chambers. And if your staff are preparing for a trip to Devon, I am sure they have more than enough to keep them occupied. I shall be able to manage on my own."

The low murmur of their voices followed her out of the room. Neither of them watched her go, so Lily paused just on the other side of the door, holding it open the barest amount. It was just long enough for her to hear Frank say, his voice pained, "I am sure he did not understand what he was doing. But what are we to do?"

She closed the door before she could hear her father's answer.

★　★　★

A detour of about fifteen minutes, Lily decided, would be manageable. Frank and her father wouldn't be done before that, and the likelihood that Frank and Lady Wyatt would speak to each other long enough to compare notes on her activity was almost nonexistent.

It wasn't much time, but it should give her a chance to slip downstairs and find Mrs. Harris, the one who had sent the message that she was suspicious about Ellen's death and the woman most likely to notice anything strange going on in the house.

The housekeeper's room was usually near the servants' hall. In a townhouse like this one, it was likely downstairs, and the easiest way down there would be the servants' stairs. Those were generally found at the back of the house, and as Lily left the front parlor where her father and Frank were talking, she headed that way. But before she got far, the sound of footsteps in the front hall caught her attention.

Footsteps in a townhouse weren't remarkable; the Wyatts, unlike her, kept a large staff on the premises. But these steps hesitated, clicking unevenly across the tile of the foyer, then suddenly becoming rapid before they became the muffled thumps of someone heading upstairs. Curious, Lily peered back around the corner and caught a glimpse of Wilkes, Lady Wyatt's personal maid, going upstairs.

For servants to use the main staircase would have raised Lily's eyebrows, but a lady's maid enjoyed a certain privileged position in the household due to her intimacy with the lady of the house. Lily wouldn't have found the sight of Wilkes on the front stairs too strange were it not for the way she moved: hesitant, a little hunched, glancing over her shoulder, then hiking up her skirts to ascend rapidly out of sight.

Lily bit her lip, momentarily torn, before making up her mind. The carpeted stairs muffled her own steps as she followed after the lady's maid.

If Wilkes had looked back, Lily would simply have asked for directions to Lady Wyatt's rooms, where she was supposed to be heading anyway. But the lady's maid, now that she had made it to the top of the stairs, didn't look back. Instead of turning toward her mistress's rooms, she went the other direction.

Wilkes walked decisively toward a room halfway down the hall before turning back to glance on more time over her shoulder. Lily stayed at the top of the stairs, shielded from view by a tall, ostentatiously gilded armoire. If she remembered correctly from her first visit, that was the door to Sir Charles's study.

The hallway carpet muffled Lily's footfalls as she made her way toward the door. Hanging back just out of sight, she could hear the sounds of drawers opening and closing, paper rustling, and an occasional quiet curse. And when she inched forward just enough to peer around the edge of the door, she found Wilkes flipping through the papers on Sir Charles's desk, looking through any drawer she could open and cursing the ones that were locked.

"Where did you put it, you damned miser?" she muttered, just barely loud enough for Lily to hear. Though her movements were as careful and quiet as she could manage while ransacking the desk, there was a frantic edge to them.

And apparently she couldn't find what she wanted. Bracing her arms against the edge of the dark wood, she let out a shaky, frustrated sigh. She glanced at the clock ticking mercilessly on the wall before straightening her spine and turning toward the glass-fronted book-cases that lined the wall.

Lily backed away, frowning in thought and unable to come up with an explanation. But according to the clock in the study, she had been gone from the drawing room for three minutes already. It was time to find the housekeeper.

She had previously noted the narrow, nondescript door at the end of the hall; a quick peek through it showed her that it was indeed the servants' stair. Lily slipped inside and was about to make her way belowstairs when she heard soft voices coming from farther up.

She knew one of those voices. Frowning, Lily changed direction and made her way up to the third floor as silently and quickly as possible.

The stairway was empty by the time she gained the top, but the door leading out into the hall was still swinging gently. Lily made her way out, glancing around as she did. This space clearly wasn't used as much; it had none of the comfort of the second floor, where the family's private rooms were located, or the ostentatious decor that was intended to impress visitors. The third floor was where children's rooms would be; above that were attics, which could be used either for storage or for servants' rooms, depending on the size of the staff and the number of rooms belowstairs.

Lily paused, listening until she heard quiet voices from one of the rooms at the end of the hall. She didn't try to hide her approach, not wanting to startle the people she knew would be waiting there. Instead she quietly whistled a well-known sailor's song that had recently made its way into the popular song sheets that hawkers sold for a penny.

The voices fell suddenly silent, and then a curly-haired head poked out of the doorway.

"Missus Adler!" Jem whispered, glancing past her down the hall to make sure there was no one else there before beckoning her to hurry. "Thought my heart was going to leap out o' my chest afore the captain said it was you. In here!"

Lily gave him an apologetic smile, placing a hand briefly on his shoulder before she slid past him into the room. Inside, Jack grinned at her, one finger on his lips.

"Thank you for warning of your approach," he said quietly. "Our little scalawag has been hanging around the kitchens enough to win over the estimable Mrs. Harris, and he convinced her that I am a man to be trusted. She agreed to sneak us up here to look around. This is Mrs. Adler," he added, turning to the woman who was watching them with barely concealed nerves.

The housekeeper was dressed severely in a stiff gray gown, her thinning hair pulled tidily back under a white cap. Her face was drawn and tense as she glanced nervously between Jack and Lily. Jack's introduction made her relax fractionally, though she still eyed Lily with wary skepticism.

"You're the one as helped Thomas? That Ellen went to?"

Lily closed her eyes briefly, fighting back a surge of guilt as she remembered Ellen's hesitant trust, her determination to protect her charge. "I am."

"Begging your pardon, ma'am, but you don't look like someone as can do much to help us."

"I shall at least listen, which is more than you can say for many of the people in this house," Lily said, looking around.

The room they were in was a bedroom, in the spot near the schoolroom and nursery that would normally be given to the nanny or governess. Lily knew there was no one in either of those positions in the household, but the room was still fitted up as a bedroom, with the austere linens and old furniture of a servant's room. Unlike most servant's rooms, however, there was only one bed, a luxury of privacy.

"I assume this was Ellen's room?"

Mrs. Harris nodded. "She slept up here near Master Arthur, so she could be close by in case he needed her in the night." She glanced nervously toward the door. "If you please, we shouldn't stay up here long. No one comes up here much, and the head housemaid took

Master Arthur to sit in the garden—he likes to draw out there—but there's no knowing when they'll be back."

The housekeeper spoke calmly enough, but her hands twisted nervously in the folds of her apron.

"We shall be quick as we can," Lily promised. "Jem, will you keep an eye out?"

He gave her a quick salute, then scampered out the door.

Jack was standing near enough to give Lily's arm a quick, comforting squeeze before he turned back to survey the room. "I had just started going through her things," he said, gesturing toward the dresser, which had three drawers and a washbasin on top. Next to it on the floor, a tattered valise was open enough to show a pile of old books, mostly novels and histories. On the wall, two pegs held a cloak and apron. "Shall I continue?"

"And I will examine the bed and nightstand," Lily agreed, moving in that direction.

"What are you looking for?" Mrs. Harris whispered, shadowing them, still nervous.

"We shan't know until we see it." Lily tossed back the linens of the bed, which were old and worn but pristinely clean, then crouched down to peer at the floor underneath. "Anything out of place. Anything surprising."

"Not much to go through," Jack said, his voice equally quiet, while he searched the drawers.

"Do you notice anything that strikes you as odd, Mrs. Harris?" Lily asked, standing and dusting off her skirts while she eyed the sparse room.

The housekeeper turned in a circle, her mouth drawn into a thin, frustrated line. "Nothing. And there was nothing Ellen said or did that . . ." She sighed, clearly frustrated, and Lily could see tears in her eyes. "She just went so sudden-like. It didn't seem natural. And what with Sir Charles being killed, and folks spreading rumors about Master Arthur . . ." She swallowed, her voice growing hoarse. "The doctor said young people's hearts can give out all of a sudden, same as old folks'. But I just can't quite credit it."

"Tell me how it happened."

Lily listened with half an ear while the housekeeper related to them how Ellen's complaints had grown more severe from one day to the next, until she was in agony during the hours before she died. When Mrs. Harris fell silent, she glanced over to find Jack looking at her.

"That sounds more like . . ." He hesitated.

"Poison?" Lily held back a shudder.

"But she never ate or drank anything but what anyone else did," Mrs. Harris pointed out. "I don't see how it could have happened."

"But you still thought something was odd?" Lily asked.

"Something just felt wrong. And with Mr. Wyatt giving her body to the undertaker before them Bow Street men could even look around . . ." Mrs. Harris shivered. "Why would someone do such a thing?"

"Do you remember Ellen doing anything odd the day after Sir Charles's death? Or the day after that?"

The housekeeper frowned. "Not that I can . . . well, yes, as a matter of fact. I saw her coming out of the library at one point. And I don't think it struck me at the time, because I'm so used to seeing maids go in and out to clean throughout the day. But Ellen's duties shouldn't have taken her in there." She glanced between Lily and Jack, wringing her hands. "Why would she do that, do you think?"

Lily had stopped searching while the housekeeper spoke; now she shivered, glancing at Jack. "She was looking for something, perhaps."

"Or someone thought she was," Jack added. "Maybe she saw something the night Sir Charles died. Or heard something afterwards."

"Or maybe someone only thought she did and feared exposure," Lily agreed. She finished with the bed and turned to the nightstand. The drawer was empty, while the top held a candle and a tattered volume of the *Encyclopaedia Britannica*.

"Was there anyone Ellen might have confided in?" Jack asked, turning back to his examination of the maid's things.

Mrs. Harris shook her head. "If she didn't tell her brother nothing, I can't imagine who else she'd have whispered secrets to. She didn't have much time to spend with the other staff her age, not since she moved up here and took over with Master Arthur. She and Edie—another of the housemaids—was good friends, once upon a time. But Edie left over a year ago. I don't know where she's ended up."

"And what did Ellen's brother think of her death?" Jack asked.

"The poor boy was too shocked to think anything at all, I fear. He hasn't said a word since she died except that he'll be taking his letter of character and going home. Wants to be there to comfort his mother." Mrs. Harris sighed, looking at the book in Lily's hands. "She liked reading, our Ellen did. Wanted to learn everything."

"She sounds like she was a clever girl," Jack said gently, closing the last drawer and standing. He glanced at Lily and shook his head. Nothing odd to report.

"She was. Spent what she could on books but saved most of her wages to send to her parents. She and Thomas come from Devonshire, like most of the staff."

The look Lily gave Jack was torn between sadness and anger. She didn't for a moment believe Ellen's death had been an accident, not coming so soon after Sir Charles's. But if the doctor had declared it due to natural causes, there would be no inquest, no investigation. And Ellen's family—a brother in service, relatives in another county—would be unable to press for more.

She set the book down and was about to ask the housekeeper another question when a mark on the top of the nightstand caught her eye.

The furniture in the room had likely been gathered piecemeal, some of it from sellers of secondhand goods, other items from family or guest rooms once they had become too worn. The nightstand was well made, but its finish was nicked and dented, with several long scratches across its top. Against the marred surface, a single circle stood out, the mark of a drinking glass set down one too many times in nearly the same spot.

It was possible that the mark had been made when the table was in another room. That could have been why it was moved here, to a maid's room. But if it had been made by Ellen . . .

Lily could picture her reading at night, her candle burning and a glass next to her bed. A glass none of the other staff would have drunk from, that it would have been easy for someone to remove from the room with no one the wiser.

Bending closer, she held her breath and put her eyes level with the top of the nightstand. There was nothing there.

But when she pulled out the drawer and looked closely, the inside edge, just under where the glass would have been, held a faint trace of white powder.

Lily straightened abruptly, glad she had been holding her breath and that she hadn't taken off her gloves.

"What is it?" Jack asked, touching her arm as he came to stand by her side.

Lily glanced sharply down at his hands, suddenly afraid. But he still wore his gloves as well. She breathed a sigh of relief and pointed wordlessly at the edge of the nightstand, noticing as she did so that her hand was shaking.

It was one thing to be suspicious of Ellen's death; it was another matter entirely to be confronted with what was likely evidence that someone had callously murdered her. Someone who didn't care that she would die in confusion and pain.

"Careful," Lily whispered as Jack bent over just far enough to see the powder before he, too, stepped quickly back.

They stared at each other, wide-eyed.

"What is it?" Mrs. Harris asked, peering over their shoulders.

Jack, after one glance at Lily's stricken face, took charge of the situation. With a gentle hand on Mrs. Harris's shoulder, he steered the housekeeper toward the door. Lily, her skin crawling, followed.

"It might not be safe in here," Jack said, quietly and urgently. "It looks like you were right and that Ellen was poisoned. But we cannot be sure until Mr. Page of Bow Street has returned. He can seek out a chemist who will be able to tell him one way or another."

"In the meantime, do *not* let your staff in there, not to clean or to fetch any of Ellen's things. Not even her brother," Lily said, pulling the door firmly shut behind her.

"What . . . what do you think it was?" Mrs. Harris said, glancing from one of them to the other.

It seemed too awful to voice her suspicions out loud. But the housekeeper had risked her position to let them look around. She deserved some kind of answer.

Every few years, the papers reported one gruesome story or another about poisoning deaths. Lily could remember three since she and Freddy first married: a woman who murdered her husband because she wanted to marry another man; a servant in the country who unwittingly prepared dinner using water from a rocky spring and ended up killing an entire family; an old man who was slowly poisoned by the green dye in the wallpaper of his bedroom.

The writers of such stories focused on the sensational nature of the deaths. But even they had to admit that there was a single poison so commonly found, so easy for a murderer to use, that the real surprise was that it wasn't used more often.

Lily swallowed and tried to make her voice as steady as possible. "Do you keep white arsenic in the house?"

Mrs. Harris's eyes grew wide, and she raised a hand to her mouth, then pressed it against her heart. "For rats," she whispered, looking as ill as Lily felt. "It's kept in the storeroom."

"Who has access to it?" Lily asked.

The housekeeper's voice was faint as she replied. "The upper staff, mostly. And Lady Wyatt has keys, of course. Sir Charles had one, but I don't know where his ended up."

Jack put a steadying hand on the woman's arm. "We ought not to linger here," he said, gesturing for Jem to return from his lookout a few doors down the hall.

"I have to go in search of Lady Wyatt," Lily said, wishing for nothing more than to go home and rage in private. The cruelty of Ellen's death almost took her breath away—even more so because the murderer clearly expected that the death of a housemaid, however odd, would go unremarked and unexamined. And it might have had it not been for the housekeeper.

Lily glanced at Jack, grateful for his steadying presence. "Captain, will you go immediately to Bow Street and find Mr. Page?"

"After I take Mrs. Harris back downstairs."

Mrs. Harris straightened, her chin taking on a firm, almost mulish set. Clearly, as horrified as she had been, she was not a woman to be easily cowed. "I'll be sure the staff stays away. And if you tell that man from Bow Street to come to the kitchen door on the southwest corner of the house rather than the front door, I'll see that he's brought up here."

Lily nodded. "Thank you for your trust in us, Mrs. Harris. We will do our best with what you have helped us learn." She turned to leave, then stopped. "By the way, what do you know of any repairs that were supposed to be done to the house?"

★ ★ ★

Once the others disappeared down the servants' stair, Lily had to run. Glancing around to make sure there was no one else in the hall, she hurried down toward the second floor, trying to move quickly without making too much noise. The stairs between the second and third floors, going as they did into the more remote part of the house, were not carpeted. Her slippers were soft, but her rushed steps still felt too loud in the chill silence of the house. When she finally gained the second floor, she didn't pause, turning the corner and trying to slow both her breathing and her steps.

But she was still panting as she found herself face-to-face with Lady Wyatt, whose eyebrows rose as she approached the stairs and found Lily coming down rather than—as a guest should have been—going up.

"Mrs. Adler." Lady Wyatt stared at her in amazement. "What were you doing up there?"

CHAPTER 18

"You are too kind to call on me once again, Mrs. Adler." Lady Wyatt's rich voice was heavy with grief and fatigue as Lily took a seat by the window, but the sentiment seemed genuine enough.

Though her expression had been frankly skeptical at first, she had seemed to accept Lily's explanation that she had become lost while coming upstairs—"Not very well done of Frank, to neglect sending a servant to show you the way. But then, I suppose we are all a little distracted these days." Now they were settled into the small sitting room that attached to Lady Wyatt's bedroom. Lily schooled her face into polite sympathy, hoping that the hectic pace of her heartbeat was noticeable only to her and trying to tuck away her anger over Ellen's death to face when she was alone once more.

"I hope you will convey my apologies to your father that I am unable to receive him," Lady Wyatt continued. "One day I should dearly love to make Mr. Pierce's acquaintance. Sir Charles always spoke so highly of him, though I rather got the impression that they were as much rivals as they were friends."

The day was cloudy outside, and heavy with the dust stirred up by the innumerable feet, carriages, and carts passing below. But there was enough sunlight coming through the glass panes to make the corner of Lady Wyatt's room in which they were seated a pleasant enough place to linger. She was dressed in mourning, with a black silk shawl around her shoulders, upright and regal as ever. But the untouched tea service before her and the crumpled edge of her shawl—as if she had been unconsciously pleating and unpleating it while she sat—made Lily suspect that Lady Wyatt's thoughts were in far more turmoil than her outward appearance.

"I am not sure my father knows how to have any other kind of friendship," Lily said, pulling her thoughts back to the conversation. "Though what they had to compete over, I could not tell you. Mr. Wyatt told us you were lately with your mother?"

"I think you will not be surprised, Mrs. Adler, if I say that I have not felt entirely comfortable here since my husband's . . . death." Lady Wyatt's voice quavered a little.

Lily waited a moment, then prodded gently, watching Lady Wyatt out of the corner of her eye for any cracks in the facade of her grief. "Do you feel unwelcome? Or something else?"

Lady Wyatt smiled sadly. "Unwelcome, certainly. I am sure you can imagine that Frank is . . ." Her lips tightened. "Well, he has always only barely tolerated me. But there is . . ."

"But there is more to it than that," Lily suggested. "It is not unreasonable, ma'am. I can only imagine how terrified I would be to live in a home where someone I love had been slain."

Lady Wyatt took a deep breath, gathering her composure once more. "Frank assures me that no one in this household could have done such a thing. But two days ago, I left because I could not shake the feeling that someone here had . . ."

"Forgive me, but are you saying you think Frank—that is, Mr. Wyatt—are you saying you think he could have harmed his father?"

"Frank? No, of course . . . that is . . ." Lady Wyatt frowned, as if reconsidering, while one hand rose slowly to her heart. Then it fell as she shook her head. "Little as I like him, Mrs. Adler, I could never see him raising a hand against his father. No, it is just a feeling . . ." She shivered and broke off. "I never thought I would say it, but I shall be glad to return to my mother's home in Hans Town." She smiled sadly. "I had once hoped never to go back there. But I've no wish to stay here any longer. I have returned only to pack my things. After Sir Charles's funeral, I'll not come back again."

"I am sorry to hear it," Lily said quietly.

"I am not." Lady Wyatt's tone had a sudden bitter briskness. "I shan't have to see these boys anymore. I shan't have to deal with that impertinent man from Bow Street." Her expression grew a little wily. "I have heard a rumor, Mrs. Adler, that you were acquainted with these constables."

Lily's heart sped up again, but all she said, as calmly as possible, was, "I told you as much, if you recall."

"Yes. But was standing by your friend all there was to it?" Lady Wyatt's gaze was verging on accusatory.

Lily, weighing her options, decided that outright denial was dangerous without knowing what Lady Wyatt had heard. Instead, she took a deep breath, affecting unconcern as she poured herself another cup of tea. "Rumors are odd things, ma'am. For example, I heard a rumor that you lied to the constable, that you and Sir Charles had a terrible quarrel the day he died."

Lady Wyatt's gasp was nearly a hiss. "Who said such things?"

"Rumor, as you said. It creeps in everywhere. Perhaps the servants heard shouting? Or perhaps one of them mentioned that you did not spend the evening with your husband as you claimed."

"It was not . . . Charles might have shouted some . . . but you know how men are . . ." Lady Wyatt trailed off, then swallowed, her eyes darting around the room before coming to rest on Lily once more. "I was not *lying*," she insisted, tears springing up in her eyes. "Yes, we had a small argument that evening, and I went to bed early. I cannot bear that we had been fighting just before he died, and over something so stupid, and now there is no chance of resolving it."

Lily sipped her tea, trying to look sympathetic. "If it was a small argument, I am sure it is nothing you need feel guilt over leaving unresolved," she said, her voice soothing. "Surely it could not have been that bad. What was it about?"

Lady Wyatt's fingers fiddled with the fringe of her shawl. "I barely even remember. Something about leaving for Devonshire sooner than we had planned. With everything that has happened, it has truly flown from my mind."

"There, you see?" Lily's quiet voice gave away none of her thoughts. But she remembered what Mr. Page had said. *Unnatural*, Mrs. Harris had heard Sir Charles yell. *Disgusted.* That didn't sound like a small argument over leaving London. "Doubtless he had forgiven you before you even made your way upstairs."

Lady Wyatt sighed. "I am sure you are right."

Lily eyed the other woman, hesitating. But she forced herself to ask the question, though she kept her voice as gentle as she could. "Did you love him?"

Lady Wyatt drew in a sharp breath. But there was no judgment on Lily's face, and Lady Wyatt's shoulders slumped. She pressed her hands to her eyes, and for a moment her shoulders shook. Then she lifted her face, and her expression was so calm and regretful that it made Lily's heart ache. "No. I respected him. I enjoyed his company. I think he loved me, and when he asked me to marry him, I hoped I would grow to love him too. It seemed like it would have been enough. And I didn't know what I was to live on otherwise." Her voice grew a little defensive. "Half the women in England are equally mercenary in their marriages."

"At least half," Lily agreed. "You at least felt fondness for the man you wed. But I wonder if that has also increased your measure of grief and guilt, knowing that you did not love him as he loved you."

Lady Wyatt flinched, as if she wanted to turn away from Lily's steady gaze but wouldn't let herself. "Yes," she said quietly. "I suppose it has."

"And I wonder—" Lily broke off as a clamoring noise arose in the hall outside, shouts and the sound of crying. She and Lady Wyatt both stared at the door, alarmed.

"What in the world?" Lady Wyatt's expression suddenly grew closed off and irritated. "Can there not be any peace in this house?"

she said, rising suddenly and crossing the room to throw the door open.

Lily followed, bemused, and found a heartbreaking scene. A young boy was sitting in the middle of the hallway, his legs crossed under him, his hands over his ears while he repeated, "No, no, *no*," at the top of his lungs. A frantic maid hovered around him, tugging on his arm and trying to pull him upright. As Lady Wyatt stormed onto the scene, the maid redoubled her efforts.

"Now see, Master Arthur, you're disturbing folks, you are. It's time to go upstairs. We've had a nice time outside, but—"

"No, no, *no*," the boy sobbed, shaking his head and pulling away from her clutching hands.

Lady Wyatt glared at the scene in front of her. "Can you please control him?" she snapped, pressing a hand against her temples. "All this racket is going to bring on a headache."

"Begging your pardon, Lady Wyatt, but you know what he's like when he's in one of his moods." The maid grabbed Arthur's arm again, tugging, but he snatched it away.

"Don't *touch*," he sobbed. "I want Ellen to come back."

"I told you, Master Arthur, Ellen can't come back, and we all miss her, but—"

"Just get one of the footmen to carry him up if you can't handle him yourself," Lady Wyatt said. "And don't bother trying to explain things; he'll never—"

"He is upset, madam. Give the poor boy a moment, please."

Lily had been so focused on watching Lady Wyatt and Arthur, unsure what to do or if she could be of any help at all, that she had missed the arrival of Percy Wyatt, who now came rushing up the stairs and down the hall. But he slowed when he came near them.

Sparing the maid only a momentary, irritated glance, he ignored her anxious attempts to explain, pushing past to crouch next to Arthur. "And all of you stop yelling, please. You know he dislikes loud noises."

Lady Wyatt let out a loud sigh. "Then why is he making such a racket?"

Percy gave her an admonishing stare. "Because he is distressed. First his father and now his companion have died. Surely you can find it in your heart to be a little kinder. You, what's your name?" He turned on the maid, scowling.

"Mary, sir."

"Go away, Mary. I will take my cousin upstairs when he is ready."

The maid hovered anxiously for a moment more before seizing the opportunity to flee. Lily watched as Percy settled down next to Arthur and put his hand palm down on the floor, not otherwise moving or speaking. Once the hall was silent again, Arthur removed his hands from his ears and looked around. When his eyes fell on Percy, a look of relief spread over his face. A moment later, he placed his own hand on top of his cousin's.

"There now," Percy said gently. "What upset you so?"

Arthur glanced at his stepmother, then hunched his shoulders. "I want Ellen."

"I know," Percy said. Lily was surprised by how softly he spoke, no trace of the impatience he had shown the maid remaining. "She was a good friend."

"She was a good friend," Arthur repeated. He straightened for a moment, then hunched his shoulders once more, glancing at Percy anxiously. "Ellen says I'm to be quiet like a mouse," he whispered. "She told me all would be well if I was quiet like a mouse."

"Then pray do so," Lady Wyatt snapped. Arthur hunched his shoulders even further, a low, anxious hum beginning in his throat, and Lady Wyatt threw up her hands in exasperation. "Give him some of Frank's laudanum, if you must."

"He doesn't need laudanum," Percy said. "He needs patience." He glanced up, his irritated gaze settling on both Lady Wyatt and Lily. "You may withdraw, if you wish," he said. "I will stay with him."

Arthur shook his head, still humming. "Don't want to stay with Winnie."

"You do *not* have permission to call me that," Lady Wyatt snapped.

"Aunt," Percy warned.

"If I have not given you permission, I certainly have not given it to him!"

"*Aunt.*"

Lily watched the exchange, trying to keep her interest from her face. It seemed her father had been right when he advised Sir Charles that the new Lady Wyatt might be unhappy to learn she would be taking on the role of mother to a child like Arthur. It made Lily sad to watch, but it didn't surprise her. Too many women would have felt the same.

What did surprise her was Percy Wyatt's gentleness and competence with his cousin.

"Whenever you are ready, Arthur, we shall go upstairs." Percy glanced at his aunt. "You needn't worry about him bothering you again."

"I hope not," Lady Wyatt said stiffly. Turning, she gestured for Lily to precede her back into the room. Lily did so, glancing only briefly over her shoulder. Percy Wyatt still sat on the floor next to his cousin, apparently content to wait until he was ready to stand and go upstairs.

"I apologize for the scene." Lady Wyatt sighed once the door was closed. "He has become so unmanageable since his father's death." As they sat down once more, she sniffed. "*Quiet like a mouse.* One can only hope."

Lily contrived some reply, but she wasn't sure what she said. She was too distracted by the cold prickle of realization that was making its way down her spine.

Ellen says I'm to be quiet like a mouse.

She told me all would be well if I was quiet like a mouse.

Lily had been too distracted by watching the interplay of family dynamics to pay much heed to what Arthur said. But she had a sudden, horrible suspicion that he might just have revealed something important.

She had been assuming Ellen was killed because she had known something important, something the killer didn't want revealed. But if she had been warning her charge into silence, that meant she wasn't the only one with incriminating information.

Arthur had been the one to see or hear something dangerous. And whoever the killer in the family was, if they found out, Arthur would be in danger as well.

★   ★   ★

Lily wasn't sure how she made it through the rest of her visit with Lady Wyatt. When she finally received word that her father was ready to leave and was able to excuse herself, it was all she could do to bid farewell politely and follow him out the door, where Frank Wyatt had summoned his carriage to convey them home.

She was so caught up in her thoughts that she almost missed the forlorn figure making its way down the street. Excusing herself for just a moment, she stepped away from the groom who was waiting to hand her into the carriage.

"I shall only be a moment, Father."

Mr. Pierce grumbled as he allowed the groom to assist him to his seat instead but didn't try to stop her.

Lily hesitated before putting herself in the approaching man's path.

"Thomas."

The footman looked up, his eyes red with grief as he stared at her blankly. "Madam?"

Lily took a deep breath. "We met briefly before. I am Mrs. Adler. And I wanted to tell you how truly sorry I am about your sister's death. She was a lovely young woman."

Thomas shuddered, his eyes closing briefly as he nodded. "Very kind of you to say, Mrs. Adler. I apologize for not recognizing you, but I remember what a help you were to me." He seemed lost for a moment, his gaze wandering to the house, before he recalled himself and looked back to her. "Thank you for the condolences."

He was waiting for her to step out of the way. Lily hesitated, wanting to leave him alone in his grief. But she wanted to find his sister's killer even more. "I am sorry to take up your time, Thomas; I know you must have many things to prepare for your return to Devonshire. But Mrs. Harris said your sister had a particular friend, Edie, who left for a new position. Is there any chance you know how to find her?"

"Edie?" Thomas's expression grew wary. "Begging your pardon, but what could you be wanting with Edie?"

He was tense, suddenly, in a way he hadn't been before when he was thinking only about his sister. Lily cast a glance at the groom, who was staring politely into the distance but wasn't too far away, and stepped closer to Thomas.

"Did your sister tell you she came to see me when she was worried for Master Arthur?"

She kept her voice low as she spoke, and Thomas followed her lead.

"She did." His eyes grew wide, shock piercing his grief. "Was she right? She'd never forgive me if I let something happen to him now she's gone."

"I think she might have been. And finding Edie could help me. Can you tell me who her new employer is?"

Thomas dropped his voice even further. "Edie didn't have a new employer, ma'am. Ellen told me Edie had to leave because she'd got in trouble and couldn't hide it any longer."

Lily caught her breath. "Do you know who the baby's father was?"

Thomas shook his head. "Edie kept it mum. All she would ever tell my sister was that it was one of the Wyatts."

★　★　★

"Which one of them do you think it could be?" Ofelia asked, scooting a glass of her husband's sherry across the table toward Lily, though she drank only tea herself.

"That is the question." Lily took a long drink before resuming her pacing around the room. She had given Thomas all the money in her purse before she left—"to help with the cost of taking her home," she insisted when he tried to protest—then suffered silently through the carriage ride home, listening with half an ear to her father's complaints about London traffic.

She couldn't call on Jack at his home, and it was too late in the afternoon to seek out Mr. Page. But Ofelia was glad to help her talk through the thorny details. And her father had been only too happy to hear that she was going to pay a call on the wealthy, connected Lady Carroway.

"And does the fact that one of the maids was in the family way actually change anything?"

"The answer to that, I think, depends on the first question." Lily stopped in front of the empty fireplace, her brows knit in thought. "We already know there is some woman in the question of Percy Wyatt, and that he has not been completely honest about his behavior."

"Which, if he were the father, could account for his nighttime excursions. You said he was surprisingly capable with his young cousin," Ofelia mused. "Perhaps he is easier with children than adults. In which case, he might be a caring father who is sneaking out at night to visit his onetime paramour and their love child."

Lily rolled her eyes at her friend. "You say that far too casually for a girl your age."

"I am a married lady now," Ofelia pointed out with pretend primness. "And you are the one who keeps lending me sensational novels."

"A fair point." Lily resumed her pacing. "So, if Percy is the father, that could exonerate him. Unless providing for his child was one of the reasons he was falling into debt. In which case he might be driven to murder in order to do so."

"But why not simply ask his uncle for assistance?"

Lily grimaced, stopping to take another drink. "So, if the child is Percy Wyatt's, that makes him less likely to be guilty. And I don't see how Frank being the father has bearing on it one way or another."

"Unless Sir Charles disapproved of his son's conduct. Or his nephew's," Ofelia said thoughtfully. "If he was a stickler like your father—they were friends, after all—he might have been disappointed enough to threaten to cut off either one of them. In which case, the baby's father might have killed him to protect his inheritance."

"But Frank's whereabouts are accounted for." Lily frowned. "Or nearly so. I don't know if Jack has succeeded in confirming that he was out all night."

"All right, then, what if Sir Charles was the father?" Ofelia made a face. "You are making me dizzy, you know, trying to watch you pace like that. Do old men do that sort of thing?"

"Frequently," Lily said, flopping down into a chair. Though both Ofelia and her husband were extraordinarily wealthy, they had chosen to rent a small townhouse near Hanover Square rather than share the family home with Sir Edward's mother and younger sisters. Lily was grateful that the arrangement allowed her and her friend to speak so freely. "And I have heard that Sir Charles was quite a skirt chaser, both when he was younger and when he was between wives." Remembering the gossiping ladies, she added slowly, "And I heard he might have an illegitimate child tucked away somewhere."

Ofelia sat up abruptly. "Could Lady Wyatt have killed him when she discovered that he had a natural son or daughter?"

Lily thought about Lady Wyatt's coolly regal bearing. "She doesn't strike me as the sort to object to her husband's amorous activities, so long as they occurred before he was courting her."

"And if they occurred after?"

"That would be another story entirely," Lily agreed. "And according to the maid Ellen, Lady Wyatt began refusing him her bed not long after they were married."

"Then we need to find this girl and determine when the babe was conceived."

"Someone does. If we can figure out where she has gone." Lily frowned, turning her now-empty glass between her fingers as she thought the matter through. "There is another possibility, if Sir Charles was the father. If he tossed her out when he found out she was pregnant . . . or if Edie was not a willing participant in their affair . . ."

Ofelia's eyes grew wide. "You think she might have been the one to kill him."

"It is not impossible."

Ofelia set down her teacup decisively. "Which makes it even more urgent that someone find out where she has gone."

★   ★   ★

Simon frowned at the papers on his desk. As one of the more experienced members of the Bow Street force, he had the use of his own office. But that experience didn't seem to be doing him much good this time.

He could feel Captain Hartley's eyes on him as he paced around the room, but to Simon's relief, his guest didn't say anything else after reporting what he and Mrs. Adler had discovered at the Wyatts' house. Instead, the navy captain leaned back in his chair, feet planted wide and hands clasped behind his head, silent but watchful.

Simon cleared his throat. "I'll send a chemist I trust to the house. He'll know how to recognize arsenic, and how to clean up the room so it's safe for the other servants." He paused by his desk, fiddling with the papers there and frowning. "But I don't want the Wyatts to know about it."

"I can have Jem introduce the chemist to the housekeeper," Hartley suggested. "She said she would let you come in by the kitchen to see Ellen's room—I assume that applies to your chemist as well."

"Good." But Simon's frown didn't move.

He had discussed the case with some of the other Runners— Simon's mouth twisted at the term, which none of the Bow Street force liked but the public insisted on using—and they all felt he was wasting his time. The family didn't want him interfering, they'd pointed out, and were uninterested in paying for his time and trouble. Better to focus on cases where the income was worthwhile and the investigation had some chance of success. And even the Bow Street magistrate he had consulted, Mr. Nares, was inclined to accept the explanation that young Arthur Wyatt was likely responsible for his father's murder.

"Poor child," Mr. Nares had said, shaking his head. "I'm sure he did not know what he was doing, but that does not change the facts of the matter. No doubt the family will find as pleasant an institution as possible where he can be secluded and kept from harming anyone else."

Simon didn't agree. But trying to force his way past the family's defenses felt like racing through a dark street only to find himself confronted by a brick wall at every turn. And then banging his head against that wall repeatedly.

Lady Wyatt had been home the night of her husband's murder. She'd had the opportunity to kill him. But she was not a large woman. As Mrs. Adler had pointed out, dragging the heavy body across the room without leaving any marks would have been almost impossible for her. And she had been gone from the house for two days, a fact confirmed by a quick conversation with the butler on his way out and a visit to Lady Wyatt's mother in Hans Town. She couldn't possibly be responsible for Ellen's death.

Frank Wyatt, with a significant fortune coming his way, had far more motive than Lady Wyatt to kill his father. And that might make him want to get rid of his brother. If Arthur were committed to an institution, Frank would have control of his share of the inheritance as well. And so far, Hartley hadn't been able to trace his movements the night of Sir Charles's murder. If he had sneaked back into the house at some point . . .

And then there was Percy Wyatt. Simon frowned, starting to pace around the room once more. Percy had lied about where he was the night of his uncle's death. While Mrs. Adler and her friends might be right that a man like that wouldn't kill for the prospect of one hundred pounds a year, that only mattered if the crime had been carefully planned. If Percy had also been lying about his conversation with Sir Charles, if his uncle hadn't pledged to pay his debts but had instead planned to cut him off, he could have acted on impulse and killed in a panic.

And who was the strange man Frank Wyatt had paid off, the one with the scar? According to Hartley, Mrs. Adler had asked the housekeeper about repairs for the house and she hadn't known a thing about them. So Frank's story that the man was a disgruntled laborer looked like a fabrication.

But was it a fabrication that had anything to do with his father's death?

Simon paused in front of his desk, staring down at his notes.

He needed to know more. And to discover it, he was going to need help.

"Well, Captain," he said at last. "I need to ask for your assistance once more. Tonight."

Hartley's heels hit the floor with a thud as he sat up, his smile grim.

Once upon a time, Simon had been fooled by the captain's air of flippancy, assuming that his personality went no deeper than the good humor he usually displayed. And as the son of a wealthy family who had prospered in naval service under his own merit, he did often seem like one of those individuals who danced through life with few cares and fewer consequences.

But any man who had seen war firsthand and survived had more to him than good humor. And while the captain could, on occasion, be as stiff-necked as Simon himself, his easy manner hid a keen intellect and a willingness to go to great lengths to help those he considered friends.

"I am at your service, of course. With what do you need my assistance? Something underhanded, I hope."

Simon glanced out the window. The sun would be setting soon. "Following Percy Wyatt."

"Excellent." The captain rubbed his hands together. "This should be fun."

CHAPTER 19

More than five hours later, even the captain had to admit that it was not fun.

"I thought you had done this sort of thing before," Simon whispered. "For Mrs. Adler."

"It was daytime then," the captain said, his words barely audible though he stood only a few feet away. His sigh, however, was quite clear. "And it was *not* raining."

It wasn't precisely raining now. But about an hour before, the air had grown suddenly cool, ushering in a misting drizzle that wouldn't have felt heavy if they had been heading someplace indoors. But standing in the shadows of a London night, even that light mist was too much. Simon could feel water soaking through the collar of his coat where it turned up around his neck, and he could see drops falling from the edge of his hat. He envied the captain his thick driving coat, with its layers of capes on the shoulders to shed the rain.

A flash of light from a door opening and closing caught the edge of the captain's silver flask as he passed it to Simon, who accepted it gratefully. He swallowed a quick mouthful of liquor to warm himself before handing it back.

He sighed. "If I'd known the weather would turn like this, I wouldn't have suggested we both come out tonight. But I thought two sets of eyes and feet would make it easier to follow him."

"They will," Hartley said mildly, taking his own sip before stowing the flask once more. "If he goes anywhere."

He clearly was not enjoying himself, but there was nothing resentful in his tone. Simon felt unexpectedly relieved. He had been half worried that the captain would decide to give up on their watch and take himself off somewhere drier and warmer. Which would have left Simon alone, in the rain, wondering if he should have listened to the rest of the Bow Street force and let the Wyatt case go. With Hartley sticking it out by his side, it was easier to feel confident that he wasn't making a foolish decision to keep going.

"Besides," the captain added. "It is actually three sets. I've set Jem to keep watch on the back of the house, just in case Wyatt goes out that way."

"It doesn't look like he's going much of anywhere tonight," Simon said, wiping rain from the back of his neck. It was too dim in the alley where they were huddled to check his pocket watch, but he knew it had to be after midnight. "We'll give it another ten minutes. Then I'll try again—" He broke off abruptly. "What was that?"

The sound of a cur dog barking three times echoed down the street again, followed by the screech of a cat. It sounded like nothing more than two angry animals, but the captain was suddenly alert.

"That's Jem's signal," he murmured. "These boys from the Seven Dials know all about keeping a low profile at night. Someone is coming out the back." The dog barked again, twice this time. "Coming this way."

It was too dark to see the face of the man who came around the front of the lodging house. Simon wanted to believe it was Percy Wyatt, but in a lodging house full of young men with plenty of money—or at least plenty of willing creditors—there were any number of residents who might decide to head out in search of entertainment at midnight, even on a night as dismal as this one. He turned to the captain, who was dressed with the unmistakable flair of a gentleman. Hartley gave a quick nod, then strolled easily out into the street, swinging his walking stick and whistling, his hat shadowing his face.

"Good evening," the man in front of the lodging house said politely.

"Sir." Hartley had given his voice a slightly hoarser sound than it usually had, and he offered the man a bare nod. They continued past each other without pause.

As the man strode off down the street at a brisk pace, the captain made a large circle, coming back to where Simon still waited. "That was him," he said, shrugging out of his overcoat. Underneath, he wore a simpler jacket in a dark color. He gave a sharp whistle, and a moment later Simon heard running footsteps as the boy Jem dashed around the corner and came panting toward them.

"Was that 'im, sir?"

"Yes. Well spotted, lad." Hartley handed him the bundled coat. "Now get home before you catch a chill, or Mrs. Adler will give both of us an earful."

Not having the driving coat would make him stand out less, and giving it up meant that if Percy Wyatt did spot them, he'd be less likely to recognize a man he had already passed once that evening. Simon was impressed at the captain's forethought, but he still gestured at the coat. "You'll get wet without it."

Hartley shrugged. "Shall we follow?"

Percy Wyatt had already reached the end of the street. Keeping to the shadows, they went after him.

★ ★ ★

"Mrs. Adler."

Lily set the book she was reading down in her lap, regarding her butler with surprise. Carstairs, always a model of propriety, almost never sought her out in her own room, preferring instead to send Anna. But now he was standing in the doorway, clearing his throat uncomfortably.

"What is it?"

"You have . . . a rather insistent visitor downstairs."

Lily's eyes widened as she glanced at the clock on her mantelpiece. The candles were drawn close to the chair where she was reading, and the dim light of the fire didn't quite fill that side of the room. But she could make out easily enough that it was far too late for callers.

If it had been someone unknown to him, Carstairs would have sent the caller on his way. Which meant that, if it was someone asking for her and not for her father, it was likely Jack. He often came by for a drink or a hand of cards if neither of them had evening engagements. But it was far too late for such a call.

Lily scowled. She had once had stern words with Jack about turning up on her doorstep too late at night, and she had expected him to respect that. Lily might push the bounds of proper behavior, but only on her own terms. And certainly not when any neighbor peeking out the front window might see.

"He seems to be somewhat in his cups," Carstairs added apologetically.

If her butler hadn't been standing right there, Lily would have muttered several choice words, none of them fit for polite company. But she would save those for Jack himself. Setting her book aside, glad she hadn't yet changed for bed, she slid her feet into the shoes she had tossed aside and strode toward the door, her face set in displeasure. Carstairs stepped nimbly aside, then followed her down, keeping up easily with her long-limbed, angry pace.

"He is in the drawing room."

Lily had been about to head to the book-room, where she and Jack often sat together. Frowning but not thinking anything of it, she changed direction and stalked toward the drawing room, throwing the door open. "Jack, what do think you are—"

Frank Wyatt turned quickly toward her, listing slightly to one side before he managed to right himself. "Hello, Lily. How about another game of cards?"

"Frank." Lily stared. "What the hell are you doing here?"

The smile he gave her was wobbly. Even in the dim light, she could see drops of rain sparkling in his hair and dampness dotting the shoulders of his coat. He held his hat and gloves in his hands. "I needed a friend tonight. I thought you and your father might—"

"My father has already gone to bed."

"Really?" Frank swayed a little as he turned to look at the window, but the curtains were already drawn. He hiccupped quietly. "Is it as late as that?"

Lily sighed. "Carstairs, do you know if there is any coffee in the house?"

"I shall investigate," he said gravely, withdrawing with a bow.

He left the door open, which made Lily feel both relieved and chagrined. She hid her discomfort by scowling at Frank. "Sit. He will fetch some coffee, and then you will leave."

"I apologize." Frank took a seat, almost missing the edge of the chair before he righted himself, then set his hat down on a side table, laying his gloves on top with the careful precision of a man who had just realized he was less sober than he believed. "I just—I needed to—"

Lily took pity on him. She sat as well, close enough to reach out and take his hand. And close enough, she discovered, to smell the sweet tang of the rum he had apparently been pickling himself in. "What happened?"

He shuddered. "A maid died."

Lily almost told him that she knew before she caught herself. She had been sitting with her guilt and anger over Ellen's death all day; it was hard to remember that she wasn't supposed to know about the girl's death at all. "Is that what your brother meant when he said someone was gone?"

Frank gave her what might have been a sharp look if he hadn't had to blink at her so many times. "You saw Arthur? Yes."

"When I was with Lady Wyatt," Lily said. "Did you . . . do you suspect anything . . ."

"That constable does, in spite of what the doctor said," Frank said bitterly, his hand tightening around hers. "I think he believes . . . Lily, I think he suspects that I . . . that I was the one who . . ." It seemed he couldn't bring himself to say it. His grip on hers was almost painful. "You know I loved my father, don't you, Lily?"

"It is the constable's job to suspect everyone," she pointed out, though she tried to make the words sound soothing. "And I know Mr. Page is a respectable man who only cares about doing his work well."

Frank narrowed his eyes at her. "You seem to have a high opinion of him. Does that mean you know him more closely than you let on?"

"No, of course not," said Lily. She had meant to comfort him, but she didn't want him suspecting that she was at all involved with Mr. Page's investigation. She quickly changed tactics. "You were gone all night, were you not, when your father died? So why should you think he still suspects you?"

"I wish I knew what he was thinking," Frank said bitterly, pulling away and dropping his face into his hands. He kept speaking, though his words were more muffled now. "Maybe a servant told him something, I don't know. And there are rumors about Arthur now; have you heard those? I don't want to believe them—he's my *brother*, you know, I love him—but perhaps he did. The doctor and the constable both seem suspicious of him. And it was his maid who died, after all. Perhaps I do need to send him away, where someone can look after . . . And maybe he *did*—God above, I just don't know." He lifted his head. "I wish someone could tell me what to do."

Carstairs arrived at that moment with a tray of coffee, and Lily was glad for the interruption. Frank had dropped his head back in his hands, so he didn't see the butler's stiff posture as he prepared a cup. But Lily noticed, and she caught the worried frown gathering between Carstairs's eyes as he hovered near the door, clearly reluctant to leave her alone.

"Thank you, Carstairs," she said, giving him a reassuring nod. "I am sure Mr. Wyatt will be departing shortly."

"Madam." He bowed, giving Frank one more skeptical look before withdrawing.

"Have some coffee, Frank," she urged.

It took a little persuading, but at last he did, and the hot, bitter brew seemed to calm him down. He took only a few sips, but he looked more alert and less unsteady.

He was able to meet her eyes again as he put the cup down. "I am behaving very badly," he said quietly, with a smile that didn't quite reach his eyes.

"It has been an awful week for you," Lily said, offering the excuse gently. "I think you are allowed a moment or two of bad behavior."

"Awful. Yes, it has been that. And unbelievable." Frank shook his head. The serious conversation seemed to be sobering him up. He glanced down at his hands, then looked up, offering her a crooked smile. "We are old friends, are we not?"

They had never been friends. The four years between them had felt like a chasm when they were young. And Mr. Pierce's obvious preference for Frank's company—combined with Frank's outgoing personality that was so different from Lily's own cautious, private one—had made her uninterested in his company, even when they were older. But now was not the time to point out that *friendly* was not the same thing as being friends.

"Of course we are," she agreed, leaning forward and setting her hand on his.

"Then you would tell me, wouldn't you?" He turned his hand over to grip hers, his smile fading as his eyes fixed on hers with unnerving intensity. "If you had heard anything? If you had seen anything?"

Lily wanted to pull her hand away. She thought of the time she couldn't explain, between leaving him and meeting Lady Wyatt on the stairs, nearly twenty minutes of creeping through his house to confirm that his brother's maid had been poisoned. But she stayed very still and gave him a puzzled smile instead. "What could I possibly have heard or seen?"

"I don't know." Frank's expression was both lost and hopeful as he shrugged. "People talk. And you notice things, I think. You know that Bow Street man."

Lily weighed her options, then decided the risk was worth it. "The only thing I have heard, Frank, is rumors about your father," she said gently. After all, it wasn't quite a lie—she had heard it directly from the gossiping ladies in the confectioner's shop. "Do you know there is talk that he had a natural child tucked away somewhere?"

"What?" Frank pulled away suddenly. He looked genuinely stunned—though Lily wondered if that was because it wasn't true or because he couldn't believe she would repeat such a rumor to him.

"Though in some tellings, the father is either you or your cousin," she added, lying with a straight face. "Have you heard any such talk?"

She watched him closely as she spoke, but he stood before she could get a good look at his face.

"My God, people will say anything," he snapped, scrubbing a hand through his hair. "I cannot wait to get my father in the ground so all this can be done."

It was a coarse sentiment, but Lily couldn't find it in her to blame him for it too much, under the circumstances. Grief and loss were hard enough without fear and suspicion being thrown into the mix. She was no closer to discovering which Wyatt was the father of Edie's child—if indeed any of them were. But there was no way to press Frank on the subject without rousing his suspicion.

"I should be leaving." Frank stood abruptly, giving her a small, lopsided smile that still looked not quite sober. "I probably should not have come."

"Probably?" Lily couldn't help asking, her brows rising.

That made him smile in earnest, in spite of the worry that still creased his forehead. "You always put me in my place. But will you do me a favor?"

She stood as well. "If I can."

"Will you tell me if you do hear anything? Any new rumors, any gossip among the servants? Any . . ." He trailed off, shaking his head. "You've no idea the strain in that house right now. All of us staring at each other and jumping, trying our best not to say the wrong thing . . ."

"You mean you and Lady Wyatt?"

He grimaced. "And the servants. Even Percy. But yes, mostly her."

That much comfort she could offer him without betraying her clandestine search. "Well, however things are between the two of you, she doesn't suspect you. In fact, she said quite firmly that she believes you could never raise a hand against your father."

Frank looked surprised. "You talked about me with her?"

"And she said something almost flattering," Lily said. They hadn't discussed Ellen, of course, because Lily wasn't supposed to know about the death of the maid. She bit her lip, then made the effort to smile. "So perhaps things are not quite as hopeless as they seem."

"Well, between us they are," he said, shaking his head and looking grumpy at being forced to think of Lady Wyatt. Or maybe his head was simply beginning to ache. He seemed far more sober than when he had first arrived. "But at least she does not believe me a murderer."

"Did you honestly think she would?"

"Not truly. But the way things are between us . . ."

"Which doesn't seem much like you, Frank," Lily said, unable to keep the puzzlement from her voice.

He gave her a smile that was almost smug. "Why, because everyone always likes me?"

"They do," Lily agreed, not rising to his bait. He had always liked to tease, but this time she wasn't thinking of her father. "But more to the point, if they do not, you go out of your way to *make* them like you. The vicar's wife was ready to whip you herself when she caught you stealing apples from the vicarage's trees, that time you were home from school. And you set yourself to winning her over so thoroughly that a month later she was *bringing* apple pie to you and your father."

"It was very good pie," Frank said, looking pleased with himself. "What is your point?"

"My point"—Lily reached out to poke him in the chest—"is that I have never seen you reduced to sniping at someone the way you do at Lady Wyatt. I don't like you either, yet you still go out of your way to be charming to me."

He stepped forward at that, smiling. His eyes were fixed on hers, and if she had judged by the expression in them, she would have believed herself the only person in the world. "You do like me, Lily," he said, his voice dropping until it was almost a murmur.

He was much too close, but Lily didn't back up. Instead, she raised her chin, refusing to drop her own gaze. "And there we are. I say I do not like you, and you act as though you are about to seduce me."

Frank chuckled, the sound so low and warm that it practically curled around Lily like a kitten. He took a step closer. "Why do you always assume it's an act?"

"Because you have been playing at it since we were children." She didn't like the breathless note in her voice. She knew she was right, that he was just pretending. But when his mouth was so close to hers, it was almost impossible not to believe it.

He shook his head, still smiling. "Not children," he murmured. "I remember when it started. You had just turned twelve. You had grown half a foot since I last saw you, and suddenly you could nearly look me in the eyes every time you told me I was wrong about something. I stole those apples to impress you."

"A gesture doomed to failure, considering that eating apples makes my cheeks swell up and get splotchy."

His smile did not falter. "A grave error on my part."

"So why not bring Lady Wyatt apples? Metaphorically speaking."

"I am inches away from kissing you, Lily, and you still want to talk about Lady Wyatt?"

"You are inches away from kissing me, Frank, because you want to change the subject." In spite of herself, Lily's heart was racing. No one had come so close to kissing her in years. She put a firm hand on his chest, keeping him from closing any more distance between them. "Why not charm her?"

They stared at each other for several heartbeats. "I did," he said at last. Under her palm, Lily could feel his heart racing, but whatever agitation he was feeling, he kept it off his face. "I tried to. Of course I wanted her to like me. She married my father, did she not? And he meant the world to me. But she is even more hard-hearted than you."

He took another step toward her as he spoke, his chest pressing against her hand and his lids lowering slightly as his gaze dropped to her mouth. He was close enough that she could feel his breath on her cheek. It didn't smell as strongly of rum as his clothes; Lily wondered for a moment if he had been drunk enough to spill the bottle on himself.

But she didn't think about it long. The intensity in his expression made her almost fearful. Which was absurd. She knew Frank, knew there was nothing to be scared of. But all of a sudden, she found herself remembering that Jack was supposed to find out whether Frank was telling the truth about where he had been when his father died.

And Jack still had not been able to.

She took a step back, keeping her hand raised between them. "Stop it, Frank."

"Why?" he murmured. He followed her, still watching her with that same unnerving intensity. And, underneath it, there was an edge of fear that he was clearly doing his best to hide. "Why do you always insist that it's an act?"

"Because it is," Lily said, shaking her head. "You are drunk, and you are grieving, and I am not the person—"

"Lily." He reached for her.

She took another step back and changed tactics. "Do you think she could have killed him?"

The question was like a cold bucket of water upended over both of them. The heat went out of Frank's expression, and he took a step back, stumbling a little, a reminder that he had shown up on her doorstep with what had to be half a bottle of rum inside him. Lily, feeling suddenly off-balance, put a hand out to steady herself and discovered he had somehow backed her nearly into a corner.

"How on earth could you ask something like that?" he said, staring at her. "I said she did not like me. I never said she was a *murderer.*"

"What about your cousin, then? He says he reconciled with your father, but perhaps—"

"You might as well ask if I was the one who killed him."

His voice was heavy with scorn and slightly shrill. When Lily did not answer, the silence hung between them like lead weights.

Frank's eyes grew wide. "You think I might have."

Lily gazed up at him in silence, then slowly shook her head. "No."

"You do." Frank swayed a little.

"No." Lily caught his arm, intending only to steady him. "I know you and he were—"

Frank pulled her abruptly toward him and kissed her.

Lily froze for only a moment, stunned into stillness. Then she yanked away and slapped him.

They fell apart, staring at each other, both of them breathing heavily. At last, Frank raised a hand to his cheek. "Ow," he said, sounding surprised.

"You are drunk," Lily said quietly, her voice shaking. "On rum and grief both. We shall forget this ever happened, and you will go home. Now."

He shook his head, swaying again, but this time Lily did not reach out to steady him. "I'll not leave with you thinking me a murderer."

She sighed. "Go home, Frank."

"But—"

"I thought I heard voices." Mr. Pierce's voice broke through the tension in the room, making them both jump a little in surprise. Lily was instantly glad Frank had already stepped away from her. God alone knew what her father would have made of stumbling upon *that* tableau.

Then she wondered how long he had been standing in the doorway and felt heat rising to her face. Behind her father, Lily thought she saw Carstairs leaving the front hall. He had fetched her father, she realized, mortified. What had he overheard to make him do that?

"Frank?" Mr. Pierce frowned as he stepped into the room. His heavy dressing gown was cinched tightly around him, but he looked too alert to have just come from sleep. "What are you doing here? At this hour?"

"I was looking for you, sir," Frank said quickly. He smiled, then swayed again, and this time the motion was exaggerated enough that Lily was sure he was faking it. Apparently he was as uncomfortable with the notion of her father having seen what just happened as she was. "It seemed like a good idea, but apparently I am not quite sober, and . . ."

"Oh, Frank." Mr. Pierce shook his head. "Shall I help you home?"

"No, thank you, sir. I will see myself out." He bowed abruptly, fumbling for the hat and gloves he had left on the table. "Good night, both of you."

He didn't meet Lily's eyes as he fled the room.

There was a long silence as they both watched him leave, and then Mr. Pierce turned slowly toward her. "What was that?"

Lily lifted her chin. "As he said, he had too much to drink and lost track of the time. No doubt he did not realize it was far too late to be calling."

Mr. Pierce sighed. "Poor boy. What a terrible time in his life."

"Indeed." Lily stared at the doorway where Frank had disappeared, then shook herself. "If you will excuse me, Father, it is late."

She had to brush past him to leave them room, and she could feel his eyes on her the whole time. But she did not turn to meet them.

She didn't notice that her hands were shaking until she saw them on the banister as she climbed the stairs.

Lily knew what grief was like, knew it could convince a person to consider many things that would never otherwise cross their minds. And when it was combined with the loose inhibitions found inside a bottle of spirits, it was no wonder that Frank's behavior had been so surprising.

But he hadn't only been drunk. And he hadn't only been grieving. He had been too close to hide his feelings from her completely.

Frank Wyatt was afraid.

Lily closed the door to her room behind her, then leaned back against it, staring unseeing at the dim light of the fire that burned low in her hearth. Was it fear of discovery?

She still couldn't believe he would raise a hand against his father, not deliberately. Accidents could happen, certainly, but he hadn't even been there that night. Though as for Ellen . . . Lily shivered, then crossed to her bed, snatching up the shawl Anna had laid out for her and pulling it tight around her.

He'd had the opportunity to poison Ellen. But if he hadn't been the one to kill his father, he would have had no reason to harm the maid.

If it wasn't fear of discovery that lurked behind his pretenses, what else could it have been?

It was desperation that had driven him to kiss her, she was sure. Desperation and panic when he thought she might believe him a murderer. Was it fear of suspicion, of rumors following him for the rest of his life, whispers behind his back that he could never lay to rest?

Lily stared at the fire. Or was it something far worse?

Two people in his home had died. Did Frank have reason to fear he would be next?

★　★　★

Simon had worried that they might have to trail Percy Wyatt for hours, lurking around whatever entertainment he chose to pursue for the night. That was another reason he had asked for the captain's help. As a gentleman, Hartley could gain entry into most of the clubs and gaming halls that Percy might patronize, whereas Simon knew he would likely be turned away at the door, at least during business hours.

But instead of heading toward the entertainments of Covent Garden or the clubs of St. James, Percy made his way farther east, toward a quiet neighborhood favored by solicitors, prosperous tradesmen, and other politely professional families just past Russell Square.

Simon and the captain exchanged a puzzled glance as they followed. This wasn't the sort of place where young men went at night.

The buildings' genteel facades didn't hide private gaming dens, and families that had to work for their living were less likely to hold parties late into the night as plenty of the residents of Mayfair did. But if Percy was planning to go farther into the city, he wouldn't have come so far on foot.

Simon was the first to realize that Percy was stopping and put out a hand to warn Hartley. The two of them waited in the shadows, watching their quarry as he stopped at the end of a block of pretty houses. He seemed to be waiting for something, or perhaps checking that no one was coming. The street was so quiet that Simon held his breath.

A moment later, Percy moved cautiously forward, disappearing around the side of the house at the end of the street. Simon motioned for the captain to stay where he was and followed after, keeping far enough back that he could see what was happening but still duck out of sight if Percy should turn around.

When he peeked around the side of the house, he found Percy carefully opening the sort of garden gate that should have been locked. Either he had managed to lift the latch from the outside or someone had left it open for him. The hinges were well cared for, and they moved silently as he swung the gate just far enough ajar that he could slip inside.

Simon was debating whether or not to follow when an odd rustling drew his attention. Before he could puzzle through what it might be, he was dumbfounded by the sight of Percy Wyatt scaling the trellis on the back wall of the house with the ease of long practice. When he was halfway up, a light flared briefly in the window above him and the pane swung open. A moment later, he disappeared inside.

CHAPTER 20

Mrs. Gregory Smythe was in a flutter of delight and nerves at the prospect of such impressive guests wanting to call on her daughter. She had come to greet them in the drawing room, clutching their cards as if they were a lifeline, her eagerness only briefly checked when she realized that the older of her two female guests was *not*, as she had assumed, Lady Carroway.

Lily was surprised by the reaction; Ofelia's marriage the previous month had been in half the papers in London, and most of them had not failed to mention, with varying degrees of emphasis, her young age and foreign background. But not everyone was well acquainted with the affairs and gossip of Mayfair society.

Mrs. Smythe, however, showed no lack of willingness to expand that acquaintance, and she covered her momentary confusion with a fawning obsequiousness. Lily caught Ofelia's eye briefly. Though the younger woman's mouth was set in a polite smile, there was a hint of bitter humor in her expression. But she played her part with aplomb, and Lily was once again impressed with her friend's easy manner and quick ability to adapt to whatever circumstances she found herself in.

"We were so charmed by your daughter when we met her the other day in the park." Ofelia, as she and Lily had planned, omitted both the day, the park, and the nature of their meeting, since it had not actually taken place. But Mrs. Smythe, as they had hoped, was so flattered by the attention that it never occurred to her to interrupt and demand more information. "We could not wait to resume our discussion. I hope you will not think us impertinent for calling without a proper introduction to you, but we were confident you would understand that no offense was intended."

"Oh no, no no, no offense indeed!" Mrs. Smythe protested quickly. "So charming indeed, Lady Carroway, Mrs. Adler, so charmed indeed to meet you. And of course . . ." She trailed off, glancing toward their companion, who bowed but said nothing.

"Our dear friend, Mr. Page," Lily said, inclining her head as she made the introduction, her voice a touch more reserved than Ofelia's.

Unlike her friend, she didn't have a title to command instant attention and respect. But she had been informed on more than one occasion that her cool manner could put any number of social climbers in their place, and she deployed it to full effect to keep Mrs. Smythe from asking further about Mr. Page.

His card had not been sent up with theirs, because the only cards he had were for business. But that didn't seem to matter to Mrs. Smythe, and she instantly let him know how pleased she was to make his acquaintance.

"My dear Louisa will be down any moment, and I know she will be delighted with your visit." Mrs. Smythe leaned forward. "I am sure I display a mother's partiality to say so, but I am not surprised that you were so pleased with her. Mr. Smythe and I attended most *carefully* to Louisa's education. She has none of those forward manners that so many girls display these days. Why"—she tittered a little bit—"I think she could scarcely number ten men among her acquaintance before her marriage, and most of them were friends of her father's."

"How delightfully sheltered an existence," Ofelia murmured after an uncomfortable pause.

A quick word with neighbors in the park had told them what to expect when they called: the house belonged to Mr. Preston, a barrister who had recently married. The young bride had come with her mother in tow as part of the marriage settlement, and Mr. Preston now lived with both the new Mrs. Preston and the widowed Mrs. Smythe.

Lily hadn't been certain, before they knocked and presented their cards, whether their quarry was the wife or the mother-in-law. But she and Ofelia didn't even need to look at each other to agree that Mrs. Smythe wasn't the sort of woman who would encourage a much younger lover to climb a trellis in the middle of the night. The daughter, then, was the one they needed.

Louisa Preston, when she entered the room, turned out to be an unremarkably pretty girl of perhaps twenty years, dressed in the height of fashion, with a shrewd expression and more polish to her manners than her mother's behavior had led Lily to expect. Even without Mr. Page's report on Mrs. Preston's likely midnight visitor, Lily would have had the impression of a girl who wasn't nearly as sheltered and innocent as her mother believed.

She was deferential enough to her mother but sized up her guests with frank confusion when Mrs. Smythe's back was turned. But either she was too polite to tell them to their faces that she didn't remember them or she couldn't find a break in Mrs. Smythe's eager conversation to point out the error.

Nearly ten minutes of the fifteen that were acceptable for a morning visit had passed before Ofelia, with a quickly hidden look of resignation, found an excuse to get Mrs. Smythe out of the room. Upon hearing that they had recently had a portrait of Mr. Preston painted and hung in the upstairs hall, Ofelia exclaimed with interest that she had been thinking of commissioning just such a thing for Sir Edward as a wedding present.

"Would it be a terrible imposition, Mrs. Smythe, for me to ask to see it? One does so worry about the style and talent of such things. But you and your daughter seem to have such elegant taste, I am sure I would love to see how Mr. Preston's portrait turned out."

The silence that fell on the room when they had departed was almost a shock, and it took Lily a moment to gather her thoughts. Mr. Page was no help; out of his element, he had done as Lily suggested when they were making plans and retreated behind the newspaper left on the table. It was Lily's job to broach the topic they wanted to discuss with Mrs. Preston. But while she was still trying to decide how to begin, the girl beat her to it.

"I would be more flattered by your visit, Mrs. Adler, if we had actually met before. But I have been searching my memory these ten minutes, and I have come to the conclusion that we have never seen each other before today." There was an edge to her smile. "I do hope you plan to explain, because I cannot account for it."

Lily exchanged a glance with Mr. Page, who cleared his throat as he set down his paper. But he still gestured for her to begin. She decided to get right to the point, thinking that Louisa Preston was the sort of person to appreciate bluntness.

"Your conclusion is correct," Lily said, keeping her voice low but not whispering, since Mrs. Smythe had closed the door when she left. "We have not met before. Mr. Page is an officer of Bow Street investigating the death of Sir Charles Wyatt."

Louisa did not freeze, but a wary stillness came over her, and she darted a quick look at Mr. Page before turning her polite smile back to Lily. "I am not acquainted with that particular family."

"Perhaps not with the family," Mr. Page rumbled, leaning forward and fixing her with a stern eye. "But with one of its members. I believe Mr. Percy Wyatt visits you from time to time, rather late at night, if I am not mistaken?"

Louisa may have been talented at presenting a bland facade in front of her mother, but she was clearly not a good enough liar to face such an accusation head on. She sucked in a sharp breath, her cheeks going painfully pale before a bright-pink flush swept from the neck of her gown all the way to her hairline. "I'm afraid I don't know what you could possibly mean," she said, swallowing. "I certainly do not receive gentlemen callers after dark. Except, of course, my dear husband, but he is out of town on business."

"Oh, perhaps it was your mother he was climbing up the trellis to pay his respects to," Mr. Page said mercilessly, standing. "I shall ask her directly—"

"No!" Louisa had gone pale again, and she leaped up to block his path to the door. Her breath was coming in sharp gasps. "You cannot . . . you *must* not . . . what do you want from me?"

"You do know Mr. Wyatt, then?" Lily asked, glancing toward the door. Ofelia would keep Mrs. Smythe occupied for as long as she could, but there was no knowing how long they had.

"No," Louisa said stubbornly, though her hands were visibly trembling.

Lily didn't blame her. The cost of such a revelation would not be as high for a young matron as for an unmarried girl. But if word of her indiscretion got out, Louisa Preston's life could still become very unpleasant. And if her husband was angry enough to sue for divorce, both she and her mother would be pariahs. Lily hated to put her on the spot in such a manner, but there was enough at stake that she didn't hesitate.

"Mrs. Preston," she said, cool but not accusatory. "We do not care about your nighttime activities for their own sake. But Mr. Wyatt, like the rest of his family, is under suspicion of murder. And we need to understand his motivations and movements."

"Mr. Wyatt had nothing to do with his uncle's death," Louisa said fiercely. "I know he did not."

"We have no way to prove that," Mr. Page said, crossing his arms. "According to Mr. Wyatt, he was home by himself all night. But according to the servants at his residence, he did not return home until it was nearly dawn. Plenty of time for a man to commit murder."

Louisa raised her head, looking resigned and terrified at the same time. "Percy could not have killed his uncle," she whispered, "because he was with me that night. He visits when my husband is traveling, as he is this week."

The silence after her words was deafening. Louisa looked as though she was going to be sick, but she clenched her shaking hands into fists and met Mr. Page's eyes.

"Mrs. Preston," he said, a little more gently. "Think carefully about what you are saying. If the matter should come to trial, you might have to be called on to provide testimony as to Mr. Wyatt's whereabouts. Do not commit yourself to something that is not true, that could damage your own reputation and well-being, simply to protect him."

He was testing her, Lily was sure. Mr. Page was too stiffly honorable to ever require a woman to sully her own reputation in such a tawdry manner. But the threat of that kind of exposure would be enough to make any woman think twice about uttering such a lie, even to protect someone she cared for.

Louisa Preston did not back down. "But it is true. And I would rather my reputation be in tatters than see Percy hanged for a crime he did not commit."

The sudden burst of voices in the hall made all three of them jump. Ofelia's was loudest of all, raised more than it needed to be to warn them to finish their conversation. Lily sank back into her chair, motioning the others to do the same. Mr. Page swiftly complied, and Louisa Preston, after a moment of frozen panic, did as well. Lily could see the girl's hands trembling, though she did her best to hide her distress.

"Indeed, such a pleasure," Ofelia was saying as the door swung open. "Mrs. Adler, what good fortune! Mr. Preston has returned home, just in time for me to compare him to his portrait, which is such a perfect likeness. I shall have to commission one for Sir Edward immediately . . ."

Talking smoothly to cover any confusion in the room, Ofelia cheerfully made the introductions. Mr. Preston was a great deal older than his wife, perhaps in his late thirties, with a pleasant-looking face and broad build that were both starting to go soft. His clothing was still dusty from travel, and he ought to have excused himself to change, but apparently he couldn't resist the opportunity to make the acquaintance of his distinguished guests.

"If I can be of any service to you, Lady Carroway, or Sir Edward," he kept repeating, mopping his brow with a handkerchief and beaming. Lily thought he came close to offering them his card at several points, though he managed to restrain himself from such a faux pas.

"Your mother mentioned that you were planning to walk this afternoon, Mrs. Preston," Ofelia said at last, when it seemed that Mr. Preston and Mrs. Smythe were going to try to encourage their guests to settle down for some refreshment. "Perhaps we might accompany you?"

Lily could have hugged her friend. It was an excellent way to extend their chance to talk with Louisa while escaping the intense attention of her mother and husband. "An excellent idea," she said, rising.

"Oh, yes, how lovely!" Mrs. Smythe burbled, while Mr. Preston added his enthusiastic agreement. "I would join you, of course, but I remember well how young people like their amusements . . ."

"It is the day for your weekly visit to the British Museum, is it not, Louisa?" Mr. Preston asked, clearly not offended that his mother-in-law did not class him with the young people. "She does so love the exhibits there; charming really, such an inquisitive girl . . ."

Louisa looked like she might have tried to protest, but a single glance at Mr. Page's stern face made her swallow, back down, and voice nothing but polite agreement.

It took another five minutes before they could make their escape, but at last the four of them were out the door, Louisa wearing the petulant, scared expression of a child who had been caught in misbehavior and knew there was no way to evade punishment.

"Well," said Ofelia at last. "I am amazed they did not come with us."

"They have aspirations," Louisa said grumpily. "No doubt, at this moment, they are scheming to get Lady Carroway to sponsor me to some society events in the winter, or even to wrangle an invitation for us all to visit her country house this fall."

"What makes you so sure Lady Carroway has a country house?" Lily couldn't help asking.

Louisa gave her a pitying look. "Her marriage was in all the papers, accompanied by a great many details about Sir Edward's family. My mother arranged an advantageous marriage for me, but my

254 Katharine Schellman

husband aims even higher. Hence my closely guarded, deeply boring life. I expected it to change after my marriage. Sadly, it has not."

"Thus your affair with Mr. Wyatt?" Lily murmured.

The look Louisa shot her was venomous. "Your father did not have a profession, did he, Mrs. Adler?" When Lily shook her head, Louisa laughed shortly. "Families like yours may have high standards for propriety and manners, but they are woefully outmatched by the moralizing of those in the middle classes with ambitions to join them."

Lily gave Mr. Page a sideways glance. "I have noticed such tendencies," she said, pleased to see him flush a little around the ears.

Louisa shrugged again. "My mother was convinced that if I was sheltered and innocent enough, she would be able to marry me off to a duke. She had to settle for a barrister who will one day inherit a country property. He intends to settle down and become a gentleman while I spend the rest of my life moldering in the country. I would rather have some fun while I still can." She scowled suddenly, rigid with tension. "Are you going to tell him?"

There was a long pause. Ofelia and Lily both glanced at the Bow Street constable.

"No, we have no intention of telling your husband," Mr. Page said, and Louisa Preston's shoulders slumped with relief. A moment later, though, she was upright as ever, her parasol adjusted to shield her from the glare of the morning sun and hide her face from any passersby. "Our next stop will be to speak with Mr. Wyatt, not your husband."

Louisa opened her mouth as though she were about to say something, closed it, opened it again, and sighed. "Mr. Preston mentioned that I regularly visit the British Museum, as I am sure you recall." She gave Lily a sour look. "I imagine you do not forget much."

"I never boast about my own accomplishments," Lily said modestly. On her other side, Ofelia gave an unladylike snort of laughter but said nothing. "But I do recall his comment. And I also know that the British Museum is an excellent place for an assignation."

Louisa Preston nodded, looking resigned. "Mr. Wyatt and I meet there once a week."

Mr. Page scowled but said nothing. Lily didn't approve either, but she was more sympathetic than he to the plight of a girl married to a much older man, not of her own volition but to better her family's standing. It was little wonder to her that the young Mrs. Preston had begun an affair with a man much closer to her own age. And her personality struck Lily as an excellent match for the snobbish Mr. Wyatt.

"Well, then," Mr. Page said. "Permit us to accompany you to the museum, Mrs. Preston."

It was not a request, and Louisa Preston sighed. "We are to meet by the corals and fossils on the upper floor."

★ ★ ★

When Lily had been an unmarried girl in London with her father, the British Museum had required all visitors to register in advance for tickets, which could be collected at set times during the day, and only a small group of people were allowed to enter at a time. Had that still been the case, they couldn't have gone with Mrs. Preston.

Fortunately, as the museum had grown, it had abandoned the system of ticketing and simply allowed respectably dressed people to enter between ten o'clock in the morning and four o'clock in the afternoon. Their group received a glance from the porter as they were handed their maps, but they were all clearly well-to-do, and he did not linger over them more than any other visitors arriving that morning.

They had debated quietly, on the way there, whether it would be best to conceal themselves from Mr. Wyatt. But, as it was the middle of the day in a very public space, Mr. Page decided it was unlikely that anyone would try to make a scene. And meeting and speaking in a public place would be far less likely to excite comment than trying to speak to him at his lodging house or asking for his attendance at the house on Wimpole Street.

So Lily and Ofelia stood with Mrs. Preston in front of the shelves of fossils, watching the door, while Mr. Page stood a couple of paces away in front of a display of beautiful corals. Mrs. Preston fidgeted with impatience but did not protest. When Lily quietly expressed her appreciation for the younger woman's cooperation, she received a decidedly unimpressed look in response.

"I've no wish to see him accused of murder," Louisa Preston muttered. "The sooner that nasty constable is satisfied, the sooner I can go back to my life without worrying that anything untoward might come to the attention of my husband."

When Percy Wyatt entered the room at last, he was nattily dressed in a fitted black jacket and gray waistcoat, with a jet stickpin in his cravat. Lily sighed to herself. She knew enough of Mr. Wyatt's finances to be sure that he could not afford a single item he was wearing; apparently his brush with the moneylender had not cured him of his expensive habits. But his being a spendthrift was not the problem she was concerned with at present.

His eyes slid past Ofelia, whom he had never met, then locked on Mrs. Preston. He smiled, but the expression slid from his face with almost comical quickness when he realized who was standing next to her. As soon as he noticed Lily, his countenance turned a sickly color, and he turned as though he would flee the room. But Mr. Page was suddenly there, smiling politely and taking Percy's arm to lead him back toward the group of women.

"Now, Mr. Wyatt, no need to look so green," the constable said, a little cruelly. "You ought to be grateful, in fact, that we've discovered your friend."

Percy Wyatt's eyes darted frantically between them, but he came meekly enough to stand in front of the display of fossils. "What happened?" he whispered to Mrs. Preston.

She turned her sour expression on him. "They found you out, of course, and came to my *house*," she hissed. "My *husband* was there."

For a moment Lily feared she had been wrong and that Mrs. Preston would indeed make a scene. But then the young matron sighed, her expression and her shoulders both drooping as if she had been deflated.

"Why did you hide that you were under suspicion, Percy?" she whispered. "Did you not think I would tell them you were with me?"

"But . . ." He looked amazed. "Your husband . . . I could not ask such a thing of you. Besides." He gave Mr. Page a look that was heavy with displeasure. "I told them I was at home sleeping all night. Surely that ought to have been enough."

Mr. Page sighed gustily. "Why should it have been?"

"Because I am a gentleman," Percy said stiffly. "The word of a gentleman ought to be enough."

Lily couldn't help the derisive sound that escaped her, and even Mrs. Preston looked exasperated with him. "You were lying, Mr. Wyatt," Lily pointed out. "So your word is hardly unimpeachable, is it?"

"But . . ." Percy frowned, clearly wanting to protest more but unable to think of a good argument. "Well, I suppose you are right. But it was rather unsporting of you to suspect my word *before* you knew I was lying."

Lily thought Mr. Page might abandon his dignity and actually roll his eyes. "Murder investigations do not generally proceed according to the rules of sporting behavior," he said instead, his voice dripping with sarcasm. "Since murderers, as you may imagine, are so often unsporting themselves."

"And since you had rather a recent history of being untruthful," Lily pointed out with false sweetness.

Mr. Wyatt looked reasonably embarrassed and cleared his throat quickly. "Well, then what happens now? Even you must admit I could not have been harming my uncle when I was . . ." He blushed suddenly, realizing what he had been about to say, as Mrs. Preston made a noise like an angry cat and kicked him in the ankle.

"What happens is that you tell us if there is any other information you have been withholding," Mr. Page said sternly. "Lady Carroway, perhaps you and Mrs. Preston would like to go view the exhibit in the next room while I speak to Mr. Wyatt?"

"Why does Mrs. Adler get to stay?" Ofelia grumbled.

"Because she would whether I asked her to leave or not," he muttered, while Lily grinned at his clear displeasure.

"Oh, very well. Come along, Mrs. Preston."

Once the two women were gone, Mr. Page turned on Percy Wyatt once more. "Where was your cousin that night?"

"Frank?" Percy frowned in surprise. "He was out gambling and drinking until something like four in the morning. Surely you've been able to verify that?"

Mr. Page didn't answer. "And what do you know of the maid named Edie who used to work in your uncle's house?"

"Edie? Lord, man, I never notice the maids."

"Try, if you please," Mr. Page bit off.

"Why does it matter?"

"That isn't your concern."

Lily could see that the answer set Percy's back up; the two men were eyeing each other scornfully, each offended by the other's manner and behavior. But there wasn't time for them to slowly realize they were on the same side. Too much was at stake.

"Mr. Wyatt," Lily said, her voice soft and serious. She took his arm and steered him toward the next case of shells as she spoke, not wanting the other museum patrons to see them standing in front of one display for too long. "However little respect you may have for Mr. Page and his methods, you must admit he is skilled at his job. He unearthed your secrets, after all. And at the moment he is doing his best to protect your cousin. Or have you not heard the rumors spreading about Arthur?"

"Arthur?" Percy stared at her in confusion. "But . . . all that is just talk, of course. Arthur has nothing to do with this."

"He does, in fact." Lily glanced at Mr. Page for permission to continue; when he nodded, she dropped her voice even further. "Arthur knows something about what happened to your uncle that night, even if he does not realize it. And his maid, Ellen, was poisoned, likely because he told her what it was."

Percy paled with shock. "But . . . the doctor said . . ."

"The doctor was wrong," Mr. Page said sharply. A woman in a mightily plumed hat turned to glare at him, and he cleared his throat as he gave her a quick, apologetic bow. He lowered his voice as he continued. "Ellen was poisoned. And unless we can find out who did it, your cousin will continue to be in danger.

"So I'll ask you again, Mr. Wyatt: what can you tell us about the maid Edie who used to work in your uncle's house?" Mr. Page's voice grew sharp. "And don't think to hide your own dealings with her. As you have learned, I have my ways of ferreting out information."

"My own dealings?" Percy looked confused and then, as realization dawned, affronted. "A gentleman does *not* interfere with another gentleman's servants," he said stiffly. "How uncouth. Anyway, that is far more Frank's style than mine." He spoke carelessly, only seeming to realize what he had said after the words had left his mouth. "Not that I know anything about any . . . business between them," he said quickly. "Just that Frank is more of a romancer than I am." His mouth twisted. "Girls like him better," he added in a petulant mutter.

Lily would have laughed at him if the circumstances hadn't been so serious.

"But I do think she got the position because she was someone's niece, or cousin, or something like that." Percy frowned again, turning the museum map around in his fingers and worrying at the edges as he thought. "Maybe Mrs. Harris? No, it was the head housemaid, that was it. Sarah, perhaps? Edie was her niece."

"Mr. Wyatt." The Bow Street constable's words sounded as though they were being forced past clenched teeth. "I spoke to all the servants in your uncle's household. The head housemaid is named Mary, and she has no brothers or sisters."

"There used to be a different one," Percy said, shrugging. "She moved into a different position when my uncle married. She serves as Lady Wyatt's maid now."

Wilkes. Lily suddenly remembered seeing the lady's maid searching frantically through Sir Charles's study. She exchanged a glance with Mr. Page, who frowned, then nodded.

Percy Wyatt was watching them. "Is there anything else you need from me?" he demanded, surly again. "Or may I continue with my day?"

"With your assignation, you mean?" Mr. Page said, his expression stern. He shook his head. "I will never understand men like you."

Percy Wyatt gave him a pitying look. "The middle classes can never hope to," he said dismissively.

"Yes, there is something else," Lily said quickly, interrupting before the argument could escalate. "Mr. Wyatt, you seem to deal very well with your cousin Arthur."

"Well, why should I not?" Percy said, looking defensive. "Do you think everyone dislikes me just because you do?"

Lily raised her brows. "I never said I dislike you, Mr. Wyatt. And that was *not* the point I was making. But now you bring it up, it is surprising that you should have so much more patience with him than his own brother."

"Well." Percy hesitated, scowling, a blush sweeping up his neck and face. "It is rather nice, isn't it, to be the person *someone* likes best?"

Lily suddenly understood. "You mean because he didn't like Frank? You wanted to be the person Arthur liked best, once it was clear that Frank dealt so poorly with him."

Percy's scowl grew. "Frank is always the favorite one," he muttered. "Everyone likes him best. And why not? He's handsome, and cheerful, and he never has to beg off going out because his allowance doesn't cover his debts. But Arthur likes me better, and I understand him better than Frank ever has. My uncle was always pleased to see me getting on well with him."

Lily couldn't help laughing, in spite of the gravity of the situation. She understood, better than Percy Wyatt could likely imagine, what it felt like to be second to Frank.

"Well, whatever the reason, I think Mr. Page could use your help."

Mr. Page looked horrified. "*His* help?"

"Yes, his," Lily said firmly. "Do you think, Mr. Wyatt, you could help persuade Arthur to speak to Mr. Page? If he did see or hear something about his father's murder, Bow Street needs to know what it was."

"Arthur does not like strangers."

"Which is why your assistance would be so invaluable." Lily managed not to grimace as she said it. She had no interest in playing to the vanity of a man like Percy Wyatt, but desperate times . . . "Please. You may be the only one who can help to keep him safe."

Percy hesitated, then nodded. "And if you truly think he is unsafe, we ought to think about removing him from the house," he added, surprising Lily with the suggestion.

But it was a good idea. "We will think of something," she promised, glancing at Mr. Page, who nodded his agreement. "In the meantime, do you think you can return to your uncle's house without exciting too much comment?"

"Certainly, since I am staying there," Percy remarked dryly.

Mr. Page's eyes narrowed. "Since when?"

"Since yesterday." Percy sighed. "Arthur needs someone to keep an eye on him."

"Then will you meet us in the kitchen of your uncle's house—"

"The kitchen?" Percy interrupted, looking horrified.

"The kitchen," Lily said firmly, thinking of Mrs. Harris, the housekeeper. There was every chance Frank and Lady Wyatt wouldn't let Mr. Page through the front door. And . . . she shivered a little, remembering Frank's odd nighttime visit to her home. She didn't want to see him again. Not yet. She glanced at Mr. Page. "Let us meet at . . ."

"One o'clock," Mr. Page said, taking her arm as if to lead her away. "And if you are not there, Mr. Wyatt, I will know where to find you."

"Yes, very well," Percy said sharply. "If my cousin's well-being is at stake, you can be assured I will be there. Now, if you would be so good as to let Mrs. Preston know she is free to go about her business?"

CHAPTER 21

"I don't see why you needed to be here as well," Simon grumbled, eyeing Mrs. Adler out of the corner of his eye as they waited belowstairs in the Wyatts' home.

The housekeeper, Mrs. Harris, had been expecting them—Mrs. Adler had sent a message through the captain's boy, Jem. After sharply telling two maids to go on with their business and keep their mouths quiet, Mrs. Harris had shown them to the housekeeper's room, where they could wait out of sight.

"They won't say anything," Mrs. Harris had said confidently, speaking in a whisper as she brought them a tea tray. "Ellen's death has left everyone that spooked. And no one will come out and say it, but there's a whisper of a feeling that Mr. Frank must be the one as is responsible."

Lily had poured for them as soon as Mrs. Harris was gone, then eyed Simon over the rim of her teacup. "Do you think they are right?"

Simon had frowned into his own cup. He wasn't thirsty, but there was, as always, something deeply comforting about the familiar ritual of serving and sharing tea. He saw a lot of ugliness in his work. He wasn't about to say no to a moment of comfort.

"He seems the most likely," Simon had said at last. "He had the opportunity to poison Ellen, especially as her room was apart from the rest of the servants. No one would have questioned him coming and going there; they would have just assumed he was visiting his brother. And he had the most to gain from his father's death. If he is the one spreading those rumors about Arthur, he potentially has even more to gain." Mrs. Adler hadn't tried to hide her grimace at his words. "But you disagree, and you know him better than I."

He saw her hesitate and thought she shivered a little, as though she was remembering something she would rather not. "He does have the most to gain, certainly," she had said at last, while he wondered what she was not telling him. "But when I try to imagine him increasing his inheritance, it is almost . . . to prove that he was indeed his father's favorite. Not for any material gain. And I could never imagine him *killing* for money. Especially not his father. They were so close. They agreed on nearly everything."

"Nearly everything?"

"Well." Her smile had been a little grim. "As we have seen, he was not terribly fond of his father's second marriage."

Simon had stirred his tea, thinking. "That could be reason enough. If Mr. Wyatt saw Sir Charles's marriage as a betrayal—of him, of his mother's memory, what have you—might he have wanted to punish his father?"

"What a horrible . . ." Mrs. Adler had trailed off at that point, her expression growing almost fearful, before she shook her head. "If his father's marriage was indeed enough to arouse such fury, he had a much easier target to set his sights on. One that would not have required him to harm a parent."

"You mean Lady Wyatt?"

"I do." She had shivered again. "Horrid thought. But as she is well and unharmed . . ."

It was a reasonable point, if one considered murder reasonable. And in Simon's experience, murder was often at least logical, if not reasonable. Very few people were driven to kill. Those who were rarely did it for no reason.

"Where does that leave us?" she had continued.

That was when Simon turned to give her what he intended to be a sharp glare but suspected had more of a grumpy pout to it than he'd wanted. When he had asked Mrs. Adler for her assistance on that first day of his investigation, he hadn't expected that she would take it as an invitation to include herself in the rest of it. But now he had no idea how to get rid of her—and even more, he suspected he didn't want to.

Still . . .

"I don't see why you needed to be here as well."

She raised her eyebrows at him. "Do you want me to go?"

"Yes."

"Shame. You will have to make quite a scene to remove me from the premises, and I somehow doubt you want to do that." She lifted her teacup to her lips again.

He had expected, after the first time she was forced to encounter the ugliness of murder, that she would never want anything to do with it again. But here she was, still insisting on being involved, no matter how many opportunities he gave her to leave. "This is not a game, Mrs. Adler."

"No, it is not." She replaced her cup sharply on its saucer, the clatter of the china loud in the quiet room. "Two people have died. And forgive me, sir, but I recall being of rather significant help a time or two in the last few days. Who's to say I will not be again?"

"Why do you care?"

"Why do you?" she demanded. It was a question she had asked him before, the last time they'd found themselves on the same side of a murder, and it made him look away, embarrassed, just as it had then. "I may not have seen Sir Charles in years, but I knew him as a child. But you? Your magistrate has given you the perfect excuse to be done. Your colleagues think you're wasting your time. So why are you still here?"

He met her eyes. "Two people have died."

"You want to believe that because your father worked for a living and mine was a gentleman, we can never see the world the same way. In some respects, you are certainly right. But I would have thought that in your line of work, you would see that people are just people, the ugly and the good and the cruel and the kind all mixed up together, no matter where or how or to whom they were born."

Simon stared at her, unable to think of a reply. He believed that with all his soul, and it was why the way men like the Wyatts treated him rankled him so deeply. It had not occurred to him, seeing the respect they gave a woman like Mrs. Adler, that they looked down on her as well. But of course they did. He had too, once upon a time.

"The world has told you that because your father worked for a living, your worth will never be but so high?" She shrugged. "Well, it has told me the same thing because I was not the child my father wanted. You do not want to admit that we are alike, you and I." She poured herself a second cup of tea, and Simon noticed that her hands were shaking. She, who always seemed so cool and calm, was trembling with emotion. "But one of these days, you shall have to."

She looked back up at him, a firm smile on her face. "And until that happens, you'll not get rid of me easily."

Simon cleared his throat. "I should have learned the last time not to argue with you."

She patted his hand. "Everyone learns not to argue with me eventually. Except my father. That man will never learn."

"He was disappointed you were not a son?"

To his surprise, she blushed. "That was the part of my rant that you want to talk about?" she snapped, exasperated. "Yes, he wanted a son. He has never—"

"Then he's a fool."

Whatever else she might have said was lost as she stared at him, mouth still open in an argument, shock in her eyes. For a long moment, neither of them knew what to say.

Mrs. Adler glanced up at the ceiling, clearing her throat. "It is rather chilling to realize there is likely a murderer in this house with us, is it not?"

Simon nodded, grateful for the change of topic. "You'd think I'd be used to it by now, but it never becomes more normal," he said.

"Although, until we find out exactly what happened to this maid Edie, I'm not ruling her out."

He was about to wonder out loud when the irritating Percy Wyatt would arrive when the man himself suddenly burst in, slamming the door behind him and staring at them with wide eyes. His normally impeccable appearance was rumpled, and his hair stood on end, as though he had been pulling at it in frustration.

"I tried to talk to Arthur," he announced. "I think you were right. He knows something."

Simon and Mrs. Adler had both started to their feet with surprise; they now exchanged a look that was equal parts excitement and alarm.

"What did he say?" Simon demanded.

Percy Wyatt strode around the small room, as though he couldn't bear to keep his feet still. "I asked him if he remembered anything from the night his father died. If he had told Ellen anything. And he said . . ." He glanced at Mrs. Adler. "He kept repeating, 'Ellen says I'm to be quiet like a mouse. I'm not to talk about it; I'm to be quiet like a mouse.' But that was all he would say. He stopped talking to me when I tried to press for more." Percy sank into one of the chairs. "Do you think I should tell Frank? He always says Arthur is a half-wit, which is *not* true, but if he knows something about my uncle's death, even Frank would believe him, don't you think?"

"No," Simon said quickly, and perhaps a bit too loudly. Both Mrs. Adler and Percy looked at him in surprise. He cleared his throat. "We don't want word getting around. This has to stay as secret as possible, for Arthur's safety, until we can discover what he knows."

"Then we ought to remove him from the house," Mrs. Adler said briskly. "Somewhere he will not be in danger. Do you think your cousin or aunt will object?"

"Lady Wyatt will have no objections; she dislikes having him around." Percy sighed. "And Frank—he may object, but he doesn't often take much interest in Arthur's care. I think I can bring him around easily enough."

"You could even tell them you are returning home and taking Arthur to stay with you, just as a precaution," Simon suggested.

He didn't add *in case it is one of them that means him harm*, though he thought it. He wasn't convinced that Percy Wyatt had realized that either his cousin or his aunt could very well be the guilty party. Instead, he crossed to the door and pulled it open. To his relief, Mrs. Harris had remained nearby, going through household inventories in the room just across the hall while she kept an eye on them. As soon as she saw Simon looking for her, she set down her pen and hurried to him.

"Yes, sir?"

Simon gestured her inside, then closed the door. "Master Arthur Wyatt will be spending some time away from the house," he said quietly. "You will need to have a maid you trust begin preparing his things. Immediately. His cousin will go to him and explain the situation."

Mrs. Harris cast a worried glance toward Percy, who nodded impatiently. "Yes, sir," she said. "How long a visit will he make?"

"Until it is safe for him to return," Mrs. Adler said quietly. Mrs. Harris looked stricken, but she nodded again.

"But where can he go?" Percy demanded. "It will need to be somewhere with the space to accommodate him, and staff with enough patience to care for him."

"And somewhere with no connection to the Wyatts. Which means none of us can take him in." Simon raised an inquiring brow at Mrs. Adler. "Do you have any ideas?"

She looked thoughtful. "I believe I know somewhere that might work."

Simon shook his head. "Of course you do. In the meantime"—he turned back to Mrs. Harris—"I need to speak to Lady Wyatt's maid, Wilkes, immediately."

"Wilkes?" Mrs. Harris frowned, looking unhappy. "Begging your pardon sir, but Wilkes isn't here. She was dismissed this morning. And . . ." Mrs. Harris's expression grew puzzled. "Mr. Wyatt just sent one of the footmen to Bow Street with a message for you, Mr. Page. He wants you to call as soon as can be."

For a moment, all of them stared at her in silence. Simon exchanged a surprised look with Mrs. Adler.

"Well," she said slowly. "You ought not to keep him waiting."

CHAPTER 22

"Mr. Page." The greeting was the most polite Frank Wyatt had yet offered him. In fact, the young man sounded positively relieved when he entered the drawing room and found Simon waiting for him. "Thank you for calling so quickly."

"I was surprised to receive your summons," Simon said carefully, his face giving none of his feelings away.

Frank grimaced. "I know you have not found me particularly forthcoming," he said quietly. "I hope you can understand that this entire situation has been so very . . . so very distressing. So very confusing. One does not know what to think. I just wanted the whole business to go away."

"And now?"

Frank wavered for a moment, glancing around the room as if he wanted to look at anything but the constable in front of him. Then his expression firmed, and he met Simon's eyes. "I am worried I know who is responsible for my father's death."

It wasn't the last thing Simon had expected him to say, but it was close. "I beg your pardon?"

"I have had to dismiss Lady Wyatt's maid," Frank said, starting to pace around the room as though he was too agitated to keep his feet still. "The official reason is that we have cause to suspect she was spreading rumors about my family. But I believe . . ."

Simon couldn't stop the skeptical lift of his eyebrows. He had met Wilkes, and she barely reached his shoulder. "You believe she killed your father?"

"No, I . . ." Frank glanced out the window, then snapped the curtains shut and spun back around. "You saw me down there, did you not? With that man with the scar? That is how you knew about him. You saw us out the window."

"I did."

"And then I told you he was a laborer whose work we no longer needed."

"You did."

"I lied." Frank swallowed, lifting his chin. "I think he may have killed my father."

Simon stared at Frank, not speaking, while the words hung in the air between them. "What reason would he have to do that?" the Bow Street constable asked softly. "And what does that have to do with your aunt's maid?"

Frank resumed his distressed pacing around the room. "He's married to a girl, a sordid little thing, who used to work here. She . . ." Frank hesitated, fiddling with an ornament on the mantel, his face flushing. "You are a man of the world, I suppose. You know the sorts of things maids get up to."

"The girl got in trouble?" Simon asked mildly.

"Yes." Frank scowled at the ornament in his hand, replacing it with a sharp click and turning back toward Simon. "She claimed, without any proof, that the child was my father's. She was dismissed immediately, of course. And I thought that was the end of it. But it seems she married, because after my father's death her new husband turned up here, insisting that he be allowed to see the will to discover if there was any money for the child."

Simon's mind reeled. It was possible Frank was telling the truth— Mrs. Adler had told him about Edie and the baby's unknown father. But there hadn't been any mention of her in the will Mr. Hammond had shown him. "Did you pay him?"

Frank sighed. "I gave him ten pounds. It was far more than they deserved, and I thought it would be enough to put an end to things." He met Simon's eyes defiantly. "And I lied to you about it because I didn't want any sordid rumors starting about my father. But it did not occur to me until now to wonder . . ."

"You think he might have killed your father with the hope of some inheritance for the child?" Simon turned the idea over in his mind. It was certainly possible. "What does that have to do with Lady Wyatt's maid?"

"If he was responsible, she could have been the one who helped him gain entry to the house," Frank said, looking ill. "There were no signs of a break-in, as you said. So someone would have had to let him in."

"And why would she do that?" Simon knew why, of course. But he wanted to see how truthful Frank would be.

"The girl, Edie, was her niece." Frank sighed. "That man said Wilkes told him my father had died, and I didn't question it at the time. But now I wonder—he might have known because he did it. And Wilkes may have helped him because she was hoping for a pay-out for herself. I don't know. But . . . but I wanted to tell you." He met Simon's eyes, his own wide and serious. "Please. He is a coarse brawler of a man. Exactly the sort who could . . ." He shuddered, turning away. "Well, you saw what he did."

Simon said nothing for a long moment, his eyes fixed on Frank. But underneath his quiet watchfulness, his heart had begun to speed up. Something about the Wyatt case hadn't made sense. Perhaps this was what he had been missing. "I'll look into it immediately. Though I wish you hadn't dismissed Wilkes before I could speak to her. Do you know where she's gone?"

Frank shook his head. "But I know where you can find the man. He had the nerve to tell me, as though I would change my mind and send him more money. Eynsford Hill Farm, in Kent."

Simon lifted his chin, going very still. "Say that once more, please."

"Eynsford Hill Farm, in Kent." Frank frowned. "Is there something wrong?"

Simon shook his head slowly. "No . . . no. Thank you for your information, Mr. Wyatt." He bowed. "We are all well served by honesty in these matters."

"Of course." Frank looked relieved. "Thank you, Mr. Page. I am glad I can rely on you."

Simon managed a polite response as Frank departed and the butler returned to see him from the house. But inside his mind was racing. As soon as he was out of sight of the Wyatts' house, he pulled his notebook from his pocket and flipped through the pages until he had found what he wanted.

As far as Frank knew, his father's will had remained a secret. But Simon had taken careful notes the one time he had been allowed to look at it. And there it was: a bequest, amounting to an income of twenty pounds per year, to Mrs. E. Patton of Eynsford Hill Farm, Kent, and her daughter Maud.

Simon let the pages fall slowly closed.

If Edie had been dismissed and Sir Charles had denied paternity of her child, why would he have included her in his will?

★ ★ ★

"Arthur, this will be your room," Ofelia said, opening the nursery door and standing aside. "We tried to make it feel like home."

Percy had brought many of Arthur's books and art supplies with him, and Ofelia and her husband Ned had been only too happy to hang the young man's artwork around the walls, just as it had been in his schoolroom back home. The room had been arranged to feel as familiar as possible, with a bedroom for him just next door and a sleeping pallet for the maid who would stay with him.

Lily squeezed her friend's shoulder as Ofelia stepped back, allowing Percy and Arthur to explore the room. "Thank you for agreeing to help," she whispered.

"Of course we agreed," Ofelia whispered back, watching Arthur as he proceeded to arrange his pencils and papers exactly as he liked them, in straight lines and neat piles. "It isn't as if Neddy and I were using the space. Do you really think someone means him harm? It is almost too ghastly to think about."

"I know." Lily turned away, wanting to give the cousins privacy as they settled in. "Shall we leave them to it for a bit?"

"And I'll go speak to Daisy, who will be looking after him while he stays here. She will need to introduce herself and spend some time with him while Mr. Percy Wyatt is here as well."

When they started down the stairs, however, they found Mr. Page coming toward them, hat in hand and dressed for travel.

"Lady Carroway." He bowed. "Mrs. Adler. Sir Edward told me it was all right to come up. If you would step aside, please, I need to speak to the boy."

"So quickly?" Ofelia frowned. "Could you not give him some time to get settled first?"

"Unfortunately, it must be tonight. I leave for Kent as soon as I am done here."

"Kent?" Lily asked, surprised. "What did Frank say to you?"

Mr. Page hesitated. "I think I have found where Edie and her child disappeared to." Speaking quickly, as though he wanted to get it all out before he changed his mind, he told them what he had learned from Frank.

Lily felt her eyes growing wide with surprise, and a glance to the side showed her expression mirrored on Ofelia's face. "So he thinks this farmer killed Sir Charles? What would have prompted him to suddenly . . ." Lily trailed off, remembering her late-night conversation with the unsober Frank. She had mentioned rumors about the baby. Was that what had made him think of Edie's husband again?

"Whatever it was, at least he told you," Ofelia said. "Do you think this man did it?"

"I won't know until I speak to them," Mr. Page said grimly. "But I saw the man. He looked more than capable of murder."

"But Mr. Wyatt did lie," Ofelia pointed out. "They were in the will, and he had to have known it. So I wouldn't trust everything he told you."

"The will," Lily said. "That had to be why Wilkes was looking through Sir Charles's study. She wanted to find a copy to see if Edie and the baby were in it."

"Most likely," Mr. Page said, nodding abruptly. "In any case, time is short. If you'll excuse me."

The passage was narrow enough that they had to squeeze past each other, Lily and Ofelia heading downstairs while Mr. Page went up to speak to the cousins. Halfway down, though, Lily paused, biting her lip and looking back the way they had come.

Ofelia shook her head. "Go on. You know you shan't be satisfied only hearing it secondhand." She smiled. "And then you can tell me, since it is unlikely Mr. Page will."

Lily didn't wait to be urged again but stepped quickly back up the stairs.

She found Arthur settled at one of the tables, busy drawing, with Mr. Page sitting next to him and Percy Wyatt hovering anxiously nearby, shooting skeptical looks at the constable but otherwise holding his tongue.

"And Lady Wyatt?" Mr. Page was saying. Lily was surprised by how unhurried he sounded, even though he had nearly three hours of travel waiting for him and any delay made it more likely that he would be arriving in Kent after dark.

"Lady Wyatt. Not Winnie." Just enough of Arthur's face was visible that Lily could see him smiling as he drew—a reaction she wouldn't have expected, given how she had seen Lady Wyatt speak to him. But a moment later she understood why. "Lady Wyatt likes art too. Like me."

Percy frowned, looking a little surprised. "Does she?"

Arthur nodded and raised his empty hand, wiggling his fingers. "Paint," he said without looking up.

"Do you remember telling Ellen anything about Lady Wyatt? Or about your brother or father?" Mr. Page asked.

He spoke with the same gentle, calm tone of voice, but the effect on Arthur was instant. He dropped his pencil. He didn't look at any of them as he shook his head, drawing his body into a smaller space with his shoulders hunched and his chin ducked down. "Ellen says I'm to be quiet like a mouse," he said. "I want Ellen to come back."

Lily caught her breath at the misery in his voice, but a sharp glance from Mr. Page kept her where she was.

"Why did Ellen tell you to be quiet like a mouse, Arthur?"

The boy shook his head, and several tears splashed down onto his paper. "No painting at nighttime," he whimpered. "I want Ellen. My drawing is ruined, and I want Ellen to come back."

His voice was rising in distress, and more tears fell in rapid succession. Mr. Page stood, his movements still calm in spite of the tension in the room. "Thank you for talking with me, Arthur. I'll leave you and your cousin alone now." Taking Lily's elbow, he ushered her from the room as Percy bent his head close to his cousin's. They could hear him begin whispering as they closed the door behind them.

"What do you make of that?" Lily said in an undertone as they made their way downstairs.

The Bow Street constable paused in the front hall, rubbing his face with one hand. There were gray smudges of fatigue below his eyes, and Lily could see the shadow of whiskers starting to prickle the skin along his jaw. "You were right, I should have given him more time to settle in." He pulled out a pocket watch, and his mouth drew into a grim line as he glanced at it. "And there isn't time to wait any longer. I'm traveling by stage, and there's only one more to catch today." The Carroways' butler waited by the front door to hand Mr. Page his traveling valise, and Lily realized he meant to depart immediately. "Will you ask Lady Carroway to keep an eye on him? And tell me if he says anything more about either his brother or Lady Wyatt? Or anyone else in the house?"

"Of course."

"And give my apologies to Sir Edward and Lady Carroway, of course, for hurrying away so quickly."

"They will understand. Good luck in Kent. Be sure to find out how old the babe is now."

"Why?"

"To find out when the affair would have happened." Lily shrugged. "Lady Wyatt might object to someone interfering with the maids while courting her, but I cannot see her being bothered by anything that occurred before."

"A reasonable assessment." Mr. Page smiled grimly. "Is it bad that I'm almost hoping I discover that she did it? Or her husband?"

"It would certainly simplify things. But I would hate to see her child left without a mother or father." Lily laid a hand on his arm. "Safe travels, sir."

He glanced down at her hand, looking surprised. She wondered for a moment, remembering what Louisa Preston had said about middle-class morality, if she had offended his sense of propriety. But a moment later he gave her a very polite nod. "My thanks, as ever, Mrs. Adler." His smile became wry. "I seem to keep needing your assistance."

"You will have to deputize me one of these days if you are not careful."

That made him laugh. "God help us." He bowed, then placed his hat on his head. "Be well, madam. I'm sure I'll see you soon."

★ ★ ★

"I had hoped we might have company for dinner tonight."

Lily, lost in her thoughts at one end of the table, started as her father broke the silence that almost always ruled their mealtimes together. She had written to Jack earlier in the day, informing him of Arthur Wyatt's change of residence and asking if he might make Jem available at the Carroways' home, to carry word if anything important should be disclosed or discovered that night. She had hoped to hear back from him, but there had been only silence for the evening.

Wrenching her thoughts back to the present, she resisted the urge to narrow her eyes at her father. Instead, she asked, as calmly as she could, "Had you said so sooner, I am sure I could have procured some. I had no idea you felt the lack of entertainment."

Mr. Pierce snorted. "Yes, you have been such a delightful conversationalist all evening," he said sarcastically. "No, I meant that *I* attempted to procure some guests for us, to spare us both the tedium of another night as each other's sole company."

Lily's hands tightened around her silverware at the thought of her father inviting dinner guests into her own home without her permission or even knowledge. "Dare I ask who?"

"Your friend Lady Carroway, as a matter of fact, and her husband." Mr. Pierce examined the wine in his cup, sighed as if disappointed, and drank a gulp anyway.

Lily put her silverware down slowly, pleased with how calm her movements were. It didn't matter that the people he had invited were friends of hers. It didn't even matter that they hadn't been able to come. She was tired of her father acting as though she were a visitor in his home, rather than the other way around.

Oblivious to her mounting fury, Mr. Pierce continued. "I had hoped she and the baronet might have joined us for dinner, but apparently they have an unexpected houseguest and could not be spared this evening. Pity."

Their unexpected houseguest was Arthur Wyatt, but Lily had no intention of telling her father that. But the thought of the youngest Wyatt made her remember the conversation she had just barely overheard between her father and Frank Wyatt, and a sudden suspicion made her feel a hot prickle of anger all over. "Was it you who suggested sending Arthur Wyatt away?" she asked, her voice cold with fury.

"Eh?" Her father frowned at her. "What has Arthur Wyatt to do with the Carroways?"

"Nothing," Lily bit off. "But I know you and Frank were talking about him while we were there. And then Frank tells me someone wants to send Arthur away to some asylum." Her voice took on a sarcastic edge that rivaled Mr. Pierce's own. "For his own good, I am sure, and everyone else's safety. Was that your idea? Are you also so willing to pin him with the blame for his father's death?"

She realized she was shaking and snatched up her own wineglass just to give her hands something to do.

"I will thank you not to speak to me in such a tone," Mr. Pierce snapped, puffing up like an offended bird. "And no, if you must know, I intended no such thing. Sir Charles would never have wanted his son tucked away like that. But I didn't think you'd object if I kept Frank talking while you slipped out to go learn what you could about Sir Charles's death."

Lily nearly choked on her sip of wine. "What?" she spluttered.

Her father rolled his eyes, a petulant, childish gesture that somehow suited him perfectly. "That is what you do now, is it not? Poke your nose into business that is not yours? Get mixed up in murder?" He sniffed. "I ran into Lady Carroway as she was leaving yesterday, and she had particularly complimentary things to say about the assistance you provided her before her marriage. And I decided, if you could help her, why not Frank? Since you may have some influence with that wretched Bow Street man after all, I decided I'd see what you could do."

Lily stared at him, dumbfounded. He'd managed to make the pronouncement sound like enough of an insult that she had trouble believing his actual words. Had he really just said he was trying to help her?

"Well? Did you manage to find anything?" he asked, looking bored.

Lily found her voice at last. "I did not attempt to."

She didn't want to tell him about the murdered maid or that Bow Street's best suspect for her death was the young man of whom he was so fond. Her father would be furious to find out that Frank Wyatt, of all people, was suspected of murder. And she didn't trust him not to tell Frank whatever he learned from her.

That might even be his tactic. The thought made her grow cold. Did Frank already know she might be assisting Bow Street? Was that why he had come by the night before? And was her father now fishing for information that he could carry back to the man she had so often felt he wished were his own son?

Mr. Pierce eyed what was left of his dinner dubiously, then pushed his plate aside to pour himself another glass of wine. "Try not to look quite so shocked, Lily," he said as he took a sip. "Where do you think you got your brains if not from me?"

Lily swallowed, trying to make her voice sound as normal as possible. She could be leaping to conclusions, but she had to be careful. "Is that your way of saying you think I am clever?"

He snorted. "I know you're clever, girl. I never had any quibble with your mind. What I wish is that you were more ladylike."

"You mean malleable."

"They are the same thing, are they not? And please stop trying to show off. No one wants to listen to a woman attempting to sound like a man."

Lily drew in a sharp breath, then let it out slowly. "And what about a woman who is trying to sound like herself?" she asked, once she had her voice under control again.

Mr. Pierce sighed, looking genuinely sad. Lily hated that she knew it was genuine. "The trouble, Lily, is that your self is rather grating."

It ought to have been hurtful. But she suddenly felt too tired to even be upset anymore. She sighed, shaking her head. "What an odd way you have of delivering compliments, Father."

Pushing back her chair, she stood. Her father, she noticed, didn't bother to do the same, though the good manners he was always harping on ought to have required it. But she hadn't the energy to point out the lapse. "I thank you for your wish to help. But I assure you, Bow Street needs neither your assistance nor mine to do their job. If you will excuse me, I believe I will retire for the night."

She didn't wait for his reply before leaving.

★ ★ ★

It would be dark in an hour, but the proprietor at the coaching inn told Simon that Eynsford Hill Farm was only a fifteen-minute walk and that Mr. and Mrs. Patton lived there with a right passel of little ones. Once Simon paid for his room, the man was even willing to offer the loan of a lantern that Simon could use on the way back.

Simon almost argued himself out of going that night—he had a nephew and a niece who lived with him at home, and he knew well enough how hectic evenings could be with young ones underfoot. But if he could talk to the Pattons that night, he could catch the first stagecoach back to London in the morning. And Lord knew he needed to get back to London before Mr. Nares at Bow Street decided to take action on the Wyatt case without him.

He accepted the lantern with ample thanks and set off in the direction the innkeeper pointed, keeping an eye out for a footbridge that would lead to a fork, where he was to take the right path and follow it a quarter mile farther.

"There's on'y one lane at the end, and Hill Farm is at the end. Ye can't miss it," the innkeeper promised. "And give them my congratulations, o'course. Tell them I'll be sending along a stew an' a pie with my Sally in the morning."

Simon, a little baffled, said something in agreement, a little too preoccupied with repeating the directions to himself to pay too much attention. He'd be able to question the man over breakfast to confirm whatever the Pattons told him—an innkeeper was bound to be a veritable font of local gossip.

It wasn't until he was crossing the footbridge that he thought to wonder what the congratulations were for. But by then it was too late to ask.

He pressed on, glad that it had been a cloudless day and that the light was lingering. The directions he had been given were good, and it wasn't long before he found himself following the single lane that led to what looked like a small, tidy farmhouse—not the home of a gentleman farmer, certainly, but prosperous enough.

The light was just starting to fade as Simon reached the house and knocked. There was a quick scuffle of movement inside, then silence.

Simon frowned. He was about to knock again when the door was yanked open and he found himself staring into the muzzle of a hunting rifle.

CHAPTER 23

After more than a decade of pursuing the criminals of London, Simon didn't freeze when confronted with a weapon. But his mind did dart through half a dozen choices in the moment it took him to draw a shocked breath.

In other circumstances, he might have tried to attack, to get inside the range of the rifle, to disarm his opponent. But if this was the Pattons' house, there were likely children around. He didn't want to put them in any danger. Instead, he took a smooth step back and raised his hands, showing that he was unarmed. There was no way he was going to smile into the muzzle of a gun, but he tried to make his expression as harmless as possible.

"Mr. Patton?" he asked, his voice somewhere between soothing and official. The spill of light from inside, after his walk through the fading twilight, made it hard to see. But it seemed a reasonable guess.

There was a pause from the other end of the rifle. "Who's asking?"

"My name is Simon Page, of London. I'm hoping to talk to Mrs. Patton about the will of Sir Charles Wyatt. I understand there is some confusion."

Another pause, and then the gun lowered slowly. Simon's eyes had adjusted now, and he recognized the man facing him as the fellow he had seen through the window on Wimpole Street, talking angrily with Frank Wyatt.

"What's the confusion?" Patton demanded, and Simon could see his hands tighten around the grip of the rifle.

"Sir Charles left a bequest settled on Maud. May I come in to discuss the details?"

"A what?" Patton frowned.

"A yearly income." Simon eyed the man in front of him. Patton was younger than he had thought when he first saw him in London, perhaps in his middle thirties, but with the fatigued look of a man who worked too hard each day to maintain a precarious living. The money Sir Charles had left would make a big difference to this family—and gave them every reason to wish him dead. "May I come in?"

Patton nodded gruffly, finally standing the gun on its butt next to the door and stepping aside. "Little 'uns are asleep upstairs, so keep y'voice down, if y'please."

The farmhouse was more spacious on the inside than Simon had expected. The front sitting room was well cared for, the furniture threadbare but scrupulously clean. Through one half-open door, he could see a kitchen and dining table, with slightly more mess visible than in the front room. A staircase presumably led to the room or rooms upstairs where the children were—a passel of little ones, the innkeeper had said—with two other doors on the main floor.

After gesturing Simon to sit down, Patton went to one of these and poked his head in. "Edie, girl?" he said, his quiet voice carrying back to where Simon waited. "You decent? There's a gentleman down from London says he's here to talk about Sir Charles's will." A pause. "I don't know, but he says there's a *be* . . . a something coming to our Maud." Another pause. "Well, bring her with you. If he minds, he oughtn't have showed up at sunset."

Simon was frowning over this last statement when Edie emerged from what he assumed was the couple's bedroom, draped in a heavy shawl and clutching a tiny bundle to her chest. She moved slowly, leaning on her husband's arm as she did so, but she smiled politely at Simon as he rose to greet her.

"Mrs. Patton? I'm Simon Page. From London, as your husband said. I apologize for calling so late; the stage only just arrived an hour ago."

"Normally I'd scold you, Mr. Page, and tell you that farmers sleep at sundown. But our schedule is all topsy-turvy these days," Edie said, her voice on the quiet side.

As she sat, using her husband's arm to balance, he realized why. The bundle she held was a newborn baby.

Simon started, suddenly understanding the innkeeper's words.

"Congratulations, Mrs. Patton. And you as well, Mr. Patton," he added, glancing at the proud father, who was beaming down at his wife and new child. "I understand this is not your first?"

"Aye, I had two boys with my first wife afore she died," Mr. Patton said, taking his own seat near Edie. "And then Maud was born soon after we was wed. This little lass is number four."

"A fine family," Simon said politely. "How old is the babe?"

Edie chuckled. "The days all blur together, no mistake. But she's, let's see . . . four days old." She bent her head to nuzzle the sleeping bundle. "Getting big, aren't we?" she cooed.

Simon counted back the days quickly. The child had arrived the day after Sir Charles died. One of them could still have. . . He cleared his throat. He didn't have a wife and child of his own, but he knew more than a little about how they made their way into the world. "You and the babe are both doing well, I see. I hope it was a safe delivery." He hesitated, then added wryly, "I have often thought our soldiers could learn a thing or two about stamina and strength from the laboring mothers of England."

Both the Pattons laughed.

"You'll hear no disagreement from me, sir," Edie said, shaking her head even as she stared blissfully at the newborn. Simon could see only a sliver of red cheek, but even that little amount took him back to visiting his sister after the births of his nephew and niece. "Took little miss here near two full days to come."

Simon nodded sympathetically, keeping his face and manner as calm as possible. Edie couldn't have murdered Sir Charles—even had she not been in labor, no one as far along in a pregnancy would have been able to travel to London, sneak into the townhouse of a wealthy man, overpower him, and kill him. But her husband was another matter.

Simon cleared his throat, adding a jovial note to his voice as he said, "I hope the lads at the inn were able to pour you a stiff drink or two while you waited it out, Mr. Patton."

The farmer shook his head. "I lost one wife in childbirth, Mr. Page. Even once the doctor arrived, I wasn't going anywhere while my girl was workin' so hard here."

It took all Simon's self-control to stay seated. If Mr. Patton had been by his wife's side for those two days, there was no way he could have murdered Sir Charles either.

Which meant it had to be one of the Wyatts.

"I think he bullied her into giving up her cozy lodgings," Edie said, rolling her eyes. "Not that I'm complaining. I was that ready to be done."

"Gave us a right scare, she did, taking so long," Patton added, taking his wife's hand and giving her a gentle smile. "Poor Edie."

"But excuse us, sir, you ain't here to talk about childbirth, of course," Edie said, looking up at last. "You want to talk about Maud, I think."

"Yes." Simon hesitated. He had what he had come for. But there was always the chance they were lying. And Mr. Patton had shown up in London demanding to know whether there was anything in the will for his wife's daughter—money that he, as her father, would see added to his own income, at least until Maud came of age.

The Pattons misread his hesitation, though, and exchanged a furtive glance. Patton sighed and shook his head. "It's all right, Mr. Page. You can speak plain. If you've seen the will, you know how things stand. Maud's my daughter under the law, but everyone around here knows the truth of things. Nothing to do about that." He shrugged. "Mr. Frank already gave us that ten pounds, which we was glad to have, believe me. But if Sir Charles left her summat more, that'll go a long way to easing her life."

"And yours?" Simon couldn't help asking, though he managed not to speak too sharply.

"I've got four little ones now, Mr. Page," the farmer said, a note of wry humor in his voice. "Nothing's going to make my life easy."

"He agreed to be stuck with us long before this, and he'll be stuck long after." Edie laughed, giving the baby a little rock as she whimpered in her sleep. Simon couldn't quite keep the shock from his face at her levity; most women would be far more embarrassed about having become pregnant and wed under such circumstances. But Edie was giving her husband a teasing smile. "I've a feeling you wouldn't have come all this way with bad news, and Lord knows poor Mr. Patton deserves some good for putting up with me."

"You're a handful, girl, but I like you well enough," the blond giant rumbled, smiling back at her.

Simon, unsure where to look when faced with such an obvious display of affection, cleared his throat and brought out a paper covered in scribbled notes. Before leaving London, he had paid a visit to Mr. Hammond once more. After being told what Frank Wyatt had done, the solicitor had agreed both to let Simon take another look at the will and to travel to Kent himself to sort out the matter of Maud Patton's inheritance. Simon had made the trip immediately, of course, wanting to see before the solicitor got there whether there was any possibility of the Pattons' guilt. He had come prepared with the details of the bequest.

As he read them out, he kept a careful eye on both Edie and her husband, watching their faces for any sign that they were less surprised by Sir Charles's gift than they should have been.

" 'To Mrs. E. Patton and her daughter Maud Patton, a bequest of four hundred pounds, the interest of which will provide an income of twenty pounds per year.' The income will go to you, Mr. and Mrs. Patton, until Maud either turns twenty-one or marries, whichever comes first. After that, two hundred and fifty pounds goes to Maud—the income will go to her husband if she marries, but the terms of the will stipulate that the money itself will remain hers, to settle as she wishes after her death—and the remaining hundred fifty pounds will belong to Mrs. Patton until her death, after which they'll revert to Maud once more."

"Twenty pounds per year," Patton breathed.

"And a dowry for our girl." Edie's eyes had filled with tears, and she quickly brushed them away. "Excuse me, Mr. Page; I'm a right waterworks when the babes are little, especially right after they come. But a dowry!" She shook her head, cuddling the bundle in her arms close and smiling through her tears. "Sir Charles gave me forty pounds, you know, when I told him I had to leave service. He wanted me to get married so that his child wouldn't be born a bastard. Mr. Patton wanted to pay off the mortgage on the farm, so it worked out well enough."

"Edie grew up near here," Patton said. "And my little ones needed a mother."

His entire face had gone red with embarrassment at having the mercenary foundations of his marriage laid so bare. But Simon saw nothing to judge. Providing the protection of his name to a woman and child who might otherwise have been ostracized and impoverished was a noble gesture, especially when he knew it meant that another man's child would be legally considered his own. And the Pattons at least seemed to be genuinely fond of each other, which was more than could be said for plenty of marriages based on economic or social necessity.

"So I knew Sir Charles was a good man," Edie said earnestly.

Simon couldn't help the way his eyebrows climbed toward his hairline. "Forgive me, Mrs. Patton, but I'm surprised to hear you say so. After he . . ." He cleared his throat, unsure how to phrase his point.

Patton's blush grew, rising to the edge of his sandy hair, but Edie shook her head. "You ain't never been in service, Mr. Page, I can see that much. I'll tell you for free, there are plenty of gentlemen as think nothing of interfering with their maids, whether the maids like it or not. Sir Charles may have enjoyed lifting a skirt or two, but he never did it unless the girl in question was willing. And he never told me to get rid of the babe once he found out I was in the family way neither. Never tried to say it wasn't his neither. Just made sure we was going to be all right."

"You was always courtin' trouble, even as a girl," Patton said, half severely, half in exasperation, as he shook his head at his wife. "No surprise to anyone around here that y'found plenty of it being in service in London."

"Well, she's your little girl now, and you couldn't ask for a sweeter," Edie countered, tossing her head a little as she gave her husband a pert look.

"Aye, true enough, and now we've this little one," Patton said, leaning over to brush a gentle hand against the sleeping newborn's head. "You don't hear me complaining."

There was, Simon guessed, over a decade of difference in their ages. But they seemed to get along well. More to the point, they both seemed genuinely happy with the way things had worked out. And he thought, as Edie turned to him, that they were truly grateful for Sir Charles's generosity.

"He doesn't, you know, much as he likes to give me a setdown every now and then," she said, tucking in the baby's blankets a little more tightly. "We was able to pay off the farm's mortgage. And the parish has a school that the children will be able to go to. With another twenty pounds a year . . ." Her eyes grew wide and wondering. "We'll have almost a gentleman's income!"

An impoverished gentleman's, Simon wanted to point out—at most that of a very young curate with no family to support. But he didn't say so. For a family like the Pattons, twenty pounds would come near to doubling their income. They would be able to hire help on the farm, which would allow their sons, and perhaps even their daughters, to get an education. Their grandchildren might even be able to enter the more genteel professions and stand shoulder to shoulder with gentlemen in truth.

"And a dowry for Maud," Patton said. There was no trace of resentment in his voice over the fact that his other children wouldn't have the same; with more than forty pounds per year now, he might even be able to provide a small dowry for his other daughter. "You was right when you said he was a kind man." He cleared his throat. "That Sir Charles, I mean."

"Well, I knew you couldn't mean Mr. Frank," Edie said, her expression darkening. "Him wanting to keep that from his own sister! I never asked them to acknowledge her," she added earnestly, turning to Simon. "It would just have made her life harder, poor thing, being caught between worlds like that. But you'd think he'd want to know she never would go hungry, or that she'd have a dowry to make a good marriage and better herself. His own sister!"

The tension in her body must have traveled through her arms; the sleeping baby began to whimper and squirm a little. Edie fell silent, though her expression was still thunderous.

"Easy," Patton said, laying a hand on his wife's arm. "If he'd kept it from her, he'd have had to answer for it one day, in the next life if not this one. And Maud would've still grown up loved and safe."

"I know, but . . ." Edie's voice was calmer now, and she rocked the baby gently as she shook her head. "That Frank has always been a nasty piece of work. Makes out like he's such a fine gentleman, but he always wants what other people have. He don't like his brother, so I suppose it's no wonder he don't like his sister neither."

"And Maud won't ever have a thing to do with him now," Patton said firmly, his hand still moving up and down his wife's arm in a soothing caress.

Simon, watching them, felt a pang of jealousy. How could two people who had such a hard life, whose marriage was founded on such odd circumstances, seem so content, so *happy* together? His work meant that he so often saw the worst of humanity, and he had come to Kent expecting to be met with more of the same. It was disorienting to suddenly be confronted with the exact opposite.

Clearing his throat, he stood abruptly. "I ought to be going. My apologies for calling so late, and thank you for speaking with me."

"Will you be by tomorrow, then?" Patton asked.

Simon shook his head. "I'll be returning to London tomorrow." He would need to talk to the local doctor to confirm that Edie had given birth the day she claimed and that Mr. Patton had indeed been by her side. But once that was done, he could be on his way back to town.

"But . . ." Edie looked surprised. "Are there papers we're needing to sign? Something we have to do? I never had to deal with a bank or solicitors; I'm not sure how it's managed."

"I imagine a representative from the solicitors will be here tomorrow, or perhaps the day after, to discuss the pertinent information with you."

The Pattons exchanged a confused look. "But you said you was from the solicitor's," Edie said, frowning.

"No." Simon shook his head, replacing his hat on his head. "I said I was from London."

A scowl slid across Patton's face, and he stood slowly, his size making the movement menacing. Simon was glad he had placed himself between the man and the rifle that still rested by the door—a deliberate choice, of course.

"Then who are you?" the farmer asked, while Edie glanced between them with growing unease.

"Simon Page, as I told you. I am a principal officer of the Bow Street police force."

Edie shrank back, clutching the baby against her so tightly that it began stirring again. "But what's that got to do with us?" she said, sounding a little frantic.

"Did the Wyatts send you here to find my wife?" Patton demanded, his burly hands clenching into fists as he took a step forward. "What does that Frank want from us?"

Simon wasn't a large or intimidating man; in fact, a fellow Bow Street officer had once described him as "remarkably forgettable" due to his average appearance. But he wasn't easily cowed, and he knew how to hold his own under pressure. He didn't back down as the farmer advanced toward him. Instead, he crossed his arms and sighed.

"Mr. Patton, if you think about it for a moment, you'll realize that Mr. Frank Wyatt had no reason to *tell* you about Maud's inheritance, so I couldn't possibly have been sent by him."

"Then who are you, and why are you in my house?"

"Did no one tell you?" Simon asked, looking slowly from one face to another. He prided himself on his ability to read people. The Pattons were afraid, yes, but they were even more confused. He had a feeling that when he talked to the doctor, he would find that everything they had told him was true. "Sir Charles Wyatt was murdered."

Edie let out a choked sort of gasp, clutching her baby so tightly that the child began crying in earnest, finally awake. Patton stared at him in shock.

"Frank Wyatt said it was an accident. That he had tripped and—"

"Frank Wyatt was lying."

"But why?" Edie asked, finding her voice at last. "Why would he do that?"

Simon shook his head. "That's what I'm trying to find out."

She had called him a nasty piece of work. Nasty enough to have killed Ellen, perhaps? But he wouldn't have done that unless he had also been the one to kill his father.

Did his trying to keep his half sister's inheritance from her make him more likely to have killed his father? If he had killed for money, he would likely want to keep as much as possible of his father's fortune for himself. That would mean cutting out little Maud, possibly even his brother, Arthur.

Mrs. Adler had said she couldn't imagine Frank killing for money. But perhaps she was deceived by her history with the family. Unless there was something he was missing . . .

Simon sat back down in his chair and leaned forward, resting his elbows on his knees. "Mrs. Patton, what else can you tell me about the Wyatts?"

CHAPTER 24

After leaving her father alone in the dining room, Lily stalked to her book-room in a blind fury, ignoring Carstairs as he tried to catch her eye in the hall. He also said something as she strode past, but she shook her head, not wanting to be interrupted.

She needed her father out of her house. He would always prefer Frank Wyatt to her—*always*—and the risk of having him there, the risk that he might tell the Wyatts what she had been up to in their home, was too great.

Someone had murdered Sir Charles. Someone had murdered Ellen. And as much as she didn't want to admit it, it seemed Frank Wyatt was the one most likely to have done so. If only they could prove where he'd been the night of his father's death.

Lily yanked open the door of the book-room and was two steps inside before she realized she was not alone.

Jack jumped to his feet as she entered, an expression of alarm on his face. "Lily, what happened?"

Lily stared at him for a moment, wondering why he hadn't been announced. But then she realized he must have information to share with her that he didn't want her father to know about. Raising a quick finger to her lips, she peeked out into the hallway, where she discovered Carstairs hovering, looking disapproving and a little nervous.

"As I tried to tell you, madam, Captain Hartley has called to see you. He asked not to be announced, which I know is highly irregular, but considering—"

"Of course," she said quickly, giving her butler a tight smile. It was hard to let go of her fury with her father so quickly, but Carstairs deserved none of her ire. "Please inform me if my father goes out, but otherwise the captain and I do not want to be disturbed."

"Of course, madam." Carstairs bowed, hiding whatever discomfort he might have felt. Such a visit, accompanied by an order not to be disturbed, was hardly proper. But Lily knew she could rely on the discretion of her servants. And more to the point, she knew Carstairs would understand that he was to keep her father far away from her if at all possible for the rest of the evening.

Lily closed the door and turned to find Jack eyeing her with a worried expression. "What happened?" he asked.

Lily rubbed her eyes wearily. "My father. He knows." She swallowed, meeting Jack's eyes. "He knows I am assisting Mr. Page. And I fear he may tell the Wyatts."

"He'd not do that, would he?" Jack had already helped himself to a glass of her whiskey. Without being asked, he poured her one. They settled into their regular spots, two chairs near each other in front of the fireplace, which had been banked to burn low, providing just enough warmth for a brisk July evening. "If he knows what you are up to, he must also realize that one of the Wyatts is guilty of murder. Surely . . ."

Lily took a gulp of her drink and stared at the embers. "If it comes down to it, I have no confidence in my father believing me over Frank Wyatt." She met Jack's eyes, feeling bleak. "Or choosing me, should he have to decide which of our reputations survives this."

"You mean he would expose what you have been doing, publicly, to prevent anything happening to Frank?"

"Yes." Lily closed her eyes, nodding, then shook her head. "I still cannot believe Frank could have killed his father. But he clearly wants to prevent Bow Street from making any arrests—of any family members or servants. If my father tells him that I am the one stirring up trouble, they have only to start *that* rumor spreading. And suddenly I am the one who is unnatural, who is behaving badly, who is the subject of gossip and distaste. And the Wyatts' scandal is forgotten." She opened her eyes, then narrowed them in Jack's direction. "But you and Mr. Page are still not convinced when I say Frank did not kill Sir Charles."

"I have no choice but to be now," Jack said, sounding a little unhappy about the fact. He stared into his glass, then sighed.

"What did you find out?"

"I visited near a dozen gaming houses in St. James and Piccadilly over the last few days, and I finally found the one where Mr. Wyatt was playing faro that night." Jack looked pleased with himself in spite of the fact that he didn't like his own news. "Faro houses keep very careful records of who won, and when, and how much. They need to know who the dangerous players are so they can keep an eye on them. And so they can spot a cheat."

"Jack." Lily sat up abruptly, eyes wide. "You did not steal the records, did you?"

"Of course not." He looked affronted. "I asked, and the owner of the gaming house showed them to me."

They regarded each other for a long moment. "I am guessing this owner was female."

"You don't think men find me equally charming?"

"I don't think that is where your particular talents lie," Lily said, her voice dry as old toast.

Jack laughed. "Well, you would be right about that. And yes, she was female. And as it happened, I knew her."

"Dare I ask how?"

"She has been the very respected mistress of several naval officers—not all at the same time, of course; that is not how these things work—and I once had the honor of bringing her to Portsmouth to welcome one of her protectors home. We got along very well."

Lily hoped she wasn't blushing. There were things that weren't often discussed in the presence of women, even when they were widows. And as comfortable as they were with each other, she had certainly never expected to discuss them with Jack. But she could see him smiling at her embarrassment, so she lifted her chin and said, "I don't suppose she was the sort of mistress you could afford to keep."

He laughed. "Most certainly not. But she was a very entertaining companion for travel. Knew lots of excellent gossip. Absolutely bested me at piquet."

"And I assume her facility with cards is what led her to run a gaming house, once she no longer wished to live upon the income of her physical charms?"

"Precisely." Jack leaned back, stretching his booted feet out in front of him comfortably. "Stroke of luck, her being there. But if it had not been at her house, she would have vouched for me with whoever's books I needed to see."

"And her records say Frank Wyatt was there?"

Jack sighed. "Well into the morning, just as he said."

Lily eyed her friend. He was disappointed with his discovery, and not just because he'd wanted to find an answer. "You wanted him to have done it."

Jack scowled but said nothing.

"Why?" she pressed. "He is hardly an unpleasant fellow. And better to know with certainty that he did not do it."

"Maybe I dislike anyone that your father so obviously prefers to you."

Lily rolled her eyes. "Then you will have to dislike Lady Carroway as well, because he finds her infinitely preferable."

"Really?" Jack looked skeptical. "And yet he still looks down on my having an Indian mother."

Lily shrugged. "She has a title. She comes from a respectable family and married in a way that pleases and betters them. She is girlish and warm and a charming conversationalist. What is there to dislike?"

"Nothing, but there is nothing to dislike about you either," Jack said loyally. It warmed Lily to hear him say it. Just as she was about to thank him, he added, "Or me."

That made her laugh. "Or you," she agreed, reaching out to squeeze his hand. The gesture made him smile, and they sat in comfortable silence for a moment before his face grew serious once more.

"But if it was not Frank," Jack said at last, "and it was not Percy, and not Arthur, then it had to be Lady Wyatt."

"Who gained nothing from her husband's death but a return to relative poverty, and who physically could not have overpowered or moved him."

Jack met her eyes. "We are missing something."

They were. But Lily had no idea what it could be.

★　★　★

"And then he told me that I might join his harem, and of course I said yes."

Lily was pulled out of her distraction with a jolt of confusion. She stopped in the middle of the path they were walking to stare at Ofelia, certain she could not have heard correctly. "What?"

"Well, that at least got you to attend." The young Lady Carroway looped her arm once more through her friend's and pulled her back into motion. "I do not think you have heard a word I said since we left Hanover Square. And I have said some very interesting words." Ofelia glanced around at the crowded pathways of Hyde Park, then lowered her voice. "I would ask you what you are thinking of, but I can already guess."

Lily grimaced. She had paid a visit to the Carroways' home that morning, hoping that Arthur might have revealed something more about his family. According to Ofelia, he and Daisy, the maid assigned to his care, seemed to be getting along well. But he had been unsettled by the transition and wasn't in the mood to speak to anyone.

"Perhaps we can go for a walk," Ofelia had suggested. "And when we return, he might be more interested in company."

They had walked in the direction of Hyde Park, and apparently arrived there, though Lily couldn't remember entering at any of the gates. She sighed, squeezing her friend's arm. "I apologize for being such terrible company. And I am very glad you are not joining a harem. You should probably save that for at least five years into your marriage."

Ofelia laughed, but without really paying attention, her eye caught by someone in front of them. "I think I spy the captain up ahead. But who is that he is walking with?"

Lily followed her friend's line of sight and was surprised to see Jack strolling arm in arm with a familiar figure. "That is Lady Wyatt."

"Hmm." Ofelia let out a thoughtful sigh. "He did say she seemed fond of his company; I think this is not the first time they have gone strolling together."

"Really?" Lily's surprise brought her to a halt without her realizing it. "He did not mention it to me."

"He did not?" said Ofelia, looking puzzled. "He told me that, since she seemed to have a preference for his company, he might as well see what information she let fall about the state of affairs at the Wyatt home. But it is odd he did not mention it to you."

"Especially since he so recently chided me for spending time in Mr. Frank Wyatt's company when he was under suspicion," Lily said tartly, taking Ofelia's arm and leading her in the opposite direction. "But if he is pursuing some bit of information, best we not interrupt."

"Hmm," said Ofelia again, though what that second *hmm* might mean, Lily couldn't guess. "I think they did not see us." She waited until they had been out of sight for some minutes before asking eagerly, "What do you think he might be trying to learn from her?"

Before Lily could reply, a voice called out, "Mrs. Adler!"

They both started, and Ofelia looked panicked for a moment before she recovered her polite, cheerful mask. Lily, who recognized the voice, felt a momentary surge of anxiety, but it too was gone from her face as she turned to greet the man coming toward them.

"Mr. Wyatt, what a pleasure."

Frank Wyatt smiled at her and shook his head. "Am I back to Mr. Wyatt again?" he said.

"Am I back to Mrs. Adler?" She didn't mind the formality at all; anything to put some distance between them after that drunken, unwanted kiss.

"We are in public." He shrugged one shoulder, swinging an elegantly carved walking stick in a lazy circle.

As he was dressed in mourning, it had a beautiful knob of jet on the top, and he wore black gloves that gave Lily a momentary pang of painful memory. She glanced down at her own gloves—pale blue now, a gift from Freddy's mother that had lain in her drawer, waiting. Then she pulled her mind back to the current moment.

"I didn't think you wanted me shouting *Lily!* for everyone in Hyde Park to hear." Frank smiled again, then turned to Ofelia with a polite lift of his hat. "Madam."

"Lady Carroway, may I present Mr. Frank Wyatt, who grew up not far from my father's property in Devon. Mr. Wyatt, Lady Carroway."

Ofelia offered her hand for Frank to bow over. "Mr. Wyatt. I hope you will not be offended when I say I have heard your name." Lily almost snorted with grim humor at the understatement, though there was an impressive lack of irony in Ofelia's voice, considering that she was currently, unbeknownst to Frank, housing his brother. "My condolences on the loss of your father. I can only imagine how difficult it must be."

Frank closed his eyes briefly, his mouth stretching out in a pained, grateful smile. "I thank you, Lady Carroway. It has been a hard loss."

"Made more so, I am sure, by the interference of those Runners," Ofelia suggested. At Frank's look of surprise, she shook her head. "One does not like to listen to gossip, of course, but word does get around. How that must have added to your distress."

Lily tried to give her friend a warning glance, but Ofelia was very deliberately avoiding eye contact. Lily held her breath, waiting for what Frank might say in response.

To her surprise, he glanced at her before he said it. "I am sure the Bow Street fellows are doing their job admirably," he said, though there was a touch of sarcasm to his voice. "As Mrs. Adler admires their work, I'll not offend her by maligning them too severely."

"Even if you wish to?" Ofelia said sympathetically, her expression growing ever so slightly impish. "You can blame me for being a bad influence, if you wish, and I am sure Mrs. Adler will not hold it against you."

At that, Frank laughed. "Thank you, my lady. I have not had many opportunities to laugh of late." He sighed, his expression growing more serious. "Truthfully, I wish the whole business were done."

"I am sure Lady Wyatt feels the same," Lily said. "How is she? The last I saw her, she seemed so dreadfully fatigued."

"Unfortunately, I cannot really say, nor will I have many more opportunities for reporting on her welfare. Winnie is preparing to return to her mother's home, permanently." At their twin looks of surprise, he shrugged. "It is an awkward business, to be sure, but the house comes to me, not her. And I don't think she is comfortable staying much longer."

"Surely you will visit, though," Ofelia said encouragingly. "Or at the very least, correspond."

"Perhaps," Frank said vaguely before he turned to Lily. "I've no wish to interrupt your walk more than I already have, but I wonder if you might ask your father to call on me this evening? We leave for Devonshire tomorrow, and I should be grateful to have his opinion on several matters that my father left in an unfortunate state before we go."

"I am sure he will be delighted. My father so enjoys telling other people what to do."

Frank gave her a wry smile. "My thanks. Good day to you both, Lady Carroway, Mrs. Adler." He bowed to each of them before taking Lily's hand and brushing a quick kiss over it. "Perhaps I will have cause to see you in Devon later this year." He smiled as he said it, his eyes meeting hers briefly before he released her hand and turned away.

Lily watched him go, feeling a little uneasy. She had been sure his behavior the other night was drunken playacting. But that final smile had been downright flirtatious. She shook her head, turning away from where he was disappearing around the bend, and found Ofelia watching her with a considering look.

"Is he *courting* you?"

"If he thinks to, he will be most severely disappointed. What did you make of him?"

Ofelia frowned, fiddling with the buttons on one glove as she considered the question. "He is not a very open person," she said at last. "Polite and charming, of course, with an excellent manner. But not open. I rather suspect he is the sort of man who could lie to your face and you would never know."

Lily blinked in surprise. "He was as a boy," she said. "But that is hardly uncommon with children."

"And thanks to the captain and his"—Ofelia waggled her eyebrows for emphasis—"*naval connections*, we know he wasn't lying about where he was the night of his father's death." She sighed as they began walking again. "Now, I must admit, the person I most want to meet is Lady Wyatt. Your reports of her are intriguing. So politely mercenary! And what a pity that she should befriend one of her husband's sons but take such a dislike to the other. And when Arthur is so perfectly sweet!"

Lily frowned. "Unfortunately, she was friends with neither of her husband's sons. That happens sometimes in a second marriage. I imagine that was why she wanted to leave Wimpole Street so quickly, even if it did mean returning to the home of her parents."

"But . . ." Ofelia frowned. "She and Mr. Frank Wyatt are friends, of course."

"No, not in the least. They are rather known for their animosity toward each other."

"But he called her Winnie. And Arthur has told me that is a name only her friends may call her."

Lily's feet slowed to a stop as she stared at her friend, eyes wide with surprise. Ofelia was right. Lady Wyatt had said as much herself on the afternoon Lily had heard her yelling at Arthur in the hallway.

It hadn't struck her because she had heard Frank call his father's wife Winnie before. And it was the sort of familiarity that should have seemed natural in a family, even between a grown man and his father's second wife.

Except there had been no such familiarity between them. And Frank Wyatt, she knew, wasn't the sort of man to be careless in how he addressed others, as he had just proven a moment before.

But he had called Lady Wyatt Winnie. Not even Winifred, her given name, but Winnie, the pet name reserved for her closest friends. He wouldn't have begun calling her that without permission.

When had she heard him say it?

Once at her home, and once the day after Sir Charles's death, when Mr. Page was interviewing them.

Lady Wyatt had been displeased with him then. Lily hadn't given it a second thought—surely she had every right to be. But what if she hadn't been displeased so much because of what he had said but because of who had heard it and what it might reveal?

"What is it?" Ofelia whispered, taking Lily's arm and urging her off the path, where their sudden pause might look odd to anyone passing by. There was a small grove of trees a few steps away, with a bench underneath. Ofelia steered them toward it, smiling politely at the people they passed to avoid any poorly timed offers of assistance. "Mrs. Adler?"

Lily sat, feeling dazed as what she'd thought she'd known about the Wyatts shifted entirely. "Ofelia," she whispered, raising her eyes at last. "The maid said Lady Wyatt began refusing her husband her bed perhaps a month after they married, though they had seemed a devoted couple before. And at some point she must have invited her husband's son to call her by the name only her intimate friends used."

Ofelia's eyes grew wide. "Had . . ." She hesitated. "Do you know whether Lady Wyatt had met Frank before her marriage?"

Lily shook her head. "I know for a fact that she had not. Theirs was a brief courtship, and she did not meet either of Sir Charles's sons until after they were already wed."

Ofelia again hesitated, looking ill. "Do you think she killed her husband because she was in love with his son? How horrifying."

"And almost too Gothic to believe," Lily said. It seemed ludicrous. But even as she told herself it couldn't be true, she couldn't help thinking back to all the interactions between Frank and Lady Wyatt that she had observed.

The animosity between them had always seemed so determined. But had there been something exaggerated about it? Something almost like a performance?

"But possible," Lily added. She stood abruptly, her hands shaking. "It is possible." Unable to keep still, she began pacing through the little woodland, away from the path they had been on before and toward the next field.

"But do you think he knew?" Ofelia asked, bounding to her feet and following. Glancing around, though there was no one promenading nearby, she lowered her voice. "Could he love her too?"

Lily halted so abruptly that Ofelia almost bumped into her. "But she could not have killed him. Whoever killed Sir Charles would have had to overpower him, then move him from where he was actually killed to a spot on the other side of the room. And Lady Wyatt was a slight woman. Her arm might have even been injured still. She couldn't have done all that."

"The maid was poisoned; maybe Sir Charles was as well," Ofelia suggested, then frowned. "But no, he died of a blow to the head. With help? Maybe Frank helped her?"

"But he was not there." Lily slammed her hand against the trunk of a tree, the sudden violence of the motion making Ofelia jump. "There is something between them; you were right, I am sure of it. They have always been so . . . there was no reason for them to air their dislike of each other so publicly. Just as there is no reason for Frank to play at courting me. No reason except convincing everyone around them that they are not in love with each other." She took a deep breath. "But I suppose their being in love with each other does not automatically mean they were the ones to kill him. Perhaps they played at hating each other because they wanted to convince themselves."

"We are still missing something," Ofelia said. Just as Jack had said the night before.

And Lily, though she felt she was only a breath away from discovering it, still had no idea what it was.

★   ★   ★

It wasn't until she was home, alone once more and pacing across her room while the light faded, that Lily thought about Ofelia's first suggestion.

Could Sir Charles have been poisoned? Mr. Page had said Sir Charles had died of a blow to the head. But was there some kind of poison that could have immobilized him? Left him vulnerable, even to a person much smaller than he?

But where would a woman like Lady Wyatt find such a thing, or learn about it in the first place? And how would she, once he was dead, have moved him to a new spot in the room?

Lily frowned, staring out the window, oblivious to the stunning sunset that was painting the skies above London in shades of crimson and gold. Closing her eyes, she pictured the library in the house on Wimpole Street, tried to remember everything she had seen or overheard while she was there.

There was something she was forgetting, but if she could just remember . . .

Lily's eyes snapped open. She needed to speak to Mr. Page.

Her father had left for the club in St. James where he kept a membership, saying sarcastically that he would dine out to spare her his company before going to pay his call on Frank. If he had expected her to protest, he had been disappointed: Lily had been glad to see him go.

And she was even more glad now. If her father had seen her departing alone in a hackney coach as dark was falling, cloaked and veiled and not dressed for an evening out, he wouldn't have held back his questions.

And though Lily knew she would have to speak to him soon, to tell him what she knew and ask for his help, she needed to speak to the constable first.

Chapter 25

After telling the driver of the hackney coach the address of her destination, she ignored his raised brows and climbed inside, clutching the paper with Mr. Page's address written on it like a talisman and trying to ignore how her heart felt like it was trying to climb out her throat.

But with the Wyatts leaving London tomorrow, what Lily needed to tell Mr. Page couldn't wait. So when the driver pulled to a halt at the end of a street that was too narrow for a carriage and told her that the house she wanted was up ahead, Lily swallowed down her fear, paid her fare, and hopped down without expecting assistance.

She had been to the area of London known as Clerkenwell twice before during the day, never at night, and certainly never alone. Parts of it, she knew, were respectable enough, with pretty walking paths over the New River canal and fields where a herd of cows still grazed. But there were at least two prisons in the area, and many of the streets were crowded with pickpockets and worse.

Her veil and cloak covered her from head to toe and—she hoped—hid the quality of her garments. Trying to move briskly enough to show that she was unafraid but not so briskly that she attracted attention, Lily set off down the street.

"Watch it, there!" A group of women and men, brassy laughter bouncing off the stone walls of the houses around them, pushed past her. Lily stumbled out of the way quickly, feeling heat rising to her face as they laughed, though none of them could see behind her veil. Once they had passed, Lily glanced at the houses, frowning. Only a few of them had numbers, and none of them were close to the number she was looking for.

Walking more quickly, Lily crossed another street. The sun was nearly set, and its straggling light did little to illuminate the narrow street, but there was enough momentary light spilling from a window that allowed her to glance around. Had the driver let her off at the wrong street?

The sound of footsteps behind her made her start, and she spun around, one hand reaching under her cloak. But the person coming behind her—a young, professional man, by the look of him, perhaps a clerk of some kind—simply lifted his hat and would have gone on walking had Lily not stopped him.

"Excuse me, sir!"

The heavy weight under her cloak made her feel both more afraid and braver as she curled her hand around it, but she kept her voice polite and unworried as she continued.

"I wonder if you might help me. I am looking for number sixteen, St. John's."

He gave her a wary, surprised look, and Lily realized her voice must have given her away as not belonging to this part of the city. But he still asked politely, "Which St. John's, miss?"

She stared at him blankly. "I am afraid I do not know."

A small sigh. "This here's St. John's Lane. If you can't find the house you're looking for, it might be St. John's Street or St. John's Square. Square's one block west, next to the church. Street's one block east."

"Oh damnation," Lily muttered.

It was hard to see in the dim light, but she thought he smiled at the curse that slipped out. He shrugged. "London, miss."

"London, indeed." Lily puffed out her cheeks and blew a frustrated breath. "I don't suppose you live around here? And perhaps know where the Page family lives?"

"Simon Page?" The young man let out a short, surprised laugh. "Sure, miss. Folks always know where the nearest constable lives. He and Miss Page are on St. John's Square." He pointed back the way she had come, indicating a narrow, dark passage that led away from the road. "Right that way. North side o' the square, red door."

Lily swallowed nervously, wondering if she should ask him to accompany her. But even in the fading light, she could see dark shadows of fatigue under his eyes. This was the sort of young man who had been up at dawn to spend all day working and likely would be again tomorrow. She doubted that he wanted to make his day longer by accompanying lost women through neighborhoods where they didn't belong. And it wasn't as if she had far to go. So she nodded politely. "I thank you for your assistance."

"Good evening, miss." He lifted his hat and hurried on his way, and Lily turned her steps back toward St. John's Square.

The walls of the narrow passage shut out all the fading light, but it wasn't long, and Lily plunged ahead without giving herself time to feel nervous. Her footsteps were muffled by the damp and moss that covered the stones, and she slowed down so that she wouldn't slip or stumble as the passage took a turn.

That was when the hand snaked out and grabbed her.

"What's a fine lady like you doing out on such a gloomy night?"

Lily yanked away without needing time to think, feeling as though her stomach had dropped out of her belly, and tried to turn back the way she had come. But the man, who had been tucked between the barrels stacked against the wall, stumbled forward, trying to grab her again.

"Here now, fine lady. Why so hasty? Stop and have a chat with me."

She couldn't see his face clearly, but she could smell him, a mixture of unwashed flesh and the faint tang of liquor. It wasn't the scent of drunkenness. In fact, she thought he had sounded sober. But it floated with him, as though it had been his companion so long that he could no longer escape it.

She could see his outline as she tried to pull away again, trying desperately to decide whether shouting would bring help or more assailants. He wasn't a large man. And as far as she could see, he didn't have a weapon.

There were reasons that ladies did not venture out alone in London's streets at night. But she had, at least, come prepared.

The metal was cold in her hand as she drew her pistol out from under her cloak. It was one half of a set of dueling pistols that had belonged to her husband. It had proved useful once before when she was investigating a murder. She had kept it close by ever since she first saw the puddle of Sir Charles's blood on the floor of the library at Wimpole Street.

The man hadn't let go of her arm, and when he dragged her back toward him, his face was close enough for her to see his leering grin. "Whatcha got under that fancy cloak, then? Pretty trinkets? Or just your pretty self? I'll take either."

Lily wanted to scream or vomit. Instead, she cocked the hammer of the gun, which now rested between them.

"Cold lead," she said, grateful that the words made it past her lips. Her voice shook, but her hands, she was relieved to realize, were steady. "And unless you want a permanent hole in your ballocks, I suggest you run away. Immediately."

She didn't want to shoot him. And he clearly didn't want to be shot. He dropped her arm and backed away.

"Come on, now, miss," he said, his tone sinking to a whine. "Just need some help, I do. I got three little 'uns to feed at home."

"That argument might have been more persuasive if you had led with it. In daylight. Since you did not, I suggest you go home to those little ones. Now," Lily bit off, taking slow steps away from him and closer to the square. He didn't move, but she didn't take her eyes off him. For all she knew, he was telling the truth about having children, but while that meant she was loath to hurt him, she knew it didn't mean the feeling was mutual. She gestured with the gun. "Unless you would rather I summon a night watchman? I hear there is a constable living just one street over."

The man hesitated once more, and Lily, barely breathing, raised her gun. He let out a whimper and fled back the way she had come.

A quick glance over her shoulder showed that the rest of the way to the square—a matter of only a few steps—was clear. But Lily didn't lower her gun or turn from where the man had disappeared until she tripped over a loose paving stone and stumbled into the open space.

She turned at last, hiding the pistol under her cloak once more. Her hands were shaking, now that the confrontation was over, and she had to take several deep breaths while she tried to distract herself by looking for the red door.

St. John's Square was a tidy spot surrounded by narrow houses, several of them with welcoming light glowing in the windows. At one side of the square was the tall facade of what she assumed was St. John's Church, though it didn't look much like the parish churches she was used to seeing scattered around London.

And there, across the way, with warm candlelight glowing in the window, was the house with the red door. Lily pressed one hand against her heart, which still felt as though it might leap out of her chest, took a deep breath, and walked toward it.

★   ★   ★

Simon had been trying to persuade his twelve-year-old niece that it was indeed time for bed when he heard three sharp raps on the front door.

"Who on earth could be knocking at this hour?" his sister, Judith, called from upstairs, where she was trying to persuade their seven-year-old nephew that it was indeed necessary to wash behind his ears.

Their niece did not lift her eyes from her book, just pulled the candle on the table closer to her pages and lifted her feet to cross them beneath her on the chair.

Simon frowned. "I don't know," he called back over the sound of splashing water. He wasn't on night duties this week, so there was no reason for anyone from the force to be calling, and the neighbors, most of whom worked during the day and had children of their own, were never out paying calls at this hour of the evening.

"Well, for heaven's sake, go see who it is," Judith called back down.

"No shouting," their niece said. It wasn't a complaint or an impertinence; she said it without inflection or emotion, merely repeating the instruction that she had both heard and given many times before.

Simon shook his head, a smile pulling at the corners of his mouth. "Of course, Fanny. No shouting. You're quite right."

Whatever he had expected to find when he opened the door, it wasn't the cloaked and veiled woman who waited on his doorstep. And he certainly hadn't expected the face that greeted him when she lifted her veil.

"Mrs. Adler!" Simon stared at her, anything polite he might have said or done forgotten in his surprise. "What the devil are you doing here?"

"Good evening, Mr. Page. Might I come in?"

There was a tremor in her voice, and he frowned as he opened the door wide enough to admit her, then closed it behind her.

"How did you come here? Are you all right?"

"I am perfectly well, thank you. I simply . . ." She lifted her chin. "It was a little difficult to find your home. The driver who brought me left me on St. John's Place. By the way, as a policeman, I think you should know that there was a man lurking in that passage across the way."

"Lurking?" Simon said sharply. "What did he do? Are you—"

"I am perfectly well," she snapped, before taking a deep breath and closing her eyes. "I am a little shaken, but I am well."

"You oughtn't to wander through London at night by yourself," he said sternly, hoping she wouldn't open her eyes and see the worried way he was looking her over.

"Concerned I will make more work for the night watchmen?" she said with an attempt at lightness as she opened her eyes.

"More like you'll get your pockets picked or worse," he said. "I thought you had more sense than that."

"I do, generally." She sighed, seeming to deflate a little, and shivered. "But I needed to speak with you. And this time, it could not wait."

Even in the dim light, he could see that the expression in her eyes was too serious to doubt. He stepped aside without another word, trying to decide what made him more uncomfortable: the fact that she was wandering through London at night—through Clerkenwell, no less!—without anyone accompanying her, or the fact that she was going to see his home. The door opened into the front parlor, and though the girl-of-all-work who came each afternoon had left it spotlessly clean, there was no fire laid there and no candles to illuminate the room. Mrs. Adler passed on through without a word and made for the open door to the cozy, well-lit kitchen where he had just left Fanny.

Simon closed his eyes in momentary embarrassment, thinking of Mrs. Adler's splendid home on Half Moon Street, which, he didn't doubt, had any number of parlors upstairs and down, all of them with fires laid by her polite and well-trained servants. But there was no help for it—and he liked his home. There was no shame in not being rich.

He squared his shoulders and followed her through.

Mrs. Adler was staring in a little bemusement at his niece, who was still bent over her book.

Simon shook his head again, the smile creeping back over his face. "Fanny, what have we talked about? When a visitor arrives, you have to greet them."

Fanny nodded to show that she'd heard him, and he could see one finger tracing down the lines of her book to show him how close she was to the end of her page. Mrs. Adler watched the girl, a puzzled frown on her face, before he saw her lips draw into a small *oh* of understanding.

When Fanny lifted her head and stood at last, there was nothing but polite friendliness on Mrs. Adler's face, and Simon felt a rush of gratitude as he made the introduction.

"Mrs. Adler, may I present my niece, Miss Fanny Andrews. Fanny, this is Mrs. Adler, who is a most distinguished guest."

Fanny looked her up and down with more assessment than curiosity and nodded. "Distinguished in this case meaning wealthy. Summer cloak, eight shillings a yard at least. Veil, Spanish lace, ten—"

"Fanny," said Simon sharply. "What have we said about discussing the cost of people's clothing?"

Fanny thought for a moment, then nodded. "I beg your pardon, Mrs. Adler."

"That is quite all right, Miss Andrews," Mrs. Adler said gently, and Simon was relieved to see that she was smiling. She gave him a quick look that had a hint of laughter in it, enough to tell him that she was not offended, before turning back to Fanny. "Your book seemed very engrossing. What is it about?"

"Botany," Fanny said, her eyes lighting up. "Do you like botany?"

"I confess I do not know much about it. But I like flowers. My Christian name is after a flower, you know. Lily."

"Lily. The genus *Lilium*." Fanny nodded, her expression serious. "Though there are many flowers called lilies that are not true lilies. Did you know the family Liliaceae was first described in the last century by the botanist Adanson? Or was it du Jussieu? No, he was the one who formally named it. But since then a number of flowers have been added to the—"

"Fanny." They all three turned to find Judith standing in the doorway, an apron over her dress and a harried look on her face.

Simon was struck, every time he saw her, by how much Judith and the children looked alike, with their delicate features, creamy skin, and hair halfway between blond and red. The sister between him and Judith—the mother of Fanny and her brother George—had looked like them too, when she still lived. He was the odd one out in the family, an average-looking man with dark hair and an unremarkable face.

Judith gave him a significant look, and he cleared his throat. "Mrs. Adler, my sister, Miss Page. Judith, this is Mrs. Adler."

Judith's smile was both distracted and embarrassed. There was soap on the collar of her dress. Apparently George had been a handful that night. "A pleasure, Mrs. Adler. Fanny, what have we said about lecturing?"

"It was not a lecture," Fanny protested calmly. "Mrs. Adler asked about my book. And her Christian name is Lily, so I was telling her where—"

"Fanny," Simon said, his voice holding a little bit of warning and a lot of patience.

Fanny sighed. "You came to talk to my uncle, not to me. And I am supposed to be going to bed." She thought for a moment, then nodded. "Yes. Good night, Mrs. Adler. Good night, Uncle."

"Good night, Miss Andrews. I hope we will have a chance to talk about botany at another time."

Fanny paused in the doorway, ignoring Judith's impatient grip on her arm. "Do you really hope that, or are you just being polite?" she asked with wide-eyed bluntness.

Mrs. Adler laughed. "I really mean that. I wish I had been half so well educated when I was your age." She glanced up from Fanny's face. "My apologies for intruding on your evening, Miss Page."

Judith nodded. "We'll leave you to your discussion. Come along, Fanny."

Simon cleared his throat. "Tea?" he asked, not sure what the correct course of action was when a lady of quality called on a policeman at his home after sunset.

"Please."

He was glad she had agreed. It gave him something to do, setting the kettle on to boil and preparing the cups. He made sure not to grab either of the ones with chips in them, then grimaced over the lack of sugar in the house before he remembered that she didn't take sugar in her tea anyway. He was used to noticing such things in his line of work.

"She is a little like Arthur Wyatt."

The quiet observation caught Simon off guard; her comment had been said so neutrally, it was impossible to tell how she felt about it.

"Yes," he said at last, a little wary. "Not exactly alike. She took her time speaking, and she doesn't like to be touched much either. But I think she lives a little more in this world than he does."

"She seems very bright."

He smiled. "She is. Right now, she's fascinated with plants and botany. She'll talk about them for hours if you don't stop her, and she doesn't always remember to check whether the person she's talking to is interested in what she wants to say." He hesitated, loyalty to his niece making him want to defend her. But Mrs. Adler wasn't attacking. "Sometimes I think she's always running the rules we've told her through her head, trying to remember the correct one. She doesn't always get it quite right."

"Well, that is true for all of us," Mrs. Adler said lightly.

She was trying to be kind. But Simon still shook his head, not wanting anyone—even in kindness—to undervalue the hard work his niece did each day. "It's not the same."

To his surprise, Mrs. Adler blushed and looked away. "No, of course not." She accepted the cup of tea he handed her, fiddling with the handle before she looked up again. "Is that why you were so good with Arthur? And so angry at your magistrate?"

Simon let out a long breath, sitting down with his own tea at last. "Yes." He gave her a stern look. "And as someone with a young girl in my charge, I hope she is never foolish enough to go wandering through London by herself, alone and defenseless."

"I am hardly defenseless, as you well know," Mrs. Adler said, pulling something from beneath her cloak. The candlelight glinted on the barrel of a pistol as she laid it on the table between their teacups.

For a moment they stared at each other, Mrs. Adler with her chin raised defiantly, Simon with his jaw clenched in disapproval. But he knew her well enough by this point to realize that she did not take frivolous risks. If she had come to see him, there was a good reason.

"Why are you here?"

Mrs. Adler turned the handle of her teacup slowly, as though thinking through how she wanted to respond. When she finally looked up, the expression in her eyes was hard to read. It might have been the triumph of a puzzle piece finally fitting into place. It might have been sorrow that she knew something and wished she didn't.

"Because I was walking with Lady Carroway today when we encountered Mr. Frank Wyatt," she said softly. "And she noticed something that I had not. Frank Wyatt, in unguarded moments, calls his father's wife Winnie."

"He calls you by your Christian name sometimes," Simon pointed out.

"Because he has known me since I was young enough to accidentally set one of my pigtails on fire. He would never presume otherwise."

"You did what?" he asked, distracted by trying to picture the elegant Mrs. Adler as an awkward child even younger than his niece.

She made a face at him and ignored the question. "Lady Wyatt is *insistent* about who does and does not have permission to call her Winnie. I have heard her making a fuss about it."

Simon frowned. "Well, then, that's damned rude of him."

"And Frank Wyatt is never rude," she said, nodding. "I have known him as both a child and an adult. Infuriating, snobbish, charming, friendly—he runs the gamut. But he is never rude, and he is never uncouth. He would never call Lady Wyatt *Winnie*, not even in his thoughts, unless she had invited him to do so."

"But they don't like each other," Simon said slowly. He didn't mean it as a protest but as a statement of fact, to be turned over in his mind as he decided whether it was indeed a fact or merely an assumption he hadn't questioned.

"And then I recalled that, according to my father, Sir Charles and Lady Wyatt married before she had a chance to meet either of his sons."

"Ahh." Simon let out a long sigh and sat back in his chair, pressing his steepled fingers against his lips as he stared at the wall, thinking. "You think that they—"

"Yes."

"And then . . ." He trailed off, but she knew what he was asking.

"Yes."

"But why that night? It wasn't a convenient moment to act. Lady Wyatt was, after all, expecting guests the next morning—you and Captain Hartley."

He glanced at her then, wondering if she had realized what the only answer could be. Of course she had. She wasn't a lady who shied away from the dark parts of human nature.

"And they were planning to leave any day for the country. And their own home in Devon is a secluded place, where they would be much more likely to escape detection." She met his eyes. "The only reason possible is they had run out of time. The housekeeper heard Sir Charles upset that night. He was disgusted, she said. That something was unnatural. An abomination."

"So Percy Wyatt was telling the truth; his uncle did intend to make him his heir. But the question is still how Frank Wyatt could have managed it." Simon stood up abruptly, beginning to pace around the room.

"Did he?"

Simon frowned at the question. "I thought that was what you were implying. Physically, he is the only one who could have. He might have killed his father before he even left for his club . . . But no, the butler came close enough to tell that Sir Charles was indeed asleep. He would have noticed then if he was dead, or even injured."

"No." Mrs. Adler shook her head. "Not Frank. Arthur told us, though he did not realize it. She likes painting, he said." She raised her fingers and wiggled them in the same gesture the boy had used. "And he mentioned painting at night."

Simon stared at her. "But that would mean . . ." He shuddered. "Dear God. But how could she have managed it?"

"If you recall, the butler saw that Sir Charles had fallen asleep by the fire. And when I thought about the fact that Ellen Cook was poisoned, it made me wonder if Sir Charles might have been too. While he wasn't given arsenic, he could have been given something else."

Simon suddenly understood. "Not a poison."

"Not quite a poison, no." Mrs. Adler shook her head. "Just enough to leave him unconscious. And if you recall, Sir Charles's gout was acting up that day, which likely meant he was in his wheeled chair."

"And Lady Wyatt was far from Wimpole Street when Ellen was killed."

"Yes."

"Ahh." Simon let out a long breath and sat down abruptly. "So you think the two of them—"

"Yes." There was a wealth of horror and sorrow in the single word.

He sighed again, then frowned. "It's a damned disaster to prove, though."

Mrs. Adler was back to studying her teacup, and she nodded. "Fortunately, I have an idea for how we might convince them to confess all on their own." When she glanced up, the horror was gone from her expression, replaced by something more uncertain, more resigned. "Unfortunately, I think that idea depends on my father's cooperation."

★   ★   ★

Mr. Pierce paced around the drawing room, his cane thumping against the carpeting. It was full dark, and he clearly had planned to go to bed after he returned from his club. But Lily hadn't wanted to wait for morning. The thought of trying to convince him that she knew who had killed his friend while they faced each other over the breakfast table, helping themselves to tea and toast, seemed too jarring.

So Lily had told him as soon as he got home. And now she watched his agitated progress, which stopped every few steps so he could turn to stare at her where she sat carefully perched on the edge of her chair.

She wanted to keep her face neutral and calm, to live up to her father's ideal of womanhood, as if by doing so she could at last persuade him to have confidence in her. But though she clasped her hands in her lap to keep them from trembling, she couldn't keep the nervousness from her face or her voice. "Well, Father?"

He stopped next to the fireplace, staring at it for several long moments as he leaned heavily on his cane. "Why should I believe you?"

"Because I am right," Lily said, her voice quiet but firm. All her life, she had wanted her father to choose her over everyone else in his life. He never had. And just when she had persuaded herself that she didn't care anymore, she found that she needed him to anyway, for very different reasons. "Because Charles Wyatt was your friend, and he deserved to live." Ellen Cook had also deserved to live, but she knew that argument wouldn't persuade her father.

"And what happens if you are wrong?"

Lily bit the inside of her cheek. "Then I am thoroughly embarrassed."

"As am I."

She took a deep breath. "But I am not wrong."

"You are a brazen hussy to even be thinking about such things."

"I am. And if I had been your son, you would have admired me for it deeply."

"But you are *not* a son," he snapped.

"No."

Lily wished she had someone standing by her side to help her persuade him. But she knew he wouldn't bow to pressure from anyone else. And—God forgive her if it didn't work—she wanted him to believe her on her own merit, not because anyone else told him to.

The ticking of the clock was thunderous in the silence that hung between them. Lily didn't look away or blink, as if somehow she could convince him just by holding his gaze long enough.

"Frank Wyatt is like a son to me." There was no knowing what thoughts were behind the words.

She lifted her chin, refusing to look away. "But he is not your son. And I *am* your daughter. You said it yourself, Father. I got my brains from you. So how much are those brains worth?"

CHAPTER 26

It had to be done in Lily's home, Mr. Page had decided, to get the staging just right. To put the players in their game where they needed to be.

Lily's part of it was an invitation that Lady Wyatt join her for the morning, delivered by Jack. When she pressed, he had—with a degree of embarrassment that surprised her—admitted that the elegant widow seemed to have a preference for his company. He was happy to put that preference to use, departing soon after Mr. Page arrived with Percy Wyatt. The constable was grim faced, the young man anxious and confused, insisting that they explain what was happening and pouting when they told him he would have to wait.

A half hour later they were in the small garden behind the house, a space barely big enough for two benches facing each other on a square of grass, surrounded by a border of summer-green shrubs. Lily held her breath as she heard Jack's chuckle coming toward them, Lady Wyatt's gentler laugh, just the right amount of amusement allowed for a new widow—calm, a little sad, perfectly proper.

Beside her on the bench, Percy Wyatt fidgeted. Standing behind them, Mr. Page shifted a bare amount, then was still again.

They had taken some time to debate where he should be. Inside, where he could be recognized later, without scaring their suspects away? But he had pointed out that it was important for him to hear whatever Lady Wyatt might say. So they waited in the tiny garden together, until Jack emerged from the house with Lady Wyatt on his arm.

As soon as she saw who was there, the young widow drew to an abrupt halt, her expression wary. "Captain, I believe we are interrupting," she said, casting an unpleasant look in Mr. Page's direction. "Perhaps we should withdraw and leave Mrs. Adler to her odd guest?"

This was the other reason Jack was there; in addition to getting Lady Wyatt into the garden at the right moment, he made it easy to keep her there by the simple precaution of not releasing her hand from his arm. She couldn't pull away without causing a scene that she clearly wanted to avoid.

"A moment of your time, if you would be so good, Lady Wyatt," Lily said, standing. "I apologize for the subterfuge, but Mr. Page has something important to tell you, relating to your husband's family."

"My husband's family?" Lady Wyatt frowned. "I am not sure . . ."

"Please." Lily gestured to the opposite bench. "Will you sit?"

Lady Wyatt hesitated, then nodded, her expression impossible to read. She sat slowly, as regally as if she were a queen on a throne. The single glance she cast Mr. Page gave away her nervousness, but a moment later she was nothing but cool composure.

Percy looked uneasy. "Mrs. Adler, what is this about?"

"I should like to know that as well," Lady Wyatt said, but her rich voice was calm as a sunny morning. Lily couldn't help shaking her head in admiration.

She sat on the bench across from Lady Wyatt, glancing briefly at Mr. Page. He, still standing, nodded and took a step back, as though attempting to remove himself from the conversation.

Lily took a deep breath. "I should like the opportunity to tell you both a story," she said, amazed that her voice sounded as serene as it did. Inside, her stomach rolled with nerves, but outwardly she was as calm as Lady Wyatt.

"A story?" Percy frowned. "Really, ma'am, I do not think—"

"A story," said Lily firmly, interrupting him without remorse. His frown deepened, but he did not protest again. "About a lady—no longer in the first blush of girlhood, of course, but still quite young. She was, as so many women are, in a difficult situation. She was beautiful, cultured, charming, and utterly without options. Her family could not afford to support her, certainly not into her old age. And so, as many ladies in difficult situations do, she married a man that she respected, who she thought would make an admirable husband, but whom she did not love."

Lily kept her eyes on Lady Wyatt as she spoke. The other woman's hands gripped the armrest of the wooden bench, but otherwise she did not move. Her eyes were likewise fixed on Lily. The motion of her chest showed that her breath was starting to come more rapidly, but she did not look panicked. Not yet.

"Because the admirable man she married was a great deal older than she was, he already had two sons, one grown, one near grown. The younger was one of those individuals who not many years ago might have been called mad because his mind did not seem to live in quite the same world as the rest of us. He was a sweet boy with no harm in him, but his father knew that having such a son in the family might lead some women to reject his suit. So this admirable man kept his courtship short, and the lady did not object. They were married before she was able to meet either of his sons."

Percy had begun to look wary. He opened his mouth as though he were going to speak. But he glanced first at Mr. Page, who must have given him some look of warning. He stayed silent, and Lily continued.

"I cannot judge the lady at all for her choice. Women without fortune are left with so few respectable options for their own maintenance other than marriage. And for what happened next, I cannot judge her either. Indeed, I pity her."

As Lily spoke, Lady Wyatt's composure had been visibly fraying. Though she was trying to keep her expression as polite and disinterested as ever, her hands clutched at the armrest so tightly that her knuckles were white, and her whole body was beginning to tremble. As soon as Lily paused, she stood abruptly.

"Mrs. Adler, I had not thought you the sort of woman to gossip and meddle in the affairs of others. My husband had nothing but respect for your father, and for you to engage in such—"

"Because what happened next *was* truly dreadful for everyone involved," Lily continued relentlessly.

Lady Wyatt turned, heading back toward the house, only to discover that Jack was blocking her path. She pushed at him ineffectually. "I refuse to sit here and listen—"

"The lady and her husband's elder son fell in love."

The words hung on the air, and they seemed to pull Lady Wyatt to a halt, so abruptly did her movement cease. She did not turn around, but her entire body was rigid, held as tightly as if she were about to shatter or fly into a rage.

Percy started to his feet, staring between his aunt and Lily, his mouth hanging open. "Of all the utter nonsense . . . Really, Mrs. Adler, what trash. Everyone knows Frank and Lady Wyatt hate each other. And it has been damned uncomfortable for the rest of us."

"Not as uncomfortable as it was for them," Lily said. It would have felt cruel to expose such a dreadful secret if she hadn't known what it had led to. "I imagine they each feigned their distaste from the beginning, as soon as they realized how much they liked each other. Only gradually did they discover their mutual attraction. And eventually, they were not able to deny themselves anymore."

Percy looked ill for a moment, then shook his head. "No, surely not. Tell them, Lady Wyatt. Tell them what rubbish it is."

Lady Wyatt was rooted in place, as though terrified to either leave or stay. At Percy's words, she turned back around, her pale face flaming with rage and embarrassment. "Have you no shame, no womanly delicacy, to say such things?" she demanded, in a voice that was choked with tears.

"Are you saying I am wrong?" Lily asked, standing at last. She held Lady Wyatt's eyes, and Lily wasn't the first to flinch and look away.

Lady Wyatt took a deep breath. Then she lifted her chin. "And what if you are right?" she said, her voice hoarse. Lily heard Percy let out a choked gasp behind her, but she did not turn away from Lady Wyatt, who was pressing on, as though by finally admitting it she had released a flood of words that could not be stopped. "Yes, I loved him! And he loved me, and I had spent so long thinking no one ever would, that respect and polite regard were all I could hope for, and I thought it would be enough, truly, and it *would* have been. But then I met Frank, and he . . . and he . . ." She stumbled to a halt, her hand rising to her mouth to hold in a sob. She closed her eyes for a moment, gathering herself. When she opened them, they were fixed on Lily with a level of hatred that almost made her take a step back. "I was his father's wife, not his mother. And it is not a crime to fall in love."

"But it is a crime to kill your husband." Mr. Page had been silent so long that when he finally spoke, his words broke through the air like the crack of a pistol.

Lady Wyatt and Percy both turned to stare at him, she in rage, he in disbelief. Lily's eyes flickered briefly to the window, where three figures were now visible, one just having pulled back the curtain slightly to watch the proceedings below. But a moment later, her eyes were fixed once more on Lady Wyatt.

"Your adultery was your business, Lady Wyatt, until you and Frank Wyatt were discovered by his father."

"*Disgusted, unnatural, abomination,*" Jack put in, his voice clipped and relentless. "Those were the words the housekeeper heard him yelling that night."

"And you locked yourself in your chambers where he could not reach you," Mr. Page added. "I imagine he planned to disinherit his son and divorce you. And that, neither of you could bear. So you decided that Sir Charles had to die."

"That was why he sent for me." Percy, looking ill again, sat down abruptly. "Five hours before, he had been saying he could never trust me again. And then he sat me down in his study and told me that he was putting me back in the will, that most of it would come to me, so long as I promised to care for Arthur." He stared at Lady Wyatt, his eyes wide with horror. "Because of you and Frank?"

"How *dare* you, all of you!" Lady Wyatt gasped, staring between them in a mixture of panic and fury. "How dare . . . Yes, I loved Frank, I have admitted it. But I had been married to my husband for nearly a year. Why on earth would we suffer that long if we were just planning to . . . And why have I not thrown myself into his arms? I am leaving, for heaven's sake. *Leaving*! Would I do that if we had some nefarious plot together?"

"Well, yes, because you are neither of you fools," Jack said.

His tone bordered on exasperated, and they all turned to stare at him, the tension of the moment forgotten in sudden surprise. He shrugged.

"They would only behave stupidly if they were stupid. And they clearly are not, to have arranged things so carefully."

"Very carefully," Mr. Page agreed, nodding. "Having decided that murder was preferable to both scandal and poverty, you two acted quickly, before Sir Charles could expose you. Sir Charles always drank brandy in the evenings, so Frank dosed it with laudanum, which we know was in the house because he took it from time to time—and so did you, Lady Wyatt, on the doctor's recommendation. And then he went out, careful to have all his movements accounted for and witnessed, and to make a racket when he returned so the butler and his valet would both see him going straight to bed—after the time when Sir Charles would have been killed."

"Frank was not lying when he said he could never raise a hand against his father," Lily put in, looking at Percy. "Which was why Lady Wyatt was the one to kill him."

He shook his head at her, his expression a mixture of queasy disbelief and dawning horror. "But . . . she could not have . . . she was too . . ." His eyes grew wide. "The laudanum. I see."

"It left Sir Charles unconscious and easily overpowered, even by a woman as small as Lady Wyatt," Lily said, her voice growing colder. It had been hard not to feel sympathy for Lady Wyatt and Frank when she described the horrible circumstances under which they had met and realized they cared for each other. But no amount of love could justify the taking of two lives. "She very thoughtfully provided herself with toweling to cover her clothing and clean up any blood, which she hid in the chimney, along with the poker she used to kill her husband. But then, of course, she had to direct attention *away* from the chimney in order to keep them hidden."

"And I suppose I lifted his lifeless body, mighty bruiser that I am, and carried him like a feather across the room?" Lady Wyatt said, her sarcasm biting even though her voice trembled. She turned to Percy. "How can you believe this drivel, Percy?"

"You didn't need to," Lily pointed out. "His gout provided the perfect means of moving him easily."

Percy's eyes darted between them, his expression blank and confused.

Lily heard Jack sigh. "The chair, Mr. Wyatt," he said. "Your uncle was in his wheeled chair that night."

Percy Wyatt drew in a sharp breath.

"It made it a relatively simple matter, so late when the servants were abed and she knew Frank would not rouse them for hours, to move him to the other side of the room." Mr. Page picked up the narrative, his voice relentless as he took a slow step toward Lady Wyatt. She, almost unconsciously, took a step back. "You were able to deposit his body on the floor, were you not, Lady Wyatt? And then you decorated the edge of the table with his blood to make it look as though he had fallen and struck his head. You simply moved his chair to the other side of the room again to give the impression that he had left it there himself."

"Then you returned to your room, went to sleep, and woke the next morning to play the grieving widow." Lily's voice shook as she spoke, remembering how easily she had been manipulated by Lady Wyatt, how ready she had been to confuse the other woman's emotions with her own. "You did it very well."

"I *was* grieving," Lady Wyatt cried. "Do you think I wanted him to die?"

The words hung on the air as all of them wondered for a moment whether that had been a confession. But they were the simple truth, Lily realized. The two lovers had convinced themselves they had no other choice.

"You may not have wanted him to die, but you were willing to choose his death over your discomfort," Lily said. "And not only his, but Ellen's as well, once you realized she knew something about what you had done."

"So the maid saw her?" Percy asked, frowning once more.

"Not the maid," Lily said. "Arthur saw Lady Wyatt returning to her room, her fingers still red with your uncle's blood. Remember, he told us that she liked painting? *No painting at night*, he said. And he told Ellen, the person he trusted most in the world. And she, realizing what he had just seen, told him to be quiet like a mouse while she went to look around the library herself."

"Mrs. Harris, the housekeeper, noticed her coming out," Jack said. "And I would bet my fortune that someone else did too."

"And then Lady Wyatt killed her!" Percy exclaimed. Then his face fell. "But she could not have . . . Lady Wyatt, you were in Hans Town. I visited you there myself." He shook his head. "She could not possibly have . . ."

"She did not." Mr. Page's voice was cold. "Frank did. A chemist confirmed that what we found in the maid's room was arsenic."

"One murder apiece," Lily said. "And each of them gone when the other acted, to confuse the matter as much as possible. Because, until we discovered the feeling that existed between them, their pretense of animosity meant it never occurred to anyone that they might have been working together. I believe they planned to wait a year or so, for appearance's sake, then wed. Odd enough, certainly, to raise a few eyebrows. But given their ages, natural enough not to cause a scandal. And then they would be together at last, both well provided for through the money that Frank inherited."

Lily had gone to stand next to Mr. Page as she spoke. Percy still hung back, but Lady Wyatt was caught among the four of them, her eyes darting around frantically as if looking for an escape. But she hadn't confessed. Not yet. And they needed a confession.

"And that is your story, Mrs. Adler? That mess of falsehoods and fabrications?" Lady Wyatt looked from one cold face to another, her eyes wide in panic, before a cool certainty settled over her features. "Ridiculous," she said firmly, though Lily could see her hands shaking. "I shall be speaking to your superiors, mark my words, *Constable.* And all of you . . . !" She turned her icy stare on Lily and Jack in turn. "How dare you throw such slanders about? I am disgusted. No, I am *enraged.*"

"We know it is all true," Mr. Page said calmly.

"You cannot, because it is all lies!" she insisted. "And even if it were not—even *if*—you have no proof." She enunciated the last three words so clearly, so sharply, that she might have been hurling each one at them like a weapon. Her face was flushed with triumph.

"We do not need proof," Lily said calmly. "Mr. Wyatt has already admitted it all."

Lady Wyatt started at her in blank incomprehension. Lily gestured to the window that overlooked the garden. "I believe he is just signing his confession now."

Lady Wyatt and Percy both turned as abruptly as if they had been spun around.

The curtain had been drawn back from the window now, and the three figures were fully visible. Frank Wyatt sat in profile by the window, signing something on the desk. Mr. Pierce stood behind him, one hand on his shoulder, a solemn look on his face. Before them stood a third man. As they watched, the third man took the document Frank had just signed, looked it over, and said something. In response, Frank nodded, his shoulders slumping, and dropped his head into his hands, a picture of resignation and defeat.

"I believe my colleague, Mr. Hammond, has everything well in hand there," Mr. Page said.

Lady Wyatt had been frozen in horror, watching the scene unfold. Now she started forward a couple of steps, then turned back to her audience, her eyes wide with fear. "No . . . He would not . . . He *could* not . . ."

"Really?" Lily said, her voice cruel and relentless in its coldness. "How do you think we knew about your affair? Did you think he would not give you up in exchange for clemency?"

"He was adamant that the whole scheme was your idea," Mr. Page said, nodding at the window. "As you see."

Lady Wyatt spun back around in time to see Mr. Pierce gesture toward the garden as he spoke, while Mr. Hammond nodded, his expression stern. Frank had leapt to his feet, staring at the two men with him, his expression halfway between furious and stunned. Then he stabbed his finger toward Lady Wyatt, his shouting audible even from the other side of the window, though they could not make out the words.

"Perhaps he did not love you so well as you thought," Mr. Page said quietly.

Lady Wyatt had gone rigid, staring at Frank's enraged diatribe. When she spun back to them, her beautiful face was livid, red and splotchy with rage, her expression twisted into something beyond fury. She looked like she could have been ready to kill at that moment. "How dare he. How *dare* he," she spat. "My idea? He said it was my idea? It was his from the beginning. He was the one who began everything, I would not—I would never—I had determined to bury my feelings forever! But he couldn't keep his hands to himself, *he* was the reason we were discovered, and he was the one who gave his father laudanum and then came to me—begged me—said there was no other choice. And then *he* killed the maid . . . The *agony* she suffered—" Lady Wyatt broke off, her whole body suddenly going rigid. "It will be nothing compared to the agony I will cause *him*!" she gasped. "The bastard, that he could betray . . . I will kill him myself!"

Lily had taken an unconscious step back, stunned by the suddenness and ugliness of Lady Wyatt's confession. It was what they had wanted, what they had planned for. But the rage that lurked beneath Lady Wyatt's calm, polite exterior was terrifying.

The others apparently felt the same. None of them was prepared when Lady Wyatt suddenly turned and dashed toward the house. Too late, Jack made an ineffectual grab at her, but she rushed past him, throwing the door open with such force that it slammed shut again behind her.

The four of them chased after her, Percy Wyatt a moment later than the rest, still too stunned by the revelations that he, out of all of them, had been least prepared for. For a moment Lily was terrified that Lady Wyatt would escape. But as they tumbled through the door after her—Lily almost rolled her eyes as Jack held it politely open for Mr. Page to rush through first—they saw her disappearing toward the room where Frank and the others had been.

Lily and Mr. Page, with Percy stumbling after them, were only a few seconds behind her as they burst into the room. Mr. Page was just in time to catch Lady Wyatt around the waist as she tried to throw herself at Frank.

"How dare you!" she shrieked. "My *idea*? You blame it on me? When every moment—both your father and the maid—they were your idea! Yours!"

"Me?" Frank roared. "I *saw* you, Winnie! Selling me out! Standing there calmly informing them that I was a murderer—when it was you, all you. I may have killed the maid, but only because you told me I had to, after *you* killed my father. How dare you tell me you love me, then *turn* on me—"

"I never—I saw you! Signing your damned confession, you bastard, you idiot! Do you think it will save you? Do you? We shall both be transported, or hanged, and it's all because of you!"

"What the devil do you mean? My *confession*?" Frank turned to snatch the paper from Mr. Hammond and shook it at her. "I was signing away nearly all my money to pay for my father's debts, you bloody fool!"

His words hung in the air, the entire room suddenly silent as both murderers stared at the paper Frank held.

Mr. Pierce stepped forward. "I am afraid, Frank, that I may have used my position as a trustee of your father's affairs to summon you here under false pretenses."

"And I may not have been quite honest, Lady Wyatt, when I described Mr. Hammond as one of my colleagues," Mr. Page said, stepping forward. "He is actually one of Sir Charles's solicitors."

"And I was lying, pure and simple, when I said Mr. Wyatt told us about your affair," Lily said from her place by the door. "I figured it out thanks to the insight of a very observant friend."

Lady Wyatt and Frank had both been utterly still as they listened, their fury slowly morphing into matching expressions of horror as they gaped at each other in stunned silence.

Lady Wyatt began trembling. "No," she whispered. "No, no, *no.*"

Percy stared around the room, his eyes latching on each face in turn. "I . . . I do not understand," he said, his voice rising nervously.

"Damn it, Perce, keep up, you idiot," Frank snapped. "They bloody *tricked* us."

"Then you did kill him," Percy whispered. As much as she disliked him, Lily's heart broke for the young man as he stared at his cousin in childlike horror.

"I didn't," Frank insisted, while Lady Wyatt moaned, slumping in Mr. Page's grip as though she were no longer able to support her own weight. "I would never have hurt my father, you know that."

"You helped someone else hurt him, and that's the same thing," Percy said, trembling. "And you killed Arthur's maid, didn't you?" When Frank said nothing, Percy's voice rose. "Didn't you?"

"It's not true," Frank insisted. He turned at last to Mr. Pierce. "You know it cannot be true, sir. I loved my father."

Mr. Pierce shook his head, apparently unable to speak.

"You loved your father, but you never could bear to share his regard with anyone, could you, Frank?" Lily asked quietly. She met the eyes of the man she had known since she was a child, and a sick, gasping feeling twisted inside her. She had to swallow hard before she could continue speaking. "You resented Arthur his whole life. You tried to shut the child Maud out of her inheritance. And when your father turned on you, said he would disinherit you, you couldn't bear the betrayal. And Lady Wyatt, who had so recently escaped one bleak future, could not bear the thought of facing another."

"No," Frank said again.

"You turned up at my home that night, pretending to be drunk," Lily continued relentlessly. His clothes had smelled of rum, she remembered, but his breath had not. And the desperation, the fear, had been there the whole time. "After Lady Wyatt saw me sneaking down from Ellen's room. You wanted to find out what I knew. You wanted to find out whether I was close enough to the man from Bow Street to have told him. And you were desperate enough to try almost anything to convince me to trust you."

"No."

"And when you realized you were still in danger, you decided to point the finger at someone else. Never mind that he was the man raising your own sister. You saw someone without the resources to defend himself, and you were happy to let him take the blame."

"No," Frank repeated, this time barely above a whisper.

He and Lily stared at each other as if there were no one else in the room. "You owe me an answer still, Frank," she said. "From our card game. Am I right?"

His shoulders slumped. He did not deny it. Mr. Pierce turned away sharply.

With a yell, Frank suddenly made a run for it, dashing toward the door. He made it only a few steps out before they heard him curse and stumble to a halt. A moment later he backed in again, slowly, his hands raised. The others stared, not understanding what had happened, until Jack followed him. He was holding Lily's dueling pistol and pointing it directly at Frank.

"Good thought that you had there, Mrs. Adler," he said cheerfully, inclining his head in a polite bow to his startled audience. "And nice to be in on the plan, for a change."

"For heaven's sake, Captain, that was one time!" Lily protested. "And this is hardly the moment to bring it up."

"As you like, ma'am," he said, winking at her. "Your very terrifying butler is waiting in the hall with Mr. Page's handcuffs. Shall I invite him in?"

"Please do," Mr. Page instructed. "I made sure to secure two pairs from the magistrate, as we expected to apprehend two criminals."

Carstairs, with the awareness of when he was needed that all the best butlers seemed to possess, entered almost as soon as Mr. Page had finished speaking. Dignified as ever, he bowed and presented the constable with two pairs of handcuffs. "At your service, sir."

"Thank you, Carstairs," Lily said quietly, stepping forward to place a hand on her butler's arm. It was an extraordinary thing to ask him to assist with, but he had taken it in stride. "Would you please step out to summon Mr. Page's carriage, which is parked down the street? I believe the captain will be accompanying him to the Bow Street offices to assist with our culprits."

"Shall I go with them as well, madam?" Carstairs asked, looking around the assembly. Though it had been years since he had boxed, his physical bulk was still imposing enough that Frank Wyatt cringed away from him. Lily cast an inquiring look at Mr. Page.

"We would be grateful for the assistance," he said, accepting both the handcuffs and the offer of help.

Percy took charge of Lady Wyatt while Mr. Page placed handcuffs on her wrists and Frank's. Though he still looked ill, Percy resolutely insisted that he would come to Bow Street as well. Mr. Page, after a moment, nodded, then asked Carstairs to summon a second carriage. "Better to separate them, anyway."

At that, Lady Wyatt, who had been silent while she was handcuffed, let out a small moan. "Frank," she gasped, her voice breaking.

They were across the room from each other, but he turned to look at her and gave her a sad smile. "Still love you, Winnie. Sorry it came to this."

"Still love you, Frank," she whispered in reply.

Lily shuddered as they were taken from the room, Percy half dragging Lady Wyatt, Jack and Carstairs marching Frank between them. Mr. Page, about to follow behind, paused and turned back to the men who were still there.

"My thanks, Mr. Hammond. I appreciate your discretion in not repeating my request to your superiors at the firm."

"My cousin spoke highly of Mrs. Adler, and he convinced me to help you once," said Mr. Hammond, packing up his papers as he spoke. He was a gangly man, and his boyish face made him look too young to already have three children. But he had proved surprisingly firm willed about assisting them, even once they had explained how they needed him to lie to Frank Wyatt. "Shall I come to Bow Street as well? The more witnesses, the better, I imagine."

"I should be grateful for it," Mr. Page said gravely. But when he turned to Mr. Pierce with an inquiring look, Lily's father merely sniffed.

"I shall *not* be dignifying that establishment with my presence," he said stiffly.

"As you wish, sir," Mr. Page said politely. "And you have my deepest thanks for your assistance. There was no one else Mr. Wyatt would have believed so implicitly on matters of his father's estate. Without your cooperation, we'd never have been able to persuade him that the estate was so encumbered with debt, nor to set and spring our trap so perfectly."

He bowed, and after a moment's hesitation, Mr. Pierce inclined his head in barely polite acknowledgment. Mr. Page, as he turned to go, caught Lily's eye, giving her a smile that was unexpectedly warm in its wryness before turning back to her father. "And by the bye, sir, I must commend you on having raised such an intelligent and tenacious daughter. She's a woman who must be a credit to any parent."

Lily held her breath, unable to believe he would say something so challenging. For a moment that seemed painfully long, Mr. Pierce was silent. Then he nodded. "She did well enough," he agreed, his voice so utterly without inflection that it was impossible to tell how he was feeling. "Good day, Mr. Page."

It was a dismissal. Mr. Page bowed to them both and, replacing his hat on his head, followed the others out of the room. Lily was left alone with her father, neither of them speaking or looking at each other.

At last Lily found her voice. "Thank you for agreeing to help, Father. Truly. And I am sorry."

He sniffed, still not looking at her. His feet were planted wide, his hands clasping the head of his cane in front of him while he stared at the door where Frank and Lady Wyatt had been escorted out. "What are you apologizing to me for?"

"I am sorry that it came to this, and that you had to be involved. I am sorry that the boy you watched grow up was party to the murder of your friend."

"His behavior has nothing to do with me." Sniffing again, he thumped his cane twice against the floor and began to leave.

"It can still hurt you," Lily said quietly. He paused in the doorway, though he did not turn back to her. "And I am sorry to see you hurting."

She watched her father, wishing there was some way to bridge the gulf between them, knowing that what had happened might have only served to make it wider. His back was to her, and she could see the rigid tension in his shoulders. She wondered if his knuckles were white where he gripped the top of his cane. She wondered if his hands were trembling.

"Branson is already packing my things. I expect to leave this afternoon."

"This afternoon?" Lily couldn't keep the shock from her voice. Her father hated travel and nights spent on the road almost as much as he hated haste of any kind. "You cannot . . . Why so suddenly?"

"Do you really have to ask?" The bitterness in his voice nearly made her pity him. But he was not finished. "I have no desire to stay here any longer, to watch you consort with lowborn persons and involve yourself in unwomanly affairs. To watch you throw yourself at men and dishonor the memory of your husband."

Lily swallowed back the angry tears that pricked at her eyes, lifting her chin even though he wasn't looking at her. "I have the right to live my life as I see fit, Father. If you do not like it, if you cannot be proud of what I have done today, then you needn't return to my home again."

He sniffed again, his cane thumping against the wood of the floor as he stalked toward the door once more.

Her father had always shown his anger either by withdrawing from the person who had caused it or by blaming someone else entirely. As a child, Lily had lived in dread of those two extremes, always there to bear the brunt, whichever way he decided to fall that day.

But this time he had, to her surprise, chosen her. When it mattered, he had agreed to believe her, had helped set a trap that would convict the man he considered the son he should have had of murder. And she was not a child anymore, to let his whims pass without comment, without asking him to be better.

"You can admit that he hurt you, Father. And if you love him still, in spite of it all, you can admit that too. I will not think any less of you."

For a moment she thought he would speak. The silence hung in the air between them.

But he walked out without another word.

CHAPTER 27

"And then he left? Just like that?" Ofelia asked, her eyes wide with surprise. As the beloved only daughter of a father without a wife, she had been his pride and joy from infancy, and she couldn't hide her astonishment that Mr. Pierce did not feel the same about his daughter.

"Just like that," Lily agreed, swallowing back the lump in her throat that her father did not deserve. "Which is a punishment to no one but him, as he left in the afternoon and will have to spend an extra night in a coaching inn as a result."

She shrugged, pretending not to care. But she could tell her friends saw through her flippancy. Ofelia's eyes snapped with fury that someone could be so dismissive of Lily's accomplishments. And Jack laid a hand on her arm. It was the only gesture that would not have raised the brows of those around them, but the gentle, reassuring touch was enough. Lily took a deep breath, laying her own hand briefly over his own, before turning to survey the extravagant scene before them.

"Your mamma-in-law has truly outdone herself tonight," she said, changing the subject.

For a moment, Ofelia looked like she would insist on remaining furious, but Lily caught the slight shake of Jack's head, warning her to follow Lily's lead. Ofelia also turned to look out over the dancers.

"She could not resist. When Neddy and I came home, she decided she would be the last one to throw a Mayfair ball before everyone leaves town." Ofelia giggled. "Truly, I am rather flattered. She wanted to be sure that everyone who was still here saw us welcomed and feted when we returned from our wedding trip."

They were at the home of the Carroway family—the real home near Berkeley Square, not the house that Ofelia and Sir Edward had rented just for the two of them—where the Dowager Lady Carroway was hosting one final ball before the members of London's upper class truly scattered for the summer. There were, Lily guessed, over two hundred and fifty people in attendance, a riot of silk waistcoats and lace dresses, white-gloved hands and jeweled necks. Laughter spilled from the supper room next door, and at least two card rooms had been opened. The ballroom floor was crowded with couples floating through the figures of the dance: touching hands, breaking apart and coming together again, watched by the dozens of gossiping observers along the edges of the room.

No few of them turned their eyes, surreptitiously or not, toward where the three of them were talking in quiet voices. Some of the attention was likely due to the presence of the new Lady Carroway, so recently returned from her wedding trip.

But some of it, Lily suspected, was due to the rumors that were spreading about the affairs of the Wyatt family. As hard as they had tried to keep what had happened quiet, talk had spread. And Lily had heard more than one whisper that she and Jack had been involved in their arrest.

Perhaps the Wyatts themselves had been responsible: Lady Wyatt and Frank certainly had no interest in protecting her reputation. And Lily did not trust Percy's discretion.

But however the talk had spread, it was enough to raise eyebrows and suspicions, especially after the Harper murders that spring. Jack was unbothered by it; the implications of a man, especially one of naval background, becoming involved in police business were less disastrous. But Lily knew that some of that talk might not be so forgiving of her.

It made her glad that summer was upon them, that she and so many others would soon be leaving town so that the gossip would have time to fade.

But it also made her a little proud.

"You are a Carroway now," Jack pointed out, drawing Lily's attention back to the conversation. "However she might have once objected to your marriage, she is not the sort of woman to have anyone question her pride in her family."

"And you are monstrously well liked," Lily said.

Ofelia laughed at that, shaking her head because, however true it was now, it had not been the case when she first arrived in London. "They like me now because I am young, rich, and married to someone they do not wish to cut."

"And because you have done your matrimonial damage and no longer pose a threat to those still seeking," Lily pointed out.

"Well, whatever the cause, we are flattered that you would take time away from your very full dance card to spend a moment with us," Jack teased. Growing a little more sober, he asked, "How are things at home?"

Ofelia smiled again, a little sadly this time. "Arthur is doing well," she said. "He still misses his father and asks for Ellen, but he has settled in well enough."

With the case against Frank and Lady Wyatt still pending, Sir Charles's estate was in limbo. Percy could neither sell nor move into the house on Wimpole Street. Though he wished to bring Arthur to live with him, and though he would likely be named heir in Frank's place, he currently had too little income to rent a new home. He remained at his lodging house for the present, while the Carroways had immediately stated their intention to have Arthur remain with them for as long as he needed.

And Percy, Ofelia had reported, came by every day to see him so they might draw together, even though the elder Mr. Wyatt had absolutely no artistic talent at all.

"I do *not* like Mr. Percy Wyatt," Ofelia added, scowling. "We almost always have to invite him to join us for at least one meal, and he is a dreadfully boring conversationalist. If he is with us in the evenings, he always tries to convince Neddy to gamble over cards. And that is besides being unaccountably rude to the servants. But . . ." Her expression softened. "For someone so annoying, he is also very kind and patient with Arthur. I suppose I ought to think better of him than I do."

"Even the most annoying fellows usually have some redeeming feature," Jack pointed out as the musicians ended their song with a flourish. The dancers bowed to each other, and the watchers clapped politely, the hum of conversation rising even as the music began again for the next set. "That doesn't mean you are required to like him."

"Thank you, Captain, that is reassuring," Ofelia said, her eyes dancing. "I shall continue to dislike him with your blessing."

The three of them were still laughing when a tall man detached himself from a nearby group and came to stand before them.

"Mrs. Adler." Matthew Spencer bowed. "A pleasure to see you this evening."

"Sir." Lily smiled, flattered that he had sought her out. After the way their ride had ended—and the favor she had asked of him—she had not expected him to show any further interest in her company. And while she hadn't been upset by that expectation, neither was she disappointed to discover that it was wrong. Especially when he turned that brilliant, disconcerting smile toward her.

He really was unfairly handsome. She resisted the urge to shake her head in dismay and instead turned to her companions. "Lady Carroway, if you are not already acquainted, I am delighted to introduce Mr. Spencer, who is a friend of the Harlowes. Mr. Spencer, the younger Lady Carroway. And of course, you remember Captain Hartley."

"I am pleased to make your acquaintance, Lady Carroway," Mr. Spencer said, bowing. "And to have the opportunity to offer you my best wishes for your new marriage."

"Thank you, sir," Ofelia said, polite as always. But she glanced curiously at him from beneath her lashes before her eyes darted to the side to peek at Lily.

"And Captain Hartley. A pleasure."

"Mr. Spencer." Jack nodded, but there was something stiff in the motion.

If Matthew Spencer had noticed, it didn't seem to bother him as he turned to Lily. "Mrs. Adler, I believe I owe you an apology. I did not realize, until I was speaking to Mrs. Harlowe the other day, how recently you had left your mourning. I hope there was nothing that I said on our ride together that gave offense."

"Indeed not," Lily said, surprised. "I rather thought I had been the more offensive one that day. And I have wished to give you my thanks, for communicating my message so swiftly to your cousin, and with such a positive endorsement."

"Well." Mr. Spencer looked a little embarrassed but not unhappy. "Seeing how things turned out, I am glad to have been of service. And"—he smiled and held out his hand—"I wonder if I might have the honor of partnering with you for one of your first dances since your return to society." His smile grew a little mischievous, and he waggled his fingers at her. "I promise, I have mastered making my way through the figures with only one hand."

"It would be the first one, actually," Lily said, hoping she wasn't blushing. She didn't glance at Jack as she said it; they had once shared a waltz while she was still in half mourning and they were both caught up in grief over Freddy. But that had been a private moment; she hadn't danced in public since before her husband died. She took a deep breath, feeling a little burst of pleasure underneath her breastbone. "I would be delighted, sir. If my friends will excuse me?"

"Of course, Mrs. Adler," Ofelia said brightly, watching them with thoroughly undisguised curiosity. "I am sure I shall manage to entertain the captain in your absence. You deserve a dance, after all."

"Then yes, I would be delighted." Lily placed her hand in his.

★ ★ ★

Jack watched as Matthew Spencer led Lily to the dance floor, sternly ignoring the uncomfortable feeling underneath his breastbone. He remembered the uncertain look Lily had given him the first day she had begun to wear colors again, as if she had been waiting for his disapproval.

He hadn't disapproved, of course. She was young, with a great deal of life left ahead of her. And he had known Freddy so well, well enough to be sure that his friend would not have wanted her to remain tethered to his memory.

But it was another thing entirely to watch her place her hand in the palm of a man who clearly admired her, to let him lead her to the dance floor and join the line of dancers, where he would have every excuse to touch her arms, her back, her waist, as they moved through the figures of the dance.

Jack hoped he wasn't scowling.

"Cheer up, Captain. It is only a dance."

Ofelia's comment caught him off guard; for a moment, he had forgotten that she was still there. He cleared his throat, looking embarrassed. "It is jarring, that is all. I am used to thinking of her as the wife of my friend. But she . . ." He sighed. "She has mourned him long enough. She deserves to move on with her life."

Ofelia raised her eyebrows in pert challenge. "You loved Mr. Adler like a brother, I know. But are you sure that is the only reason you look as if you have a toothache?"

Jack scowled at her. "I haven't the faintest idea what you mean, Lady Carroway."

She shook her head, casting her eyes heavenward as if he had said something deeply amusing. "Yes, you do, Jack. And if you don't yet . . ." Ofelia smiled and patted his arm, her expression sympathetic. "You will soon."

AUTHOR'S NOTE

Arsenic's history as a chillingly accessible poison made it a frequent cause of both accidental and deliberate deaths in many countries. For years it was known as "the inheritance powder" because it was so commonly used by those who wanted to get their hands on the family fortune quickly. It was rumored to be the favored poison of the ruthless Cesare and Lucrezia Borgia in the fifteenth century, but its use for murder continued well into the twentieth century. (It was also a common cause of accidental death. The story of a servant accidentally poisoning a family with spring water that Lily recalls is based on a real incident: in the nineteenth century, a girl poisoned her father and sisters by serving them pears boiled in water from a nearby mine.)

Arsenic was popular because it was easy to administer and accessible. White arsenic could be added to food and drinks without dramatically changing their taste, and it was used for pest control as well as found in cosmetics, wallpaper dye, and other everyday places. Another factor in its favor? Death due to arsenic could be difficult to spot. The symptoms of arsenic poisoning often imitate those of other illnesses and include stomach pain, vomiting, dizziness, and shortness of breath. Dr. Shaw's misdiagnosis of Ellen's cause of death would not have been the first time an arsenic death was attributed to heart trouble.

To learn more about various poisons, as well as how the development of forensic chemistry began to make it harder for poisoners to escape detection, I highly recommend *The Poisoner's Handbook* by Deborah Blum (which I picked up for another project and ended up finding extremely useful for this one as well!).

It is a common misperception that because terms like "neurodivergent" are modern inventions, the people they describe are found only in modern times. But plenty of historical accounts show the presence of individuals with what we would consider sensory processing disorders or autism spectrum disorder. The lives of neurodivergent individuals in history varied widely, as they do now, but could be especially challenging if their families did not have the funds for their care. The early interventions and coping techniques that pediatricians and occupational therapists provide today were obviously not available. As a result, the lives of neurodivergent children and adults were often kept separate from those of the rest of their families and communities. For more on the study of neurodivergent and autistic children and adults in history, I recommend the research of John Donvan and Caren Zucker.

Finally, a note on charades: though the principle is the same (clues to help the audience guess a word), the version that would have been played in Regency England would have involved word games in the form of riddles, rather than acting out or staging the puzzle. The version Lily and her friends play is more similar to the Victorian game found in *Jane Eyre*. But it was more fun to write it this way than to have the characters sitting around making up riddles.

ACKNOWLEDGMENTS

Writing a book in the middle of a global pandemic is not an experience I ever expected to have, and it's one I hope I won't have to repeat. Still, I feel incredibly privileged to have had the opportunity and to have had so much help along the way. Many more thanks are due than I can possibly include here, but for a start . . .

. . . to Faith Black Ross, for her unerring guidance and incisive edits.
. . . to Whitney Ross, for being the best partner and advocate a writer could hope for.
. . . to Melissa Rechter, Madeline Rathle, Rachel Keith, and the entire Crooked Lane team, for their endless hard work.
. . . to Margeaux Weston, for her generous and insightful sensitivity read.
. . . to Alexander Gillies and Shannon McLeod, two of the very best writing buddies.
. . . to Neena Narayanan and Gemma Furman, who always have words of encouragement.
. . . to the Beach Crew, for their endless excitement and weirdness, even from far away.
. . . to my parents, siblings, and in-laws, who all believe in me so beautifully.
. . . to every reader who enjoyed Lily's first adventure and wanted her to have another.

And last but never least, to Brian, who joyfully took on so much at home so I could write this book faster than I thought possible (and who, even as I write this, I can hear arguing with a four-year-old and making dinner while I squeeze in just a few more minutes of work). You are my beloved partner in everything, and I am so grateful to have you by my side.